Fighter's Kiss

SIENNA BLAKE

ISBN: 9781690946359

Stock images: depositphotos
Content editing services by Book Detailing.
Proofreading services by Proof Positive: http://proofpositivepro.com.

For "broken" souls.

Your cracks are how your light shines out.

You are perfect and wonderful and deserve love just the way you are.

Declan

"*You'll never fight again.*"

The doctor's words were an echo over and over in my brain.

A terminal prognosis.

A death sentence.

I shook my head, trying to agitate those words out. But they were sticky and vicious, clinging to me.

Danny let out a curse, reminding me that my two best friends were also in my private hospital room. Except the two of them were standing and I was the fucking cripple in the wheelchair.

You'll never fight again.

"But with rehabilitation…" Diarmuid trailed off, the future—*my* future—hanging in the silence.

"With rehabilitation, he'll learn to walk again. To run. To fight. But to compete at that level…" The doctor forced a pathetic excuse for a sympathetic look to his face. "Sorry."

Sorry? I'll fucking show you sorry.

I gripped the arm of my wheelchair with my left hand, my good hand. My right arm was in a cast, having broken my forearm bones in several places. Apparently, it was crushed when the steering wheel crumpled.

I glared at the doctor. "I will fight again. I *will.* And I will *win.*"

Pity shone through the doctor's light blue eyes and baby face. He couldn't be much older than my twenty-seven years. What the fuck did this child know about anything? Did he even graduate from medical school?

"I'm just telling you the facts, Mr Gallagher."

"Facts?" I spat out, blood heating my face as my control started to snap. "*Facts?*"

"Dex—" Diarmuid warned.

In my periphery, I could see Danny and Diarmuid looking at each other with worry. They'd seen me lose my cool. They knew the warning signs.

I ignored them and their damn worry. "Here are some fucking *facts*," I yelled, "I am Declan Gallagher, world number one MMA champion. I'm number fucking one. *You* are fucking nobody."

The blood drained from the doctor's face.

Diarmuid, ever the mammy, was trying to calm me down in that soothing voice of his that he used for his kids, the troubled youths he worked with.

Danny was silent.

But I could feel him stewing with anger. Anger with me. Anger for me.

He knew what this meant.

If I didn't compete, I'd lose my title.

To *him*.

Dominic "The Spider" St Pierre. My blood seared at the very thought of his name. That fucking despicable excuse for a human, Dominic. He couldn't beat me in the ring, so he went for what was mine outside of the ring. And *she* let him take her.

The image of him pounding my wife from behind splashed across the backs of my lids like a gruesome murder scene, her low moan in my ears like a swarm of insects.

I heard a roar. It was coming from me. "Get out. Get the fuck out!"

Suddenly, this fucking room was too crowded. This whole fucking planet was too crowded. I wanted everyone gone.

My body was thrashing. I was grabbing onto whatever I could and throwing it. Underneath the surge of adrenaline, I could feel my broken body screaming.

I felt arms holding me down. Danny and Diarmuid are around the same height as my six two, both of them strong boys having kept up with their training even after we stopped training at the same boxing gym. They weren't as strong as me, but together and with my ass fucked up right now? They had me. Just.

I felt a sting of a needle in my arm and I let out a groan, not because it hurt. But because they were putting me down like an animal.

I no longer felt human.

I fought against it. I fought because that was what I did. That was who I was. I fought until the very last second. Diarmuid and Danny lowered me onto my hospital bed as alarms went off. I growled at Diarmuid as he whispered everything would be okay. I flinched as Danny placed a hand on my good arm.

I fought as my vision closed in, even after I lost touch with my limbs.

I fought, because if I stop fighting, I died.

Before the blackness took me, thoughts circled my carcass like a vulture.

Who am I if I'm not a fighter?

What am I worth if I'm not number one?

River

Nine months later…

What the hell have I done?

I leaned my forehead against the cold glass portal window of the plane that was flying across the Atlantic, carrying me away from New York, the States, Miley and everything I'd ever known. Too late now to turn back.

Miley had kicked up a fuss, of course.

"I can't believe you're leaving me," Miley had squealed, slamming into me just as I'd dumped my backpack—all I owned in this world—into the trunk of the cab ready to take me to JFK a few hours earlier. The lazy-ass cabbie hadn't even gotten out to help. He was just sitting there in the driver's seat scrolling through his phone.

This did not bode well. My nerves were shot to shit. I hadn't slept at all the night before.

"Maybe I shouldn't go," I said, staring over her shoulder at the backpack in the trunk.

Not too late to retract my things and pull the plug on this whole mad idea. I could email the Irish agency that had offered me a position as PA to one of their country's sports stars and tell them I'd made a mistake in taking the position. I had barely read the offer before I accepted. The job would give me a visa for Ireland. The job would get me out of here. So I took it.

Only a tiny part of my heart tightened at the thought of having to start over again in a new place.

"Don't you fucking dare," Miley said, slamming the trunk shut and shoving me toward the open back door. "Go. Get out of here."

I let out a snort. "Love you too, Cyrus." She hated it when I called her that.

"Love you more." Miley grabbed me right before I ducked into the cab and squeezed the living daylights out of me one last time. She might have looked sweet, her blonde hair cut into a short style like a tiny pixie, but she was strong. And had no qualms about punching you in the face if you pissed her off.

Miley was my neighbour and the closest thing to a best friend I'd ever had. She was a painter by day and waitress at a strip club downtown by night to pay the bills. She'd spotted me walking out of my apartment with my second-hand camera slung around my neck and let out a squeal. We'd argued over SLR versus DSLR and bonded over the colour wheel and Romanticism while exploring the graffitied lanes of New York City. We'd gotten drunk later on Student Night with cheap shots of tequila. We've been friends ever since.

On the way to the airport, I'd felt certain I was doing the right thing. I wasn't running away. I *wasn't* running away, okay? I was running *to* something. Something better.

Now on the airplane, stuck against the foggy window in economy, the armrest taken up by a beefy hairy arm, I felt…alone.

I should be used to this feeling. Before Miley barged into my life and demanded my friendship, I had no one. At least no one I could rely on.

I shoved those thoughts down where they couldn't bubble up and cause any more trouble.

I wasn't alone, I was free. *Free.* About to embark on an adventure of my life.

I didn't need anyone.

Declan

Every night before I fell asleep, I prayed that the stiffness would lessen. I prayed that the pain would go.

Every day when I woke, I felt like I'd been hit by a car again. I moved slowly at first, reaching automatically for the industrial-strength pain pills that I kept in the bedside drawer.

One.

Two.

Three.

I swallowed them with water. I took more than I should because the lower dose had stopped working.

My physio, Niall, kept telling me I needed to *stop*. He didn't understand. If I stopped, I died.

Only Seamus, my manager and coach, understood.

I groaned and stretched my arms over my head, waking my limbs, getting the blood flow back into them.

Worse than the physical pain was remembering how easily I used to move, how strong I used to be, how fit, how fast. My mind kept getting smacked around when it realised that *this* body couldn't do what it thought it could.

Every day, I woke and the clock ticked louder. Every day was another day I couldn't defend my title. And The Spider got closer to stealing it from me. Bitter hatred flooded my veins like an anesthetic. It was all I felt. I used that rage to get up out of bed. But the relief was only ever temporary.

My recovery wasn't moving as fast as I needed it to.

I almost forgot my new assistant was arriving today. Lucky me, I had my manager to nag me about it.

"Don't fecking send this one off, Declan," whined Seamus as he jogged to keep up with me as I strode through my country home toward the gym.

I snorted. "If they can't handle the pressure of the job then they deserve to scamper out of here with their tail between their legs."

Seamus sighed. "At least try not to scare him off before your comeback announcement. I have too much shit to do rather than worry about your social media and admin crap."

"Relax."

"That is the last thing I ever feel like doing around you," he muttered.

Fuck you, too, Seamus.

I didn't *like* him, not that I liked a lot of people, but he was good at his job. And he only pissed me off half the time. In his forties, ginger beard covering the lower half of his face, a scowl marring his thick brows over watery blue eyes, he'd been managing fighters for over a decade after retiring from semi-professional fighting. He'd not kept up with his training, an obvious paunch folding over his belt.

"Are you going to go meet him?" Seamus asked. "He should be arriving here soon."

"I have training." I had training every day. From eight till midday, then again from three till six.

Seamus let out a disapproving sound. "I had to go outside Europe to hire this time. None of the local agencies will work with you anymore."

"Pussies," I grumbled under my breath. I worked hard. My coaches were tough on me and I was tough on them. I was tougher on myself. If this new assistant couldn't function as part of an elite team, he could fuck right off.

"I'll bring him to meet you when he arrives."

"Bring him after." Nothing interrupted training. Nothing. Not even my own pain. I had to pass out for training to stop.

"Fine," he replied.

I pushed into my home gym, a huge well-equipped space that would rival any top gym in the country. I'd designed it with the help of my coaches, knocked out several walls to create it. A training cage, a weights area, calisthenics and stretching area. Directly above it were treatment rooms: massage, a sauna and spa. I breathed in a deep breath, letting the familiar space soothe me.

"His name is River, by the way," Seamus said.

Was he still following me? I grunted. "That's not a name, that's a landmark."

"He's American. They like to be different. For God's sake, don't tell him you don't like his name."

I rolled my eyes as I wrapped up my fists with one of the used but dry boxing wraps hanging on a bar. At least with an assistant I'd have someone to clean my wraps again. Maybe River wouldn't be so bad. Maybe he'd last more than three weeks. "Anything else, *Ma*?"

Seamus narrowed his eyes at me. "Try to be…not to be so…like *you*." He turned on his heel and strode away, the door swinging shut behind him.

Try not to be like me. What the fuck was that supposed to mean? Fuck knows. Fuck cares.

With my wraps securely on, I turned to the empty gym. My solace. My space.

This is where the fight was won or lost. Not the cage.

And I would not lose.

River

When the car that picked me up from Shannon Airport on the west of Ireland finally pulled to a stop on a narrow gravel road, I reached for the door handle only to fall forward as it opened on its own.

"Miss?" the driver, a tall, thin, pale man, held out his long, bony hand.

I pushed myself up and blinked at the ivy-covered stone

mansion in front of me. "Umm, I think there's been a mistake." I pointed at the goddamn *castle* compared to my shoebox apartment in NYC. "Sleeping Beauty must be waiting for you back at Terminal 3."

The driver did not laugh. The thin, pale corners of his lips didn't even twitch.

"Her fairy godmothers must be worried."

Nothing.

"Better hope Maleficent can't get that spindle through TSA."

Still nothing.

"I assure you, miss," he grumbled after a long sigh. "This is the residence of Mr Gallagher."

"Oh, is that the name Prince Charming is going by these days?"

The driver glanced over his shoulder at the imposing stone façade. "Charming isn't exactly the word I would use to describe him."

I climbed out of the backseat of the black sedan without the driver's aid and stretched from the long journey. "Well, that's fine." I grabbed my backpack from the driver's hand as he pulled it from the trunk. "Because I am certainly no damsel in distress."

I slung it over my shoulder and marched toward the arched double doors.

"Miss, I can help you with that," the driver called after me.

"You want to help? Go get *Miss* Beauty an espresso instead."

The irritated grumblings of the driver faded as I approached a scowling brass lion. I knew Miley wouldn't believe this shit, especially considering the "Under Repair" sign covering my doorbell for the past year. I lifted the heavy knocker and heard it reverberate loudly inside.

"Coming, coming," a voice shouted.

The door swung inward and I was greeted by the back of a redheaded man already walking away and this hospitable welcome, "You're late."

Yanking the door closed behind me required more strength than I expected, and so I had to hurry to keep up, backpack bouncing off one shoulder as we crossed the expansive grand entrance to the mansion.

"Name's Seamus and I'm far too busy training Declan to hold your hand as you learn the ropes, alright?"

I barely heard a word as I craned my neck to stare up at the ornate moulded ceiling of the two-story foyer. Two wide staircases descended on either side, the kind a princess would know how to hold on to just so as she daintily floated down.

My prince, however, was barking at me as he marched away. "Declan likes his help to look presentable, right?" Seamus grumbled. "So we'll get you fitted right away for a new suit. It's a waste of time in my opinion because none of the others have made it past a week, but what the hell do I know? Mate, do you know your inseam?"

I hurried after the blunt Irish man, my thrift store sneakers echoing against the polished hardwood floors beneath the antique chandelier high above. "Um, I usually just grab whatever fits from the bargain bin at Goodwill."

Seamus stopped so abruptly that I almost ran into him. He whirled around, his thick red eyebrows raised in surprise. He looked me over from head to toe in shocked silence. Finally, he said, "You're not a man."

I glanced down at my cleavage before looking up at him again. "You're not wrong."

"Fuck, fuck, fuck," Seamus muttered as he circled me while I tried to peek down the hallway of the mansion. "You're supposed to be a man." He stopped again in front of me, crossing his arms over his stomach as he assessed me. "You're not supposed to be a—a…"

I lifted an eyebrow as he wiggled a finger at me. "A woman?"

Seamus scratched at his thick ginger beard. "The agency said your name was River when I approved you for the gig," he said. "What kind of woman is named River?"

"Um, *this* woman." I placed my hands on my hips, pushing back my rain jacket.

Seamus immediately groaned and threw his arms up in exasperation. "You have tits." He glared at my chest like they'd mugged him in some dark alley. "You're not supposed to have tits!" He groaned. "You're supposed to be a middle-aged balding man from Kentucky or some shitehole like that with a Blackberry and no fucking tits that look just like hers."

"*Excuse me?*"

"At least you don't wear makeup like her." His tone was hopeful as he studied my bare face. "And you *clearly* don't care what you look like the way she did." He eyed my mismatched tie-dye tank top and floral skirt.

"Hey!"

"She would never be caught dead in those…things."

I followed his eyes to my sneakers. "I like these," I protested.

"Might just escape this," Seamus muttered to himself. "Might just escape this."

I glared up at Seamus.

He noticed and immediately shook his head. "But those eyes…" His head dropped back and he stared at the ceiling. "Those are her eyes."

I glanced around the empty foyer. "Umm…whose?"

"He'll know those eyes, those wild eyes a man can't resist." Seamus gave me a pointed look. "She almost ruined him, you know? With those wild eyes just like yours."

"Who?"

He buried his face in his hands.

"Listen," I said, staring at him in utter confusion, "I didn't fly all the way from New York to—"

"And you're American like her," he muttered through his fingers. "He's going to lose his fucking mind."

"*Who?*" I asked.

Seamus ignored me as he pulled his hands away from his face, grabbed me by the arm, and dragged me back toward the front doors. "He shouldn't see you," he said quickly as he glanced nervously over his shoulder. "I'll get a room for you at the inn in town."

"Who shouldn't see me?"

"We need to hurry. He'll be finishing his training any second."

"You need to tell me right now—what is going on?" I demanded as I tried to tug my arm away from his strong grip.

Seamus he held me in place as he managed to get the massive door halfway open.

"Who is that?"

The voice made him freeze.

With Seamus's fingers still digging into the flesh of my upper arm, I craned my neck around. From the shadow of the hallway, a man emerged.

So here was the Beast.

His broad, toned chest riddled with white jagged scars heaved as he stopped and assessed me with blue eyes, narrowed, dark and angry. He wore exercise shorts and sneakers with a white towel slung over his muscular shoulder. Tape bound his knuckles, and I thought I could see patches of red. Sweat beaded on his forehead as he pushed back his dark auburn hair and sucked in a shaky breath.

I pushed away the sudden thought that I wanted to fish through my bag, pull out my camera, and take his picture, just as he was there in that moment: raw and unfiltered and animalistic. He intrigued me. And the glare of those piercing blue eyes with a scar just above the left one both unnerved me and thrilled me.

Don't get attached.

Don't fall in love.

Those were the rules. They'd served me well all my life and I wasn't going to start breaking them now, especially not for my boss. This was just a job. A job I *needed.*

"Declan, listen," Seamus almost sounded fearful as he clearly fought to keep his voice calm. "There's been a mix-up with the agency, okay? I'll get it all sorted out."

Taking advantage of his distraction, I finally wrenched myself from Seamus's hold, straightened my jacket, and confidently strode toward Declan. I extended my hand. "I'm River," I said, suddenly feeling nervous so close to him. "Not any specific river. Just a river. Any river, really. Just River. Yeah, that's it. River."

"I think her name is River," Seamus muttered sarcastically from behind.

Declan remained silent, his eyes daggers of ice.

"I'm your new personal assistant," I explained, trying not to cower before him.

Why was he so angry with me? Why did it look like it was

taking everything in his power not to push me away from him with those muscular tree trunks of arms?

When Declan finally spoke, his voice was as if from the grave: rough, haunting, lifeless. "Get her the fuck out of here."

Declan

It wasn't the first TV I'd broken. It certainly wouldn't be the last.

But as I finished my training in my personal gym, I couldn't handle listening to a single syllable more of some "expert" discussing how unbeatable Dominic was in the ring. Sweat stung my eyes. Pain consumed my arm and blood seeped through my white hand wraps as I pummelled the flat screen I tore from the wall.

It should have been easy. Before my accident, I would have been able to wrench that TV from the wall like a magnet from a fridge. But after the accident and even after months of physical therapy, it still took my whole weight several times to rip away the cords and mountings. I heaved it to the ground and drove my fist through the screen. Glass sliced at my skin, but I couldn't stop. Stopping was death.

I punched it again and again and again till I finally fell back, exhausted in every possible meaning of the word. I gasped and drank in the agony of my body as I lay there. I deserved it, after all. I wasn't where I needed to be in my training. I needed to push myself harder, train longer, heal faster.

I needed to beat Dominic "The Spider".

I needed to show *her*.

Dragging myself up from the floor, I held onto the pain that coursed through my veins as I walked toward the kitchen for Chef's lunch. I squeezed my knuckles and the cuts tore. As I crossed the foyer, I was nearly shaking.

It was an entirely new kind of pain seeing the woman standing in the corridor with Seamus. It was the kind of pain that made the cuts on my knuckles look like paper cuts. It was the kind of pain that was more dangerous than any car crash. The kind of pain I couldn't bear.

She looked at me over her shoulder, and it was like a punch to my gut. On her face, freckles dotted her nose between wide, doe-like brown eyes. Wild, kinky hair fell across her rosy cheeks as she stared curiously at me, a gypsy child brought in by the wind.

And she needed to leave.

Now.

It only got worse when she moved to stand right in front of me and held out her hand, enticing me to touch her. My chest tightened.

The girl looked like *her*.

She sounded like *her*.

She intoxicated me with her eyes like *her*.

I had to hold myself back from tightening my bleeding hands around her delicate throat covered in string necklaces.

“I’m serious, Seamus.” I finally managed to tear my eyes from her. Looking at her was painful, but her absence left me numb. I wasn’t sure which was worse. “I want her gone. Now.”

“No problem, Declan. No problem at all. She’s gone.”

Seamus stepped forward and tried to grab her arm.

She shook him loose. “Gone?” The girl’s eyes were fire as she spoke.

I wondered briefly if she’d ever been in the ring. She didn’t have the frame for it, but she sure as hell had the spirit for it.

“I’m not some stray that showed up on your front steps in the night.”

Seamus again stretched out his arm for her.

She spun around and pinned a finger to his chest. "That doesn't mean, of course, that I won't bite."

I had to hold back a grin as Seamus eyed me over her shoulder, silently asking me what he was supposed to do.

"You haven't even given me a chance," the girl said, turning back around to face me. "You need to give me a chance before booting me."

It was already too much, being this close to her. "The position is closed." I kept my voice monotone, unemotional. "We no longer require your services."

"Bullshit," she said before quickly covering her mouth. "I mean, with all due respect, Mr Gallagher, you need me."

I almost spit out a wicked laugh. Need her? *Need* her? I *needed* to stop wasting my time with her and get back to training. I *needed* to get back into shape and defeat Dominic. I *needed* to win back my title and my fame and my reputation. That's what I needed.

I needed her like a shot in the head.

"Please," she continued.

I said nothing, only stared at her blankly.

"I'm hardworking and I'm smart and I'm resourceful. Anything you need from me, I can do. I promise I'm worth it. Just give me a chance. That's all I'm asking for." Her eyes were earnest, almost desperate as she stared up at me.

"It's not going to work out. Sorry." I'd wasted enough time. I turned to leave when she surprised me again by rushing in front of me to block my way with arms crossed over her chest.

"I want a chance." Her shoulders were squared, feet planted wide. She looked like she was ready to stand her ground in the ring. "I'm not leaving without my chance."

"You need to leave." I tried to step around her, but she swerved to the side.

"My visa will be revoked if you fire me."

Yes, there was definitely desperation now. Why did she want this job so badly?

"I'll have to go back to the States," she pleaded. "And I can't do that."

I pressed my fingers into my eyes to ease the throbbing pain in my head. "Seamus will arrange payment for your flight back."

She shook her head. "It's not that, it's just…"

I saw something in her eyes that I couldn't quite describe. Pain? Fear? ...Terror?

"I just…please."

Hope filled her eyes as I hesitated, silent for a moment. Hope is for fools. The sooner she learned that, the better.

"No."

I moved past her.

She then shouted, "Wait, wait!"

When her hands grabbed ahold of my arm, I flinched. Her touch seared my skin, branded it, tattooed it, permanently and irrevocably changed it. My eyes, nothing more than slits, moved from her hand on my arm to her eyes. My voice almost quivered as I whispered in a low, dangerous tone, "Most men that try what you're doing right now come to regret it very quickly after."

She did not flinch from my imposing glare. "Good thing I'm not a man."

My eyes ghosted over the curves of her body, her hips, her long, slender legs, her chest. She might have been a nuisance, a pain, an irritant. But she was certainly *not* a man.

"Just give me a week," she pleaded. "Give me one week. If you want me to leave after a week, I'll go. No questions asked." Her fingers squeezed my arm just slightly.

I sighed. "A week?" I asked.

"A week."

This was a bad idea. I knew it was. I knew it was a terrible, horrible, life-ending idea. I was jeopardizing my body, my title, my reputation. Everything. I was risking everything.

And yet I couldn't say no.

"Some rules then," I said.

"Fine."

"No personal questions."

She frowned. I lifted an eyebrow.

"A problem already?"

"No, no," she answered in a rush. "I got it. No personal questions."

"No more of whatever this is." I gestured toward her hideous, colourful shirt.

"Tie-dye?" she asked, pulling at the fabric to better see it.

"I don't care what it's called," I said. "Don't wear it."

"Alright…anything else?"

"Yes."

She looked up at me.

"No touching me. Ever." I wrenched my arm from her touch and marched past her without another word.

"Declan, where are you going?" Seamus called after me.

His rushed steps to keep up with my long, aggravated strides irritated my ears as I turned down the hallway. I wanted to be alone. I needed to be alone.

"Declan?" he shouted again.

"I'm going to train."

"You just finished training."

I scoffed. "No shit." It wasn't like I couldn't still feel the sweat on my brow and the ache in my sore muscles.

"You'll kill your body if you hit the gym again so soon, Declan."

I ignored him.

"You need to eat and sleep and rest. Chef has lunch ready."

"Leave me alone, Seamus."

"I'm your trainer," he shouted, running to catch up with me. "I don't have the luxury of leaving you alone."

"I want to be alone, Seamus."

"You'll never beat The Spider and show her that she picked the wrong guy if you kee—"

I wheeled around, caught Seamus by the throat, and pinned him against the wall. Old paintings in gold frames rattled on either side of his wide, fearful eyes.

"I'm going to train," I growled. "And you're going to fuck *off*."

I could snap his neck in an instant. I saw in his eyes that he knew that, too. I gave his body another slam against the wall for good measure before stalking away.

He should have listened.

The girl in the tie-dye should have listened, too.

River

In the suddenly empty foyer, I gasped as if I had just emerged from the rapids of a freezing, dark, churning river. My lungs burned as if I had been drowning, my mouth sucking in relieved breaths. My fingers felt numb.

This close. I had been *this close* to being fired not even two minutes into the job. I would have had to go back to the airport. I would have had to fly back to NY. I would have…

No, I wouldn't think about it. I had a week. One week to prove to Declan that I was worth keeping around. The details of exactly how I was going to convince the angry, anti-social, irritable man were still a little foggy. But I wasn't lying when I said I was resourceful. I'd figure it out.

Somehow.

"No, no, he only wants organic," a new voice echoed from somewhere close. "He doesn't care if it costs triple. He wants organic." A man wearing a white chef's jacket and burgundy silk loafers stepped from the hallway, pausing when he saw me. He covered the bottom of his phone with his palm and leaned toward me. "You're the new one?" he whispered.

I nodded.

He frowned as he looked me over from messy airplane bedhead hair to my universally adored baby-blue high top Converse sneakers. "Has Declan seen you yet?" he asked before pressing the phone back to his ear. "Yeah, yeah. I'm still here. Still waiting."

"Just met him," I answered when he again covered the phone. "Charming man."

He grabbed me gently by the chin and turned my face back and forth. He twisted a finger around a particularly kinky curl. "And he's letting you stay?" he asked, doubt obvious in his voice.

I nodded.

"Girl, you must have brought some Louisiana voodoo magic with you to manage that feat."

"I'm from New York."

"Well then, some Brooklyn voodoo magic, baby." He laughed. "The strong stuff."

I smiled. If I did have voodoo magic I wouldn't use it on some rude, arrogant boxer or whatever it was Declan did.

"I'm Declan's personal chef." The man balanced his phone against his cheek as he extended a perfectly manicured hand. "You can call me Oisin or Chef or Cat."

I frowned as I shook his hand. "Cat?"

He winked. "Cookies Any Time, my little voodoo queen."

I narrowed my eyes as I maintained my grip on his hand. "Mint chocolate chip with rainbow sprinkles?"

He grinned and swept into a low bow. "Your wish is my command."

Awestruck, I dropped his hand and whispered, "Maybe I am Sleeping Beauty."

"Don't you fall asleep yet," Oisin said. "We have to get you to your room. Come along, I'll show you the way."

I slung my backpack back on my shoulder and followed.

Oisin returned to his phone call. "I've told you a hundred times now. I need the limes by Friday. I'll stay on hold all day long if I have to." Oisin pointed to a swinging door to my right. "There's the kitchen, aka where I live. It's state of the art. Anything and everything you'll need you can find in there and if you can't, you know who to ask."

"You?" I guessed.

"Hell no!" He laughed. "Go bother Seamus."

I chuckled as he held up a finger while we walked on. "Yes, this Friday," he complained. "Yes, it has to be this Friday. I'll hold." He shook his head at me and whispered, "There's tons of parklands and woods and flowers and dirty stuff out there if you aren't allergic to the sun like me."

I stared out at the beautiful green grounds of the mansion as we passed a row of tall, narrow peaked windows. I loved Central Park in NYC, but here it seemed I'd be less likely to get stabbed by a junkie's needle while cloud gazing.

"Declan's gym is here to the left."

Through floor-to-ceiling glass panels, I could see the massive gym full of exercise equipment, weights, machines, and its own boxing ring.

As we passed I spied Declan pounding away at a punching bag. I thought it was going to explode. "So, the boss is a little, umm..." I shrugged as we went on. "A little beastly."

Oisin placed a hand on my shoulder to guide me toward a staircase to the right. "Trust me, his bark is worse than his bite." He suddenly held up a finger to me as he paused on the stairs and rolled his eyes. "Yes, George. I'm still be here. You don't have to keep checking. I'm not going till I get what I need." We started to climb again and Oisin continued, "Declan has been going through a rough time. I've worked for him for a long time and he's a good guy, the best guy, really. He just...pain makes us all a little mean, I guess."

I nodded, wondering what exactly he meant.

"The treatment area is here, directly above the gym," Oisin pointed out. "Declan spared no expense. Massage, spa, sauna, steam room. Afraid you might not have much time to use it, though. Declan will keep you pretty busy." As we followed the long hallway, Oisin again stopped and huffed in frustration. "Give me just two seconds, dear." He squeezed my arm. "I have to go all Momma Bear on this asshole."

"No worries."

"Listen here, George-y Boy," Oisin said, stalking off back down the hallway. "Getting back into fighting shape means everything to Declan, and I'm not going to be the one who gets in his way because I can't find a single organic lime on this entire feckin' island."

The echo of his voice faded as I wandered a little farther. A half-cracked door down a small hallway caught my eye. I glanced back at Oisin, who still waved his arm about, despite the person on the phone not being able to see him. Chewing at the inside of my mouth, I hesitated for just a moment before tiptoeing down the hall and slipping inside.

A grand canopy bed, pressed and made, stood in the centre of the room with drapes drawn tight. I peeked into the closet to find it filled with sequined evening gowns, fine silk blouses, and a Sax Fifth Avenue worth of heels. My scuffed sneakers squeaked on the white marble floor as I toured the gorgeous en suite bathroom with a gold clawfoot tub and a vanity still filled with high-end makeup.

Back in the bedroom, I found a picture frame turned face

down on the bedside table. I knew I shouldn't look. I should have left, closed the door behind me, and never returned. But I could only fight the curiosity for so long and after a few moments of staring at it, I quickly flipped it over.

It was a picture of Declan and a gorgeous woman on a yacht in crystal blue waters off of some white sand beach. I leaned in close and noticed he didn't have the scar near his left eye. The scowl was missing, too. It was shocking to me, but he was actually smiling—a big, wide, happy *smile*.

I jumped as Oisin poked his head into the room.

"My little voodoo queen, get your cute ass out of there," he hissed.

The picture frame slipped from my fingers and clattered to the table. I darted out of the room, leaving behind the mysterious woman and the man who appeared just as much a stranger.

"You're not supposed to be in there," Oisin said as he reached over me to quickly close the door.

"It was open."

Oisin frowned.

"Open?"

"Cracked."

"Curious." He tapped his chin for a moment and then grabbed my hand and spun around on his heel, dragging me along behind him.

"Whose room is that?"

"A ghost," he said with a shudder.

"A ghost?" I glanced up at him, trying to search his face.

"Don't ever go in there again, alright?" Oisin wouldn't look down at me as he increased the speed of his steps next to me. "It's off limits."

Over my shoulder, I looked back toward the hallway with the strange room.

"Trust me." Oisin shook his head. "You don't want to go near there."

I didn't understand. "Why not?"

I watched as Oisin practically shuddered. "It's a cursed place," he explained. "There's nothing but pain in there."

Slowly, I said, "You're not making any sense."

"It doesn't have to make sense. Just know that if Declan saw you in there, at the very least you'd be fired on the spot."

I hesitated before asking, "And at the very worst?"

Oisin stopped and leaned down so he was face-to-face with me. He placed a hand on each of my shoulders. Before he spoke, he looked down the ornate hallway in each direction. "It's Giselle's old room," he whispered.

"Giselle?" I racked my brain.

"They had separate rooms and that was hers."

"What happened to her?" I asked.

Oisin poked my nose. "No more questions."

"Where is she now?"

"Nope."

"Why does Declan keep all of her stuff in there?"

"Not a chance."

"What's the worst Declan will do if he sees me in there?" It hadn't escaped my attention that he hadn't answered that question earlier.

Oisin shook his head again. "You will not work your voodoo magic on me, little lady. I've already said too much." He mimed locking his mouth and throwing away the key. "You know what they say about loose lips."

I shrugged. "They sink ships?"

"Worse." He winked down at me. "They waste lipstick." He nodded over my shoulder at a door. "This is you."

"Me?"

"Your room." He pushed the door open for me and flipped on the light.

I stepped inside and looked around. It certainly wasn't as luxurious as Giselle's room, whoever she was, but the bed looked comfy with lots of fluffy pillows and the windows overlooked a pretty little garden. "This is great," I said. "I'm ready to sleep for thirty hours."

As I headed toward the bed to deal with my looming jetlag,

Oisin clicked his tongue. "Eh, eh, not so fast." He pointed to a binder on a small wooden desk in the corner. "You've got homework."

Tossing my duffel bag onto the bed, I wandered over to the desk. "Homework?" I asked.

"Declan expects you to have read and memorized it all for your start tomorrow at 7 a.m."

I whirled around in horror. "Seven a.m.? I haven't slept in two days."

Oisin just shrugged.

I returned my attention to the large binder. "Job Manual," I read the intimidating bold black letters on the front. "I've had high school textbooks thicker than this." I thumbed through the dozens of pages. Hundreds?

"I wouldn't worry about it too much, my little voodoo queen," Oisin said, lingering in the doorway to my room. "No matter what you do, Declan's going to find a way to get rid of you."

I nodded as he closed the door behind him.

Not if I had something to say about it. I wasn't going back. Wouldn't go back.

River

In the quiet kitchen, I drummed my fingers against Declan's detailed weekday morning schedule thoroughly outlined in the Job Manual folder Oisin left with me the night before. I rubbed at the drool stain from where I fell asleep on the pages sometime past 2 a.m. Turns out the pages of Declan's dietary restrictions and appropriate healthy substitutions isn't exactly thrilling late night reading.

Yawning and glancing around the kitchen for the coffee pot, I considered what to make for Declan's 8 a.m. *prompt* breakfast. As I opened the cabinets and meandered through the pantry, it was quickly obvious that the options were endless. Oisin's kitchen was better stocked than the Whole Foods store I couldn't afford that had been located beneath my NY apartment.

I wanted to impress Declan on my first day, so I picked a meal even the grumpiest of grumps couldn't resist smiling at.

Within minutes I had my apron tied on, my ingredients laid out across the large marble island, and a steaming cup of coffee in my hand to fuel my culinary genius. But something was missing. Standing in the centre of the kitchen, I eyed the auxiliary cord connected to a state-of-the-art surround sound system. A little music never hurt anybody. I would keep it down, just loud enough to hum along to it.

And honest to God, it started off low. It's just that when I passed the stereo to get to the fridge to put the milk away, I turned it up just a smidge. And while I stirred the blueberries into the pancake batter with the bowl held against my chest, I just happened to dance over on my bare toes toward the stereo and *oops*, the music got a little louder. It wasn't my fault that while the pancakes cooked in the skillet, I had nothing else to do but turn the knob higher and higher and higher between each flip.

By the time I was arranging a fresh mint leaf on top of the fruit salad, drizzling the pancakes with maple syrup, and pouring a big glass of freshly squeezed orange juice, I was singing at the top of my lungs to my girl Whitney Houston, belting out "I Wanna Dance with Somebody" in the kitchen.

"I wanna feel the heat with somebo—"

The music abruptly stopped and I whirled around, dropping my microphone—I mean, spatula. It clattered to the floor as I stared at Declan, who frowned at me by the stereo with his finger still on the power button.

"Oh, hi, morning," I said cheerfully as I untied my apron and slipped it over my head. "How are you feeling?"

His dark auburn hair was wet from a shower and it hung low over his blue eyes. I thought I could still see tiny drops of water clinging to his thick, long eyelashes. I wanted to lean in to see closer, but the ferocity of his glare stopped me. He remained silent as I waited for him to speak.

He wore gym shorts again, all black, sneakers again, all black, and had a towel slung around his shoulders, also black.

I glanced down at my rainbow-striped sweater where there was not a trace of black. Shifting uncomfortably under Declan's unwavering angry eyes, I scratched at the back of my neck. "Um, did you sleep well?"

Declan ignored me as his eyes moved to the dirty kitchen surrounding me.

To distract him from the mess and to distract myself from the contour of his abs, I walked around the kitchen island and pulled out a bar stool. "Breakfast…" I swept my arm across the masterpiece, "… is served!" I patted the seat of the bar stool.

Declan did not move an inch.

"I thought we could start with fresh squeezed orange juice." I pushed the glass closer to him.

He didn't even look at it, his eyes were fixed on me.

"And here's some fruit I picked from the garden, and then for the grand finale…" I imitated a drumroll on my legs. "Pancakes!"

Declan blinked. I think…

"My friend, her name is Miley," I was starting to babble, "she swears they're the best in the tri-state area." I held out a fork for Declan to try it.

He seemed set on just glaring.

"Then before your training, I was thinking I could lead you through some yoga," I continued, hurrying over to the binder now stained with both drool and pancake batter. "It's not on the schedule here, but I've found it can help to calm the mind, prepare the body, open the heart space and stuff, you know?"

He did have a heart space, right?

"Have you tried meditation?"

Declan did not answer.

"Have you had your chakras cleansed recently?"

After several moments of long, drawn-out awkward silence, I drummed my fingers against my leg and started to ask, "Have you had your chakras cleansed recen—"

I stopped mid-sentence and watched in confusion as Declan

suddenly crossed the kitchen, grabbed the platter of golden, fluffy, warm blueberry pancakes smothered in steaming butter, glistening with maple syrup and lightly and lovingly dusted with powdered sugar and promptly dumped the entirety of it into the industrial-size blender on the counter. I gasped in horror as he then shoved in several raw eggs, milk, a bundle of kale, two whole carrots, and half an eggplant. He fit the lid on top before turning to me.

He waited till I met his eyes and then shoved his finger down on the pulverise button.

A piece of my soul died as the bright blue of the berries and the golden brown of the cinnamon and butter turned into a stomach-churning greenish brown.

Without even taking the time to reach for a glass, Declan tipped back the monstrosity and chugged it down without coming up for air.

I resisted the urge to gag as he tossed the blender into the already overflowing sink of dirty dishes and stormed right past me out of the kitchen. The last of the maple syrup dripped to the floor from the empty platter Declan left haphazardly on the edge of the counter. With a quick glance down the hallway, I stuck out a finger to catch a drop, licked it off, grabbed the binder, and hurried after my new boss.

I certainly wouldn't be getting any sweetness from him.

Declan

Seven days.

I only had to last seven days.

Seven days and the girl would be gone.

As I stalked toward my gym, trying to repress the frustration and anger igniting my blood, I heard the echo of fast little footsteps behind me. I groaned and rolled my eyes.

"I can cook something else tomorrow if you don't like pancakes," the girl said as she ran up beside me.

I kept my eyes straight forward.

"French toast, maybe?" She had to jog to keep up with my long, brisk stride. "I can do a *mean* French toast with strawberries and basil. I like to use croissants instead of brioche, actually."

Out of the corner of my eye, I noticed the girl struggling under the weight of the binder containing her Job Manual. My first thought was to hold it for her, but I immediately strangled that urge. Those were dangerous thoughts. I would kill each and every one of them.

"Do you want to know my secret?" she asked with that endlessly merry singsong voice I hated so much.

I walked faster toward my gym.

"My secret…" she caught up with me, nearly running now, "…is to take the recommended amount of butter for the recipe and double it."

We passed the foyer where I should have given her the boot yesterday and still she didn't shut up.

"So what do you say? French toast tomorrow?"

"No." My voice felt raw, hoarse, rough.

"No?" She shifted the binder to the other arm. "Okay, well, how do you feel about bacon and maple donuts?"

"No," I growled. "Christ, did you read the manual?"

"Of course!"

I hazarded a glance over at her when she paused. Her hair bounced wildly as she struggled to keep up with me. Why couldn't she tie it back? It was driving me crazy.

"I mean, most of it, at least," she finally said quickly before moving on. "I've got a sure winner here. What about banana bread pudding? Just minus the raisins. Nobody likes the raisins. Maybe chocolate chips instead."

That was it…the last straw.

I stopped so abruptly that the girl had to walk back a few steps to stand in front of me. She looked up at me with such sweet, innocent eyes.

I had to crush that. "Banana bread pudding?" I crossed my arms. "For breakfast?"

The girl looked oddly confused. "Sure, why not?"

I laughed incredulously. "Why not? Why not?" I shook my head. "Because banana bread pudding is a dessert, first of all."

"Says who?" she protested.

"Second, it's unhealthy."

"Very good for your mental health." She lifted a finger to point out, nearly dropping the binder in the process.

"And third, I don't have the time for it." With this, I spun on my heel and marched past her into the gym, shoving the doors open in frustration and enjoying the sound of them slamming against the walls. I grabbed my jump rope off the peg and started as the girl pushed her way inside, struggling against the heavy doors.

"Don't have time for it?" she asked. "How long can it take to eat banana bread pudding?"

"Too long," I answered.

The buzz of the jump rope whipping past my ears soothed the anger that had been boiling up inside my chest since I saw the girl in the kitchen that morning. I spun it faster and faster around me, trying to block out the sight of her next to me. That worked well enough, but no matter how fast I went I still saw my memory of her dancing in the kitchen: carefree, happy, joyful.

Disgusting.

The girl bit at her plump bottom lip as she continued to muse over my words. Finally, she said, "Surely a minute or two can't matter."

I dropped the rope and stalked toward her.

She looked up at me in surprise, her eyes widening.

"A minute or two is all that matters," I growled. "A minute or two can mean the difference between knocking someone out and being the one lying there on the floor with blood in your mouth."

I loomed over her as I stepped closer.

Her eyes flinched, but she did not retreat.

"A minute or two more can mean the difference between

reclaiming my title as MMA Champion or never stepping foot in the ring ever again."

Why wasn't she retreating from me? I was shouting, my biceps were bulging as I clenched my fists at my sides, and anger surely burned in my eyes.

"A minute or two is the difference between decay and rebirth." My red face was mere inches from hers as I ranted on, "Between ruin and fame, fortune, pride, between death and life itself."

My chest was rising and falling painfully as I gasped for breath. The whole time the girl just stared up at me with those eyes I couldn't stand to see and couldn't stand to look away from.

Then she asked a question I never expected in a million years, "A what champion?"

Her question caught me so off-guard that I stumbled back a step. "What?" I asked.

"You said something about a champion," she said. "An M something?"

Anger flared in my chest. "Are you fucking with me?"

The look of confusion on the girl's face only grew. "What, no, I just, is that some sort of Irish thing?'

I laughed. "MMA?"

The girl nodded.

"Mixed martial arts?"

"Oh, so like a hobby then?" She glanced around the expansive gym. "A very important hobby apparently."

My nails dug into my palms to keep myself from grabbing onto her neck. "No, not like a fucking hobby," I gritted out through clenched teeth. "Like the international sport watched by half the fucking globe."

"Never heard of it."

She said it so casually, so uninterestedly that I nearly bristled in irritation. Then the thought hit me. If she didn't know what MMA was, then… "You don't know who I am," I said slowly. It was not a question.

The girl shook her head.

"You've never heard of me before?"

"Sorry."

I was dumbfounded. "You didn't see me fight Manny Ortiz five years ago?"

"No."

"You didn't see me knock out the then champion, Killian Horne, within nine-tenths of a second?"

"No."

"You didn't see me beat sixty-three guys in a row?"

The girl shrugged. "To be honest, the only thing I've seen you beat is those blueberry pancakes back there." She thumbed over her shoulder.

I stared down at her in shock.

"So you hit people?" she asked as if she didn't buy any of it.

"I'm a fighter," I said. "I fight. I beat other men till they're bloody and unconscious on the floor." I waited as patiently as I could as the girl pondered this over. Who was she that she'd never heard of the great Declan Gallagher, hell, never heard of MM-fucking-A?

I wished it wasn't true, but this only intrigued me more. She was driving me out of my mind, and all I wanted to do was know more about her. What was wrong with me?

Finally, the girl looked back up at me and asked one single question with one single word. "Why?"

It was the wrong question to ask.

Roughly and without mercy, I grabbed her wrist and dragged her after me. The binder fell from her thin arms as I pulled her toward the small study at the back of the gym. She stumbled behind me to catch up as I flung open the door and pointed to the chair inside.

"Sit," I ordered.

As she stepped inside I went back, snatched up the binder, and walked back to find her looking small and out of place in the desk chair. I slammed the binder on the table. "You have your Job Manual here." I pounded my fist on the cover. "If you have any questions, don't ask me."

The door rattled on its hinges as I hurled it closed behind me and finally stopped wasting my time.

I had work to do.

River

At the end of my long first day, the manor's kitchen was again empty as I wandered inside with a grumbling stomach. I was expecting to open the fridge and try to scrounge up something tasty from the hordes of kale and chard and lemongrass. But instead, I found a silver cover over a large plate with a bright pink sticky on it that read in looping, dramatic cursive: *Enjoy dinner, my little voodoo queen.*

I lifted the cover and the mouthwatering aroma of a chargrilled steak with the creamiest garlic mashed potatoes I've ever seen and gorgeous honey-glazed carrots wafted up to my nose as I closed my eyes and breathed in deeply. Licking my lips, I quickly found a fork and knife in a nearby drawer and scooped up the plate that was so loaded up with food, it almost made my knees buckle.

I made my way down the hall to the cosy dining room with a roaring fire at one end, large windows with green velvet drapes drawn tight. At a large wooden table set with gold plates, shining wine glasses and polished silverware, a brooding and slumped over Declan sat, aimlessly pushing his uneaten food about his plate.

Sitting down at the end of the table opposite him, I scooted up in the big chair with the plush leather armrests, comfy cushions, and wooden feet carved like lions' paws. I grabbed the burgundy silk napkin and spread it out over my lap as the heat of the fire danced across my cheek. I reached for a wine bottle set on the table and poured myself a generous amount of deep red wine. Sighing contently, I was finally ready to dig in.

I glanced over at Declan. "So how was your—?"

"I eat alone."

His abrupt words and clipped tone caught me by surprise as I held my fork and knife suspended just above my juicy, oh so juicy steak. I don't know why it surprised me, though. It wasn't like Declan had been a rainbow-coloured box full of kittens so far. "What's that?" I asked, though I was fairly certain I had heard correctly.

"I eat alone," Declan repeated without looking up at me.

I watched him roll a carrot over and over again as my irritation grew. "I have to leave?"

"I eat alone."

"Are you serious?"

"I eat alone."

Staring longingly at the roaring fire and cosy, warm room, I hesitated. "Well, I'm already here so is it alright if I—"

"I eat alone."

I dropped my fork and knife in frustration. They clanged against the table as I shoved back my chair and grabbed my plate, the pool of butter wobbling in the middle of my mashed potatoes. I hadn't meant to take my anger out on the food.

Pausing in the doorway, I glanced back.

Declan sat still as he stared morosely at his plate.

"So, is this just 'cause you're in a bad mood today or is it—"

"I eat alone."

I turned to leave, but again leaned back into the dining room. "Like, every night?"

"I—"

"Yeah, yeah," I grumbled as I walked back toward the kitchen. "I get it already. You eat alone."

Back in the kitchen, I slammed my plate down on the marble island and sank into a metal bar stool that was cold, hard, and uncomfortable. There were no merry, twisting, twirling flames in here. No velvet or plush rugs or beautiful silk napkins. I grumbled incoherent obscenities under my breath to myself as I ate alone – cold and alone.

"Food's not good?"

I looked up from aggressively stabbing my carrots with my knife to see Oisin walking across the kitchen toward the fridge. "What?" I said. "No, no, why would you say that?"

He nodded toward my mutilated carrots.

"Oh, no, the food is out of this world." I brushed my hair out of my face and sighed. "Company's not good."

Oisin pulled out a naked chocolate cake and brought it to the island next to me. "You tried to sit with Declan?"

I nodded. "What is his problem?" I waved my fork around as my emotions started to take over. "I mean, there's twelve chairs in there and I can't sit in one of them? I know nothing about his life and I can't ask a single question? I have to make him breakfast, but I can't make pancakes or French toast or even a simple bread pudding?"

Oisin paused as he loaded a heap of chocolate icing into a piping bag. He lifted a curious eyebrow. "Bread pudding for breakfast?"

"He's insufferable." I ignored his inquiry in favour of more complaining. "He's rude and antisocial and a jerk and arrogant and prideful and rude – had I said rude already?"

Oisin chuckled as he began to cover the cake with dollops of icing. "It might have been mentioned, dear."

Chewing on the last bite of steak, I grumbled, "Like where does he get off treating people like that? Who does he think he is?"

Oisin nodded along to my rant as he continued his work on the cake.

"He's an asshole!" I huffed in frustration and shook my head as my heart rate began to return to normal. I guess I could check off my workout for the week/month/year. I dragged my pinkie across my plate to pick up the last of the mashed potatoes. "That's just it," I said as I licked it off my finger. "Declan Gallagher is an asshole. Plain and simple."

Oisin finished piping the cake and cut a slice that he pushed across the kitchen island toward me followed by a fork. He sighed and said, "I know you may not want to hear this, my little voodoo queen, thus the cake, but consider that he may have a reason to be."

I forked a big piece into my mouth. "Doubt it," I grumbled. I had to admit it was hard to maintain my current level of fury when I was tasting something so sweet and delicious.

Oisin cut a piece for himself and smiled over at me. "Give him a chance, darling," he said.

"I don't see why."

"You will."

I smiled at him as I ate my cake.

"You know," he started, "cake is a good pick-me-up, but do you know what works even better?"

"Cookies?" I guessed.

"Alcohol." Oisin laughed. "Lots and lots of alcohol. Why don't you come drinking with me and the staff this Friday night at the local pub?"

I drummed my fingers against my chin in contemplation. "David will be there?"

On one of my allocated fifteen minute "free time" breaks during Declan's minute-by-minute schedule, I wandered outside and found David trimming the hedges outside. He was a young Irish guy with an impressive knowledge of flowers.

"If his mom lets him." Oisin chuckled.

"What about Joan?" I asked.

I met her when she came into the gym during Declan's lunch to clean the equipment. She was an old, kind-hearted woman who spent fifteen minutes showing me pictures of her grandchildren.

"Joan's the craziest drinker of us all," Oisin answered. "I'm on my second appletini and she's put down five fingers of Jameson and three pints of Guinness."

I laughed. "And Declan?"

Sorrow shadowed Oisin's face before he shook his head. "Never Declan."

I grinned. "Then count me in."

River

The next morning, in my tiny, windowless prison—aka "small office at the back of the gym" if you were asking Declan—I opened YouTube and typed into the search bar: Declan Gallagher.

Miley insisted I do it while talking to her on the phone the night before.

"Bitch, it sounds like you're living in fucking Cinderella's castle," Miley said after I described the manor, its sprawling green grounds, and fantastic, warm, accommodating staff.

My feet waved back and forth in the air as I lay on my stomach across the bed. I frowned and said, "No, no, I think Cinderella lived in a dirty attic or something that looks more like our place in New York."

"Umm, excuse me," Miley mocked offense. "Our place is shabby chic and you know it. And I meant after she met her prince and all that shit. *Then* she lived in a castle."

I rolled over onto my back and sighed as I stared up at the ceiling. "Oh, well, you tell me when my prince is coming along then."

Through the line, I could hear the blare of a siren's horn and suddenly felt homesick for the bustle and noise and chaos of NYC. It was so quiet here. I could hear too many of my thoughts.

"Your boss sucks?" Miley asked, probably after the drag of a cigarette out on the emergency staircase where we used to sit and talk over too many bottles of cheap Merlot.

"He wanted to fire me the first day."

"What the fuck?" Miley shouted.

"I know." I laughed. "I may be back much sooner than I said."

Miley sighed. "We both know you didn't say when you were coming back, River."

I was silent for a moment. She was right. It was just that I never quite figured out how to tell my best friend that I was never coming back. "He's really fucking hot at least." I tried to change the subject back to Declan. "Washboard abs, chiselled jaw, piercing blue eyes."

"Damn," Miley said, a little less enthusiastic than before. "Is he a model? Is that why he needs a personal assistant?"

Picking at my cuticles, I shook my head before realising Miley couldn't see that. "No, no, he's some sort of boxer or something," I said, bored and entirely uninterested in the subject. "MMA? Have you ever heard of that?"

Miley laughed. "Who hasn't?"

I was silent.

"Jesus, River," Miley groaned. "I knew I should have taken that camera away from you and made you watch more TV with me."

"You mean our neighbour's TV that you watched from across the alley?" I grinned.

"Yeah, yeah, yeah." Miley was probably rolling her eyes, probably still covered in sparkly blue eye shadow from her last shift. "So who is he? Is he any good? Is he professional?"

I sighed. "Umm, I don't really know," I admitted. "I guess he won a few fights here and there. Or at least that's what Declan clai—"

"Declan?" Miley interrupted.

"Yeah, that's my boss' name."

"Declan Gallagher?"

I raised my eyebrows in confusion at the phone screen. "Yeah, how'd you kn—"

An excited screech cut me off and I dropped the phone at the unearthly volume.

"Jesus Christ, Miley," I complained as I held it back up to my ear.

"You're working for Declan Gallagher?" she continued to shout. "Wait, fuck, you're *living* with Declan Gallagher?"

My mind went to the memory of me getting kicked out of the dining room earlier that evening. "I wouldn't say living necess—"

"You slut, I'm so fucking jealous!" Miley screamed. "He had been the best for years. He's a legend. You have to find a video of him fighting. You have to see this shit."

"Definitely not into that kind of thing," I said firmly.

"Trust me, River, you want to see this," she insisted rather seriously. "The way Declan Gallagher fights…it's just…listen, you want to be a photographer, an artist. Well, the way he fights is art."

I frowned hesitantly. "I don't know, Miley."

She was quiet a moment and I thought I had lost the connection.

Then she spoke again, "It's beautiful. It is. It's fucking art."

So there I was in the prison-office the next morning, clicking on the first video I could find for the search "Declan Gallagher." It was for some championship, apparently.

I kept the volume down low even though I could hear Declan's fists pounding against the punching bag just outside. I leaned in close and winced at the first punch Declan delivered to his opponent.

It was violence, pure violence.

The muscles all along Declan's back rippled as he drew back his arm before his fist collided with his opponent's jaw, a splatter of blood erupting into the air dense with heat and sweat. Despite his opponent stumbling back at the bone-rattling strength of the blow, Declan showed no mercy. He launched himself onto his opponent like a wild, blood-thirsty animal about to sink in his fangs for the kill.

I continued to watch, shocked and horrified at the two men circling around the ring. Declan was clearly playing with his prey, drawing the roars of the adoring crowd as he effortlessly toyed with his opponent. He was the ultimate showman. He allowed the other man to land a punch merely to be able to spit blood back into his face, grinning manically as he did so.

Mesmerized and horrified, I forgot to listen for the sound of the punching bag as I was drawn into the spectacle.

"What are you doing?"

I looked up in surprise to find Declan at the doorway to the office, sweaty and glaring. No surprise there. His eyes fell to the video of him fighting on my computer screen. "This isn't work," he snapped rudely.

No surprise there either.

"Turn it off," he demanded.

The only surprise was when I ignored his command.

"This is what you do?" I pointed to the screen, my finger almost shaking.

He hesitated, glancing down at the screen before looking back up at me. "I already told you I fight," was all he said.

I watched the referee drag a kicking and screaming Declan off of his then unconscious opponent. The crowd was deafening as he thrashed, trying to get back for more.

"You didn't say that you liked it," I said softly. "You didn't say that you *like* hurting people."

Declan shook his head. "It's physical chess," he argued. "And I like winning it."

I stared up at him. "It's not chess," I said. "It's an excuse."

Declan leaned across me suddenly and stopped the video. "Your one-week trial is off to great start," he growled. "Get the fuck back to work."

I expected the door to slam behind him, but it didn't. It simply closed. Well, weren't we all just full of surprises? Even me.

Because despite protesting the unabashed celebration of violence in that video, I couldn't deny that it excited me. I couldn't deny that I thought about it all the rest of the day. I couldn't deny that I dreamed about Declan circling me in the ring that night, his muscles rippling, his skin covered in a sheen of sweat, his blue eyes trained on me, his prey.

I couldn't deny I wanted, just the tiniest bit, to feel the sting of his fangs along my neck.

River

That Saturday morning I was dealing with quite the dilemma. I wanted to groan because of the horrible pain of a thousand needles stabbing my brain, but the sound of my groaning would only multiply the number of said needles stabbing my brain.

I was lying in bed, contemplating this dilemma in the dark of the drawn curtains in my bedroom, when a pounding erupted at my door.

Thud!

Thud!

THUD!

"What the fuck!" I shouted as Declan crashed into my room.

I pulled the sheets up over my naked chest because I was butt-ass naked. I apparently forgot to put on the t-shirt and shorts I normally wore to bed after drunkenly stumbling into my room early that morning when Oisin and I returned, swaying arm in arm, to the manor from the local pub. "What are you doing, Declan?"

He ignored me as he stalked over to my curtains and flung them open. I groaned in pain as the rays of morning light accosted my light-sensitive eyes. As I suspected, the sound of my groan and my shouting made my head explode. I cradled it in my hands as Declan stood over my bed.

"Where's my breakfast?"

"Breakfast?" I blinked with squinted eyes up at him. "It's Saturday."

He crossed his arms, somehow making his biceps appear even bigger than usual. Usual…meaning the size of tree trunks. "So?"

I tried to keep the comforter against my naked chest as I stretched over to pull back the drapes to block the harsh glare of the morning sun.

Declan easily pulled them out of reach. "*So* I don't stop training just because you decided you wanted to go out and get shit-faced the night before," he said with obvious irritation.

Closing my eyes, I rubbed at my temples to attempt to ease the relentless throbbing. Foggy images of a small, crowded, smoke-filled pub flashed in my mind. There was a drinking contest with Joan, who wore a sweater with a kitten on the front she knit herself. Mistake. There was begging David's mom on the phone to let him stay longer with us. Mistake. There was dancing on the bar with Oisin. Mis—no. No, that one was a great decision.

"You train on the weekend?" I asked, noticing Declan's black athletic shorts and sneakers.

Declan sighed. "You still haven't finished the Job Manual?"

I glanced at it, untouched on my nightstand. "I have…" I lied.

"Employer trains every day without exception, including both public and private holidays, birthdays, or social engagements," Declan recited. "Employee must request for approval a day off of normal duties with a minimum two weeks' notice." He glared down at me. "So get up."

I gazed longingly at the cool, soft comfort of my pillows before sighing in resignation of my pain-filled morning. "Fine," I grumbled.

That was that, but neither of us moved. I remained in bed, staring up at Declan. Declan remained standing next to the bed, staring down at me. I waited…and waited…and—

"Well?" Declan asked with a raised eyebrow.

"You need to leave." Over the edge of the covers still pulled up close to my chest, I pointed a finger toward the door.

He glanced over his shoulder at it. "I'm not leaving till you get up," he said as he faced me again, face resolute. "You're not going back to bed."

I rolled my eyes. "That's not it. I—"

"In case you've somehow already forgotten, you're still in your trial week at this position." Declan planted his feet, obviously not intending on going anywhere.

I wasn't even sure a bulldozer could move him out of my room.

"I suggest you get up to make my breakfast."

I clenched the balled-up comforter in my fists and said through gritted teeth, "I will get up… once you leave."

"You're going to go back to bed."

"I'm not."

Both of us glared at one another as we each grew more and more frustrated.

"I need my breakfast now."

"The sooner you leave, the sooner you get your breakfast," I retorted.

Declan was clearly not used to someone challenging him as his eyes grew angry and he bristled with obvious frustration. He jabbed a finger at me and tried to keep his voice from shaking.

"Listen to me and listen to me real good…" His voice rose to yelling. "Get up now or you can pack your bags and get your ass out of this house this after—"

"I'm naked!" I finally shouted.

Declan froze with his mouth still open, half a word still on his lips.

"I'm naked, okay?" I waved one hand up and down the length of my body. "Under here? You see, yeah? Under here, there's nothing but me. Head, shoulder, knees, and toes, all naked. Tits, pussy, ass and hips, all naked. Naked, naked, naked."

I jutted my chin up in defiance as Declan ducked his gaze. But before he did, I could have sworn I caught his eyes skim the outline of my body beneath the sheets: the subtle hint of the roundness of breasts, the soft protrusion of my hipbone, the long line of my slim legs. He certainly couldn't get the whole picture, but even with the comforter pulled up high, he could catch a glimpse.

I couldn't help but imagine what would happen if I pulled back the sheets with Declan standing there. What if I lay there completely exposed before him? Would he look? Would he like what he saw? Would he take a step closer?

My heart rate spiked and the brush of the cool sheets against my now hard nipples sent heat between my legs. I was trying and failing to send the image from my mind when Declan finally spoke.

"Well, then," he grumbled after clearing his throat. "Put some goddamn clothes on." Eyes to the floor, he turned and stalked out of my room without another word.

After the door slammed, I sank back into bed and slung an arm over my eyes with a pain-filled groan. Why was I thinking of my employer like this? Why was I thinking of my asshole employer like this?

I was in trouble. I was in serious trouble. If the thought of alcohol hadn't made my stomach churn, I would have needed a drink and it wasn't even… I peeked an eye open to squint at my phone. Fuck.

It wasn't even 7:45 a.m.

* * *

It wasn't even 1:45 p.m. when my bedroom door crashed open for the second time that day during an impromptu dance session while cleaning.

"You've got to be kidding me," I shouted over Whitney Houston as she belted out "How Do I Know." "Don't tell me you need an afternoon snack. Because I have no idea where the Cheerios are."

Declan crossed my room without looking at me and smashed his fingers on the buttons of the speakers, cutting off the song.

"What do you want?" I placed my hands irritably on my hips. "I can do ants on a log. Little raisins on a celery stick filled with peanut butter. Is that what you want?"

"No music from 1 to 3 p.m.," he said in an emotionless voice as he walked back toward my door. "Page 23 of the Job Manual."

He was already halfway into the hall when I shouted after him, "Are you kidding me?"

"No!" His voice echoed back to me from the hallway.

"Why?"

Declan returned to stand in the doorway of my room. He crossed his arms over his broad, bare chest.

I couldn't help my eyes from following the trail of his chiselled abs straight down toward the v-shaped muscles at his hipbones that pointed down, down, down before disappearing below the low-slung waistband of his thin cotton lounge pants. I blushed and looked away to stop myself from hungrily searching for the shape…and length of anything lower. I focused on Declan's blue eyes, but dear God, they turned me on just as much as his body.

"I'm sleeping," he said.

I nodded while realising my gaze had drawn to his mouth. I quite liked the shape of his lips as well. They were full and soft and perfect for kissing down my stomach toward my— "Right, right," I shook my head to clear my dirty thoughts. I reminded myself I was supposed to be aggravated, not aroused. "But it's a mansion," I argued.

"No," Declan said. "It's *my* mansion. So no music from 1 to 3 p.m."

I squeezed my hands into fists in an attempt to hold back my frustration. I wasn't used to this…rules for this, rules for that. Rules, rules, rules. "I can't listen to music?" I asked as calmly as possible.

Declan shook his head. "You can't do anything that disturbs my training," he said. "If your music disturbs my training, you turn it off. If your endless questions disturb my training, you stop speaking. If your presence disturbs my training, you leave."

"If my breathing disturbs your training, I quit breathing," I mumbled.

Declan's perfect lips curled into a mock smile. "Glad we're finally on the same page."

I glared at him as I snatched my headphones up from the nightstand, ripped my phone from the speakers, and blasted Whitney into my ears. "I'm listening to music, Declan, and it's 1:45," I shouted over the song as I began to dance again. "What are you going to do about it?"

Swinging my hips to the rhythm, I spun around and shook my ass at Declan. "Huh, Declan?" I shouted. "What are you gonna do about it?" As I continued to dance, I glanced over my shoulder and paused. "Oh."

Declan was gone and I was alone.

"Well, I showed him," I mumbled to myself as I snatched up some dirty clothes from the floor.

I kept the door open the rest of the day because I wasn't sure the hinges of the door could handle much more. I wouldn't admit to myself that I secretly wished Declan would come storming in again.

I wouldn't admit that I was secretly a little disappointed when he didn't.

River

Declan wasn't exactly the smile-for-the-camera type, and the preapproved photos for his social media account certainly confirmed that. In my office at the back of the gym, I clicked through photo after photo of blank-faced, dead-eyed, straight-lipped stares in obviously posed positions of Declan "“training.” I sighed as I tapped the arrow key in boredom.

Click…click…click…

Declan pretending to kick a punching bag… Declan pretending to duck under an opponent's jab… Declan pretending to naturally wipe the sweat from his brow after a hard training session…

Click…click…click…

It wasn't a surprise at all that his social media engagement was at an all-time low. These pictures lacked all traces of authenticity, energy, *soul.* I'd seen Declan kick the black punching bag in the corner of his gym, his eyes locked in as his foot collided with the swinging bag again and again and again. I'd seen the ferocity of his gaze, the tension of his muscles, the vibrations through the bag.

None of it looked like these still, lifeless, dead pictures.

If only his followers could see what it *was* like…

With my foot, I pushed open my canvas tote and tapped my fingers on the desk as I eyed my camera just visible beneath my balled-up rainbow sweater. It wasn't the best camera in the world, far from it. But it was all I could afford and even then, it took three months of eating a diet of exclusively SpaghettiOs and leftover—only slightly mouldy—bread from the deli down the block before I could purchase it used from the local consignment store. It was old, glitchy, and a bit scratched here and there, but I'd learned everything I knew about photography on it and it hadn't failed me yet.

I looked from the camera in my tote to the Job Manual on my desk. The Job Manual gave specific instructions regarding which photographs to use for Declan's social media presence. They were even labelled on his computer as "Approved

Photographs." But if I could show him how the world responded to a non-staged picture of him…

Before I could stop to consider what a terrible, idiotic, *dangerous* idea this was, I snatched up my camera and rushed to the door. I only paused to peer through the crack in the door at Declan.

He was training with a dummy set up in the centre of the fighting cage, which was raised up a few feet from the floor. Seamus was nowhere to be found. Declan was alone.

I took a breath and slipped inside. Declan's back was to me as I tiptoed through the dumbbell racks, weight machines, and cardio equipment. The sound of his laboured breathing and the harsh pounding of his fists against the dummy was the only noise echoing through the gym.

His back was still to me as I checked the settings on my camera and adjusted for the dim light of the gym. I winced at the unexpected beeps as I clicked through, but Declan remained fixated on the dummy as he delivered a series of brutal uppercuts to its chin. Inching closer toward the cage, I raised the camera up to my face and leaned my shoulder against the wire panel.

Through the lens, I watched Declan duck and weave in front of the dummy, so light on his toes. He delivered a powerful jab to the chest and the dummy swayed on its stand before falling back into place with a loud thud. The muscles along his back tensed as he pulled back for another strike.

I frowned as I fidgeted with the zoom. Declan's body looked strong, powerful, fit, but it wasn't quite the picture I was looking for to put up on his social media accounts. I needed to see his face. I wanted to see his emotion, his passion, his raw, animalistic aggression. I wanted to capture that. To do that I needed to get closer.

The sound of my footsteps was masked as Declan punched the dummy faster, faster, faster. Harder, harder, harder. I followed the edge of the cage till I could just make out the profile of his strong, defined jaw. My heart raced as I lifted the camera again, closing one eye and nervously blinking open the other.

Through my camera, I saw a different Declan than the one I knew, or the one I thought I knew. The Declan I saw through my camera was completely unguarded despite the deadly fists protecting his face. He had no defence up even as he artfully evaded an invisible onslaught of furious punches. He was entirely vulnerable in that moment regardless of the impressive display of strength and speed. I saw that through my camera. I saw it and I knew.

Declan was in pain.

As he wailed endlessly against the dummy, I knew this wasn't a normal kind of pain. It wasn't the good kind of pain. It wasn't the pain of lungs gasping for air after sprinting a mile or muscles begging for relief after bench pressing a new personal best. It was the kind of pain that made people scream. The kind of pain that made people reach for medicine. The kind of pain that no one wanted to endure.

But Declan did not stop.

Instead, he moved faster, he attacked harder, he pushed himself further. Lines of agony etched his face as he punched the dummy again, again, again.

Why wasn't he stopping?

Again, again, again.

Why didn't he just stop?

Again, again, again.

Why couldn't I look away?

Again, again, again.

I took the picture and immediately I knew it was a mistake. The shutter sounded loudly in the gym and Declan whirled toward me. He chest heaved up and down as sweat dripped down his face. His hands were still curled into fists that hung low at his sides. His eyes, dark and savage, fell on me.

Then my camera.

"Delete it," he commanded, his voice low.

I glanced down at my camera and then back up at him. His breathing seemed not to be slowing, but spiking. "Listen, Declan, I was looking through the folder of your preapproved photos and I thought that I could help you take a more authentic one and—"

"Delete it."

I frowned at his rude interruption *again*. "You didn't even give me a chance to explain what I was trying to do," I said, squaring my shoulders and preparing myself for a fight.

Declan stepped closer to me as he neared the edge of the ring.

I tried not to take a nervous step back as his imposing form loomed above me.

"I don't give a fuck what you thought you were doing," he hissed. "Delete it. Now."

Crossing my arms, I glared up at him. He looked even more like a dangerous animal behind the cage wires. He wanted to consume me. I saw it.

"Delete the picture," he demanded. His voice was ice cold; his eyes, even colder. His single step closer to me was an obvious threat. He stood tall, high above me. Every muscle along his arms and chest was tense to the point of shaking. His chest rose and fell like he was still punching the dummy and not standing still above me. "Delete. The. Picture," he repeated.

I jutted my chin defiantly up at him. "No." The word was out of my mouth before I could stop it. "You hired me to help you and—"

I gasped and stumbled back as Declan kicked open the cage door. He leaped down and stalked toward me, pointing a finger at my chest as I retreated as far as I could before my back bumped into a weight machine. My eyes were wide as I stared at him in shock.

"Let's get one thing straight here." His voice was shaking with anger that only burned brighter in his narrowed eyes, the piercing blue replaced with the deepest of blacks. "I do not need your help. I need your *obedience.* I say blend a smoothie, you blend a smoothie. I say turn off your music, you turn off your music. I say delete a picture, you fucking delete it!"

Before I even realised that Declan had moved, the camera was already ripped out of my hands. I lunged for his arm, but was too late—far too late—as he lifted my camera high above his head, drove it down with inhuman speed and strength, and smashed it to the floor.

Gasping, I fell to my knees and lifted up the shattered pieces of glass and plastic that, only moments before, shaped my dreams.

They weren't going to fit back together. No amount of time or patience or super-strength glue could make my camera whole again. It was ruined. The pieces fell from my fingers as I stood slowly and looked Declan straight in the eyes.

I wanted to make sure he saw me.

I wanted to make sure he *heard* me.

I wasn't afraid that he would interrupt me this time. I wasn't afraid because I knew. I knew he wasn't going to fucking interrupt me, because I had only two words to say.

"I quit."

Declan

The wilted spinach was bland, the sweet potato had no seasoning, and the chicken breast was poached with not a trace of salt or pepper, and that's how I knew I fucked up. I'd become well accustomed to Chef's passive aggressive tendencies over the years. He knew I couldn't go more than a few days of intentionally sabotaged cooking that he slopped out on a plate, entirely lacking his normal pristine presentation. He knew I would relent and apologise for whatever asshole thing I did that time.

But this time I wouldn't give in so easily. Not for her.

In my dining room, *alone* just the way I liked it, I shovelled the cold and mushy, oily and yet somehow burnt, tasteless and ugly spinach into my mouth like I was a starving man and it was a five-star Michelin meal.

It wasn't even a good camera. I'd seen enough cameras outside the cage, along the red carpet, hidden in the goddamn bushes to know what a professional-level camera looked like. Hers was a piece of shit. Really, I did her a favour.

I wasn't going to apologise for doing someone a favour. That was madness, after all.

No, I wouldn't apologise.

My knuckles were white from where I gripped my fork as I stabbed the wilted spinach, squelching from the overload of tasteless oil.

All she had to do was delete the picture. That wasn't an outlandish request. Really, it was quite reasonable. I was perfectly reasonable.

I chewed the spinach and resisted the urge to immediately spit it out.

Chef told me the girl hadn't been out of her room since yesterday afternoon. Like I was supposed to care? I didn't.

I didn't.

As I forced down the spinach, it occurred to me that *she* should apologise to *me*. She broke the rules. She invaded my personal space. She took a picture without permission, a picture no one could ever see, especially not me.

I knew I was pushing myself too far. I was spending just as much effort on attacking the dummy as I was on keeping myself from screaming or passing out or both. Every inch of my body was in agony, but I kept going. Because I had to. I needed to feel strong, to feel powerful, to feel ready.

And I was terrified that if I saw that picture, I would see a man who was weak, helpless, never to fight again. A picture is a permanent mirror and I couldn't face mine. So I shattered it.

But it was her fault.

Her fault.

Not mine.

Fuck, this tastes like shit, I thought as I scooped up another forkful.

But why did she have to look at me like that after I broke her camera? I was fine till she looked at me like that, eyes watery and filled with hurt despite the resolute set of her jaw. That one look stabbed a part of me I thought was long ago callused over with thick scars.

Fuck her.

Fuck her camera.

Fuck this food.

I was attempting not to gag on the hard, lumpy sweet potato

when I heard the front door slam shut and angry footsteps echoing toward the dining room.

Three…two…one—

"Declan, you need to go apologise."

"Hey there, Seamus." I jerked my chin toward him before returning to my delicious plate of food. "Nice of you to let yourself in."

He pulled out the chair closest to me and slouched into it, scratching irritably at his beard. "Stop fucking with me, Declan," he grumbled. "Just go apologise. Go apologise now, you hear me?"

I ignored him as he scooped up the nearest fork and stabbed a piece of chicken from my plate. I held back a laugh when he immediately spit it out into the silk napkin in front of him.

"Chef's trying to give you salmonella, Declan." He paused to rub the napkin against his tongue. "You know if Chef's pissed, you need to go apologise. Is the spinach any better?"

I shook my head before I proceeded to dig my fork into the unappealing lump.

"So are you going to go apologise then?" Seamus asked as he reached for the bottle of wine in the centre of the table. He quickly found out, like I had just earlier, that Chef poured it all down the kitchen sink before setting the bottle back out. "Shit, Declan," he said as he sagged deeper into the chair. "Just go apologise already. I need a fucking drink."

I kept my attention on my meal.

Seamus finally grew irritated enough to lean forward and prop his elbows on the table. "Declan?"

"Buy her a ticket home," I finally ordered. "Or a ticket to wherever the fuck she wants to go. Just as long as it's not here."

Seamus's forehead thudded against the table, making the silverware clatter and a wine glass wobble. "Please don't do this to me!" he wailed. "Please, Declan, I can't go through the process of finding you yet *another* assistant again. I just can't."

"She's no good," I grumbled after forcing down the last bite of sweet potato. I wasn't going to give Chef a crumb of satisfaction, literally. "She has to go."

Seamus sat up and threw his arms into the air. "No good?" His voice echoed around the dining room. "No good?! Declan, we both know she's the best assistant you've had."

I slammed my knife down onto the table. "She made me blueberry pancakes," I argued. "With enough syrup on them to fill up a plane. A plane like the one she needs to be on. Now."

Seamus rolled his eyes. "Blueberries are high in antioxidants."

I scoffed. "And syrup?"

"Eh…" He waved his hand at me dismissively. "Surely, there's some anti-inflammatory shite in there or something."

"She kept me awake during my scheduled rest hours."

Seamus crossed his arms. "We both know you couldn't hear her." He lifted his eyebrow as he gave me a pointed look. "And we both know you don't sleep."

"She wears too many colours."

"You're reaching now, Declan."

"She asks too many questions."

Seamus shrugged. "Why don't you answer them? Maybe it'd be good for you."

I spit out a laugh at that.

"You need to talk to someone someday."

I ignored that too. "She took a picture of me during my training," I said with finality. "That's unforgiveable, Seamus."

Seamus sighed and rested his elbows on the table as he leaned closer to me. "Tell me this, Declan…" he nodded back toward the door, "…that stability ball in the gym back there. Why do you use it?"

I frowned in confusion. "What the fuc—"

"Just indulge me, asshole," Seamus grumbled.

Sighing, I leaned back in my chair and sighed. "It makes you stronger and better balanced by forcing your muscles to adjust to the shifting beneath your feet," I said rather irritably. "The stable floor can't give you that."

Seamus grinned and tapped his nose. "That girl is your stability ball, like it or not."

I stared at him.

He pushed back his chair from the dining room table. "You need her in your life, Declan." Seamus stood and squeezed my shoulder. "And I need those blueberry pancakes in mine. So for the love of God, just go apologise."

I watched Seamus disappear into the hall and heard him cup his mouth to shout toward the kitchen. "Chef, please tell me you didn't dump all the wine. I need wine!"

I stared at my empty plate while somehow feeling emptier than when I started eating. There was no fucking way I was going to go apologise to the girl. Seamus was dead wrong. Dead wrong. No, it wasn't going to happen. Chef could punish me as long as he wanted. I would never taste a grain of salt again before admitting to her that I was wrong. I wasn't going to apologise.

I wasn't.

No fucking way.

Absolutely not.

No.

No.

No.

River

My duffel bag was packed.

My passport was ready.

My mind made up.

All I needed before heading to the airport was a ticket.

I had no ticket.

Seamus, I sent you my resignation at 3:43 p.m. two days ago and I still haven't received my ticket home as per the employment conditions we both agreed upon. In case the problem is that you somehow missed my resignation email (or the ten I sent after that) I will summarize it for you: I quit. I'm leaving. Send me my ticket. So, in conclusion, send me my ticket!

- River

Ps. I quit.

Pss. Send me my ticket.

I pressed send on the email and groaned as I rolled over on my bed to wait. If I had enough money to cover the cost of the flight home, I would have paid for it myself and been out of there after a quick goodbye—and good luck—to Oisin, David, and Joan. Hell, I would have upgraded to first class just to drink that fancy champagne in celebration of escaping this place. But I was broke.

So I was stuck.

My phone beeped as I stretched out to grab it and check the message.

River, I'm sure there is something I can do to convince you to stay. Please, just name it and it's yours.

I read through quickly and typed in a quick reply, *Anything?*

Moments later, he responded again, *Anything. Seriously anything. You can't leave. You just can't. Anything, anything, anything!*

Great. I'll tell you what I want, alright?

Yes. Tell me. I'll make it happen.

Promise?

Seamus messaged back, *Yes. Absolutely. What do you want?*

I typed in, *A flight back to NYC ASAP. Is first class too much to ask? I mean, he did shatter my only camera. So I think it's fair.*

My phone was then silent. Crossing my arms stubbornly despite being alone in my room, I grumbled at the ceiling. There was *nothing* that could convince me to stay. Nothing.

It wasn't till a few minutes later that Seamus replied to my list of demands, well, demand.

River, listen, I'm begging you to reconsider your resignation. You're needed here, believe me. Probably more than you know yet. I know what Declan did was terrible. Just terrible. And I know he's difficult. That's hard to argue. He's been different since the accident. But he'll get better once he fights. Please, just give him a little more time. That's all that I ask—a little more time.

I skimmed over the email, shaking my head in disgust at every other word. I was about to reply with the classic American threat that "my uncle is a lawyer" when I paused and frowned in confusion. Accident? What accident?

A sudden knock at my door startled me and my phone slipped from my fingers. I clutched my chest and rolled my eyes.

"Unless you've got that ticket you can go away, Seamus," I called out.

His answer was simply to knock on the door again.

"I prefer window seats," I said. "Aisles are alright. But I will not accept a middle seat under any circumstances."

When another knock on the door reverberated through my room, I groaned, rolled off the bed, and stalked forward to yank at the door handle. "In-flight entertainment, too—oh."

Standing outside my room was not Seamus, but Declan.

I stared into his blue eyes for a second before promptly slamming the door in his face. I hopped back onto my bed even as another *knock, knock, knock* rattled my door. "Go away," I called out.

There was silence for a few moments as I listened for the

sound of his footsteps moving away down the hall. Surely, he would leave. But right when I was certain he was gone another knock came at my door.

"Seriously, Declan," I shouted. "I don't want to see you. Go away." I stared at the closed door. He would leave this time. But the hall was silent.

Knock.

Knock.

Knock.

I was starting to inform him where *exactly* I wanted him to go when the door handle twisted round and Declan stepped into my room.

"Hey!"

Declan ignored me, strode forward, and extended a box toward me. "Here," was all he said.

I glared up at him.

He was avoiding my eyes, clearly uncomfortable as he stood before me.

"Get. Out. Now," I hissed.

Declan just moved the box closer to me. "Take this."

I crossed my arms and shook my head defiantly. "No."

Declan's tense jaw twitched, his eyes still on the floor. "Just take it."

"No."

"Take it."

"No."

Instead of just leaving, Declan then tucked the box under his arm, pulled my arms easily away from my chest despite my struggles, and then plopped the box down on my lap.

I tried to grab it and shove it back toward him, but he quickly stepped away, just as fast as he was in the cage. "I don't want this," I told him. "Whatever it is, I don't want it."

"Just open it."

"No."

"Open it."

I spit out a laugh. "I said, 'No.'"

Declan stepped toward me as if to forcefully open the box himself, and I relented after shoving him away with my palm against his rock-solid chest. "Jesus, alright," I complained. "I'll open the damn box."

After glancing over at him to find him shifting from foot to foot and still avoiding my gaze, I tugged open the cardboard flaps and pushed aside the packing peanuts. My eyes widened as I pulled out a brand new, top of the line, I'd-stab-Miley-to-get-my-hands-on-one-and-not-even-feel-that-bad SLR camera. I stared up at Declan.

"This is your apology then?" I asked him.

His eyes flickered over to me as his fingers fidgeted in front of him. "You can stay on past the trial week," he said without looking over at me. "As my permanent assistant. I, umm, I want you to stay."

His words sank in while I held the beautiful camera gently in my hands as if it was the rarest of butterflies with the most delicate of wings. This camera was a dream, my dream.

But it came with a nightmare.

"No."

Declan looked over at me in surprise. "What?"

I placed the camera back in the box and held the box out for him. "I don't accept," I said. "You can take it back."

Confusion played out across Declan's sharp features, making him look younger and more vulnerable than I'd ever seen him. "I don't understand."

I nodded toward the box I still held suspended between us. "It's just not enough," I answered. "Please take it."

Declan shook his head. "That's the best, most expensive camera on the market right now," he said more to himself than to me. He looked up at me with hints of anger and frustration in his blue eyes. "How could that not be enough for you?" he demanded. "I can't get you a better camera. I—how—it doesn't, you—"

"I don't want a camera," I said.

Declan stared at me, his eyes searching mine. Slowly,

hesitantly, he asked with narrowed eyes, "What *do* you want?"

I set the box next to me on the bed and stood up. This was a negotiation, after all. I wanted Declan to know that we were on equal footing.

He eyed me suspiciously.

I squared my shoulders. "I want two days off."

"Two?" he sounded incredulous.

"Two. Per week."

I watched as Declan considered this. "You'll prepare my breakfast smoothies in advance, I presume?"

I chuckled. "Presume again, Mr Gallagher." I pointed a finger at his chest. "*You'll* be preparing your own breakfast smoothies."

He opened his mouth to protest, but I interrupted him.

"I'll show you where the power button on the blender is."

Declan's hand curled into fists at his sides, but when he caught me noticing, he slowly relaxed. "Fine." He sighed. "Two days off and you agree to sta—"

"I want to eat dinner with you."

Declan stepped back as if we weren't in my room but in the cage, and I'd just punched him in the face. "What? Why?" He asked the question as if I was asking something preposterous.

"Because I'm tired of eating alone," I answered simply.

Declan bit his lip and hesitated. "I eat alone," he said, eyeing me warily.

"Then buy me a ticket."

He dragged a tired hand over his face. "I don't have to talk to you, do I?" He looked nervously over at me. "Ask you about your day or the weather or that kind of shit?"

I shook my head. "Nope. I just have to be there."

Declan considered my term and finally nodded. "Fine." He turned toward the door to leave.

"And finally—"

"You're pushing it, girl," Declan said, turning around again to face me.

I could see in his face and hear in his voice how hard he was struggling to maintain his composure. Why? What did this man care if I stuck around? Could it be that hard to find another personal assistant? Why was Declan, a hardened, callused fighter, bending over backwards to please a flower girl from NYC?

"I want permission to paint my room," I finally said, studying the reaction in his eyes.

They flickered toward the stark white walls around us.

"White walls remind me of a hospital room." I answered his question before he had to speak it.

I expected a struggle for this last concession. I was asking to change Declan's home. I was asking to take something from him and make it my own. I was asking to make this place, his home, my home as well. That was commitment. That was finality. That was permanence.

But Declan did not protest. He merely nodded. And that was that. "Anything else?" he asked sarcastically.

I shook my head.

"Good," he said.

I watched Declan hurry to my door as if eager to escape my presence.

Why did I have such an effect on him? Was it the same effect he had on me?

Declan was halfway out my door when I suddenly called out to him, "Wait!"

He leaned back inside my bedroom with an annoyed, quirked eyebrow.

"I want one more thing," I said.

Declan waited.

I swallowed, for some reason more nervous to ask for this than any of three requests earlier. I forced myself to keep Declan's gaze. I raised my chin. "I want you to call me by name."

He stared at me for a silent moment. "Is that it?"

"Yes."

He nodded. "Goodnight, River."

Declan

"Where is the kale? Where the fuck is the goddamn kale?"

Grumbling irritably to myself, I shoved aside tomatoes, eggplants, and zucchini in the walk-in fridge at the back of the kitchen. A red pepper rolled off the shelf and after leaning down to grab it I smacked my head on the wooden shelf above me.

"Motherfucker," I growled.

I hurled the pepper across the empty, quiet kitchen, not caring as it bounced off the rain-streaked window and rolled across the floor as I rubbed at the painful bump on my head that was already throbbing.

Why was I doing this? Why was I making myself my own breakfast smoothie? Why was I stuck in the kitchen on a Sunday morning when I should still be in bed getting the rest my body needed to get back into fighting shape? Why the fuck did I agree to any of this?

I was Declan Gallagher. I busted in faces, shattered jaws, bloodied eyes. I didn't *do* breakfast smoothies.

I'd overheard Chef calling the girl his "little voodoo queen," a ridiculous nickname. Absolutely ridiculous. But maybe he wasn't too far off after all. Because she somehow made me—the *employer*—agree to doing her—the *employee's*—job, while still paying her the same salary! If that wasn't some voodoo magic, then I wasn't sure what was…

It was those goddamn eyes, I thought as I gave up searching for kale and instead grabbed the first bowl I found, swept my arm across the vegetable shelf, and accepted a smoothie of whatever didn't fall on the floor.

Tucked under wild, dark curls and nestled amongst light freckles like little mountain flowers were the most alluring green eyes I'd even seen. They seemed to call out to me like a siren's song, even when the softest of whispers failed to escape her full, pink lips. I couldn't resist them.

I was crashing against the rocks for her and I didn't even care. I was spellbound in her presence, and that was the reason I was stuck wandering the kitchen, searching for the blender with a bowl of vegetables I hoped would make a smoothie when I should have been doing literally anything else.

I finally found the blender tucked behind the espresso machine, but when I went to throw in a tomato, I quickly realised there was a problem.

"Now what in the hell happened to the top part?"

I whirled around in a circle in the centre of the kitchen, searching the counters for the missing piece where you actually put the shit to blend. It was nowhere in sight. I began randomly opening drawers and cabinets, growing more and more irritated each time I saw knives and forks, bowls and plates, wine glasses, martini glasses, and champagne glasses and not a goddamn thing that looked like it belonged on top of a blender.

As I continued my rampage through the kitchen, I cursed the girl for putting me through this. Really, I should have been cursing myself. I was the one who relented when there was no reason to relent. *I* relented to the days off, *I* relented to the paint, *I* relented to dinner – fuck. I'd forgotten about that.

Tonight was the first night the girl would be joining me for dinner. She would be the first person to join me for a meal since…

Despite there being no chance in hell that what I needed was in there, I nevertheless clanged around a utensil drawer just to make enough noise to drown out her name in my head.

What was I supposed to even wear tonight? What was I

supposed to say? Was I supposed to look at her? Acknowledge her? Perhaps I could just pretend she wasn't there, I pondered as I finished my first pass through the kitchen without success.

If I was being honest with myself, I was nervous for dinner. I felt nervous to be so close to her for so long. Nervous to have her eyes, those intoxicating eyes, just a glance away the whole time. I was nervous I would find a way to fuck it up and drive her away.

I was nervous I wouldn't fuck it up and I'd just grow closer to her.

That couldn't happen.

It couldn't.

It just couldn't.

I stood at the sink with my hands on my hips with no fucking clue where to look next. At the end of my rope, I pulled out my phone and quickly texted Chef. *Hey, where do you keep the bowl part of the blender?* Leaning against the counter, I waited till my phone vibrated.

The bowl part?

I sighed in frustration. What else would someone call it? Did it even have a name? I was a fighter, not a cook. *You know, the part where you put the stuff.*

Ah. River normally puts it in the dishwasher.

The dishwasher, of course. I glanced up and tapped my fingers against my leg before picking my phone up again. *Right. And where's the dishwasher?*

Twenty-seven minutes after walking into the kitchen bleary-eyed and half asleep that morning, I had the blender out and the vegetables, eggs, and protein powder ready for my breakfast smoothie. Twenty-seven minutes of wasted sleep, missed workout, thrown away physical therapy.

Fan-fucking-tastic.

My morning just kept getting better as I tried to shove the head of broccoli into the blender. It wouldn't fit. Of course it wouldn't fit. I was trying to pound it in with frustrated growls when I caught a flash of bright yellow out in the rain. Leaning across the counter to see, I searched the back lawn just past the gardens.

There, out in the rain, with no jacket, no boots, not even an umbrella was the girl, barefoot and smiling from ear to ear, in a bright yellow sundress.

There was no sun.

"What the fuck is she doing?" I mumbled to myself without realising that I was stretching closer to the window to see.

I watched as she ran out to the centre of the lawn, craned her neck back, reached her arms out wide, and spun around in circles as she caught raindrops on her outstretched tongue.

She was crazy. That explained it. She was simply insane.

On a dreary, miserable day, when everyone else bundled up under the covers next to the fire inside, she ran outside *barefoot.*

I found myself worrying about her catching a cold and immediately pulled my attention from the window and focused again on my smoothie. The head of broccoli still wasn't fitting, so I raised a fist and punched it inside. Little florets snapped off and flew in all directions, rolling across the counters and off onto the floors.

"She's picking all this up," I irritably said aloud to myself. "The deal was I make myself breakfast. We said nothing about me cleaning. I'm not fucking cleaning."

Shoving the lid on, I jammed the button for the highest power. The blades whined loudly, spinning around and not blending a goddamn thing. I tried whacking the sides. Nothing. I tried wobbling the whole thing back and forth. Nothing. I tried pounding the lid. Nothing.

"Fuuuuuck," I shouted, angrily turning off the blender.

I looked out the window to see the girl still outside in the rain.

"This is what she needed a day off for?" I threw my hands up in frustration. "She needed a day off to go feck about in the rain?"

The girl splashed merrily through puddles, kicking at the muddy water with her bare toes. I leaned forward to see her more closely as she began to dance under the raindrops, her lips moving to some song, maybe one of the horrendous ones she insisted on blasting full volume. All alone and in the pouring rain, she danced and danced and danced.

Splashes of water kicked up around her, making her look even more like a mystical creature come to tempt me away from my path. There wasn't a trace of sunlight in all of Ireland most likely, but her in her sundress looked brighter than any golden afternoon ray. I found myself smiling and immediately chastised myself.

I forced a frown as I continued to watch, unable to pull my eyes away.

As the rain soaked her yellow dress, it clung more and more to her body. It outlined her shapely hips as she rolled them to some unheard rhythm. It traced her long legs as she jumped and twirled. I knew I was in trouble when the water plastered her dress to her chest, revealing the shape of her breasts, the peak of her nipples.

She was beautiful.

She was dangerous.

She was a distraction.

Wrenching my eyes away from the window, I focused on the smoothie. I jammed the veggies in, added the eggs, and ended up with something that looked nothing like it was supposed to.

It was nasty, lumpy, and foul smelling, and I suddenly had a craving for the goddamn blueberry pancakes I knew I couldn't have.

River

I hopped into the dining room on one foot that evening while simultaneously cleaning off my dirty toes with a towel and pulling leaves, twigs, and clumps of grass from my still damp hair.

"I'm here, I'm here," I hurriedly said as I pushed my curls out of my face and sagged into the chair across the table from Declan.

He sat frozen with his arms crossed over his wide chest, his frown set in its perpetual scowl. He wore a black V-neck cashmere sweater and his hair was styled for the first time.

I was surprised to see him in something other than workout clothes. I was even more surprised to see that he hadn't started eating without me. The Beast had manners after all. I thought I could even smell a hint of cologne over the burning wood in the fireplace.

Smiling politely over at him, I arranged the silk napkin in my lap and asked, "So how'd the smoothie go this morning? Did you find the power button?"

"You're late," he grumbled as he eyed my yellow sundress that I adjusted around me.

I watched him lean over just enough to frown at the hemline stained brown from the puddles speckled across the back lawn from the rain. "And dirty."

I stretched my hands out toward the roaring fireplace and sighed contently at the warmth. "The rain is just wonderful, isn't it?" I asked, smiling over at him.

"Dinner starts promptly at 6:30 p.m," was his cold, unemotional answer. "I shouldn't have to inform you that it's now 6:39 p.m."

I ignored his usual grumpiness and reached across the table for the closest bottle of red wine. "Have you explored the forests at the edge of your property?" I asked. "They're incredible, especially in the rain."

Declan watched as I poured my glass almost to the point

where the deep red liquid sloshed over the lip of the fine glassware. His own glass couldn't have had more than a few sips worth. "Perhaps it was my mistake to assume this was obvious, but I expect a certain level of decorum at my dinners. For instance, shoes are unfortunately not optional."

I wiggled my toes beneath the table, inching them toward the heat of the flames. Feeling the rich, dark earth beneath my feet centred me and calmed me. I wasn't going to let two minutes with Declan unravel me. "People think that everything is dull and grey in the rain," I said after taking a healthy sip of wine. "But that's not the way I see it. The rain saturates colours, gives them a depth, a richness. Greens are greener. Reds are redder. And wow, oh wow, don't even get me started on the yellows."

Declan stared at me, blinking slowly.

I smiled across the long table at him.

"I would really prefer you arrive to dinner properly washed," he finally said, a mischievous flash lighting his narrowed eyes. "Joan can show you how to find the 'power button' in your shower should you require aid."

Gritting my teeth to keep myself from reacting, I forced a pleasant smile. "I'm really quite a fan of the smell of rain," I went on, unwilling to sound anything but perfectly cheerful despite how easily Declan got under my skin. "What about you?"

He shrugged nonchalantly. "There is this one scent I quite like." He drummed his fingers along the edge of the table. "Perhaps you've heard of it. It's a relatively new one. I believe most people call it soap." The corners of his lips curled up in a smirk.

I glanced down to see the white of my knuckles where I gripped my butter knife. Releasing it and moving my hand away, I breathed in deeply. "You know…" I leaned forward onto my elbows and rested my chin in my hands as I looked across the table at Declan, who was at the edge of his seat. "…I enjoyed exploring the forests so much that I was thinking I'd take another walk tomorrow before dinner. Barefoot, of course."

Declan smiled and nodded. "That sounds lovely," he said as his jaw twitched. "I'll inform David to be ready to hose you down before you come back inside."

I smiled sweetly over at him and he smiled sweetly over at me, but there was no sweetness in either of our glaring eyes. We stared at each other in a polite, antagonistic silence as the fireplace popped and snapped. Neither of us was going to relent, that was obvious.

We were at a standstill when a familiar voice behind me asked, "Is it safe to come in?"

I glanced over the high back of my seat to see Oisin poking his head inside the dining room.

"No knives have been thrown?" He eyed both of us warily. "No chairs hurled? Bottles heaved? Forks flung?"

"We're having a marvellous time," I answered quickly, checking Declan.

He nodded. "Fucking fantastic."

"Beautiful evening," I added.

"Best night of my life," Declan mumbled.

At the door, Oisin rolled his eyes. "Yeah, there's no tension in here at all."

Whatever was going on between Declan and me was quickly forgotten when Oisin wheeled in a cart covered in a white cloth and piled high with silver-topped plates.

I licked my lips and rubbed my hands together in anticipation as my stomach growled.

"I've prepared a very special dinner tonight, sir and madam," Oisin announced after unloading everything onto the table. He sent me a wink before unveiling the main course.

It was the most stunning roast I'd ever laid eyes on. He removed silver cover after silver cover and I drooled more and more each time. There were caramelized vegetables, roasted red potatoes with fresh herbs, thick, fragrant gravy, and a loaf of French bread dripping with garlic butter and parsley and still steaming from the oven. Oisin swept into a deep bow as I clapped enthusiastically despite Declan's exaggerated eye roll.

"Bon appetit." Oisin then left the dining room, but not before calling back to us, "Don't drown each other in the gravy, you two!"

"I don't know what he's talking about," Declan said before promptly stabbing his roast with the biggest knife on the table.

I smiled a sickly-sweet smile. "Nor do I." I squeezed my fork a little too tightly. "We're having a lovely time."

"Indeed." Declan dove into his plate with an animalistic ferocity.

I took the time to breathe in the divine smell of the food first. I intended to enjoy this, regardless of present company.

Carefully, tenderly, oh so gently, I pulled apart the roast and eased it onto my fork. It was already melting and it hadn't even touched my tongue yet. My eyes fluttered closed like the typical girl in a romance movie during the first kiss as I tasted it for the first time… So succulent, flavourful, and *incredible*.

I chewed slowly, savouring each bite, not wanting it to end. I was on a butter and garlic and pepper river and I wanted to float down it for hours and hours and hours. Happy little noises escaped my lips as I chewed and swallowed, a bittersweet moment. Good thing I still had a literal *table* full of food left to enjoy.

When I finally opened my eyes to select my next bite, I found Declan, with a massive forkful of food suspended halfway to his mouth, staring at me. I couldn't quite tell if he was confused, irritated, or amused.

I raised a curious eyebrow. "What?"

Declan shook his head, grumbled something incomprehensible, and returned to shovelling food into his mouth.

I shrugged and next selected a beautifully roasted potato that was perfectly golden brown and covered with bright, fresh herbs.

I was slipping it between my lips when Declan suddenly

shoved his chair back from the table.

"Where are you going?" I asked over my potato as he stalked out of the dining room.

"We agreed to eating dinner together," he called back. "I'm done eating."

I glanced over at his plate and found it empty.

Declan's footsteps echoed down the hallway before disappearing entirely.

I sighed as I stared across at the chair where he sat moments before and told myself I didn't miss him.

The potato suddenly didn't taste quite as special.

River

Miley's voice filled my room from my cell phone set to speaker in the centre of my messy sheets and dirty clothes piled on my bed. I barely heard her as I wandered the room, snapping random photos between fiddling with the features on my new SLR camera.

"Hello? Bitch, you still there?"

I still couldn't believe how amazing the pictures of just bras, toothpaste, and dirty sneaker shoelaces turned out. I couldn't imagine the picture of a sunrise over the emerald hills or a dew-covered flower in the garden. Though what I really wanted to shoot was Declan.

There was something that drew me to him past just his strong jaw, defined muscles, and piercing blue eyes. I wanted to capture whatever that was I couldn't quite place my finger on.

"River? Hello?"

I wanted it to just be him and me, somewhere in these forests. I wanted to cup my hand along his jaw to tilt his face toward the light. I wanted to brush my fingers through his hair so it fell just right over his long, dark eyelashes shadowing his blue eyes. I wanted his eyes on me, only on me, as I unbuttoned his shirt, only my camera between our chests as they started to rise and fall more rapidly. I wanted—

"Bitch, I just told a hilarious story involving a unicorn, a rat on the subway stealing a pizza, and my ex, the magician, in a tutu and you didn't even laugh!"

Miley's irritated voice interrupted my thoughts and I quickly shook them from my mind. "Sorry, sorry!" I pulled the camera over my head, set it carefully on my nightstand, and leaped onto the bed like I used to do when Miley and I spent hours talking in her bed late into the morning hours. "I was just messing around with that camera," I said, which wasn't a lie.

"I still can't believe he got you that."

I sighed. "He's certainly full of mysteries," I said, which reminded me of something Seamus said in his last email. I grabbed my phone and pulled up Google. "So apparently he was in some sort of accident." I typed in *Declan Gallagher accident.*

"No shit," Miley said. "It was all over the news."

I covered my mouth in horror as I scrolled through paparazzi pictures of a terrible car crash. If I hadn't touched Declan and felt how solid he was, I would have guessed I was working for a ghost. Because no one should have walked away from that mangled mess of iron and flames.

"Ended his career, obviously," Miley continued after I heard her take a drag of a cigarette. "It was all over the news. Pretty sad it had to end that way."

I frowned at the phone. "He's training."

"What?"

I nodded. "Yeah, he's training to fight again," I said.

Miley paused. "Are you sure it's not just physical therapy?"

I remembered the ferocity with which he attacked the dummy in the cage. His face read murder, not healing. "No," I answered. "No, he wants to fight."

Miley laughed. "Sounds like he's delusional."

"He's not," I quickly insisted. "He's strong. He really is." I wasn't sure why I was defending Declan all of a sudden. I hadn't meant to. It just…came out.

"River…" Miley said my name with heavy implication.

I stared at the phone and huffed. "What?"

"You know."

I rolled my eyes. "No, I don't know," I said grumpily. "So you better just go ahead and tell me, Miley."

Miley sighed. "You can't get close to this guy, River."

I knew that was coming. Of course I did. "I'm not." I was becoming defensive and that should have scared me more than anything that Miley said.

"That's not the way it sounds."

"He's just my boss," I argued, my tone biting. "An arrogant, asshole boss who gives me a paycheque and who I feel nothing more toward than slight disdain and occasional irritation."

I imagined Miley holding up her hands as she said, "Alright, alright. Don't bite my head off, dude. I'm just saying."

"There's nothing there," I insisted a little too strongly.

"Fine, fine," Miley said, clearly trying to calm me down. "I believe you, okay?"

I stared up at the ceiling, chastising myself for reacting like that. That's not the way someone reacts who doesn't have feelings for someone. "Sorry," I finally said.

"We're cool," Miley replied. "I just wanted to warn you so you don't get hurt. Man's got a wife, you know?"

Her words sent ice running through my veins. I felt paralysed as I stared at the phone. "What?"

Miley sighed. "If you hadn't been living in the same building as me for a year in one of the biggest cities in the world, I would assume you've been living under a rock, River," she paused. "Or some hippie commune, I guess."

I appreciated her trying to bring levity to the situation, but all I could focus on was that one word: wife.

"Everyone in the world knows her but you, obviously," Miley explained. "Her name's Giselle and she's some super-hot model, you know, bikinis and wings and all that shit."

I remained silent, still unable to speak.

Wife?

Declan has a *wife*?

"Listen, dude," Miley continued, "he's got baggage. And lots of it. That chick ditched him for his biggest rival. It wrecked him, literally." She laughed darkly.

I stared unblinking at the phone.

"Yo, you still there?" she asked after a silent moment.

"Yeah, yeah," I tried to sound casual, nonchalant. I tried to sound like my throat wasn't tightening and my heart pounding. "Just got caught up in checking out this camera again. It's amazing."

"Good," Miley said. "I really didn't want to upset you or anything. I just thought you should know, you know?"

I forced a laugh. "No, no, I really don't care." I smiled even though I didn't want to smile at all. "I don't have feelings for

Declan." I hesitated a moment before adding something else, more to convince myself than to convince Miley: "I really don't."

River

I tried a quick cup of chamomile tea.

I tried focusing on the gentle wind through the trees outside my window.

I tried the old classic of closing my eyes and counting sheep.

Nothing was working. As I blinked up into the darkness at the ceiling of my bedroom, my fingers twitched toward my phone on the nightstand next to my pillow. I wasn't going to look, I told myself. I wasn't.

Rolling over with a frustrated exhale, I folded my pillow over my ear and squeezed my eyes shut.

Lavender...periwinkle...lilac...amethyst... Listing my favourite shades of a particular colour always helped. If I listed enough colours, I'd forget about my phone, ready and waiting just inches from my head. Mulberry...magenta...boysenber—

It wasn't working.

Pushing myself up onto my elbow, I reached for my phone, squinted at the brightness of the screen, and opened Google. My fingers hesitated over the keypad. This was a bad idea. Nothing good could come from it. I was only asking for trouble. Nodding to myself, I reassured myself I had enough self-control not to look.

After placing my cell phone carefully back on the nightstand, I put my hands into prayer, pressed my thumbs against my third eye, and repeated a calming mantra as I inhaled and exhaled deeply. My mind stilled, I slipped back under the cocooning warmth of the covers, ready for a restorative night's rest, and closed my eyes.

They popped back open approximately 3.2 seconds later.

Snatching up my phone, I again winced at the glare, opened Google, and typed into the search bar. My thumb pressed Go, but before the page could load, I tossed my phone away like it suddenly burned my fingers.

I growled in frustration as I tugged at my hair and flopped

back onto my pillow. I shouldn't look, I told myself. It would be much better if I didn't look, I reassured myself. I can totally not look and go back to sleep right now, I fooled myself.

Still staring up at the ceiling, I stretched my hand down and patted around the comforter until I found my phone. I squeezed one eye closed before looking the way children do when they're watching a scary movie for the first time; as if that would help.

Holding the phone up above me, I finally looked at the screen and immediately groaned. It wasn't as bad as I expected; it was worse.

Way worse.

I had searched what I knew I shouldn't have searched…Declan's wife, Giselle. As I scrolled down through the image results, she only grew more and more beautiful, more and more stunning, more and more *perfect*. She was a professional supermodel, and I could see why.

She was tall with long, thin limbs, but still somehow had a full, perky ass and massive tits that defied gravity. Self-consciously, I tugged at the opening of my tank top and glanced down at my own breasts in the light of my cell phone screen. I squeezed my arms together to create cleavage and frowned. It certainly didn't look like Giselle's, that was for sure.

I clicked on a photo of her at a beach shoot and my eyes moved from her smooth tanned skin—cellulite-free, of course—to her flat, toned stomach, all the way up to her prominent clavicle and elegant neck.

Did I have an elegant neck?

It was a question I'd never considered in my entire life, but suddenly it was all I could think of as I patted the shape of my own neck in the dark while comparing it with Giselle's in the photo. Despite seeing my neck daily and not noticing anything out of the ordinary, I was then convinced that it was impossibly short and awkwardly wide with a horrifically prominent oesophagus.

If Giselle's body hadn't made me feel thoroughly inadequate, one glance at her face up close finished me off for good. Her features were sharp and defined, while I was certain mine were lacking and unremarkable. Her makeup was flawless, just like her smooth, long, shiny golden—not blonde, but *golden*—hair.

I tugged down a kinky curl between my eyes and went cross-eyed assessing it. Little flyaways made it slightly frizzy, despite running my fingers over it to tame it. My hair was wild and I thought I liked my curls just the way they were, bouncy and free. But maybe it was just because I hadn't seen Giselle's sleek, not-a-hair-out-of-place locks.

With a sigh, I sagged against the pillow and let my phone fall from my hand haphazardly onto the floor. So that was who Declan fell for.

It made sense. Obviously, it made perfect sense. He was a successful, rich, famous fighter and of course, he could get anyone he wanted. When you could get the chocolate fudge brownie with multi-coloured sprinkles and a cherry on top, why would you settle for a vanilla cone, single scoop? My stomach grumbled at the prospect of ice cream and I laid a hand over it. There was no six-pack here.

As I stared up again at the ceiling and found it impossible to close my eyes, I wasn't sure why I was letting all of this affect me the way it was. I chastised myself for looking, but I was really more upset at myself for caring.

What did it matter if Declan's wife was gorgeous? What did it matter if that was Declan's "type"? And what did it matter if I wasn't that, wasn't even close to that?

I already promised myself I wouldn't get involved with my boss. I wasn't even sure I had feelings for him, I tried to tell myself. None of this should matter. I was Declan's employee. That was it. He surely didn't see me as anything more than that.

Which was great.

Just great.

Because I wasn't falling for him. I *wouldn't* fall for him.

That way I wouldn't get hurt when he obviously didn't feel the same way.

It was great.

Everything was great.

Just great.

Sapphire…indigo…cerulean…cobalt…navy… I sighed. It was going to be a long night.

Azure…

Sky…

Turquoise…

The blue of Declan's eyes…

Declan

My phone vibrated in the pocket of my workout shorts as I climbed the stairs to the second floor.

Seamus: *Where are you?*

I frowned and checked the time…our training session wasn't for another five minutes.

Me: *Why?*

Seamus: *You're not here.*

Pausing at the top of the stairs, I sighed in slight frustration. *It's five to.*

I waited for his response, drumming my fingers along the railing impatiently. My eyes skimmed over his message when it popped up on my screen.

You're ALWAYS in the gym AT LEAST a half hour before training.

ALWAYS.

Are you sick?

I rolled my eyes as I sent my reply. *No.*

In pain?

I was always in fucking pain. *No.*

Is it the arm?

My arm was still fucked, but that'd never stopped me before. *The arm's fine.*

Hungover?

Of course not.

There was a pause between Seamus's replies before a flurry came through.

Kidnapped?

Shit. Did someone kidnap you?

Are they asking for ransom?

If they are, it's coming out of your pocket, not mine. I hope you know that before I agree to their terms.

I sighed. *I'm upstairs. I'll be down in a minute.*

Seamus: *Seriously, are you kidnapped?*

Ignoring Seamus's last text, I continued on my way to... A few steps down the hall, I paused. Where was I going? Why was I up here on the second floor in the first place instead of down in the gym already training? I stared down the hall with the same confused expression as someone who walked into the kitchen and promptly forgot why.

That's when I heard the humming.

Sweet, cheery, *loud*, it could only be coming from one person: the girl. I realised with surprise that I was just around the corner from her bedroom. I wasn't coming to see her. I wasn't. I knew that for certain.

I couldn't for the life of me remember what I *was* up here for…but it wasn't her.

It wasn't.

At that point, I should have turned around, marched back down the hall, hurried down the staircase, and got down to training. But I wanted to go see her, the girl. There was a driving need inside of me to see her that I couldn't explain.

Maybe I was irritated by her humming.

Or I wanted to complain about my breakfast smoothie that

morning.

Maybe I had to make sure she'd finally finished reading the complete Job Manual I provided her with on the first goddamn day of employment.

Or maybe I just wanted to see her.

Rounding the corner, however, the first thing I saw at her open bedroom door was not her at all, but a horrendous, godawful, assault-on-the-eyes horrific, irreparably burn your retina it's so terrible, bright-ass yellow paint *all over my walls.*

"What the fuck is that?" I demanded from the doorway, staring unbelievingly at the monstrosity.

With a paint roller in one hand and a glass of wine in the other, the girl turned around in surprise at the sound of my voice and at least mercifully stopped that incessantly happy humming. "Oh, hey there!" She smiled at me before assessing her own handiwork. "You like it?"

I couldn't look away from how ugly the '80s yellow was as I shook my head a definite *no.* "It's awful." I stepped inside and groaned when I found it already on three of the four walls. "It's the worst colour I've ever seen."

"Well, good thing we agreed that I would get to paint my walls whatever colour I wanted," she said.

I expected to look over and find her wearing a neon headband, a spandex one-piece, and leg warmers. But the girl stood across the room barefoot with baggy vintage jeans and a light blue lace top that was tied dangerously loosely between her tits. With one side already hanging off her shoulder, it appeared ready to slip off of her entirely, leaving her exposed in front of me with nothing on but a smear of yellow paint across her chest.

The thought turned me on more than I was willing to admit.

The girl wiped the back of her hand across her brow, spreading a smear of paint over her forehead.

I found her eyes on mine with the quirk of an amused smile on her pink lips. Had she caught me staring at her chest? "You're not keeping it this colour," I quickly commanded with my usual gruff, all-business, no-nonsense tone. I needed to address her as an employer speaking to his employee. Because that was our relationship. And that could not change.

Heedless of the paint dripping on her jeans, her wine nearly spilling onto the floor, and her blouse slipping further off her shoulder, the girl placed her hands defiantly on her hips. "We said I could paint it," she argued, stubborn as fucking usual.

I pointed to the garish yellow colour. "I thought you meant cream or light grey or beige."

The girl mimicked throwing up.

I stared at her in confusion. "What?"

"*Beige?*" She said it like the word itself caused her pain.

I crossed my arms and levelled my gaze at her. "Don't you think you're being just a little bit dramatic?"

The girl looked me straight in the eye and said as if it was a simple matter of fact, "Beige is, without a doubt, the worst colour in the whole spectrum of colours, seen and unseen, discovered and undiscovered, dreamed and to be dreamed. There will never in the history of colour be a worse colour than beige."

She stared at me and I stared at her and the only sound in the room was a dollop of paint falling from the roller onto her jeans with a loud smack.

"The yellow stays, I say," she finally said with a curt nod. "If the yellow goes, I go."

Well, I was in quite the fucking dilemma, wasn't I?

Because I wanted to tell her just how badly I hated the colour and how much I wanted her to paint it something else. I wanted to tell her that I didn't like her meddling with my house. I wanted to tell her that this was too much change, too fast. But if I said all of that and still allowed her to keep this hideous yellow, I would be admitting I wanted her to stay more than I wanted my house my way.

I would be admitting that I could change for her.

I would be admitting that there was hope for me.

And I didn't want that.

"I don't give a fuck what you paint your room," I grumbled before storming out of her room.

As I made my way back down the hall, I pulled out my phone to a string of missed texts.

Seamus: *You're officially late to training.*

You've never been late before.

What are you doing?

Hello?

Are you dead?

You always get on my case for being late.

Now you're late.

What are you always telling me?

"This is the most important thing in the world to me."

"Nothing is more important than fighting again."

"There is nothing else."

I stared at the last missed text on my phone when I arrived at the doors to the gym.

Do you still believe that?

River

While I waited for Declan to arrive for dinner, I stood near the centre of the long dining room table instead of taking my seat for two main reasons.

One, I brought out a beautiful, multi-coloured glass vase I found tucked in the far back of a top cabinet in the kitchen. Then, after filling it with the brightest yellow flowers I could find in the garden, I wasn't entirely certain that Declan, upon entering the dining room and seeing it, wouldn't merely walk over, snatch it up, and hurl it promptly out the window.

So it was mostly precautionary that I was standing and holding onto the vase.

But the second reason I was standing when Declan arrived for dinner that night was one…I was less willing to admit to myself. Before coming down, I took nearly an hour getting ready. I stood in front of my full-length mirror with my nicest lavender sundress on, the one with the sweet butterfly sleeves I liked so much because of how they fluttered softly when I moved. I stared at myself and then took it off.

I put it back on.

Then took it back off.

I arranged my curls into a twist with bobby pins.

Then ripped them out and messed up my hair.

I arranged them again.

I ripped them back out.

I applied lipstick Joan lent me from her purse that afternoon after I shyly, sheepishly asked.

I wiped it off.

I carefully put the pretty red back on.

I hastily smeared it away.

I was out the door on my way downstairs in my paint-dotted

jeans and a t-shirt with my hair down and not a trace of makeup when I stopped at the top of the staircase. Rolling my eyes at myself, I ran back to my room and quickly threw on the lavender dress, pulled up my hair, and ran the lipstick over my puckered mouth, blotting on a piece of toilet paper the way Joan motherly showed me to.

Although I would never admit it aloud, I was standing as Declan entered the dining room mostly so that he would see me.

He entered with his normal brisk stride, laser-focused on his plate already set at the table. It wasn't until he pulled out his chair, sat, and spread his napkin across his lap that he spoke. "Why are those on the table?"

Certain he wouldn't hurl the vase out the window, I adjusted it a smidge and walked toward my end of the table. I swallowed back my disappointment that he hadn't noticed me. It was silly to expect that, after all. "I thought the place could use some brightening up," I said as I pulled my chair in, forcing a smile.

"I don't like it," he grumbled. "It's too bright." Declan chewed on a piece of meat, not bothering to look over at me.

I pushed a couple peas around my plate and wished I had kept on my jeans. I was promising myself not to make the same mistake again.

Declan spoke again. "You look nice."

It was said so softly and so quickly that I almost missed it. *Almost.* But I heard it. Declan was already slicing into his meat, his attention fixed on his plate, but I smiled at him nonetheless. Because he said it. And I heard it.

Unable to stop myself from grinning, I spooned up a heaping pile of peas glistening with butter and closed my eyes as their fresh flavour popped in my mouth. It wasn't like I could stop the giddy, delighted purr that escaped my lips even if I wanted to. And I definitely didn't want to.

I opened my eyes to survey the plate and consider the agonising choice of what to eat next. Everything looked so divine, how could I pick? As my fork hesitated over the peas versus the carrots, I noticed Declan giving me that look again from across the table.

"What?"

He quickly shook his head. "Nothing."

But as I was chewing on a tender, flavourful, oh so juicy piece of chicken breast and making little sounds of pleasure, I heard Declan clear his throat *loudly*. Upset that I was forced to rush through my bite, I opened my eyes and levelled at look at Declan. "What?"

His eyes flickered up at me from his plate before he continued to eat.

"What?" I insisted. "What is it?"

"Nothing." He shrugged. "It just seems like you're enjoying your dinner."

I leaned back in my chair and crossed my arms over my chest. "I am."

Declan twirled his fork in the pasta and I was about to return to my own plate when he spoke again. "Perhaps a little *too* much."

I frowned across the table at him. "What does that mean?"

He carefully set down his fork and knife, then bridged his fingers, elbows resting on the table. "Those little noises you make…" He paused. "They sound like noises a woman makes during…"

I saw what looked like a blush on his cheeks. I narrowed my eyes. "Sex?"

If Declan wasn't blushing before, he was definitely blushing now.

I tried to hide the little hint of a grin on my lips at his obvious discomfort. "Well, it makes sense, you know," I said, grabbing my glass of wine and giving it a swirl. "Eating a good meal is just as enjoyable as sex. So why shouldn't I make those noises?"

Declan scoffed, crossing his own arms. "I've never had a meal anywhere near as good as sex," he argued.

I nodded. "Well, yeah. Why would you when you're over there just dry humping your chicken breast with the only goal being to finish."

Declan stared at me in shock. "Excuse me," he finally said slowly and calmly, "but I am *not* 'drying humping' my chicken breast."

"With all due respect, you are."

Before Declan could protest, I pushed back my chair, threw my napkin on the table, and walked around to his side of the table. "Here, let me show you."

Declan's eyes widened as I approached him. "What are you doing?" he asked.

I sat on the table and crossed my legs.

My knee brushed his arm and he looked at it like he wasn't sure what human touch felt like. "This isn't your chair." He looked up at me. "This wasn't part of our agreement," he said. "Go back to your chair."

I ignored him and grabbed a chicken leg from his plate. "Close your eyes," I said.

Declan immediately leaned away from me. "Abso-fucking-lutely not. Are you out of your goddamn mind?"

"Close your eyes."

"Not happening."

I reached for his face and he quickly caught my wrist in his strong grip. I did not flinch. I was not going to relent. I stared at him and he stared at me. "Close your eyes," I said softly.

I was almost surprised when Declan stared at me for a moment longer, as if checking to see if I could be trusted, and then closed his eyes as I asked. I momentarily got distracted looking at him with his eyes closed: he looked younger, gentler, sweeter, even. "Keep your eyes closed," I said as I pulled a tender piece of chicken from the bone. My fingers brushed his lips as I fed him and I quickly sat on my hands to keep myself from touching them again. They were so soft, so full. "Let it sit on your tongue at first," I instructed, checking to make sure Declan kept his eyes shut. "Inhale the smell, just like you would a woman's perfume at the base of her neck."

I could see Declan moving to peek open an eye and quickly chastised, "Keep them closed!"

I heard him grumble, but he obeyed.

"Move slowly," I said. "Don't rip off her clothes. Unhook a single button, slide a single strap from her shoulder, start with her bracelet, your fingers ghosting along her wrist bone." I shifted on my hands as I stared at Declan's hands and imagined them undressing me. "Breathe in deeply." My eyes moved to his lips again. "The kind of sigh you let out before you kiss a wom—"

"This is ridiculous." Declan's eyes popped open and I saw him swallow before quickly grabbing his fork back up like a starving caveman. He stabbed his chicken leg and brought the whole thing up to his mouth.

I rolled my eyes, slid off the table, and took my place back in my chair. But as I continued my meal, I heard a little noise from Declan's side of the table. I glanced up at him and found his cheeks red.

"That wasn't me."

I smiled. "Okay."

"It wasn't."

"I said, 'Okay.'"

It was totally him.

Declan

I thought I heard it over the steady drone of the treadmill, but when I paused to measure my heart rate the gym was again silent.

Later, I swore I heard it when I pulled out my headphones between sets of squats. But if it was actually there and not in my mind, it was quickly drowned out by the clang of metal on metal as I began again.

It wasn't until the whirl of the jump rope in my ear stopped as I gasped for breath that I was dead certain I heard it. Won over by curiosity, I dropped the jump rope and moved toward the small office at the back of the gym where the girl was working.

Or *supposed* to be working.

As I got closer and closer, the noise got louder and louder…humming.

Again.

Always with the fucking racket.

Couldn't I get just one moment of silence? I hurried my steps toward the office door and raised my fist to pound on it, ready to shout at the girl to get back to work. I wasn't paying her to sing, goddammit. But with my fist raised, ready to strike the wood grain of the door, I paused.

I suddenly couldn't do it.

I suddenly didn't want to do it.

To my horror, instead of asserting my rules in *my* house like I should have done, I leaned forward and placed my ear against the wood grain so I could listen to the girl humming.

Thirty seconds went by. Twelve squats, eight burpees, thirty-six doubles on the jump rope went by. Gone forever.

A minute passed with my ear against the door, listening. Just listening. A quarter-mile sprint, a round in the cage with Seamus, a circuit on the leg press passed away with my body doing nothing but just listening.

Two minutes disappeared and I would never get them back as I stood at the door and listened to the girl. Two minutes closer to getting back into fighting shape wasted, two minutes closer to winning back my title wasted, two minutes closer to getting the only thing in life I wanted wasted as I stood at the door and listened to the girl.

And smiled.

I left the girl to her humming and went back to my training without saying a word. I didn't use my headphones or the gym speakers for the rest of the afternoon.

Later that night, after dinner, I went to the kitchen for a frozen bag of peas for my arm. It wasn't uncommon for me to do so, with the pain in my arm often reaching unbearable levels after a hard day of pushing myself during training.

I normally walked downstairs, my bare feet against the marble floor the only sound. The kitchen was normally dark, so dark that I would blink against the glare of the freezer as I opened it. Without a soul in sight in the quiet, empty manor, I normally returned alone to my room…alone to my thoughts, alone to my pain and nightmares.

But that evening, as I tiptoed down the hall on the first floor, the echo of my footsteps was impossible to hear over the loud, unfettered, merry laughter practically booming from the kitchen. It wasn't dark either. Quite the opposite, it appeared that every light was still on despite the time of night.

Careful not to make a sound, I snuck toward the door and slowly peeked my head inside the kitchen. At the large marble island in the centre was Chef, an older woman who I was fairly certain was the maid, and the girl.

In a light-pink tank top and matching shorts, she sat on the island, swinging her bare feet back and forth with a massive metal bowl of cookie dough in her lap. She giggled as she dug in a wooden spoon and licked dough directly off of it.

At the sight of this, I had three immediate thoughts:

First, I hoped that she didn't use that wooden spoon while making my breakfasts.

Second, it was a waste of resources, *my* resources, to keep the lights on when not necessary for the normal functioning of the kitchen staff.

And third, I wanted to join.

I wasn't sure where the desire came from, but it hit my chest like the fist of a heavyweight champion. I couldn't remember wanting anything other than to train and to get stronger and to *win* for so long that it was almost strange to me to want something as simple and silly as to go eat chocolate chip cookie dough with my employees late on a weeknight.

I wanted it and that was undeniable.

I hesitated at the doorway, certain they hadn't noticed me, and simply watched. The girl said something and Chef grabbed his stomach, throwing his head back in laughter I hadn't seen in months. Even the maid couldn't stop chuckling as she reached for the almost empty bottle of wine.

It was all so simple: happy people, eating and drinking and laughing. It felt so out of reach to me. It seemed like a life I might have had for myself, once. A life of laughter, joy, and simple pleasures.

But that life was gone.

He stole it from me.

She stole it from me.

And there was no way to get it back.

Without my frozen pack of peas, I turned around and silently left the kitchen, returning down the hallway, back up the stairs, and into my room. I closed the door and I was again alone, in my darkness, in my silence.

I held my pillow over my mouth to hide my screams of pain and did not sleep.

River

I wasn't used to silence.

In NYC, there was always the blare of some emergency vehicle, the honk of some cabbie, the screech of some bicycle to avoid crashing with said cabbie. There was the drone of TVs through the paper-thin walls, the 3 a.m. arguments of the couple upstairs, the incoherent shouting of the drunk on the corner. It was always noise, noise, noise.

When I was with my ex, Ricardo, he never wanted silence. There was always some kind of pretentious experimental "music" screeching from his music player, and if it wasn't that, some snippy art critic podcast, and if it wasn't that, he was gushing or verbally disembowelling something to someone on the phone.

Even while alone, I always reached for the nearest auxiliary cord to blast music – let's be honest, by music I mostly meant '80s diva pop—I thought something was missing without it.

So the silence of the dining room in the manor as Declan and I ate dinner was foreign to me. We again sat across the long table from one another, the only sound between us was the occasional clatter of fork against knife.

I assumed a lack of noise meant a lack of joy, a lack of happiness, a lack of life. But I was surprised to find that the silence between Declan and me seemed to lack nothing.

It felt comfortable. It felt easy. It felt natural.

With the crack of the fire and his presence across the table, nothing at all was missing. I was completely satisfied with our silences. And I fully expected them to continue.

So it was quite the surprise when Declan blurted out this rushed question, "What were you laughing at?"

I looked up at him with wide eyes.

He had set down his fork and knife on either side of his plate, as if the question was so pressing that he simply couldn't eat a bite more without receiving an answer.

The only problem was that I had no idea what he was talking about. "What?"

Declan bristled a little with obvious irritation. He was clearly uncomfortable and my confusion was only dragging it out. "The other night," he clarified with an annoyed sigh. "When you were in the kitchen with Chef and that older lady. What was so funny?"

My mind scrambled to figure out what he was talking about. Older lady? "You mean Joan?"

"I don't know her name."

I stared across the table at him. "She's been working here for you for six years."

Declan's cheeks brightened with embarrassment, and he quickly grabbed up his fork and knife again. "Never mind," he grumbled, sawing into Chef's rosemary pork chops. "It was stupid to ask in the first place. I don't give a fuck either way."

"No, no, no," I quickly said as I reached my hand toward him, afraid to let the baby step of progress go to waste. We were almost having a real, adult, mature conversation. *Almost.* "Joan was telling us a story about her seven-year-old son, Liam."

Declan's eyes were focused again on his plate, but I knew he was listening so I continued, "He was trying to steal parts of his neighbour's chain link fence and accidentally let their dog loose. Joan spent the whole night driving around to look for it and couldn't find it. She got home and the dog was right back in the yard, sleeping next to his bone."

After my laughter—and my laughter alone, at recalling the

story—died, the dining room again fell into silence. I thought our "conversation" was therefore over, so I returned to my meal.

Then Declan asked barely loud enough for it to be audible, "Why was the kid stealing a chain link fence?"

I rushed to swallow my bite of pork chop. "Oh! Right, right." I explained hurriedly while I still had Declan's attention, "He wanted to make his own cage so he could be an MMA fighter. He's a huge fan of yours, apparently."

I glanced over at Declan but he wasn't looking at me and he didn't respond. I sighed softly and mindlessly twirled some pasta around my fork. I was considering a way to engage Declan in more conversation. Perhaps I just had to put out a tiny bit of bait... "It's kind of violent for a child, in my opinion," I said nonchalantly as I tried to keep my eyes from checking Declan.

After another few moments of silence, he bit. "MMA is far more than violence, you know."

I reached for my wine glass to hide my grin. "What do you mean?"

"Brute strength and unfettered aggression will only get you so far," he explained. "To really master the sport, you need the mind. That's where you need to be toughest. It's all about strategy, like chess. You have to outwit your opponent. Your mental endurance has to last longer than his. It's far more than just 'violence'."

I nodded, remaining silent as I contemplated his words. Maybe he was right. Maybe I was missing something. Maybe there was more to the sport than I thought.

Maybe there was more to the fighter than I thought.

Declan then surprised me by adding under his breath, "Sounds like a smart kid to me."

I grinned as I scooped a heap of buttery pasta into my mouth. That was a conversation. It had all the necessary requirements: I said something. He said something in response. Progress! "Um, since you asked me something," I started slowly, knowing I was pushing my luck at this point, "maybe I can ask you something?"

Declan's eyes darted over to me. "I was just asking for clarification on an employee as an employer," he said. "That wasn't 'get to know each other time'."

I dropped my eyes in defeat and my shoulders slumped.

An exaggerated sigh came from across the table. "One question."

I smiled at my plate as I considered what I would ask. I knew I should ask something simple, something impersonal, something like 'Where do you like to go on vacation?'

Not, "What happened with your accident?"

Of course, that's *exactly* what I asked.

I fully expected Declan not to answer. I wouldn't have been surprised in the slightest if it caused him to storm out of the dining room. I wouldn't have even been startled if I heard the crash of glass or porcelain.

But after a moment of silence, Declan was still seated calmly and undisturbed in his chair. "I'm surprised you didn't look it up," he finally said. "You could find all the answers you're looking for online about what happened."

"I only saw the car," I admitted truthfully. "I want to hear what happened from you."

Declan shrugged, tapping his fork on the edge of his plate. "Nothing much to tell," he said, looking over at me. "It was my fault. I got drunk, got in my car and crashed. Simple as that." He returned to eating.

I didn't reach for my fork. Instead, I stared in confusion at Declan's nearly untouched glass of wine. From what I'd seen of his regimented routines, health-conscious eating, and drive to keep his body in tip-top shape, I couldn't see Declan doing something as reckless as getting drunk and driving. "You hardly drink," I ventured softly, not expecting him to reply.

"I did that night," he practically whispered.

I watched him closely and it seemed like he was about to say something more. It seemed like he *wanted* to say more. Pain, hurt, and anger seemed ready—*eager*—to spill from his lips. But Declan opened his mouth and promptly closed it. That was that. He chewed on a bite of pork chop and remained silent.

I didn't push him to say more.

I grabbed my fork and settled back into the comfortable silence I was growing to like so much. I knew there was more to the story. There had to be. I just had to gain more of his trust for him to let me in. We had a conversation for the first time and that was enough for tonight.

Baby steps.

Baby steps, River.

River

To the relief of my liver, the staff and I decided to skip the pub that Friday night and opt instead for a relaxing night in. Oisin cooked up enough hors d'oeuvres and finger food to feed a village, David brought his playlist to teach Joan what the 'kids were listening to these days', and Joan, of course, brought the wine. I brought my portfolio to show everyone my photographs of New York City.

It was a wonderful evening of laughing, eating, drinking, talking, and listening to music that David insisted was good. I couldn't stop shovelling Oisin's bacon-wrapped dates into my mouth, and I thought someone was going to have to wheel me to my room after we were done. As I plopped another one onto my salivating tongue, Oisin flipped through my portfolio, commenting on this photo and that photo. He was turning the page when Joan gave out a startled, "Oh."

All at once, our heads turned toward the door of the kitchen.

There stood Declan: silent, unmoving, face unreadable.

David jumped off the counter and placed his hands behind his back as if Declan was his drill sergeant at boot camp. His eyes darted to his beer and he not so subtly shifted to block it from Declan's view.

Joan set down her wine glass for the first time that night and Oisin hurried past me.

My eyes, widened in surprise and confusion, shifted between all three of them in turn. Why were they so afraid of him?

"Sorry, Declan," Oisin said as he quickly switched off the stereo. "We just lost track of how late it was. We'll keep it down."

"Sorry, sir," both David and Joan promptly chimed in, averting their gazes and stepping back.

Declan did not say a word. He just stood in the doorway.

We all watched him, waiting…waiting…waiting…

"Did we wake you?" Oisin prompted when there was still no response from our boss. "We're terribly sorry if we woke you."

Still in the doorway of the kitchen, Declan remained silent, his form imposing in the narrow space, nothing but darkness behind him.

I expected him to yell at us for being loud or yell at us for wasting his money on beers and chips or yell at us for, who knew, breathing too much of his air. But Declan didn't yell at all.

In fact, he didn't even open his mouth.

He merely stepped forward awkwardly, pulled a gym bag from his broad shoulder, and extended it toward Joan, whose eyes were still trained on her scuffed white sneakers.

Joan's eyes lifted hesitantly. She stared at the gym bag warily before glancing over at me, clearly unsure of what to do.

All I could manage was a quick shrug of my shoulders. I had no clue what was in the bag or why he wanted Joan to take it.

Declan cleared his throat as he pushed the gym bag toward her again. "It's, um, well, I signed some stuff," he said. I could have sworn he sounded…*nervous.* "And, well, it's in here."

The confusion on Joan's face only intensified as she stared at the bag, too unsure to cross the small distance between her and Declan to accept it.

"Take it."

She jolted forward, grabbing the bag, and then looked over

uncertainly at Declan for further instruction.

"I think you're supposed to open it," I whispered, staring at Declan, who appeared ready to bolt right out of the kitchen.

Joan nodded.

Oisin and I both leaned closer as she unzipped the gym bag.

Joan glanced over at Declan one last time for an approving nod, which he did not give, before reaching into the gym bag. She pulled out a rolled poster first.

I watched Declan step back in discomfort as she unrolled it…a poster of Declan fighting in the cage, and it was signed.

My eyes travelled over to Declan as Joan more and more eagerly pulled out shoes, shorts, gloves, hats, and all other kinds of memorabilia, all signed by him.

He wasn't looking at me as I stared at him, but instead he looked awkwardly at the laces of his sneakers. Who was this kind, generous, humble man?

"You know his name?" Joan asked, startling me from my thoughts.

I stepped toward her and looked over her shoulder to see that not only was all the gear and memorabilia signed, but it was also personalized. I even caught a glimpse of a letter he wrote Joan's son. I wanted desperately to read it, but it was quickly covered by a t-shirt that Joan pulled out of the bottom of the gym bag.

"I didn't know that you knew I had a son," she admitted a little sheepishly. "Let alone that he was a fan. And his name, I had no idea that you knew his name."

He was listening.

He heard me.

He *remembered.*

I mentioned Joan's son's name offhandedly while I told Declan the fence story. I wasn't even sure I would have remembered his name if the roles had been reversed, and I always made a point of remembering names. But he remembered.

I couldn't help the small smile that tugged at the corner of my lips as Joan held one of the many t-shirts close to her chest.

"You don't know how much this will mean to Liam," she said, choking up.

Oisin reached over and softly rubbed circles on her back.

David eyed a signed cap enviously.

Joan was still trying to get it out. "It's just, this is so...so..."

Thoughtful.

Kind.

Generous.

Sweet.

Tender.

Not exactly the words one would think to use to describe

Declan Gallagher, ruthless fighter, MMA champion.

Joan continued incoherently trying to express her thanks. "Sir, it's just so...so—"

"It's nothing," Declan muttered under his breath before promptly turning to leave.

"Wait!" The word fell from my lips before I even knew what I was saying. Even to my own ears, it sounded loud in the expansive kitchen.

I winced and bit my lip as Declan stopped and slowly turned around. His eyes landed on me.

I immediately blushed. "Um, it's just that…" I tugged at a random curl nervously. "It's just, um, would you like a snack or something?"

His eyes held mine.

I could see the struggle play across his face. I wondered why it was so difficult for him—talking, laughing, smiling.

My heart sank in disappointment as he opened his mouth to obviously decline.

Joan jumped in, "Yes, sir, please?" She stepped closer to him before realising she was getting too close and stopping. "Come have a drink with us. We have plenty."

"You'd better stay before River here completely destroys the bacon-wrapped dates," Oisin chimed in.

I tossed a balled-up napkin at him, but he just laughed and winked.

"You can even pick the music, if you want," David said. He offered up the auxiliary cord after disconnecting his phone.

"Stay," Joan insisted as Declan hesitated.

"Yeah, stay for a bit," David added.

Oisin walked over and slung his arm over Declan's shoulder, and despite a little flinch of discomfort, Declan did not knock him out on the spot. "You know you want to," Oisin said.

Declan looked at me last.

I could tell from his eyes that he was on the edge and he needed just one last shove. I was more than willing to give it. *"Stay,"* I mouthed.

Declan sighed and threw his hands up in defeat. "One beer."

Everyone cheered. I grinned as Oisin popped the cap of a low calorie (shit) beer. Declan let David put his music back on, and the little impromptu party in the kitchen resumed.

Declan remained silent, just listening, as the group chatted casually, but as he sipped his mostly untouched beer, I noticed him glancing at something behind me on the counter. Curious, I took the opportunity when he wasn't looking, engrossed in one of Oisin's enthralling cooking disaster stories, to check what was behind me.

There on the marble counter I found, still flipped open to a picture of my reflection stretched across a graffitied wall, my photography portfolio.

When I turned back, I caught Declan looking at it again. This time, he noticed I'd caught him and his eyes darted away in embarrassment. He didn't look at it the rest of his time in the kitchen till he drank half his beer and excused himself to bed.

As he left the kitchen, he looked back and I saw it. He looked again at the picture.

What was it that intrigued him so?

I couldn't see it myself as I stared at it. But when I lifted my head to ask him, he was gone, back into the darkness.

Declan

It was stupid.

As I made my way to the gym for my morning training session, I stared down at the little pink flower from the blooming tree in the garden resting so delicately in my palm. It was entirely by chance that I noticed it among the first rays of golden morning light outside my bedroom window. It was just a single bud of colour amongst the frost-covered branches.

It wasn't even particularly noteworthy. But as I dressed and went down for breakfast and stood against the large windows along the garden with my smoothie, I couldn't stop thinking about it.

After failing to convince myself to forget about it, I checked both ends of the long hallway to make sure it was empty before stepping outside, my bare toes wincing at the cold of the stones. I crossed the garden, tugged the flower from the tree, and hurried back inside to shake off the chill of the morning.

I smiled down at the little thing as I laced up my shoes. It was petite, bright, and pretty, and I wanted to give it to the girl.

As I neared the gym, I began to doubt myself. It was stupid. She deserved more than a frost-covered flower from the garden. She deserved a whole bouquet of flowers. She deserved a whole room filled with flowers. She deserved a mountain meadow all her own, a field of tulips, a thorny hill of wild roses, a lake of the brightest and most beautiful water lilies.

It was stupid.

But I couldn't bring myself to throw it away.

It was stupid, but I thought she just might like it.

Turning into the gym, I was resolute on giving it to her. I stopped dead in my tracks when I saw the girl, not in her office, but talking to Niall, my physio.

The sight of it immediately caused a surge of jealously that tightened my chest and made my blood run hot.

The two were just chatting near the door to the spa at the back of the gym, just chatting. But it looked so *easy*, the way it never was for me. Niall said something and the girl laughed, looking up at him as she tucked a stray curl behind her ear. They stood close, closer than I ever dared to stand next to her, and both of them seemed perfectly comfortable. Her presence near him didn't make Niall's body tense, his chest rise and fall more and more rapidly, his jaw clench or his brow sweat the way it constantly did for me. Everything between them just seemed natural.

They looked better together than she and I. Her dark, curly hair complemented his chin-length hair that somehow fell right back into place every time he ran his hands through it. They both had soft green eyes, they were both slim, both quick to smile, slow to frown. Together, they were a sweet, happy, normal couple.

She and I were a mismatch. She was the delicate rose and I was the jagged, sharp thorn. The sharp lines of my face clashed with her soft cheeks, her soft lips, her soft eyelashes. I was brooding, dark, stormy. She was a pure beam of light.

Niall and she were two puzzle pieces that fit. Where did that leave me?

Niall laughed and touched the arm of the girl, making my jaw clench. He was clearly interested. And why wouldn't he be?

The girl was a magnet. Everything about her drew you in closer and closer, and the more you fought against it, the tighter the attraction pulled. Her eyes, soft, kind, and curtained by those long lashes, dragged you to the edge and you had no choice but to fall, fall, fall. I wasn't even sure I had hit the bottom yet.

There was something about her. Anyone who met her could sense it. She saw the world differently and she made you want to see it differently, too. She was unique.

She was special.

Why the fuck would she be interested in me?

Crushing the little flower in my hand and tossing it behind me, I stalked over to the two of them.

They each stepped back from one another when they caught sight of me approaching. Only guilty people would do that.

Niall tried to smile casually at me as he extended his hand. "Declan, hey, what's the—"

"Is my watch wrong?" I asked, my tone clipped, anger thinly veiled.

"What?" Niall asked.

"That clock there on the wall." I pointed to the wall above the cardio equipment. "Is it off?"

Out of the corner of my eye, I caught a look on the girl's face. I wasn't sure, but it looked something like disappointment. For what, I didn't give a fuck.

"Declan, man, I don't know what you're talking about." Niall glanced at the girl for support.

She had her gaze on her ridiculous colourful sneakers.

"Are all the clocks in this goddamn gym suddenly wrong today or is it 8:07?"

Niall glanced at his wristwatch and scratched sheepishly at the back of his neck. "Sorry, I was just talking to River here and—"

"I don't pay you to talk," I interrupted. "Either of you." I looked toward the girl.

Her eyes were narrowed on me. Anger had clearly replaced her disappointment.

How dare she be angry at *me*. She was the one not working when she was supposed to be. I was the one with the right to be angry, after all. Not her.

She didn't flinch from my glare, but glared right back for a prolonged moment before she promptly, with a word of apology, turned on her heel and walked away. She marched straight to her little office and went inside, slamming the door behind her. It rattled in the high ceilings of the gym.

"If you're ready, sir," I said sarcastically to Niall, nodding toward the door of the spa.

"Yeah, yeah." Niall jumped and moved to hold the door open for me. He jabbered on as we climbed the stairs to the therapy room. "How are you feeling since our last session? Any discomfort? I'm sure you have some soreness, but is there any unbearable pain still?"

Not answering him, I went straight to the massage table and lay down. I stared up at the ceiling as Niall poked and prodded around my shoulder.

"Hey, um, so that new girl," he started hesitantly as he gave my arm an experimental rotation in its socket. "Is she—"

"She's not your type."

Niall paused and stared down at me.

I continued to look up at the ceiling.

"No, no, that's not what I meant," he insisted, shaking his head. "I just meant—"

"I know exactly what you meant," I grumbled irritably. "You meant you want to fuck her."

Niall laughed uncomfortably. "Ah sure look, if you like her, I'll totally back off—"

"I don't want her."

"Okay, but…"

I turned my head to send an imposing glare up at Niall. "She's not your type," was all I said, making it more than clear to him that the conversation was over. Finished.

Dead.

But the truth was that the girl would be perfect for Niall and he would be perfect for her. They would laugh together, smile together, sing together.

I could not give the girl laughter.

I could not give her cheer.

I would never sing with her.

My chance with a girl like her was as withered as the petals of the flower crushed and abandoned on the gym floor.

River

I was licking my fingers from a brownie sundae Oisin made me for a Monday pick-me-up when I heard the shouting. It caused me to stop and strain to listen as the rain pattered loudly against the tall windows in the hallway overlooking the garden below. I didn't have to struggle for long, because the shouting from the gym just up ahead grew louder and louder.

My first thought seized my heart and made my veins run with

ice-cold blood: Declan was hurt.

Sprinting toward the gym, I ignored the black scuff marks my sneakers left on the polished hardwood floors. Chest heaving, I shoved open the gym doors and scanned the floor for Declan.

But I found him, not injured, but instead arguing loudly with Niall. I sighed in relief. I barely had time to worry that I was starting to care for my employer a little too deeply when the argument dragged away my attention.

"It's my fucking choice!" Declan shouted, jabbing his finger at Niall's chest. "Mine and mine alone."

"Right, right, Declan." Niall crossed his arms and moved his face up to Declan's. "Because you've had a great streak of choices recently. Real good choices, pal."

When Declan spoke, his voice was low and threatening, like the rattle of snake: a warning before its deadly strike. "Shut your fucking mouth."

Niall continued nonetheless, "Giselle was a fantastic choice, obviously." Niall lifted one finger.

"I won't say it again, friend," Declan hissed. "Do not speak another word."

Niall counted on another raised finger. "Getting locked off your tits drunk that night, another great choice in the history of Declan Gallagher's great, great choices."

From across the gym I could already see Declan's fingers, one by one, tightening into a white-knuckled fist.

"Oh, am I missing one?" Niall tapped his chin before lifting a third finger and waving it in Declan's face. "Right! Throwing away your career by crashing your fucking car!"

"Woah, woah!" I shouted as Declan's arm whipped back, lightning fast.

Both men turned toward me as I ran over to them. I placed myself between them and extended my arms to shove them away from each other.

"What is going on?" I demanded, looking up from one to the other as both sent glares at one another over the top of my head. "Someone better tell me."

"Why don't we get the opinion of your pretty little assistant here," Niall spat, grinning sardonically as he crossed his arms. "She's seen you the last couple of weeks."

Declan's chest was still heaving as his dark eyes sent daggers toward his physio.

"Hello?" I said, but I still couldn't get Declan to look at me. "What. Is. Going. On?"

"Should I tell her or do you want to?" Niall said, jutting his chin toward Declan.

Declan remained silent save his furious exhales like some sort of wild bull.

"This fucking *idiot* here thinks that he's ready to fight again," Niall said to me, pointing a finger at Declan. "Without consulting his doctor, without consulting his physio, *me*, he's gone ahead and announced his return."

I looked over my shoulder at Declan in surprise. He didn't see me. In fact, I wasn't sure he was seeing anything other than bright, all-encompassing *red.*

"He's going to get himself killed out there if he goes back now," Niall said as I continued to look at Declan. "He's going to fucking get himself killed."

In my head, I replayed the videos of the MMA fights I'd seen, and they were brutal. There was no place for weakness in that cage, not an ounce of it.

"Listen, River." A gentle hand on my arm startled me, and I turned around to find Niall leaning over so we were face to face. I couldn't help but contrast the feel of the sweet-faced, mild-mannered physio's touch with Declan's. They couldn't have been more opposite from one another. Niall was tender, soft, gentle. He was a friendly breeze on a sunny afternoon.

Declan was a goddamn crashing wave in the heart of a storm across a shoreless sea.

I glanced back at Declan before focusing my attention on Niall's earnest light brown eyes.

"Please, you have to tell him," Niall insisted. "He'll listen to you. Declan cannot fight."

He must have seen the hesitation on my face, because he squeezed my arm before pressing his case further. "Has he told you the extent of his injuries from the accident?" he asked. "Do you have any idea how badly he was injured?" Niall looked over my head at Declan. "Did you tell her?"

I couldn't see Declan's face, but whatever was on it, Niall just scoffed and shook his head. "Of course you didn't tell her," he spat out angrily. "Because if she knew, she'd never agree that you should fight this soon, if ever." Niall focused his eyes on me. "Seven fractured ribs, a collapsed lung, an absolutely shattered clavicle," Niall listed in rapid succession, barely pausing for breath. "Orbital fractures in two places beneath his left eye, four broken fingers, three on his right hand, hairline fractures in both the ulna and radius of his right arm, a humorous practically snapped in half, a dislocated shoulder, and as a cherry on fucking top, a goddamn torn rotator cuff that isn't even close to being healed."

I stared in shock up at Niall as his chest heaved up and down and his fingers squeezed deep into the flesh of my arm. My mind flashed with images of a winding road, slick with pouring rain, a mangled car reduced to jagged pieces of bent metal with a body trapped inside, unconscious, bruised, and bloody.

Declan.

I'd seen the pictures of the crash. I'd heard the story of that night. I'd known there were scars. But it'd never felt real like it had in this moment. My palms grew clammy and my heart seemed to skip a beat as it fluttered nervously in my chest.

"River." Niall levelled his eyes to mine.

I could barely breathe as I stared at him.

"He'll never tell you, ever, but for Declan every jab, every uppercut, every right hook, left hook, every cross, overhand, round kick, choke, guard pass, sprawl, and strike is agony. Pure agony." Niall released my arm, straightened, stepped back, and sighed as he pushed his fingers through his hair. "He cannot fight," he concluded. "And you need to tell him."

I stared at Niall for a moment longer before turning my head to see Declan. I was surprised to find him not defeated, not slumped over with his glassy gaze on the floor, not avoiding my eyes at all, but instead staring straight at me, chin high, shoulders back, eyes intense. There was a challenge in the ferocity of his glare that was locked on me. He was daring me to tell him. His fight wasn't in the cage at all. It was right here. Right now.

And he was ready.

"He's stronger than you think." I didn't speak loudly, but in the near silence of the gym, every word sounded like a bullet from a gun.

"Excuse me?"

I turned to find Niall staring down at me in surprise. "You're underestimating him," I repeated, refusing to cower under the physio's scrutiny.

"You need to really consider your next words carefully," Niall whispered, his voice nearly shaking.

I checked over my shoulder back at Declan and found all the strength I needed to see without even glancing at his muscles. I turned back to Niall, who was waiting, leaning forward. "I think Declan should fight," I said.

Niall threw his arms up into the air and shouted, "For fuck's sake!" He stormed past me, shouldering me out of the way and cursing under his breath as he hurried in a rage out of the gym.

I watched his back till he disappeared, slamming the door behind him. Did I just make a huge mistake?

Was I just being rash? Was I just swept up in my feelings for Declan? Was I ignoring my head to follow my heart?

Did I just doom Declan to more pain, suffering, and defeat than he'd already experienced over the past few months, more than any one man should ever experience in a lifetime?

Out of the corner of my eye, I noticed Declan staring at me. One eyebrow was slightly raised as he eyed me from head to toe. It was as if I wasn't the same girl who had been standing in front of him the whole time. It was as if he was seeing me for the first time.

When he caught me looking at him, he blinked, frowned, and turned on his heel to march to the treadmill. "Get to work," he ordered before putting it on max speed.

"Please don't prove me wrong."

The sound of his feet on the belt drowned out my response.

Declan

As the first star appeared in the sky, I stepped out onto the balcony overlooking the garden at the back of the manor, only to find the girl standing at the stone railing. She tugged a blanket tight to her neck as she sipped a steaming cup of hot chocolate loaded with a mountain of whipped cream.

"Dammit," I heard her whisper to herself as the wind swept a curl across her face just as she was drinking, lashing it directly into the cream.

I held back a laugh as she clumsily tried to wipe off her hair and keep the cup from spilling. After the accident, I thought I had closed up my heart, nailed shut the doors, locked every lock, boarded over every window. How had this girl so easily slipped inside?

Shaking my head, I walked forward to join her at the railing as one by one, stars dotted the sky as if switched on as easily as the lamp at my bedside.

She glanced over at me with chocolate-covered lips and a dollop of whipped cream on the tip of her nose, cheeks rosy in the chill of the night air. "Do I have anything on my face?" she asked as she attempted to tuck her unruly hair behind her ear.

I opened my mouth to tell her she had everything on her face, but at the sight of her wide, innocent, sweet eyes, I closed my lips and changed my mind. "No," I said instead. "You're perfect."

"Good." She sighed, taking another sip and making those little noises of pleasure. "That would have been embarrassing."

I forced back a smile as that silence that was becoming so familiar to me wrapped its comforting arms around the two of us. The sky darkened, but with each new star, the girl's pretty face was bathed in more and more delicate light that seemed made just for her.

I wanted to thank her for taking my side with Niall regarding my decision to announce my return. I wanted to tell her that it meant more than I could possibly put into words, especially considering the way I already struggled to express myself. I wanted to explain to her that these last few months I'd felt more alone than I thought was possible. My world had been an empty, dark, isolated void. And I liked it that way.

At least I was able to convince myself of that only until she came like a gust of colourful blossoms through my front door.

But as I stood next to her at the stone railing and looked over the outline of distant hills in the moonlight, I found the comfortable silence between us spoke more than I could. Her presence calmed me. Normally, silence meant chaos, panic, anger. Because in silence I could hear most clearly my own raging thoughts: *You should be training. You should be working. You need to win back your title. You need to defeat Dominic. You need to show them you're strong. You need to show everyone. It's all that matters.*

But in the silence with the girl, I didn't think about training. I didn't think about fighting. I didn't think about winning. It was peace.

Peace I hadn't thought was possible.

"I'd missed the stars in the city."

I glanced over to find the girl's neck craned back, her eyes searching the constellations above us.

"The first night I arrived in New York, I stepped off the bus, looked up to see Times Square with such anticipation, and in the glare of the lights, found myself willing to trade it all in for just a single star in a black sky," she continued. "I almost got back on the bus right then and there."

Her long, soft eyelashes seemed to skim the night sky itself as I drank in the sight of her elegant neck, her pink cheeks, her curly hair in the wind. "Why didn't you?" I asked.

"Hmm?"

"Why didn't you get back on the bus?" I clarified. "Why did you stay?"

"Oh, umm…" The girl finally looked over at me. She bit her lip and hesitated. "You're going to laugh."

I raised a curious eyebrow. "Why would I do that?"

"Because it's silly."

Leaning against the railing, I crossed my arms and levelled my gaze at her. "Have you *ever* heard me laugh?" I asked.

A small grin made the girl's face even prettier as she considered my question.

"I don't think I'll start giggling now," I said. "Trust me."

The girl laughed. "Fine, fine." She pointed a finger at me. "But still promise."

I made the sign of an x over my heart.

She looked back up at the stars before beginning. "It was a ridiculous idea, but I went to New York because I had this marvellous, wonderful, colourful dream of being a photographer and opening up my very own studio."

Still not understanding, I asked, "Why is that ridiculous?"

The girl avoided eye contact with me as she continued to bite at her lip and shift nervously from foot to foot. Finally, she answered, "Because I ran out of money in a week. I had to work three jobs to pay rent, because it took me three months to save enough money to buy my shitty camera and I had to volunteer at a studio to get lessons. Because people in that city use you and throw you away when they've gotten what they want from you and you're left with nothing but a broken dream and—" She stopped and glanced over at me with red cheeks, flushed with embarrassment. "Sorry," she said with a sheepish smile.

"It doesn't sound like you have anything to be sorry for," I whispered.

We looked into each other's eyes, and I again wanted to speak to her. I wanted to tell her I understood. I wanted to tell her I'd been used, too…tell her I was the king of broken dreams.

But our silence was enough.

"Anyway," she said, breaking eye contact and smiling, "I'm just happy to be back with the stars. That's all I need, really. Stars and a camera."

Guilt flooded my chest at the memory of breaking the camera she'd saved up for. "I didn't know it meant that much to you," I admitted, scratching at the back of my neck. "Not that it's an excuse or anything. I just…I'm sorry."

The girl turned her head to smile at me. "The camera you replaced it with is a thousand times better than my old one. Don't be too sorry."

"Still," I said.

She remained silent for a moment, but I could see a debate playing across her delicate features. I thought she had decided to remain silent, but I was obviously wrong when she blurted out this question, "Do you hike?"

I bit back a chuckle. "Hike?"

"Yeah," she awkwardly continued. "Well, it's just that tomorrow, I was planning on going up through the forest and taking pictures with the camera and stuff and, well, if you wanted to come along, you totally could."

She was speaking so quickly I could barely understand her.

"I mean, if you don't want to or can't or, you know, don't want to, then it's obviously totally fine. I mean it's not a big deal at all. Like you can come or you don't come. Wow, I'm saying come a lot. Shit. Umm, yeah either way I'm totally cool. No pressure. No pressure at all. Like totally no press—"

"I want to."

She looked over at me in surprise. "Huh?"

"Come," I said. "I mean I want to come."

She stared at me.

I felt my own cheeks warm. "I mean I want to go hike with you. Tomorrow."

The girl nodded, a sweet smile growing on her pink lips. "Great," she said.

"Yeah."

"It's a date." The girl's smile disappeared and she quickly corrected, "I mean, not a date, but—"

"It's a date," I repeated her words.

It was obvious the girl was trying to hide her grin as she nodded and returned her gaze to the stars.

Our silence returned.

Then I realised what I had agreed to without thinking. I had training in the morning, as always. When was I going to catch up on those missed hours? How far behind would it put me? I couldn't miss training. If I missed training…

What?

What terrible thing would happen? I'd not be in the best shape I could be in for my fight? I'd lose? I'd never reclaim my title? I'd never prove Giselle wrong?

As I stood there next to the girl, I couldn't quite bring myself to care as much as I had before. I couldn't even quite remember why I had in the first place. Because all my dreams in life were erased for just one single desire—to walk next to this girl beneath the trees and hear only our breaths and nothing else for miles.

I glanced over at the girl.

I'd never been more thankful for the stars. Because as she got to stare at them, I got to stare at her.

River

Declan Gallagher had been full of surprises the last few days. But none was more shocking than, when halfway through our picnic at the lookout point in the forest, he leaned forward and unlaced his sneakers. Then slipped them off and his socks, as he wiggled his bare toes in the soft breeze that tugged at my curls and danced through the green leaves above us.

Sitting next to him on the red-and-white chequered blanket

with nothing but a wicker basket between us, I gawked at him with my mouth open and my eyes wide.

Reaching for another grape, he said before plopping it into his mouth, "Don't say a fucking word." He kept his gaze, stern-faced as usual, on the view of the rolling hills beneath us.

I could swear I caught the tiniest quirk of his lips slip into what could possibly be described as a smile. I grinned and leaned back on my elbows to enjoy the stunning emerald scenery around me.

That morning, I packed a picnic basket of fresh fruits, a hot-from-the-oven baguette the length of my arm, and the biggest wheel of cheese I could find in Oisin's pantry along with my new camera and my sunglasses, hoping for just a few precious rays of sun. As dawn illuminated the fog-covered horizon, Declan met me at the front door of the manor. Then we set out through a narrow, overgrown path that wound its way around ancient moss-covered roots, along trickling brooks with the clearest of waters. Then through tiny meadows that seemed to dazzle like a gem mine from the reflection of the first rays of hazy sun on the delicate dew-covered petals.

We moved slowly along the path as I paused nearly every other step to take another picture that I simply couldn't resist. It was all just too beautiful to pass up. But I was afraid that Declan would quickly grow bored or impatient. If he had his way, I thought, we'd surely be sprinting through the awakening forest with weights around our ankles and twenty-five-pound dumbbells in each hand. Only to reach the lookout point at the top of the hill, to do a thirty-five-minute workout complete with burpees and push-ups. Then sprint back down to the manor, pausing only to swallow some raw eggs and chug some protein powder before heading back over to the gym for an afternoon training session.

But every time I glanced over my shoulder after snapping a picture of a tangle of mossy limbs or a single dandelion amongst tall wild grasses, I found Declan not huffing or sighing with his arms crossed over his chest, but gazing at me with the strangest expression. I couldn't quite figure out what it was as he looked away immediately when I caught him. It took me the whole hike to piece it together from stolen glances.

There was a softness to his features as he looked at me, the hard lines gentled and smoothed. He didn't seem to be searching for anything, asking for anything, demanding anything, or expecting anything. As we neared the lookout point, it appeared more and more clear to me that the way Declan looked at me was the same way I was looking at the trees, flowers, streams, and birds I wanted to photograph along the path: I simply wanted to admire them.

I didn't want to change them or alter them or take anything from them. I didn't want to pluck a flower to keep in a vase beside my bed. I just wanted to be near it, in that quiet, sweet moment.

Maybe I was crazy. Probably. Likely. But I *thought* perhaps this was the way Declan was looking at me. Maybe it was the way…I *hoped* Declan was looking at me.

The path ascended to a small grassy peak with a full view of the lush land surrounding the manor. We were greeted with a clear blue sky and a rare merry sun as we laid out the blanket and arranged the various picnic foods. I, of course, kicked off my shoes the first chance I had. I never in a million years expected Declan to do the same.

"Feels pretty good, doesn't it?" I asked him after a few quiet moments.

"I said not a word," he grumbled.

I watched a pair of hawks circle in the blue sky above while trying to hold back a grin. Finally, I couldn't stop myself and added, "Imagine what else I'm right about."

Declan pushed himself up from his elbows and reached for his shoes.

I laughed, quickly stopping him. "No, no, I'll stop," I said. "I'll stop."

Declan eyed me warily and hesitantly reclined again.

Again, I thought I maybe, just maybe, I saw the corner of his lips raise just the teeniest, tiniest bit. But again, maybe I was just crazy.

"This has to be the most beautiful spot in all of Ireland." I sighed happily as I tore off another chunk of baguette warmed by the sun.

Declan scoffed.

"What?" I turned to him.

"Have you seen all of Ireland?"

I shook my head. "Nope."

He rolled over to face me. "Then please do tell me, how could you possibly say this is the most beautiful place in all of Ireland?"

I grinned. "I just know."

Declan's eyes narrowed at me.

I laughed. "I just do," I insisted. "In my heart, I just know it."

Declan rolled his eyes.

I crossed my arms defiantly and asked, "What can you trust if not your heart?"

Declan shook his head. "You going to quit this job and go write pretty little cards for Hallmark, hippie girl?"

Grumbling under my breath, I ignored him and instead focused on the breathtaking view. "I'm going to travel all of Ireland just to prove you wrong," I said. "Then I can say my heart knew this spot was the most beautiful."

Declan sent me a sarcastic thumbs up. "Good luck with that."

I clenched my fists in frustration. "Surely your wife saw more of Ireland than me," I argued. "What did she say?" I realised too late that I shouldn't have mentioned Giselle. The words just came out. Shit. I deserved a kick in the shin for that.

Declan was silent as he rolled back away from me and stared up at the blue sky with his hands behind his head. I was considering how to apologise when he spoke first.

"She never came up here," he admitted.

I looked over at him in confusion. "What?"

"Can't hike in Louboutins," Declan said darkly.

I scanned the 360 view of the green hills stretching into the distance and found it unbelievable that someone would find no interest in it.

"I tried a few times to convince her to come with me," Declan continued. "But I always ended up going by myself."

Was I the first to come up with him?

"I was by myself most of the time I was with Giselle," he said.

There was a sadness in his voice, and I wasn't sure what to say.

"It wasn't much different after I caught her with Dominic, I guess."

Dominic. Declan's MMA rival? "Caught her?" I asked softly. I wanted to see Declan's eyes, but they were glued to the sky.

"Came home early from the gym to surprise her with takeout from this little Italian place we went to on our first date," he said with anger painting his tone. "Walked into the bedroom and found out she was already plenty stuffed."

I picked at a blade of grass as the wind whispered through the trees. Finally, I glanced over at him. "And that's when you..."

"Emptied the liquor cabinet and got in my car."

And crashed, I filled in for him. There was the rest of the story I had been searching for. There was the reason. "That must have been terrible," I said. "To, you know...see someone you lov—"

A dark laugh came from Declan. "That's the funny part of it all, isn't it?" He shook his head. "I crashed my car, destroyed my career, and doomed my body to a lifetime of pain, and I'm not even sure if I ever loved that woman."

His words shocked me. "What do you mean?"

Declan sighed. "I don't know," he admitted. "It's just, the more I think about it, the more I wonder."

I waited patiently as he pieced together the words.

"We were perfect for each other, Giselle and I," he started. "We boosted each other's careers, our relationship made a fuck ton of money, she looked good on my arm and I looked good with her on my arm. Perfect, right?"

I remained silent.

"But is that all love really is? A good PR package?" Declan finally turned his face to me. "That can't be it, can it?" His eyes were earnestly searching mine.

The normal icy blue storm of his gaze had stilled and in its place was a deep, still pool with depths I hadn't noticed before.

"I'm not sure," I admitted in a soft voice after a few quiet moments. "I wish I did, though."

"You've never been in love?" he asked.

There was no pretence between us there on that craggy hillside above the trees. It wasn't MMA champion and his assistant. It wasn't billionaire and not-a-dime-to-her-name nobody. It wasn't employer and employee.

It was human to human.

It was heart to heart.

It was soul to soul.

"For a little while, I thought I had been," I said, "…in love, I mean."

Declan was patient as I chewed at my lower lip, unsure whether to open up so much of myself to him. I was playing with fire and I knew it. But he'd been honest with me. The least I could do was reciprocate, right? "Ricardo. The owner of a photography studio in New York City," I admitted.

"The one you volunteered at?" Declan asked.

I nodded, once again surprised at how closely he'd listened to me. "He thought I was talented. He said I could be somebody. He promised me I could have the world if I wanted." My mind flashed with images from those first few times together. His whispered words, his feather-light touch, his entrancing eyes I couldn't escape. "It was intense and fast and passionate, but it wasn't love," I said. "At least I don't think so."

"Why?"

My eyes flicked over to Declan.

He seemed eager to know.

"Because I wasn't me," I said with a shrug. "The whole time I was trying to fit into a world I didn't belong in: fancy clothes, sophisticated manners, shoes all the fucking time."

Declan laughed and it took me by surprise. I wanted to hear it again. And again. And again…

"So no orgasm sounds during dinner?"

I blushed and laughed. "No, no orgasm sounds. Only very serious conversations about *very* serious art."

Declan nodded. "What about very, very, *very* loud singing?"

I grinned. "Nope."

"Not even in the kitchen when you're supposed to be working?"

I shook my head.

"Surely there was very, very, *very* loud singing when people were trying to sleep?"

"Believe it or not," I said, "there wasn't."

"Incredible."

Declan was quiet for a moment. After my laughter died down, he looked back over at me.

His eyes held mine and I realised I wanted his gaze on me the same way I wanted his arms to hold me.

His voice was soft when he spoke again. "What about dancing barefoot in the pouring rain while wearing pretty yellow sundresses?"

His words were like silk sheets against my skin, and goose bumps travelled down my arms. He'd seen me? That day in the rain, he'd seen me?

I hadn't known.

"No," I whispered.

Declan didn't break eye contact as he said, "That's a damn shame."

He saw all of it, I thought as he moved in just a hair's width closer. It was such a small distance that no one watching us would have caught it. But I caught it.

He'd seen it all. He'd seen my quirks; each and every annoying quirk, he'd seen. He'd seen my weird habits, my odd dinner manners, my unconventional clothes, ideas and wants.

When I danced, I was me. Fully and entirely and completely *me*.

And he'd seen it.

Declan saw *me*.

I found myself leaning closer just the tiniest amount, no farther than the breadth of one of the blades of grass quivering in the wind around us. No one would have noticed me move at all if they had been standing nearby. But I moved closer.

And Declan saw.

I saw it in his eyes.

And that was when I pulled away. I pulled away and breathed deeply like I'd been under water for the last five minutes. I pushed my hair off from my suddenly sweaty forehead.

I couldn't do this, I thought. I couldn't make the same mistake all over again. I couldn't.

I had my rules.

I had my rules and I was going to follow them.

I had to.

"Beautiful day," I said, forcing my attention out over the hills again.

"Beautiful," Declan agreed.

Out of the corner of my eye, I could see that he wasn't looking at the hills at all. He wasn't looking at the trees or the grass or the birds circling above or the bright, clear blue sky.

He was looking at me.

River

"Declan, I really don't have time for this."

I looked up from my computer in the small office at the back of the gym and rubbed my temples.

Declan stood at the doorway with his normal scowl, his normal crossed arms, and his normal irritated sigh. "It'll just take a minute," he said in his normal monotone.

"I don't have a minute," I practically whined as I glanced over the flood of rainbow-coloured sticky notes plastered everywhere on my desk. "I don't even have thirty seconds. I still have to post to your social media accounts, reply to comments from the last one, arrange media interviews for the fight, set up—"

"I need you to come now."

I shook my hand loose of five or six sticky notes stuck to my fingers and groaned. I was prepared to argue again when I saw the dark set of Declan's eyes.

He quirked his head to the side. "Do you not understand what *now* means?" he asked sarcastically. "Or should I write the definition on the line where I normally sign your cheques as your *employer*."

"Fine, fine," I grumbled, shoving my chair back and following Declan out of the office.

He walked with fast, determined strides past the cage as I hurried to keep up.

"Can you at least tell me where we're going?" I called after him.

"No."

How out of shape am I? I thought as I broke into a jog. I blamed Oisin's delicious food. "Well, can you tell me what we're doing then?"

Up ahead, Declan turned the corner down the hall, and I found him already at the landing as I caught up.

"Hurry up," was his only answer.

I huffed and puffed as I pulled myself up the stairs after him. "Do we really have to do this right now?" I moaned, my lungs burning.

Was I dying?

"Are you hurrying?" Declan glanced over his shoulder to ask.

I resisted the urge to give my *employer* a certain finger. Why did we have to go so fast? Where were we even going? And why?

"Shouldn't you be doing like thirty thousand burpees right now?" I asked. It felt like I was sprinting next to his manly amble. "Isn't there a bag somewhere that you can kick or punch or head butt?"

Declan just rolled his eyes next to me as we moved past his room…then Giselle's…then mine…where in the world were we going?

"Aren't you supposed to be training right now?" I asked, clutching at the stitch in my side.

Wait.

He *was* supposed to be training. It was right there in the *War-and-Peace*-length Job Manual: 3 to 6, afternoon training session. Declan didn't miss training sessions. So what could possibly be so important that he decided to abandon it today?

"Hurry up," Declan again ordered.

We entered a wing of the manor that I had never bothered to explore because Oisin had simply waved his hand as we passed it and said, "Eh, that's all storage and shit."

As our rapid steps echoed on the hardwood floor, I imagined all the terrible tasks Declan could be assigning me in this forgotten hallway. *Organise my jump ropes by length, width, and material… Watch this archived film of my matches and take detailed notes about punches my opponents have landed. There's only like four thousand and sixty-seven hours' worth… Dust and polish this closet of MMA trophies…*

Did the MMA even give out trophies? I considered as Declan stopped in front of a door at the end of the hallway.

I was busy catching my breath, but Declan was just...standing there.

"Well?" I asked, looking between him and the door. "What was the big rush all about?"

Declan scratched at the back of his neck and his blue eyes suddenly appeared nervous. "Umm, you can open it."

How bad of a mess was this storage room?

I frowned up at him. "Huh?"

He jutted his chin toward the door. "You can open it," he repeated.

I stared warily at the door and hesitated. "Do I need a hard hat?"

This inquiry clearly caught Declan off-guard. "What?"

I tapped on the door. "Is stuff going to topple down on me when I open this door?" I asked. "Like if it's jump ropes, I guess I should be fine, but if we're talking about a mountain of trophies, then this is really a workplace hazard."

Declan's eyes were wide and unblinking as he stared down at me. "What in God's name are you talking about?"

Huffing in frustration, I crossed my arms and leaned my shoulder against the doorframe. "Listen," I started as Declan listened with growing bewilderment. "I don't want to be a sad story in the local newspaper, you know? American girl lampooned by falling MMA trophy. She is survived by her best friend, Miley Miles, and her negligent employer, Declan Gallagher. I don't want that, you know?"

Declan had no response.

"It's just that we haven't even discussed workman's comp and I'd have to talk with Seamus and—"

"For fuck's sake," Declan grumbled as he reached over, twisted the handle, and shoved open the door.

I got a glimpse of the inside of the room. Holy…crap. I could do nothing but stare. My mind tried to comprehend what I was seeing but it was just error message after error message. "But..."

Afraid it was all a mirage that would disappear any moment, I tried not to blink. I couldn't believe it. This couldn't be real. It just couldn't.

"No trophies in here," I managed to whisper. My eyes searched the space, as much of it as I could see from the doorway. "No jump ropes either."

The toes of my sneakers toyed with the line between the room and the hallway. If I stepped inside, I'd know: I'd know it was just a dream and I was really just in a dusty, crammed closet to organise. Or I'd know it was real. Marvellously, unbelievably, stupendously real. With a shaky breath, I closed my eyes and stepped inside.

When I peeked an eye open, it was all still there: my very own darkroom.

Slowly, just as slowly as I savoured any bite of Oisin's food, I circled the room set up with everything I would need to develop my film. My fingers ghosted over the enlarger, a stack of photographic paper, baths for the developing chemicals—and it was all solid—it was real.

It was *all* real.

Back in the centre of the room, I turned around to find Declan watching me from his same place out in the hallway.

"This is for work," he grumbled.

I nodded.

His lips were still set in a straight line with no hint of a smile. "I set this up only because I require high-quality pictures for my promotional items." He said this with the same icy monotone he used for all his other work assignments.

I again nodded, but I couldn't help grinning just a *little* bit.

Declan frowned. "Stop smiling."

"I'm not smiling."

Declan pointed toward my lips. "I can see you smiling."

"Nope."

"Stop."

This only made me smile more. How in the world was I supposed to stop when I was standing in my very own darkroom?

"Stop smiling."

"I'm not smiling."

"I didn't do this for you," Declan insisted. "I did it for my career."

"Okay."

"I don't want you thinking this is all for you or any nonsense like that," he continued, prickly as always. "So get that through your mind, alright? You've always got your head stuck in the clouds and I need you to understand this is for work and work alo—"

Declan's words were abruptly cut off as I suddenly rushed forward and wrapped my arms around his broad, strong chest. It was like hugging a steel beam—cold, hard, and unmovable—but I squeezed tightly because I knew there was a heart deep in there and I wanted it to feel me.

Declan tensed immediately as I laid my cheek against his chest. He held his arms out like a stiff coat rack, and I wasn't entirely sure whether he was still breathing or not. I knew he could throw me off of him like a rag doll and I could do nothing to stop him. But he didn't.

After a few breathless moments, Declan tentatively rested his big, callused palms on my back. His skin was warm through my thin periwinkle sweater. We stood together like that long enough for our heart rates to leap against one another's.

Then Declan cleared his throat, patted my back like a dog, and stepped back awkwardly. "I have to get back to training," he muttered, placing the scowl back on his stern face.

He turned without another word and marched back down the hallway with hurried steps.

"Thank you," I shouted after him as I watched him go.

He called back grumpily, "Not for you, hippie girl."

I grinned. "Okay."

Before he turned the corner, I heard him grumble without looking back, "And stop that incessant smiling."

I laughed and shook my head before going back inside the darkroom that definitely, without a doubt, in no uncertain terms, absolutely *wasn't* for me.

River

"Cancel your plans this Saturday night."

I glanced up from my plate of rabbit ragu gnocchi to raise a curious eyebrow at Declan across the corner of the dining room table. "Excuse me?"

Without giving me the courtesy of eye contact, Declan raised another forkful of pasta to his mouth and said, "I need you for a black-tie event in the city on Saturday."

I narrowed my eyes, leaned back in my chair, and crossed my arms over my chest, doing the impossible—temporarily ignoring my deliciously steaming gnocchi and the mouthwatering scent wafting toward my nostrils.

"Saturday is my day off," I said. "Surely you haven't forgotten the terms of my employment already?"

Declan still kept his eyes focused on his plate as he tapped a finger against his knife.

"Well?" I pushed. "I don't want to spend my Saturday night holding your BlackBerry or fetching you diet-approved hors d'oeuvres, or live streaming rich people drinking champagne and talking about stocks and bonds."

I waited for a response.

"Declan?" I finally asked irritably.

"It's not work." His words were mumbled under his breath.

I wasn't sure I heard him even though we were sitting on the same corner. "What?"

"It won't be work, alright?" Declan looked up at me then, and his eyes searched mine as he hesitated. He set his fork and knife carefully down, then placed his hands in his lap. "You'll be going *with* me."

I unfolded my crossed arms. "You mean...?"

Declan rolled his eyes and sighed. "You'll be accompanying me."

"Like…no Job Manual?"

Clearly uncomfortable, Declan rubbed his temples.

"No BlackBerry?" I continued. "No to-do list? No—"

"You'll be my date, okay? Satisfied?" he barked. "Is that clear enough?"

A tense silence settled between us, and I reached for my glass of wine to take a sip. As I twisted the sweet wine around my tongue, I twisted his words around my mind, tasting each and every syllable.

Declan bristled impatiently as the length of my silence stretched, stretched, stretched.

"Ask me," I finally said in a voice barely louder than a whisper.

"What?" Declan growled.

Past the bottles of wine, past the glassware, the table runner, the flower vase, past the flames dripping wax down the tall silver candlesticks, I levelled my eyes on him. Warm green against icy blue. A morning ray of sunlight against a raging storm. A velvet petal against a deadly frost.

"Ask me," I repeated. I made sure he heard me this time. "If you're asking me," I said, "if this isn't work, if this isn't an order from an employer to an employee, then don't command me."

Declan's gaze was fixed on me.

Mine did not waver. "Ask me."

The length of the flames dancing on the wicks of the candles didn't grow, but the temperature of the dining room seemed to raise significantly as we stared into each other's eyes.

We were two opponents in a cage, he and I. Nothing but ferocity, challenge, and intensity in our locked gaze. The only thing left to be decided was whether we would step away and each leave the cage…or whether we would crash into each other.

The spell snapped instantly as Oisin sashayed into the dining room with two chocolate souffles and a bellowing voice. "Dessert ti—oh shit, I just interrupted something, didn't I?"

Both Declan and I shook our heads and sank back in our chairs, as far away from one another as possible. I hadn't realised how close I had leaned toward him, and I was sure after a quick glance in his direction that he felt the same confusion.

"What's going on?" Oisin asked warily. "Should I leave? I should leave."

Oisin was hurrying to escape the tense dining room after placing the desserts on the table when Declan insisted he stay.

"There's no need to leave," he assured the chef. "There's nothing going on."

My heart sank at the sound of his words. I'd pushed him too far. I laid my cards out on the table and he didn't care. He would find someone else to attend the event with him. Or better yet, he would go alone.

He said it plain and clear—there was nothing going on between him and me. Nothing.

My rabbit ragu gnocchi tasted like cement in my mouth as I chewed a small bite, and I knew it wasn't because of Oisin's cooking.

"We were just discussing that black-tie event in Dublin this weekend," Declan continued, though I barely heard him. It felt like there was cotton stuffed in my ears. "And I was just about to ask River something."

My name on his lips surprised me. I looked up from pushing food about my plate to find both Oisin and Declan assessing me.

"Well, don't stop on account of me." Oisin's grin was practically giddy as he glanced back and forth between us.

I watched as Declan adjusted himself in his chair across from me, showing again how uncomfortable he was with all of this. Finally he settled, looked over at me, and even attempted a smile. "River, would you like to accompany me this Saturday night?" he asked. "I'd very much enjoy your company."

A squeal escaped Oisin's lips before he slapped his hands over his mouth. "Sorry, sorry," he whispered through his fingers. "Act like I'm not even here."

I shook my head before returning my attention to Declan.

He was looking at me expectantly, waiting.

"Okay," I said.

"Yes!" Oisin shouted.

I caught what looked like a relieved exhale, but Declan quickly covered it up by reaching into his back pocket and pulling out his wallet. I frowned in confusion as he pulled out a black credit card for Oisin. "Get her anything she needs," Declan said as he handed over the card. "A dress, shoes, whatever."

I frowned between the two of them. "Umm, I already have a dress." I'd wear my yellow sundress, maybe. Or the lavender one even.

"My little voodoo queen." Oisin walked over and cupped my cheek. "You may have a dress, but for this you need a *dress*."

"But I—"

"Get ready for the most extravagant shopping trip of your life, baby doll." He gave me a wink. "Better get a good night's sleep." He patted my cheek before disappearing through the door leading out of the dining room. "And before you ask, no," he shouted back to me from down the hallway. "You can't go barefoot!"

I glanced nervously at Declan. A new dress, new shoes, the whole makeover thing, that wasn't me. I thought I was done trying to pretend to be someone else, acting this way, dressing that way, laughing at jokes that weren't funny, wearing shoes… I was already getting uncomfortable just thinking about a formal event, tugging at my collar and wiggling my toes in my sneakers.

"This thing," I asked slowly, afraid to hear the answer. "It's fancy?"

Across the table, Declan shrugged. "I guess."

I drummed my fingers nervously on the edge of the table.

"Um, like how fancy would you say?"

Declan stretched his arm past his untouched wine glass for his souffle. "I don't know," he answered with disinterest. "It's black tie."

My heart rate skyrocketed. "Black tie?!"

Declan's lips pursed in confusion around his spoon. "Didn't I say it was black tie?" he asked.

"Did you?" I tried to remember back to what he had said, to what exactly he had said.

"I'm pretty sure I did," Declan said.

Peculiar, I thought. Very peculiar. I hadn't heard him say black tie. In fact, as I considered it over my chocolate souffle that melted in my mouth, I really had no idea in the slightest what exactly I had just agreed to going to. I didn't have a clue.

All I had heard was that Declan wanted to go with me.

Me.

River

It was a stroke of good Irish luck that the first dress boutique Oisin and I hit that morning in Dublin had a full-size kelly-green tufted velvet couch in the posh dressing room, because just one glance at the price tags hanging from the dresses Oisin picked out to start with, and I was ready to pass out.

"What's taking so long?" Oisin shouted from just outside the burgundy silk divider.

He was already three mimosas in from our breakfast at the Merrion Hotel after checking our bags in early.

"I'm coming, I'm coming," I grumbled.

I was still slightly irritated at him from earlier that morning. It had just been the two of us in the warm, elegant Garden Room at the Merrion since Declan decided to get in a training session at his gym down the road. Yes, *his* gym. The man also owned a chain of gyms across Europe.

"Alrighty then, let's see here…" I had been scanning the most glorious breakfast menu I'd ever seen as the poised and polished waiter held his black pen in his crisp white glove at the ready above his cream notepad. "So I'll have the raspberry and toasted coconut pancakes, the croissant French Toast with blackberries, the fresh herb and zucchini frittata with, um, let's make it two servings of the maple candied bacon, and—"

Oisin had slipped the menu from my fingers and smiled up at the waiter. "She'll have a black coffee and a spinach smoothie. And ask the chef to throw in some cayenne if he can, please. Thanks, doll." Oisin winked up at the waiter.

I glared at him. "What was that?" I asked when he walked away.

"I was flirting to get his number, obviously," Oisin answered, tucking his napkin into his shirt to prepare for *his* pancakes.

"No." I rolled my eyes. "I mean with my breakfast. I'm not Declan. I don't want a smoothie."

"I'm doing you a favour," he insisted. "Have you ever tried slipping into a formal dress with a full stomach?"

I pouted the whole breakfast, eyeing his maple syrup-smothered pancakes enviously, but as I struggled to tug up the first body-tight evening gown in the dressing room, I realised he might have had a point. Not that I would ever admit it…

Once it was up…mostly, I nearly tripped on my way out to show Oisin. I grabbed onto the silk drape and feared I'd yank the whole thing down on top of me. Thankfully, Oisin hurried to my aid, catching me as I stumbled forward and somehow managing not to spill his mimosa in the process.

"Such elegance, my little voodoo queen," he joked before he downed the rest of his drink, set down the glass before arranged me in front of the trifold full-length mirror.

I wobbled a bit as he zipped me up, arranged the dress around me, and fidgeted with bits here and there till he was fully satisfied with the finished product. Finally, he stepped back, shaking his head slowly back and forth. "Wow," he whispered in awe.

I could only frown at the image in the mirror in front of me. I was in a strapless black chiffon dress that was pleated from head to toe in such a way that it hugged my body so tightly, it accentuated every womanly curve and at the same time hid all the "maybe I didn't need two chocolate souffles after all" ones. I had to admit that the woman standing in front of me looked beautiful, but that woman was not me. I was struggling to express this when Oisin stepped close to me and caught my eye in the mirror.

"Not quite right, eh?"

I shook my head before raising a curious eyebrow up at him.

"How'd you know?"

Oisin grabbed the end of my chin and squeezed. "Because, my dear, you're standing like a plastic manikin on a stick instead of a gorgeous dandelion dancing in the sun."

I laughed and he reached for the zipper at the back of the dress.

"We have plenty more to try on." He smiled at me in the mirror. "I want to see you dance." He paused and glanced over at his empty mimosa glass. "Plus, I haven't had *nearly* enough mimosas yet."

All the rest of the morning and late into the afternoon we bounced from expensive boutique to expensive boutique to "fuck, I didn't know things could be this expensive" boutique, trying on dress after dress after dress. It was unlike anything I'd ever experienced in my life. The staff in each boutique greeted us with champagne bubbling with raspberries or wine spritzers topped with a bouquet of beautiful, brightly coloured edible flowers or gin and tonics complete with an artfully twisted burned lime zest. There were plates set up with French cheeses, berries, and tiny sponge cakes Oisin kept smacking my hand away from. Women with sharply tailored black suits helped me into extravagant dresses, each more lovely and stunning than the next. It was a day out of a fairy tale with Oisin being my fiercely dressed godmother, and yet I couldn't help but sag to the floor and flop onto my back in the last dress at the last store.

I groaned and stared up at the crystal chandelier above my head in a gold silk dress with a thigh-high slit, plunging back, and a price so large they barely managed to fit it on the tag.

"I'll have to go naked," I moaned as I blindly reached for the tray of Belgian chocolates that Oisin quickly snatched away from me. My hand flopped in defeat onto the white marble floor. "That's it!" I cried. "I'm going naked."

The store attendant with a tight bun and severe black glasses eyed me from the dress rack. "Umm, she really shouldn't be lying on the ground if she doesn't intend to buy the dress," she said to Oisin with a cold stare.

"Can't you see the girl's having a breakdown?" Oisin replied. "I'll buy the dress if it makes you feel better. I'll buy the whole store, the floor included, if it makes you feel better."

I heard a huff and then the aggravated *click, click* of sharp heels and then a sigh as Oisin joined me on the floor. He patted my arm as I wallowed in my self-pity. All that delicious food left unconsumed and for nothing! That was the real tragedy.

"Really, dear, don't fret. We'll find you something," Oisin attempted to cheer me up. "There are more stores still open for a little bit and—"

"None of them are going to work and you know it," I said, turning my head to him. "You know it."

Oisin opened his mouth, hesitated, and instead leaned over to grab a wine glass of a crisp, sweet rosé. He took a swig and then passed it over to me.

"They're all so tight I can't even walk," I bemoaned before raising the glass to my own lips. "How am I supposed to talk to all those rich people about like, I don't know, which offshore banks they recommend for tax evasion or where to buy a baby tiger and shit when I'm busy tugging up the front of my dress or making sure my leg slit isn't showing my hoo-ha. Or resisting the urge to tug at my wedgie because the material is so thin I had to wear a thong the width of dental floss?"

I passed back the wine glass to Oisin. This dress was beginning to suffocate me as I imagined being lost in a crowd of formally dressed strangers, shoulders bumping into me, angry, irritated words shot at me to get out of the way. I could feel my ribs closing around my heart, which was thudding more and more rapidly. Oisin was actually going to have to end up purchasing this dress after all, because I was sweating. And not like model-in-yoga-pants-commercial level of sweating. I mean *sweating*.

"I'm not meant to be a part of this world." I shook my head. "I shouldn't be here." I sat up and struggled to get the zipper down so I could rip off the restrictive dress and go running butt-ass naked down Grafton Street.

Oisin stopped me with a gentle hand on my shoulder. "You know, my little voodoo queen," he said with a grin. "This isn't the first time I've heard nearly those exact same words."

I looked up at him and listened while resisting the urge to squirm in the dress.

"Years ago I was in a locker room with a young, wide-eyed, fire-souled kid right before his first big fight," Oisin explained, his eyes twinkling in remembrance. "He was a nobody kid with an unconventional fighting style no one had ever seen before, an unconventional fighting style no one believed could win in the cage. He was told to change or lose."

"What happened?" I asked with whispered breath.

Oisin smiled down at me and plopped the tip of my nose. "He fought his way."

"And won?"

Oisin winked and then leaped to his feet, downed the rest of his rosé, and held out a hand for me.

I lifted a wary eyebrow at him.

He wiggled his fingers impatiently. "Come on," he said as he tugged me unsteadily to my toe-pinching stilettos that I wanted to burn. Oisin rubbed his hands together and smiled. "I've got an idea."

Declan

The Merrion Hotel had a gnat problem and its name was Seamus Barry Flanagan.

In the hallway of the top floor of the Merrion Hotel beneath the row of crystal chandeliers, he buzzed around me despite how many times I shooed him away.

"Alright, so Tina and Patrick from Nike will be sitting at table six." He spoke as quickly as the flutter of a fly's wings as he flipped through page after page on his clipboard. "Bollocks, you and River are at table five, but maybe if you arrange your seats you can butt up against them and—"

"I'm not listening, Seamus."

"Yeah, yeah, that could work." It was obvious Seamus hadn't even heard me as he studied the layout of the ballroom, red pen held between his lips just beneath his bristling mustache. "Snag seats on the east side of the table. South would be alright. Definitely not the north. Jaysus, that would be disastrous. Did you get that?"

Leaning against the brocade wallpaper just outside the girl's hotel room, I tugged at the collar of my starched white shirt. I hated these fucking suits. Always have. They were always too tight. Always too uncomfortable. Always just a little…off, like they belonged to someone else and not me.

"Declan?"

The gnat was back. I'd really have to inform the desk downstairs about their pest issue. It was getting out of hand.

"Declan? Hello?" Seamus circled around to shove his face up toward mine. "Did you hear me?"

"Yes, yes," I grumbled irritably. "North side of the table."

It took every ounce of strength to keep from grinning as Seamus exploded into an aggravated flurry of movement.

"East side, Declan!" he shouted as he flung his clipboard into the air. "Jaysus me fuck, *east!*"

I held up my hands, suit jacket already pulling at the seams. "Eh, eh, easy man, okay? I heard you, alright? I heard you."

Seamus exhaled shakily to calm himself before he burst that pulsing blood vessel in his forehead. He leaned down to retrieve his clipboard from the plush hotel carpet and dragged a hand through his hair. "Sorry, sorry." He sighed. "It's just there's a lot riding on tonight, and I really need you on your best behaviour; no messing around, right? It is *imperative* to snag some sponsors before your return fight."

I clamped a hand on his shoulder and squeezed. "Relax, man," I said as I shook him a little. "I've got it, okay?"

Seamus sighed again. "Alright, alright."

"Relax."

He nodded. "Yeah, yeah, you're right."

The corner of my lip quirked up despite how hard I tried to stop it this time. "North side."

"Motherfucking Christ!" Seamus exploded into another tirade in the hallway, but at that exact moment the girl's door opened. "Motherfucker, motherf—"

Despite the wildly waving arms and frustrated pacing, I heard nothing more of Seamus when I saw *her*. I was transported out of the hallway, far from the hotel, away from Dublin, away from streetlights, away from cars and noise and concrete. She swept into the hallway and I was swept into a meadow of wildflowers in a small grove of delicate aspens alight with a full, bright moon overhead.

I could smell the intoxicating jasmine, primrose, and lily of the valley as she smiled at me from down the hall. The dress was unlike anything I'd seen in the windows of the city's shops. A mesh the colour of the deepest port wine grazed her clavicle and hugged her arms down to her petite wrist bones. Etched all across it were little flowers with purple sequins that flashed like drops of dew in the hazy, warm midnight. The flowy, delicate skirt swept like a cool breeze to her feet.

Her hair was pulled up with soft curls falling down like gentle wisps to frame her makeup-free face. The twinkle of her eyes and the natural blush of her cheeks couldn't be achieved by even the most expensive products in the city.

She was fully and entirely herself. She would bring sunlight to any dimly lit ballroom, soft moss to any hard, cold marble floor. To any crowd of women drenched in exorbitantly priced perfumes stinking of fake flowers…she would bring the scent of velvet petals bathed in starlight.

"Declan, are you even listening to me?" Seamus hissed.

I didn't even look toward him when I answered, "No." Without waiting for his response, I approached the girl, whose eyes quivered with nervousness as she searched my face.

She fidgeted with the delicate lace hem of her sleeve. "I wasn't sure if this would be appropriate," she started, mumbling quickly as her nerves took over. "I mean, I can put on some mascara, I guess. There's a straightener in there if you think I need to straighten my hair or maybe the dress isn't right. Maybe it's too much. Maybe I should change. Maybe this isn't a good id—"

"No."

The girl blinked up at me. "No?"

I swallowed heavily, suddenly finding it hard to breathe. "No," I managed to breathe out.

Her eyelashes fluttered innocently as she waited in anticipation. "No what?" she whispered.

Why couldn't I breathe? What was wrong with me?

"No," I repeated, voice low. "Don't you fucking dare go back into that room."

I noticed a little flutter of her chest like a butterfly, and her perfect lips pulled up into the sweetest smile I'd ever seen. She was beautiful, absolutely beautiful. I wanted to study every inch of her, from head to toe. I wanted to trace every petal on every flower of her dress even if it took till the early hours of the morning when dawn stretched its golden arms above the slumbering city. I wanted to—

"Limo's here."

I turned around to find Seamus waving at us from down the hallway.

"We've got to go."

My heart beat faster than it ever had before, even the biggest of fights, as I reached for the girl's hand. I felt her pulse in her small, soft fingers and found it easily matched mine. Her green eyes watched me as I guided her hand under my elbow and onto my arm. Her fingers hesitated slightly, hovering over the fine silk of my suit as she looked up into my eyes. I knew what she wanted to see—she wanted to see if she could trust me.

Looking down into her eyes, I brushed my thumb along her wrist bone and held back a smile as her hand came to finally rest comfortably on my arm.

"Ready?" I asked, close enough to her that I could make out light freckles dotting her nose.

She smiled and nodded. "Ready."

With the girl on my arm, we walked together down the hall, and it felt right. In every way that the suit felt wrong, this—*this*—felt right.

Annoyingly, the gnat managed to follow us into the elevator. He was again flipping through his clipboard, and it was pissing me off because all I wanted to hear was the girl's quickened breath as I held her arm tighter to my side.

"So I haven't talked to you about the reps from Optimum Nutrition who are going to be there tonight yet," Seamus droned on. "Protein powder is where the money is, so we really need to make those guys like you. Which, as you know, will be quite a challenge for you and your lovely personality."

I rolled my eyes as the lights flashed on each floor as we descended.

"It would be best if I could sit next to you on the ride over to discuss this, Declan," he continued. "So River, dear, you'll sit up front in the limo and I'll—"

"Seamus, you're in front," I ordered as the elevator doors

opened with ding. "River sits with me."

River

I'd always wanted to see Dublin, the narrow cobblestone streets, the ornate old-fashioned streetlamps, the cosy, bustling corner pubs, and it was all right there just outside my window in the limo, but I barely caught a glimpse of any of it.

I spent most of the drive through the busy city streets staring at the black screen dividing Seamus and the chauffeur in the front from Declan and me in the back. I would stare at it and stare at it, telling myself…

Don't look.

Don't look.

Don't look.

Until, dammit, I couldn't fight the temptation any longer. I'd glance over at Declan, quickly looking away before he caught me. Then I would go back to staring at the black screen in the back of the limo, promising myself that was the last time.

Until the next time…

And the next time…

And the next time…

It wasn't my fault really, the fact that I couldn't take my eyes off him. He just looked so damn beautiful in his black suit. If Declan, in that suit, climbed out of the water or stood on top of some skyscraper on my television screen and told me to buy some overpriced cologne, I would have done it. And I wasn't even a man.

I just wanted to look at him. As I stared at the black screen again, I cursed myself for not bringing my camera along. If anything needed to be captured on film, it was Declan.

It didn't help that despite the fact that there was more than enough room in the back seat of the limo for space between us, we sat pressed up tight to one another as if there were ten other people squished in next to us. It made my body burn, his thigh against mine, and I should have scooted over. The feelings it was giving me were not appropriate boss/employee feelings. I didn't want to scoot over.

I wanted more. More touching. More closeness. More heat.

More, more, more.

I was reaching for a bottle of water to cool myself off when the driver announced through an intercom system, "Sir, we'll be arriving in just a minute or two."

Gulping down the water, I wiped my sweaty palms against my dress as nerves started to make me fidget even more. "I'm gonna trip," I blurted out suddenly, unable to contain myself.

Declan turned to look at me, his piercing blue eyes twinkling in amusement. "What?"

I twisted a curl nervously around my finger. "I am totally going to trip," I repeated. "What happens if I trip on the red carpet?"

Declan hesitated a moment before answering. "You won't trip."

"But what if I do?"

"You won't."

"But—"

"You won't." Declan laughed. "You won't."

I wasn't entirely convinced as I eyed the long hem of my skirt gathered around my ankles. Definitely a tripping hazard. No doubt about it. "But what if I *do* trip and I drag you down with me? Right there on the red carpet in front of everyone."

Declan chuckled. "You're not going to trip and you're not going to drag us both down."

I chewed at my bottom lip nervously. "Is there anything special I should do?" I asked, mind whirling. "I've never walked a red carpet before."

Declan shrugged. "Smile?"

I frowned. "Are you going to smile?"

"No."

"Why?"

Declan pondered this. "Because I don't smile."

I glanced over at him. "You should smile."

"I'm not going to smile," he said firmly.

I grinned. "You might like it."

Declan shook his head. "I definitely won't."

"You might."

Declan rolled his eyes and sighed. "I'm not smiling."

I winked at him. "We'll see." I was silent for a moment as I imagined what the night would be like. But then another question popped into my head and I asked it before thinking, like the biggest friggin' idiot ever, "Is Dominic going to be there? Is Gis—" I clamped a hand over my mouth and whispered, "Sorry."

Declan shook his head. "Don't be. I shouldn't let her have that kind of control over me. She…" Declan paused, "*Giselle* won't be there tonight. She and Dominic are on vacation in the Amalfi coast celebrating his last MMA win."

Well, at least that was a relief.

"We're here, sir," the chauffeur announced moments later.

Already, outside I could hear a large crowd of people, and I shrank back into my seat. "Maybe this isn't a very good idea," I whispered, hearing the chauffeur's door open.

He'd be opening ours any second. The shouting and cheering outside only grew louder. I needed to get out of there. I needed to leave. I—

"River." Declan laid his hand on my arm and my wild, nervous eyes found his. "I'll catch you."

We stared into each other's eyes.

He squeezed my arm gently. "If you trip and fall, I'll catch you."

"And if I drag you down with me?" I whispered.

He smiled softly. "Then we go down together."

The cheering and shouting, dulled by the frame of the car, exploded as the chauffeur opened the door.

Declan climbed out of the limo first. He reached back a hand for me to take that I barely saw over the blinding flash of dozens of cameras.

I blocked the glare with one hand as I took Declan's with the other. He guided me out of the car and I wobbled before he immediately pulled me in tight to his side. People shouted his name as we started down the red carpet: kids calling for his autograph, reporters bellowing out questions, fans cheering.

"Who's the pretty lady?" one man shouted, shoving a microphone at Declan.

Declan kept walking as if he hadn't even seen him.

"New girl, Gallagher?" asked another.

"What's your name, sugar?"

I flinched away from a reporter with a recording device held out to me. All it took was one glare from Declan and he slinked back into the crowd as we continued on.

It was chaos, and if it hadn't been for Declan's protective arm around me, I would have turned right around and climbed back into the limo. I think Declan sensed my discomfort because he traced little circles on my arm that nobody but I would have ever noticed. It surprised me, that kind, soft, gentle gesture. Declan was all rough edges and scowls.

Or at least that's what everyone thought. I was starting to believe that there was something more under all that gruffness and all those intimidating muscles. I just wasn't sure why he wouldn't want anyone to see it.

As we were making our way down the red carpet, a particularly loud voice rose above the rest.

"You're a has-been, Gallagher."

I couldn't help but look over my shoulder and search the throng of people for the source of the heckling, finding a man with a dingy baseball hat pulled over his eyes.

"Ignore it," I heard Declan whisper in my ear.

We took a few more steps and again, the voice shouted over the crowd.

"Washed up piece of shite."

I whirled around, escaping Declan's arm, and pointed at the man in the baseball cap. "Instead of demeaning other human beings you don't know even the first thing about, why don't you go buy a bar of soap and wash up, you piece of shi—"

"Woah, woah!" Declan's arms were around me, pulling me away from the heckler.

I tried to push away from him to go back and finish my business with that asshole, but Declan's strong arms pulled me into a hug.

"Easy, easy," he whispered against my hair, laughter in his voice as I struggled against him. "Easy, fighter."

"No," I growled, frustrated I couldn't free myself. "That's not right that he says that and he has no idea what you've gone through and—"

"I know, I know." Declan held my head tight to his chest.

I could tell he was smiling, amused at my outburst. I'd gone through enough of his mail. Apparently, the sheer mountain of hate mail had started to affect me—the fan mail, marriage proposals, and unrequested naked pictures were an entirely different matter. The Declan the media knew was not the Declan I knew. It wasn't fair how people treated him.

"It's not right," I protested.

"Hey, hey." Declan lifted his chin so I could see him. "Watch, okay?"

I frowned.

"Just watch. Don't go attacking people while I'm gone, alright?"

"Fine," I said as I rolled my eyes.

Declan grinned and strode to a section of young kids clinging to the barrier, waving posters and pens to get autographs. Declan greeted them, chatted, and signed their posters before returning back to me. "Those are the only voices I care about," he said, wrapping his arm around me again. "The rest I just ignore."

"I don't get how you can," I admitted.

I'd found new respect for Declan tonight. What he did seemed impossible to me. Such a bright spotlight, such a high level of judgement always focused on him.

"I pretend I'm in the cage," he explained as we walked farther through the crowd along the red carpet. "All these lights are gone and it's just me and the cage."

I was silent for a moment. And then I looked up at him. "Can I be in the cage with you?"

Declan stopped. "Just you and me?"

I nodded.

A small smile tugged up the corners of his lips. "You and me," he said. "We'll pretend it's just you and me."

I grinned. "You and me."

Declan smiled down at me.

My eyes suddenly widened and I pointed up at him. "You're smiling!"

Declan's smile immediately disappeared. "No."

"You were!" I laughed. "I told you that you would."

Declan laughed and shook his head. "Nope, wasn't smiling at all."

But as he looked down into my eyes, a small smile was on his lips. And it stayed there as we gazed into each other's eyes amongst the cheering and flashing of cameras.

"You and me," I whispered.

Declan's face moved in closer to mine and my heart leaped in my chest. "You and—"

He didn't finish his sentence because someone called his name.

A female.

Declan

Some words are a slap in the face. Some catch you by surprise with a pop to your jaw from your blind side…leave your eye bruised and bloodied like a strong left hook.

Some words are a caress. Some brush against your cheek like the tenderest of touches. Or cause your eyes to flutter peacefully shut as you breathe in deeply and sigh contently, perfectly contently.

But some words, a few rare, dangerous, deadly words, are a knife in the spine, dug in, twisted, forced in deeper and deeper. They clench icy fingers around your throat and kiss your lips with poison that paralyses your heart.

All it took was two words called from across the room for the blood in my veins to run cold and the scars on my shoulder to burn as if my skin was on fire. I was back in that metal death trap, the remains of my crashed car. Rain trailed blood into my eyes as I blinked numbly at my mangled arm. Sirens wailed in the distance as I waited for the pain to crash over me like a flood. Again and again, I saw them together: her on top, his fingers digging into her rolling hips, her eyes when she saw me…

"Declan, darling."

Moments earlier, I would have found it nearly impossible to drag my eyes off of the girl in front of me, her magical eyes, her sweet smile, her gentle hand on my arm. But at those two words spoken like an ancient curse, the girl I couldn't stop looking at practically disappeared from sight.

I whirled around and scanned the crowd half with desperation, half with fear. I searched for *her* the same way prey searches for their predator in the encompassing dark—you don't want to see the claws and gnashing teeth, but knowing they are just out of sight is even worse.

Faceless men in black tuxedos and faceless women in long evening dresses parted. From them stepped Giselle on Dominic's arm. Her eyes found mine and she smiled as if she hadn't ripped out my heart and sunk her pearly white teeth into it, as if my blood wasn't running down her chin.

But I supposed the snake eating the mouse wasn't anything personal—it was simply nature.

With cold, cold blood and a forked tongue, Giselle betraying me with Dominic was simply nature.

She smiled as she approached me with swaying hips so similar to the hypnotic dance of a dead-eyed cobra. She wore a skin-tight, blood-red dress with a slit along her tanned, toned thigh all the way up to her protruding hipbone. A plunging neckline revealed all of her breasts save the nipples and even at that, anyone could see them straining against the thin silk. On her miles-high stilettos next to Dominic's lumbering frame, she walked toward me like she always walked…as if the carpet was her runway, as if the whole world had eyes only for her.

And it was true.

A hush fell over the crowd as whispers spread from ear to eager ear like a wild fire.

"It's Giselle..." "They haven't seen each other since..." "This could get ugly..."

They weren't supposed to be here. My mind clung to that thought as its last bit of desperate hope. They weren't supposed to be here. He wasn't supposed to be here. *She* wasn't supposed to be here.

And yet there they were, less than ten feet away.

I couldn't move. I couldn't speak. I couldn't even breathe.

But all of that changed when Dominic, his arm wrapped around Giselle's bare shoulders, caught my eye to make damn sure I saw his finger brush against the side of her breast before he sent me an amused wink.

Anger boiled over in my tight chest as my hands balled into white-knuckled fists, and I tensed to lunge forward for the motherfucker who grinned openly, ready for it, *wanting* it. I was about to throw myself at him when something moved in front of me to block my path. Blinded by rage—red, burning, searing hot rage—I grabbed the nuisance to toss it from my warpath.

"Declan."

I hadn't thought it possible that I could even hear a whisper with the loud rush of blood in my ears, but I heard her.

Because some words are a lifeline thrown out in the dark, crashing waves… Some could pull you back from the edge of the staggering cliff and the jagged rocks down below. Some words can save you.

"Declan," the girl whispered again.

Her soft, wide eyes were waiting for me as I blinked and looked down at her. She laid a gentle hand, fingers quivering just slightly, over mine, which I realised with horror was squeezing her arm like an iron vice. I exhaled shakily and released her, stumbling back as guilt washed over me. I never wanted to hurt her. "Sorry," I muttered rapidly as I wiped a clammy palm over my forehead. "Sorry, sorry."

"It's okay," she whispered, closing the distance I put between us. "Just focus on me."

I tried to keep my eyes on her, but Dominic's voice just beyond her was too much.

"Have you forgotten your manners, Declan?" he joked darkly. "You're not going to come give us a kiss?" He pursed his lips at me.

Again, I lost control at his taunting and was ready to drive his nose up into his brain with just the flat of my palm.

Again, the girl placed herself in my way. This time, she grabbed my face, one hand holding each cheek, and pulled my attention down to her. "Hey," she whispered as she smiled. "It's just you and me."

"What?"

Could anyone else hear the pounding of my heart? It was like a hammer in my ears. I needed to move. I needed to hit something. I needed to hit *him*.

"Declan," the girl brushed her thumb along my cheekbone sweetly while firmly holding me still. "It's just you and me."

Why wasn't I moving her aside? Why wasn't I pushing her away from me? Why wasn't I doing anything?

It would have taken the strength of my pinkie alone to get her out of my way. She wouldn't have stood a chance if I decided to brush her to the side. There was nothing she could do to stop me and yet—she was stopping me.

"It's just you and me," she repeated as my darting, fury-filled eyes fell back on hers. "You and me."

My heart thudded against my ribs and my veins were about to burst, but she held my face close to hers and in that tight space between us, there was silence.

Our silence.

The silence of our dinners together. The silence of our hike through the sleepy, fog-filled forest together. The silence of her body against mine in the dim light of the dark room.

I stared down into her eyes and it was just her and me.

She gasped as my lips crashed against hers, as inevitable as any wave against the Cliffs of Moher.

The girl froze against me, shoulders tensed, lips still, heart stopped entirely. But as my lips melted against hers, she melted against me. I wrapped my arms around her, feeling the delicate flowers under my hands, and we weren't even in the city any longer. I was laying her down beneath the starlight, dewdrops sparkling in her wild curls spread around her head like a halo.

My fingers clung desperately to her as her hands slipped behind my head to tease through the hair at the nape of my neck.

I wanted to say I was kissing the girl because Dominic and Giselle, my rival and my ex, were standing no more than a few steps away from us. That the only reason the heat of my tongue was brushing against the heat of hers was because I wanted to spite the woman who'd betrayed me. How fiercely I wanted to convince myself that I was pulling the girl in tighter as she sighed against my chest only because I wanted to hurt Giselle, make her see what she gave up, realise how badly she fucked up.

Because if I couldn't say that, then I had to admit to myself something far more terrifying, far more painful, far more ruinous. I would have to say something else I wasn't sure I was ready to say. I would have to say that the reason I was kissing the girl in front of the crowd was because I had feelings for her I couldn't shove aside, bottle up, hide, destroy, or push down.

Feelings I couldn't escape.

Feelings I couldn't run away from.

Feelings that would kill me.

River

His kiss came like a current, swift and strong, and I was dragged under before I could even gasp for one last breath of air. I could have fought against it. I could have thrashed, kicked, and struggled to the surface of the waters encompassing my body like the finest flowing silks. I could have fought against the tide…against the pull of his body, the draw of his cologne, the tug of his teeth against my lower lip. I could have fought against Declan's kiss.

But I didn't want to.

I wanted to drown in him. I wanted him to hold me tighter in his arms till I couldn't breathe any longer, till I didn't want to breathe any longer. Tie rocks to my ankles and drag me down deeper and deeper and deeper into the warmth of his embrace.

The moment his lips touched mine with the softest of lightning, the red carpet disappeared. The reporters were gone, the flash of cameras, the microphones and notepads and audio recorders all gone. Dominic never existed and I'd never even heard the name Giselle.

I'd been confusingly apprehensive at the sight of her when I turned around after Declan to see her approaching. She was everything that I was not. Her blonde hair sleek and shining in a dramatic slicked-back style with not a hair out of place, green eyes flashing beneath dark eyelashes. Her seductive red dress might as well have been painted onto her long, lean body, made even longer and leaner by stilettos. Ones I would have snapped an ankle in within three minutes of putting them on. Giselle looked ready for a photo shoot right then and there, and I couldn't help but think Declan in his fine suit would look like more of a match next to her than next to me.

But his lips, soft and full, pressed eagerly against mine. Suddenly, I felt beautiful, strong, powerful. I felt desired. And it had nothing to do with what I was wearing.

It had to do with the way his fingers clawed into my lower back when I gasped against his lips. It had to do with the way he scraped his teeth against my lower lip when I leaned further against his chest…with the way every single tiny movement of my body created a reaction in Declan that I wasn't sure even he was able to control.

I wasn't sure how long we kissed, as time itself seemed to disappear with the flashing lights and whispered gossip and wide-eyed stares. But when Declan finally pulled away, I was left breathless.

The fresh air outside the hotel should have revived me, but after that kiss, I was certain I didn't need it.

I needed him.

But as reality flooded in to drown my starry-eyed, princess-in-a-fairy-tale, head-in-the-clouds, Hallmark-card-worthy sentiments, I realised what had just happened:

1) My boss had just kissed me.

2) My boss had just kissed me in front of more cameras than I could count.

3) My boss had just kissed me in front of more cameras than I could count and I had definitely, absolutely, assuredly, without a doubt, totally and undeniably kissed him back.

Fuck.

My cheeks warmed as I averted my gaze and stared at the hem of my dress along the red carpet. Declan cleared his throat next to me, and I braced myself for what he would surely say.

"I'm sorry, that was a mistake."

"I'm sorry, I already regret that."

"I'm sorry, that was stupid. Very stupid."

"I'm sorry, I'll never do that again."

But before Declan could utter the words I was certain would tumble from his lips that I still yearned for, Seamus walked up and slapped Declan on the back. "Well, well, well, that was quite…" he eyed the two of us with an amused grin, "…entertaining."

I blushed even more.

"Where did Giselle go?" Declan asked.

I glanced over at him at the sound of his voice. Even though he only stood a couple feet away, I couldn't help but wonder if he was purposefully putting more distance than necessary between us. Was he trying to send the message that he didn't feel the way I could no longer deny I felt myself?

"Thanks to your little publicity stunt—quite brilliant, by the way," he added, elbowing Declan and me playfully. "It was about halfway through that when they headed inside. Should have seen the look on Giselle's face."

Publicity stunt? Was that all that was?

I tried to read Declan's face, but he wasn't looking at me. Was he avoiding my eyes on purpose? Why wouldn't he look at me?

I wanted to pull him aside and talk to him. At the same time, I hoped we wouldn't be alone for the rest of the night, because I was afraid of the truth that would come out—the kiss meant nothing.

"All the colour drained from her face, and she dragged Dominic away, stomping off in those heels of hers," Seamus continued.

I kept studying Declan's face.

"Surprised you two didn't hear the thump, thump, thump."

I hadn't heard anything. Nothing at all except my heartbeat and his.

Why wouldn't he look at me?

"We should get inside," Declan grumbled under his breath, still not even glancing in my direction. His tone again sounded dark, melancholy, and monotone. He was again the emotionless robot with big muscles who I never expected could kiss the way he'd just kissed me.

"Of course, of course," Seamus said quickly as he guided Declan and me back toward one another with a hand on each of our backs. "Go get us Nike, you two lovebirds."

Declan gave me his arm without giving me his eyes.

I hesitantly rested my hand at the crook of his elbow. I could feel how tense he was even through the thick material of his suit jacket. He was a bow pulled tight, and I wasn't sure if it was because of Giselle or because of the kiss. Declan stepped forward without a word.

"Or at the very least Adidas!" Seamus called after us as we walked toward the ballroom for dinner.

It was for the best, I told myself as we stepped into the bustling room with fine linens dressing the tables, servers with white gloves weaving expertly about, and a live band playing jazz in the corner.

I'd broken my rules, yes, but it wasn't going anywhere. Declan and I would have a few awkward days, but then we would go back to normal. He just needed a distraction from his ex and that was me. When you think about it, I considered as we found our seats, it was simply an employee completing an assignment for an employer. I was his assistant and I assisted him. And it wasn't like I slept with him.

Nope.

Couldn't think about that.

Wipe that thought from your brain, I told myself.

It was just a kiss.

It meant nothing, the kiss.

Just a kiss.

Everything would go back to normal.

It had to.

It would be fine.

Everything was fine.

Yeah, it was fine.

Totally fine.

Fine.

Fine…

River

"Well, goodnight then," I said, rubbing my eyes sleepily as I stumbled out of the elevator on the top floor of the Merrion Hotel. "Don't let the bedbugs bite."

I waved back lazily at Declan as I walked to my door and fumbled in my purse for my key card. I squinted at the key slot as I failed again and again to get it in the key hole probably due to the complimentary champagne I kept reaching for all throughout the event. But, hey, at least I didn't care at all about that kiss anymore. Like I'd totally already forgotten about it.

Totally.

"Here." Declan reached over my shoulder and easily inserted the key, unlocking the door.

Well, isn't that just great. He's fantastic at kissing *and* opening doors. Whoop-de-do… "Thanks," I said as I stepped inside and turned on the light.

But as I turned to close the door, Declan's big hand stopped it.

"Umm, what are you doing?" I asked, frowning up at him.

"I'm coming in with you."

I blinked as my brain tried to process the words. "What?"

"I'm sleeping with you."

These words didn't take nearly as long to understand. "Excuse me?"

"Don't be so dramatic." Declan rolled his eyes. "It's just business."

I crossed my arms over my chest, and my voice practically squeaked as I repeated myself. "*Excuse me?*"

With an annoyed sigh, Declan pointed over my shoulder at the window overlooking Dublin. "The paparazzi out there are expecting one light to turn on, not two," he explained. "We have to keep up the ruse."

I narrowed my eyes. "What ruse?"

"That we're together."

I stared at Declan. And stared...and stared...and stared... "Together?"

Declan pinched the bridge of his nose before shrugging. "You know..." He scratched at the back of his neck. "With one another."

"With one another?"

"Together."

I shook my head. "You already said that one."

Declan exhaled loudly. "You know what I mean, River."

"I have no idea what you mean, *Declan*."

"Together," Declan repeated, emphasizing the word.

"It's getting late," I said, grabbing the door. "I think you should be heading over to your ro—"

Declan's hand again stopped me from closing the door to my hotel room. "A couple, okay?" he hissed, checking each side of the hallway behind him before looking down at me. "A couple."

I stared up into his eyes. All throughout the evening, I'd been on Declan's arm. I'd met potential sponsors, fellow athletes, and loads of media personalities. He'd never introduced me as his girlfriend, but he'd also never corrected anyone who mistakenly assumed.

Is that what Declan saw us as? I wondered. A couple?

I couldn't lie. The thought of it made my heart swell. He'd never told me he felt that way about me, but Declan wasn't exactly skilled at crystal-clear communication, especially regarding emotional aspects of life. Did he really care about me? Did he really see me this way?

Could it be that I'd wanted this all along?

"We're a couple?"

"No. I mean, no, obviously not," Declan quickly said, obviously not realising how casually he stabbed a dagger into my heart.

In that moment I hated myself for being so foolish, so stupid, so goddamn hopeful all the fucking time.

"Seamus just thinks it would be a good idea to make people think that, at least for a little while."

I remembered a time during the night when Seamus pulled Declan aside. I saw him pointing at me as he talked emphatically, but I had only cared as long as it took for another tray of champagne glasses and bacon-wrapped dates to make their way around the ballroom. This must have been what they were discussing, strategizing with my fucking heart.

I fought to maintain my composure as Declan continued.

"The media is intrigued by you," he said. "They like the drama of me with a new woman, my rival with my ex. Seamus said people eat that shit up."

I nodded.

"The more people talk," he said, "the more the media covers it."

I listened numbly.

"And media coverage means money," he explained, "and money means sponsors and sponsors mean—"

"More money."

He stared down at me after I finished his sentence. He was silent.

"And that's what you want?" I asked, focusing on Declan's eyes. "More money?"

You don't want dancing in the rain? You don't want picnics in the sun? Dewdrops at midnight?

"I want to win," Declan's answer was as cold as the tone of his voice. "And I want to go to sleep." Without another word, he pushed past me into the room.

Angrily, I shoved the door closed and huffed in frustration. My shoulder bumped into him as I marched toward the bed, grabbed one of what seemed like dozens of crispy, white pillows, and tossed one onto the plush oriental rug in front of the bed. "Sweet dreams," I said sarcastically before flopping onto my stomach on the bed, arms and legs stretched out to each corner of the mattress.

Not caring that I was still in my evening gown, I reached for the bedside lamp, turned it off, and closed my eyes. But a few seconds later it was right back on. I winced against the glare as I peeked open an eye.

Declan, with his tie loosened and the first button of his shirt undone, was standing next to the lamp with his arms crossed over his chest. His lips were drawn into a tight, firm line. "I'm not sleeping on the floor."

"Well, then the bathtub it is, *honey*, because you're not sleeping on this bed," I replied. My fingers fumbled for the light switch and the hotel room was again plunged into blissful darkness. I groaned when Declan immediately turned the light back on.

"You're being unreasonable, *sweetheart*," he said through clenched teeth. Declan unbuttoned his shirt and tugged it off his shoulders, which was a totally unfair move because he had the body of a Greek god, and chiselled abs were my Achilles heel. "Move over," he demanded.

In response, I stretched my fingers and toes even further to take up even more room on the bed, making sure not to make eye contact with his perfect pecs. "Maybe Seamus will share," I grumbled before turning off the light. "Goodnight, *darling*."

Declan turned it back on within half a second. "*Sugar*, you're testing my patience," he growled. "I'm sleeping in this bed. So move over."

When I reached for the light this time, Declan grabbed my wrist. I glared up at him. "I'm not in the mood for bondage play right now, *sweetie*."

Declan released my hand and I stuffed a pillow over my face to block out the light. I yelped when he then easily scooped me up into his strong arms and dumped me on the far opposite side of the bed. I nearly tumbled right off the bed onto the carpet. With half my body hanging off the edge of the mattress, I stared at him with wide, unbelieving eyes as he climbed into bed, settled himself in against the fluffy pillows, and turned off the light.

Now it was me turning it back on. "Hey!" I barked.

Declan flopped an arm over his eyes and groaned. "*Honeycomb*, turn off the light."

I shoved at his bicep, but it was like pushing a boulder up a mountain. Or a very, very, *very* stubborn ass. "*Dumpling dearest*, you're taking up too much of the bed." I tried moving his legs over with my feet up against his rock-solid thigh with little to no success.

Declan ignored me and again turned off the light.

"No, no, no." I immediately turned it back on, pointing a frustrated finger at him. "No way in fucking, goddamn *hell* am I sleeping like this…*baby*."

When Declan feigned an unperturbed snore, I bristled, my fingernails digging into my palms as I clenched my fists.

"You asked for it," I warned before leaping into a bellowing rendition of Whitney Houston's "I'm Every Woman" horribly out of key on purpose.

Rolling his eyes in frustration, Declan tried to drown out my beautiful, stunning, "bring a single tear to the eye that rolls down the cheek in slow motion"-level singing, but I only belted out the chorus even louder.

"Fine, fine, you win!" Declan shouted as he scooted over to his side of the bed. "Fuck, stop that racket."

"Whitney Houston is not racket," I grumbled.

"You're not Whitney Houston."

I glared at him and grabbed a pillow off the bed, smacking it down in the middle of the bed between us. "This is how this is going to work," I declared as I added pillow after pillow to the middle of the bed. "You stay on your side of the bed and I stay on mine."

"Great."

I started with a second layer of pillows. "No coming onto my side," I insisted.

"No coming onto mine then."

I stared down at him. "Fine."

He glared up at me. "Fine."

"No snoring," I added.

"Not a problem."

"No stealing the covers."

"Not a problem."

I hesitated and then said, "And no snuggling."

"*Definitely* not a problem." With that, Declan reached over and turned off the light.

Cursing him under my breath, I lay down on my side of the pillow wall and closed my eyes, trying to fall asleep. He was insufferable. How could he ever think that I would even *pretend* to be with him? It was ridiculous. Absolutely ridiculous. My thoughts bristled as I readjusted myself to get comfortable, still in my evening gown; it wasn't like I could take it off. Because he so rudely barged in. Because he was selfish and inconsiderate. Because he was the worst.

Sleep refused to come.

I was too distracted by the sound of Declan's breathing, the smell of his cologne, the impression of his body next to me, the warmth of his skin just past the line of hotel pillows.

Pillows I wanted there.

Pillows I wanted gone.

Pillows that could never move.

Pillows that could never stand in my way.

Pillows I couldn't see through.

Pillows my heart could.

River

Alright.

That was it.

The last straw.

That was *it*.

I could deal with a little moving. Miley used to shift around in her sleep, too, on the nights she crashed in my bed after a late boozy night in. That wasn't a problem. I could handle the noise of some heavy breathing, even some mumbling while someone slept. After all, it was nothing compared to the honking of horns, screeching of tires, and blaring of '90s hip-hop from beat-up boomboxes at three in the morning. No, noise wasn't the problem either. That wasn't nearly enough to make me want to shove Declan out of the bed and onto the floor.

But I drew the line at stealing the covers. *That* was unforgiveable. *That* was a violation of bed code. *That* was the last straw.

I tugged the covers back over my shivering shoulders once before falling back asleep, only to have them wrenched back over to his side. Grumbling, I snatched them back a second time. By the third time, I'd had enough.

Sitting up, I opened my mouth to shout his name, but after one glance toward Declan, I did neither of those things.

He wasn't just moving in his sleep, he was thrashing. It wasn't just incoherent mumblings escaping his lips, but panicked whimpers. Because he wasn't stealing the sheets to just be a greedy asshole. He was kicking, tossing and turning in the grip of a terrible nightmare.

Fear etched deep lines across his forehead as his breath quickened and his struggles to escape some unknowable foe intensified.

"Declan," I tried whispering his name. "Declan, wake up."

I watched as he continued to thrash his head back and forth on the pillow. Swallowing nervously, I extended a finger to tap his shoulder, which I found slick with sweat.

"Declan," I repeated, voice hushed.

When I laid my hand fully on his arm, he flinched away from my touch with a whimper. He kicked at the sheets as his breathing grew ragged and strained. I knew I had to wake him up. No one deserved to go through whatever horror he was experiencing, even if it was just in a dream. But I feared what would happen if I woke him up the wrong way. If he wasn't aware of where he was…I imagined his hand around my throat. I knew I'd be helpless, completely and utterly helpless.

Instead of reaching over for the lamp with its harsh, bright glare on the bedside table next to me, I slid out from under the silk sheets and tiptoed across the plush carpet. I held up my wrinkled skirt as I pulled back the heavy, velvet curtains covering the French doors that led out onto the quaint balcony overlooking the cobblestone street lined with bars and cafes. Soft moonlight swept in like a gentle breeze across the hotel room as I hurried back and sat hesitantly on the edge of the bed next to Declan.

The white light from outside illuminated his chiselled chest, his huge biceps, his defined abs. But this was not a strong man. In fact, he'd never looked weaker, more vulnerable. His body was drenched in sweat as he curled in on himself, quivering uncontrollably.

With my own shaking fingers, I slid my hand across the bed toward his hand. I watched his face as I brushed my pinkie against his.

His clenched eyes tightened with fear, but he did not wake.

"Declan," I whispered as softly and gently as I could. "Declan, wake up. You're okay."

Everything inside of me told me to stop. The rational part of my brain screamed at me that this wasn't safe; I was going to get hurt. He was going to wake up, confused and panicked, and I could do nothing if he attacked. But still I continued. "Declan, you're okay," I said in a hushed voice as I slipped my fingers beneath his. "You're safe, you're safe." I wrapped my hand around his and squeezed gently. "Declan, you're safe," I whispered. "I'm here. You're not alone."

His palm was searing against mine as I traced circles on the back of his hand with my thumb. He whimpered and shook, but I did not leave.

"I'm here," I cooed. "Declan, I'm here."

I held my breath as he slowly started to still. The tension in his face eased, his shoulders relaxed and his breathing evened out as he grew quieter and quieter. I sighed in relief as his eyes no longer darted back and forth wildly beneath his eyelids.

"I'm here," I whispered one last time.

It was one too many times.

Declan's eyes shot open and he immediately wrenched his hand from mine. "What are you doing?" His tone was angry, angry at *me*.

"You were having a nightmare," I tried to explain calmly.

"So?" he barked, eyes glaring up at me in the moonlight. "What excuse is that to wake someone up?"

I shook my head, not understanding why he was so upset. "You looked like you were in pain and—"

"I didn't ask for your help."

"I know, but—"

"I don't want your help."

I stared down at Declan, whose chest was now heaving, his forehead again glistening with sweat. There was anger and frustration and rage in his eyes, but there was something more, too.

There was fear.

Nodding nonetheless, I pushed myself up from the edge of the bed and returned to my side of the line of pillows. "Sorry," I mumbled as I slipped back under the covers.

Across the bed, Declan sagged into the bed. I expected his breathing to slowly return to normal. But as I stared up at the ceiling, I heard him continue to gasp for air like he'd been training in the cage for hours, for days. It was a desperate, hopeless kind of wheeze.

Declan struggled alone for minutes before I felt the pillows shift slightly next to me. Beneath the covers, Declan's hand searched for mine till his thumb, burning with heat, brushed up against my pinkie. As if afraid to scare off a wounded animal in need of aid, I kept myself as still as possible as he slowly, slowly, agonisingly slowly interlaced his fingers with mine. I feared every pounding beat of my heart would send him retreating back to his side of the bed. I hardly dared to breathe.

Declan's racing heartbeat pulsed against my palm as I remained still and silent in the bed next to him. With his hand in mine, I heard his harsh gasps for air soften, his wheezing lessen, the rise and fall of his muscular chest slow, slow, slow…

After a long span of stillness and quiet, I suspected Declan had thankfully fallen into a peaceful sleep.

Then I heard him sigh. "I thought I'd gotten them under control."

I wanted to look over at him, but I was afraid to even move my head. I breathed in deeply to try and calm my racing heart. "This has happened before?" I asked quietly.

A dark laugh escaped Declan's lips. "Yeah, you could say that."

I stared up at the ceiling of the hotel room, hyperaware of Declan's hand still in mine. "Is it always the same dream?"

Declan sighed. "No, not always…" His voice seemed far away even in the absolute quiet of the room. I thought I felt him squeeze my hand tighter before he added, "Always the same fist, though."

The silence was heavy, oppressive. I wanted to know more. But I didn't know how far I should push. So I remained silent and still, my hand in his.

Finally, it was Declan who spoke. "I never wanted Giselle to know," he said, his voice soft, uncertain.

I remembered Giselle's room at the manor…separate from Declan's…

"I never wanted anyone to know," he continued. "*Anyone*."

I glanced over to see Declan staring at the ceiling.

Then he turned his head so his blue eyes, soft in the moonlight, fell on mine. "I'm a fraud," he said. "People think I'm strong, but I'm not. I'm not." His fingers between mine again began to quiver as I waited, anxious and terrified. "I never did anything…" His voice faltered. "Every night he beat me and I didn't fight back. I didn't stand up to him. I was a coward. I am a coward."

I couldn't tell which pain was worse: Declan's shaking hand gripping mine to the point where I feared my bones might snap in two or my heart wrenching in two. "Declan, I—"

"I shouldn't have yelled at you," he said, immediately changing the subject. "I'm sorry." He looked into my eyes.

I could see him begging me not to ask more questions. He had done what he had never done before—he had told someone. He hadn't told anyone, but he told me. That was a huge step and I understood that.

I had a million questions I wanted to ask, a million things I wanted to say, a million caresses I wanted to comfort him with. But I knew if I pushed, he would retreat back into himself, back into the cage, back into his lonely world of pain and darkness. "You don't have to apologise, Declan."

"I do," he quickly said, averting his gaze for a moment. "You scared me."

I nodded. "I know," I said. "I tried to be as gentle as possible when waking you up, but—"

"That's not what I mean." Declan's eyes again met mine. "You scared me because of how easily you calmed me," he whispered, as if afraid to even hear the words aloud. "From those nightmares I've only ever awoken screaming, paralysed so I can hardly breathe, shaking uncontrollably for hours after. But with you, with your touch..." His voice trailed off.

I waited.

His eyes were locked on mine. "I'm afraid I'm starting to need you, River," he said softly. "And that scares the shit out of me. When I get scared, I get angry. Because it's weakness."

I wanted to tell him he was wrong. I wanted to grab his face and scream into his face that he was wrong, wrong, wrong. I wanted to shout at him that he'd never been more wrong about anything in his entire life.

Fear wasn't weakness. Admitting you needed help wasn't weakness. Accepting help wasn't weakness. Far from it.

I wanted to tell him there was nothing stronger.

But in that moment, Declan slipped his hand from mine and rolled over without another word.

I stared at his back, feeling the cold like a frigid winter's night where his hand had been the sun itself. I bit my lower lip and hesitated before laying my hand on Declan's arm. He flinched slightly, but he did not shrug me off or curse me out or move away.

If I couldn't tell him, I wanted to show him.

Slowly, I cuddled up next to him and wrapped my arm tightly around his chest. My eyes fluttered closed as I felt his steady, even, calm breathing against me.

Declan must have thought I was asleep when he again moved his hand.

And slipped his fingers between mine.

River

"Wakey, wakey, eggs and bakey!"

The door to my hotel room crashed open and I jolted awake. With one bleary eye open, I watched as Seamus swept into the room in a flurry of noise and movement.

"How are my favourite lovebirds doing this fine Dublin morning?" he bellowed as he stalked over to the cracked curtains and flung them wide open.

Declan stirred against me. My cheeks burned as I quickly pulled my arms from where they were wrapped around his waist and scooted away from where I had been snugged tight against his back.

He cleared his throat and moved over toward his own side of the bed as he ran a hand through his hair, each of us avoiding eye contact with the other.

"No, no," Seamus pointed between the two of us. "Get back close together. That's perfect. They'll eat that shit up, all that cuddling, lovey-dovey stuff."

Declan and I glanced at each other before nervously looking away.

I winced as Seamus clicked on the television and blasted a news channel. I was shocked to see my own face there on the screen. Even after rubbing the sleep out of my eyes and pinching myself to make sure I wasn't still asleep, there I was…on television…with Declan…

"Thanks, Tom. Former MMA champion, Declan Gallagher, caused quite the stir last night on the red carpet when he was photographed kissing a mystery girl, get this, right in front of his ex, supermodel Giselle and his rival, Dominic "The Spider" St Pierre. Who is this mystery girl? What does Giselle have to say about her? And, most importantly, ladies, just how was that steamy, passionate, seductive kiss? All those answers coming up!"

Chills snaked down my spine as I stared numbly at the television. I never wanted this much attention. What had I gotten myself into?

A knock at the door startled me from my panicked trance.

Seamus hurried over to the door to let in a server, who pushed a cart laden with silver trays into the room and silently disappeared. Clanking loudly, Seamus pulled the covers off platters of eggs, bacon, ham, pancakes, and French toast. There were chocolate croissants, fruits, yogurts, and jams, anything and everything you could want for breakfast.

Normally, the sight would have brought an excited rumble to my stomach. I only felt sick.

I exhaled in relief when Declan grabbed the remote and clicked off the television. "Are you okay?" he asked softly, resting a gentle hand on my forearm.

"I—"

"Okay? *Okay?!*" Seamus wagged a finger over at me as he poured coffee into three cups. "She's goddamn brilliant is what she is. Fucking brilliant."

He handed each of us a cup of coffee; I took mine with shaking fingers and struggled to keep the steaming dark liquid from sloshing over the edges.

"Defending Declan on the red carpet, stepping between him and Giselle and Dominic in that tense moment, holding his face like that…that kiss," Seamus winked at me. "Brilliant. Just brilliant. The media is eating it up. They love you two."

I frowned. "But I didn't do any of that for the med—"

"There's already polls about who Declan should be with: the poor, wild American hippie or the famous, rich model ex."

Seamus was scrolling through his phone. "The drama is *delicious*. And we need to capitalize on it."

Declan groaned next to me. "Jesus Christ, Seamus."

I shook my head, trying to keep up as I placed my overflowing coffee cup on the nightstand. "No, no, Seamus, I think there's been some sort of misunderstanding," I said. "It wasn't my idea to pretend to be Declan's girlfriend."

"Eh, eh, don't be so modest." Seamus laughed as he dropped a massive plate of breakfast in my lap.

I stared at the fluffy golden pancakes with no desire at all to cut into them. I was afraid not even a river of maple syrup could change my appetite.

"So listen," Seamus continued, "I've got Oisin dropping by after breakfast to get you dressed, River. I'm thinking we need to pick something sexier than that crazy dress of yours. Maybe something with some cleavage, something that creates juicy competition between you and Giselle."

I frowned. "Dressed? Dressed for what?"

Next to my side of the bed, Seamus picked up a curl before I swatted his hand away from my head. "Can we do something about this hair, though?"

"Hey!" I shouted indignantly.

"I'll check with Oisin before."

"Before what?!"

Seamus was back on his phone, clicking away. "They want to

see a kiss," he said to us. "Think you can do one like last night for the camera?"

My confusion was only growing. "Camera?" I asked.

"Yes, yes, yes." Seamus waved an irritated hand at me. "Keep up, River. There will obviously be cameras at an interview. Do you need more coffee? I can get you more coffee if that will help. We need you on your A game."

I could barely hear him as blood rushed against my ears. "Interview?" I managed to croak.

Just the thought of those bright, glaring, harsh lights made me sweat. Imagining the questions made my throat tighten. I couldn't even fathom how many people would see it, and maybe that was a good thing because if I knew the number, I probably would have thrown up.

As my palms grew clammy and my heart rate jumped, out of the corner of my wide, panicked eyes I noticed Declan studying me.

"Seamus, I think you need to leave," I heard Declan say as if through a long, long tunnel.

"We have a lot of prep to do," Seamus countered. "We need to go over the story of how you two met so that you each have it straight, maybe beef it up with some juicy details."

"Seamus," Declan warned in a low voice.

I couldn't turn to see what his face looked like in that moment. I was frozen with fear, stuck staring at my reflection in the black television screen.

"We need to practice how you two sit together and touch each other," Seamus continued nonetheless. "I'm thinking flirty and seductive. Anything to increase the buzz."

"Seamus, get out." Anger rang in Declan's voice.

"River, we'll go over some of the personal questions they'll ask you so—"

"Get the fuck out, Seamus!" Declan moved off the bed and forced Seamus out the door despite his protests. The floor practically shook when Declan slammed the door. Then he was back at my side, sitting on the edge of the bed and pulling my hands into his. "Hey, hey," he whispered. "Look at me."

I dragged my eyes to him.

He smiled sweetly. "Hey."

"Hi," I said softly, shakily.

"You don't have to do anything you don't want to do," he said. "Seamus is a fucking idiot."

I found myself comforted by the gentle tone of his voice and the steady hold of his eyes.

"I'll tell Seamus you're not coming, alright?" Declan moved to push himself off the bed.

I squeezed his hands to keep him where he was. "What about you?" I asked.

He shrugged. "It's promotion for my comeback fight. I have to go."

I saw the bright, glaring, harsh lights again. I saw the camera. I heard the questions. I felt the stares. But now it wasn't me in that unforgiving spotlight. It was Declan.

And he was alone.

"Do you want me to come with you?" I whispered.

"River, Seamus just gets these big ideas in his head and—"

"Do *you* want me to come with you?"

Declan hesitated, his eyes searching mine. We were silent together on the bed in the hotel room.

Declan waited and waited and—

"Yes," he said in barely a whisper.

I raised an eyebrow.

"I want you to come with me." He shifted a little on the bed and fidgeted slightly with my fingers, but he looked me firmly in the eyes and repeated himself, "I want you to come with me."

I nodded. "Then I'll go."

River

"Right, so take Elizabeth Taylor-level of eyeshadow…" I said over the phone.

"Emhmm," Miley replied.

"Add Kim Kardashian-level bronzer."

"Yikes."

"Then imagine Dolly Parton's boobs."

"Okay…"

"And that's how plump my lips are."

Miley paused on the other end of the phone as I stared at myself in the illuminated mirror, alone in the makeup room at the news station.

"Hello?" I pulled my phone away from my ear, grimacing at the thick orange makeup that came off on the screen before checking to make sure I hadn't lost the connection. "Cyrus, you there?"

It was then that I heard a stifled snort. I rolled my eyes as Miley's laughter grew more and more impossible to contain. Soon she was giggling uncontrollably into the phone.

"Miley, this is serious!" I shouted into the phone.

"This is hilarious is what this is!" Miley laughed. "I remember when I tried to put makeup on you and you were twitching so much, I stabbed you in the eye with the mascara wand."

I groaned as I sagged into makeup chair with my hand flopped over my eyes. "You flirted with that doctor in the ER while I suffered in agony. Pure agony."

Miley giggled. "Fun night."

I threw my hands up into the air in frustration. "Not for me!" I bellowed. "Oh, shit…"

"What?" Miley's voice was heavy with concern. "What happened? Is everything alright?"

"No, yeah," I responded as I shifted closer to the mirror. "I think one of my eyelashes is wonky." I blinked uncomfortably as I prodded at a long row of fake lashes still sticky with glue that had come loose from my lash line. I supposed it was a no-no to rub your eyes…I hadn't known. I was entirely new to all of this fuss.

In all fairness, I *had* told the makeup artist—a petite, curvy girl whose heavy, layered foundation gave a bad name to the word "caked"—that I didn't want the false lashes. She had paused, the black row of spider legs suspended next to my face by a pair of tweezers she had held between long, manicured nails.

"You need them."

That's how the whole morning in the small, dark dressing room had gone.

"Oh, I'm alright without that shimmery stuff," I'd said.

"You're not."

I'd be sneezing unicorn dust for a month.

"Um, hey, listen, you really don't have to put on that lipstick."

"Yeah...I really do."

At least that tacky, sticky stuff in a tube tasted like blueberries—plastic blueberries I'll admit, but blueberries nonetheless. This lady just kept telling me to stop licking my lips.

"I think it's best without more eyeshadow."

"I think you're wrong."

"I like it better without the eyeliner."

"We're keeping the eyeliner."

"Can we lay off the bronzer?"

"Can we lay off the chatter?"

So I sat in silence as I was transformed into a sad circus clown stuffed into a tight, cleavage-baring pale nude dress. I frowned into the mirror, trying to avoid looking at my contoured cheeks, darkened brows and overlined lips, as I tried to squish the fallen false lashes back into place.

"It won't stick," I whined to Miley.

My efforts only succeeded in smearing my eyeshadow and eyeliner all over my cheeks.

"You need glue," Miley instructed.

"Glue, glue, glue..." I mumbled as I searched the makeup table, blinded in one eye.

"It usually comes in a tube."

I snatched up the first tube I found. "Now what?"

"Put it along your lashes, silly."

I frowned as I applied the glue. "Is it supposed to be bright blue?"

A laugh erupted on the phone.

I blinked and blue got all over the top and bottom of my eye. "It's just getting worse, Miley," I moaned. "I look like I just woke up in a stranger's bed on a Saturday morning and I'm about to do my walk of shame past families in the park swinging and shit." I tried to rub at the blue that I was beginning to suspect wasn't lash glue after all.

"Why are you doing this anyway?" Miley asked. "You hate attention. You stabbed me with your fork when I got the staff to sing happy birthday to you at that little Mexican restaurant in Hell's Kitchen."

I leaned back to assess the damage I'd caused in the mirror. Fuck. "I wouldn't say 'stab'," I said, licking my finger.

I practically heard Miley placing her hands on her hips. "What would you call it then?"

I grinned at the memory of that night. "I don't know." I laughed. "A little poke."

Miley sighed dramatically. "Tell that to my scars."

I laughed, knowing she was full of shit. "Good times." I grimaced as I again rubbed at my eye.

"You know you still haven't told me why you're doing this," Miley said.

"Oh…" I tried to sound as casual as possible. "It's my job."

"It's your job to get all dressed up and pretend to be his girlfriend on TV?" she asked.

I immediately caught the scepticism in my best friend's voice. "It's going to help him get sponsors," I tried to defend myself. "Marketing and PR is part of my job as his assistant."

"Bullshit."

I stopped trying to fix my face and spun around in my chair. "It's not bullshit," I lied.

"You're doing it because you care about him," Miley said. "Just admit it."

"No."

Miley laughed. "Why won't you admit you like this guy?"

I threw my hands up. "Because I don't."

"Right."

"I don't," I protested.

"Then why are you doing this, River?"

I sighed in frustration. "Miley, for the last time," I said, "I absolutely, positively, do not—"

The man in question stood in the doorway in dark grey pants and a black V-neck cashmere sweater.

"I gotta go," I said quickly to Miley.

I heard her making juvenile smooching sounds before I managed to hang up.

"Do not what?" Declan asked with a wry smile as he closed the door behind him.

"Um…um…um…" My mind scrambled for an answer. "…do not know how to fix this." I pointed lamely to my eye.

Declan grabbed a chair and pulled it close to me, examining me with a confused look. "It looks like you went a round or two in the cage," he said with a frown.

"It's supposed to look like this." I turned my face for him to see the other side.

Declan nodded slowly before catching my gaze. "Is it?" he asked.

"Huh?"

"Is it?" he repeated. "Is that what it's supposed to look like?"

I glanced at the mirror, frowning in confusion. "Yeah, I mean, I didn't touch that one after the makeup artist finished so that's what it's supposed to look like."

"Hmm," Declan studied me. "Maybe I can help."

This surprised me greatly because as far as I was aware, Declan Gallagher was more likely to know how to bite off a nose than contour it, more likely be able to fish hook a lip than smother it with plumping lip gloss. And far more likely to be an expert in eye gouging rather than be an eyeshadow "lewk." How exactly, I thought, was he, an MMA fighter and a *dude*, going to help with fixing my makeup?

Curious, I studied him with a raised eyebrow as he surveyed the available options of blush brushes, sparkly eyeshadow palettes, application sponges, mascara tubes, and compacts of highlighter and bronzer galore. His fingers drummed the edge of the makeup counter before he clicked his tongue and snapped. "Here we are," he announced. "Close your eyes."

I narrowed my eyes at him in suspicion.

"Trust me." He smiled as his fingers brushed against my knee. "Close your eyes."

After another moment of hesitation, I allowed my eyelids to flutter closed. My body tensed as I heard him grab something off the counter. I could sense his hand moving toward my face and I imagined another trip to the emergency room with a mascara wand lodged in my eye socket. I wondered for a moment if my contract with Seamus included workman's comp. After a brief flinch at Declan's first touch, I quickly relaxed and a small smile tugged at the corner of my lips because it wasn't an eyeshadow brush or mascara wand or eyeliner pen that was going to fix me, but a makeup remover cloth.

I peeked open the eye opposite to the one that Declan gently, carefully, delicately wiped clean. His blue eyes were soft as they focused on his task.

"What are you doing?" I whispered.

"You're moving," he said with the tiniest of grins. "You're going to mess up my work."

This caused me to smile even more, the laugh lines around my eyes crinkling in delight.

"Stop it," Declan playfully chastised. "Perfection is hard work."

I laughed. "But you're taking all the makeup *off*."

Declan's eyes found mine. "Exactly." He pulled his hand away from my face and folded the makeup remover cloth over to a clean side before offering it to me.

I stared down at the mix of colours and streaks of black across the damp cloth. I raised my eyes to Declan. "You said you were going to fix it," I said.

Declan smiled. "I did." He nudged the cloth toward me.

I eyed it warily. "Everyone is going to expect *this* girl to be next to you," I said, pointing to my eye still laden with what felt like ten pounds of makeup.

Declan reached over and brushed his thumb along the cheekbone beneath my makeup-free eye. "Of course they're going to expect *that* girl," he said, his voice low. "They have no idea that *this* girl can possibly exist."

I wanted to shake my head. I wanted to tell him that I wasn't anything special. I wanted to stop him from saying anything else. But for some reason I couldn't find the will to open my mouth.

"They have no idea that someone so special, so unique, so colourful and full of life and joy and hope could ever exist today," he said with a passion I'd only ever heard in his voice when he was discussing the cage. "So of course they're not going to expect you." He smiled as his fingers brushed against mine, his touch electric. "Show them who you are, River."

He placed the cloth in my palm and gently folded my fingers over it. His skin was warm against mine as he cocooned my hand with both of his. "They're going to love you," Declan said. "They're going to love you just like—" He suddenly cleared his throat and dropped my hand, averting his gaze from mine. His cheeks reddened as he pushed his chair back from mine and stood, scratching at the back of his neck.

Just then, the door to the makeup room opened and the studio assistant poked her head in. "You ready?"

I quickly rubbed my other eye with the makeup remover cloth and was about to say I was ready when I looked down at the skin-tight dress I was stuffed into.

Declan noticed, too. "She just has to get dressed," he told the assistant.

The assistant looked with confusion at my dress. "That's what she's supposed to wear."

Declan winked at me as he corralled the assistant out of the dressing room. I heard him out in the hallway say, "Change of plans."

You don't fucking say, I thought as I wiggled out of my dress.

The plan was to move away from NYC for a fresh start.

The plan was to keep things simple, uncomplicated.

The plan was to never, ever, *ever* again fall for my boss.

Change of plans.

Shit.

River

Well, my palms weren't dripping pools of sweat onto my skirt, and I was able to sit comfortably in my chair without shaking so terribly that it rattled against the floor, and the contents of my breakfast with Declan remained in my stomach, so there was nothing else to say other than that the interview was going…fine. Grand, as they'd say here in Ireland.

The producer had caught one look at me without makeup and

in a simple floral skirt and tangerine lace top before we started filming and made a beeline toward me.

Declan quickly blocked his path.

"What happened to her makeup?" he asked.

"She doesn't need it," Declan replied, arms crossed over his chest.

The producer had frowned, leaning over to see me past Declan's wide shoulders. "But—"

"She doesn't need it," Declan repeated. It was clear to everyone in the studio that the conversation had ended.

The production staff set up the microphones on both Declan and me, arranged us in chairs next to one another, and blinded us with hot, bright studio lights.

The interviewer arrived. With her cleavage practically spilling out of her low-cut dress and a pearly white smile, she introduced herself to Declan without even a glance toward me.

"This is River," Declan said.

The interviewer nodded disinterestedly over at me. "The assistant?" she asked.

"The girlfriend."

The interviewer's sickly sweet smile faltered. "Right then." Her eyes avoided me as she tugged back up the corners of her bright pink, shiny lips. "Let's get started, shall we?"

Declan then reached over and squeezed my hand. He smiled

over at me. "Thank you," he whispered. "It's nice not to do this alone."

I nodded. "I'll try not to say anything too stupid or embarrassing."

He laughed. "Anything you say will be perfect," he said as the producer counted down the start of the filming.

And so it began. I was on television, the last place on earth I had thought I wanted to be just days ago, with Declan Gallagher, the last person on earth I had thought I wanted to be with just two days ago. Life sure was funny.

It started off easy enough. Most of the questions were directed at Declan: questions about his training, about his diet, his comeback, his strategy, his title and championship history.

I mostly nodded along, adding in here and there quips about how hard he'd been training or how regimented he'd been or how I supported him without reservation.

Soon the interviewer's questions pivoted toward me.

"Now, River, darling…" The woman uncrossed her legs, shifted in her chair toward me, and crossed them again, her shiny black stiletto with the bright red sole bouncing. "…all of this must be very new for you?"

I cleared my throat only to realise it was threatening to close shut. "Umm, yes," I somehow managed to croak out.

"Declan here isn't the only one with pressures, now is he?" she asked, her shiny pink lips curling up into a stiff smile.

My brows furled in confusion. "Umm…"

"Well?"

"I don't know what you mean," I admitted.

"You've got quite large shoes to fill," she said before her eyes travelled to my chest. "Or shall we say, quite large *cups* to fill."

It was an insult, obviously it was, but she laughed like we were the best of friends sharing an inside joke, as if she meant nothing at all by it.

Beside me, Declan leaned forward, but I quickly placed my hand on his leg. "If we're talking Guinness," I said, "I'd be happy to fill any size cup."

Declan laughed along with the rest of the production team off set.

The interviewer gave a half-hearted chuckle before diving right back in, talons poised.

I knew what she wanted, of course I did. She wanted a sound piece to churn drama. She wanted a feud between Giselle and me, because nothing would boost ratings more than a high-profile catfight. She wanted something *juicy*.

"Yes, but," she started again, "surely, it must be difficult knowing who Declan used to be with."

"I think it's important to look forward, not back," I said, keeping my demeanour calm.

The interviewer didn't even seem to have heard what I said. "The comparisons don't hurt then?" she asked, leaning forward, going in for the kill. She drummed her long manicured nails against her notepad as she studied my reaction with a small grin.

"Comparisons?" I asked, my voice small.

The interviewer chuckled casually. "Well, of course," she said. "Giselle: international supermodel, multimillionaire entrepreneur with her own fashion line and one of the largest Instagram followings in the world, named *People*'s Most Beautiful Woman for three consecutive years, I could go on."

I suddenly felt uncomfortable with my bare face and simple floral skirt. The interviewer shrugged.

"And then there's you," she said. "A personal assistant and…" Her voice trailed off, making the statement a question with the unspoken "what." A personal assistant and *what?*

It was left to me to fill in the blank. And what? And what? And *what?* I had to answer something. But what? "Um…"

The studio lights that hadn't felt so bright after all, they suddenly felt like the summer sun reflected off the black pavement on a busy New York street. It was sweltering and I kept waiting for a cool breeze that wasn't coming. And what?

"Um…"

What was there? I wasn't a celebrity. I wasn't rich. I wasn't stunningly beautiful. I didn't have a fashion line. People, let alone *People*, didn't even know who I was. And what?

"Um…"

And what?

"Um…um…"

And what?

"And kind."

The male voice that spoke was strong, confident, sure. The voice inside my head was none of those things.

"What was that?" the interviewer asked.

I glanced over at Declan.

His mouth opened, his lips moved, his voice strong, confident, and sure, cut through the heavy silence. "A personal assistant and kind," he said. He smiled over at me and reached to intertwine his fingers with mine in full view of the cameras. It was a message, one he seemed to wish to convey loud and clear—she was with me.

"Kind?" the interviewer asked, as if hearing the word for the first time.

"Yes," Declan said, sounding totally self-assured. "If people are so eager for a comparison, then I'll give them a comparison. River learned the names of my staff the first day she arrived. The next time you're interviewing Giselle, ask her if she can name a single one. And 'the gardener' doesn't count."

The interviewer sat stunned as Declan leaned forward. On his face was the same determination and ferocity as when he sparred in the cage with Seamus. This was no longer an interview; it was a fight.

A fight for *me*.

"River doesn't know the word grudge, but you best believe it's Giselle's middle name," Declan continued. "River is a 'yes', Giselle is a 'no'. River is a 'you', Giselle is a 'me'. River's camera is pointed at others, the world around her, nature and its infinite beauty and mystery and majesty. Giselle's never leaves her own face."

Flabbergasted, the interviewer's jaw dropped as she was left completely mute. Though it wouldn't have even mattered if she managed to come up with something to say. Declan wasn't finished.

He had yet to deliver the final knockout punch.

"Giselle was the one who dragged me down to my lowest, sank me down to my darkest, pulled me down toward my destruction." Declan's eyes contained fire. "River was the one who found me down there and did not run, did not leave, did not flinch. She was the one who showed me there was light. River was the one who believed I could fight."

My eyes widened in surprise when Declan suddenly stood, pulling me up beside him. "So I'm going to fight," he said. "And from now on, I'll let my fists do the talking. This interview is over."

I just caught the look of disbelief on the interviewer's face as I hurried after Declan as he stalked quickly off the set, ripping his mike from his suit jacket.

"Shit, Declan," Seamus hissed as he hurried after us. "What the fuck was that?"

Declan didn't even glance back at him as he shoved the back door open to where our black sedan sat waiting for us. "That was my final word," he said as I climbed inside the back seat.

After he climbed in, Declan slammed the door closed in Seamus's face. Immediately his callused palms were on either side of my face. His eyes searched mine earnestly. "I am so sorry," his said quickly. "I'm so sorry, River. I'm so sorry. Christ, I never should have agreed to do any of that stupid shite. I'm sorry, I'm so, so sorry. Ah, fuck. Fuck. Fuck, I'm sorry. Fuck, I'm so—"

"Thank you."

"I can't believe I dragged you into this. I am so— Wait…what?"

I smiled as I laid my hands over his still holding my face. "Thank you."

In the dim light of the back of the sedan, Declan frowned. "Thank you?" he asked with obvious confusion.

I nodded.

"But— I-I'm the reason you had to go through that." He shook his head. "Thank you for what?"

"For reminding me of the answer," I said.

When Declan's eyes remained unsure, I continued. "I froze back there," I explained. "When she said 'and…' I had no answer. I'd forgotten who I was, with all of…well, all of this."

I brushed my fingers against his. "And you reminded me," I finished. "So…well, I just wanted to say thank you."

Declan studied me for a moment before awkwardly pulling his hands from my face and turning in his seat to face the front. He cleared his throat and stared forward. "Well, um, you're welcome then," he said stiffly before calling toward the front, "Driver, we're ready."

As the car pulled out onto the street, I stared out the window and traced the lines on my cheeks where Declan's hands had been. It was another chance to see Dublin and again, I saw nothing but Declan placing the makeup remover cloth into my palm, Declan reaching over for my hand, Declan storming off the set.

Maybe the spotlight wasn't so bad. Maybe I could handle it after all. Maybe it wasn't all that terrible. At least, with him by my side.

River

I hadn't bothered with a spoon…no, I'd gone straight for the ice cream scooper.

It was weeks later. The bowl of cookie dough wobbled where it was balanced in my lap as I dug in deep for another mountain-sized mouthful. I squinted at my computer screen, the only source of illumination in the otherwise dark kitchen. It was, after all, sometime past midnight. As I crunched into a chunk of dark chocolate, my fingers flew furiously over the keyboard before reaching for the bottle of merlot on the marble island.

I'd skipped the glass as well.

The last few remaining swigs sloshed at the bottom of the bottle as I pressed and held down the delete button to erase what I'd just written. I was left again with just a blank email draft. I growled in frustration as I tried to dig out more cookie dough from the nearly empty bowl. I was licking the ice cream scooper when footsteps approached and a light switched on.

"Uh-oh."

Wincing at the glare, I looked up from my frantic typing, the ice cream scooper stuffed into my mouth, to find Oisin shaking his head in the kitchen doorway.

"My, oh my." He clicked his tongue as his eyes travelled from the bottle of wine to the bowl of cookie dough to my laptop. "This does *not* look good, my little voodoo queen."

"I'm leaving, Oisin," I announced matter of factly before returning my attention to the keyboard. "So don't try to convince me otherwise. I've made up my mind. Hey, can you grab me some more wine while you're up?"

I reached for the bottle next to me to finish it off before Round 2, but Oisin snatched it up faster than I could wrap my fingers around it.

"Hey," I whined.

He narrowed his eyes pointedly at me before marching over to the sink and pouring the rest of the bottle down the drain.

"*Hey!*"

Oisin leaned against the counter, crossed his arms over his silk night robe, and levelled his eyes at me. "River, what are you doing?"

"I'm quitting."

Oisin frowned at me. "No, you're not."

"I am," I insisted, pointing to my computer screen. "I'm writing the email to Seamus right now. I'm out of here. Out. Of. Here."

Oisin assessed me. "You wouldn't…" he said slowly.

"No?" My chin jutted forward in a challenge. "Watch me." My fingers typed out a quick "I quit, loser" and my mouse was hovering over the "Send" icon when Oisin rushed over.

"Woah, woah, woah!" He pulled my laptop away from me. "Let's think about this, shall we?"

"I have thought about this." I lunged for the keyboard, but Oisin easily kept it out of reach. Pouting, I again grabbed my ice cream scooper and dug into the cookie dough.

Oisin scooted my laptop a little farther away, eyeing me to make sure I wasn't going to stretch for it, before pulling out a bar stool next to me. He laid a hand on my shoulder. "What's going on?" he asked softly.

"I'm quitting," I repeated over a mouthful of cookie dough. "I'm quitting and that's that."

"River." Oisin squeezed my shoulder.

I glanced over at him and saw in his soft but determined gaze that I wasn't getting out of this one: I was trapped in a friendship web.

I sighed and sagged over my bowl of cookie dough. "Everything's been so different since Dublin," I admitted. "I thought Declan and I were making progress. I thought even…" My voice trailed off as I stared down at my hands.

The first time he missed dinner I hadn't thought much about it. After our time in the city, I understood the pressure that Declan was under for his upcoming return fight. As I glanced again and again at the clock on the wall in the dining room, I assumed he simply lost track of time in the gym. It was nothing. I ate alone and went up to bed. I fell asleep without giving it a second thought.

The second time he missed our dinner together, I started to worry. I remembered Niall's words regarding Declan's injuries. Was he beginning to push himself too hard? Was he going to hurt himself? Anxiety filled my chest because I was the one who said he could fight, that he *should* fight. I wasn't sure I could stand to be the reason for Declan's pain. Alone again, I finished my dinner, and on my way upstairs I stopped by the gym. I peeked inside to find Declan at the punching bag, fists pounding faster, faster, faster as the muscles along his back rippled. I went to bed but tossed and turned the whole night.

The third night he didn't show up for dinner I waited fifteen minutes, thirty minutes, forty-five minutes with my favourite pesto farfalle with grilled chicken getting colder and colder before slapping my napkin on the edge of the dining room table and marching straight down to the gym. I shoved open the doors and stormed across to where Declan was in full-out sprint on the treadmill. I moved to the front of the machine and pressed the emergency stop button.

"What do you think you're doing?" I shouted as the belt slowed and stopped.

Declan pulled out his headphones. "What?" he asked, clearly confused.

"It's 6:58," I said, folding my arms across my chest. "What do you think you're doing?"

Declan had glanced down at his watch. "Oh." Without another word, he had hopped down from the treadmill and walked out of the gym.

Relieved, I followed him along the hallway toward the dining room. I chastised myself for worrying; everything was fine. He just lost track of time, just as I had suspected.

But as I turned into the dining room, I nearly crashed into him as he was leaving the room with his plate. He slipped past me without a word, without a glance.

"Where are you going?" I shouted after him.

"I'm going to watch the film of my last practice with Seamus while I eat," he called back before disappearing around the corner.

That night I didn't sleep. I was far too busy staring up at my ceiling.

As the days went on, I saw Declan less and less. He no longer ate dinner with me. Every time I went into the gym to get to my office, he was busy on a phone call or in the spa or just mysteriously gone. He even gave my morning breakfast routine to Oisin so I no longer saw him then.

Soon, I realised what was right beneath my nose, what I hadn't wanted to see: Declan was avoiding me.

Our time in Dublin had blinded me. His lips, hot, desperate, and hungry, had placed a blindfold over my eyes. His arms, strong, firm and possessive, tied it tight. And his eyes, soft, kind, and yearning, had double knotted it, then double knotted it again, so I had no choice but to feel my way around the dark with my heart and my heart alone.

So I didn't see it coming.

The old Declan had returned and I hadn't even known it till I was already out in the icy cold, alone and in the dark.

"So I'm quitting," I said with a determined nod of my chin after explaining all of this as best I could to Oisin. "And that's that."

Sitting next to me at the kitchen island, Oisin sighed and pinched the bridge of his nose.

I frowned over at him in confusion.

Oisin opened the laptop. His fingers clacked on the keyboard and he squinted. I watched in growing curiosity as his eyes scanned the page back and forth. In a whirl of motion, spun the laptop around to face me and jammed his finger at the page.

"Look at this," he commanded, pushing the laptop even closer to me.

My head flopped back and I began to protest with a whine, "Ois—"

"Look," he interrupted. "Just look, alright?"

I groaned in response.

"I'll make you a deal," he said, laying a hand on my arm. "I'll leave you to your decision. I swear I won't say a single word to stop you."

I narrowed my eyes warily at him.

"All you have to do is look at this, okay? Really look."

I sighed. "Fine."

Oisin squeezed my arm and pressed, "You'll look?"

"Yes," I grumbled.

"You promise?"

"Yes, yes," I complained, "I promise I'll look, okay?"

Oisin patted my arm before standing and giving the top of my head a kiss. "He's crazy about you, my little voodoo queen," he whispered. "He just doesn't know it yet."

With that, his quiet footsteps echoed through the kitchen and then out into the hallway before they faded away, leaving me alone with just my tumultuous thoughts and the computer screen.

I didn't want to look.

I wanted to wobble over to the wine cellar, grab another bottle, and stumble upstairs to drown my sorrows in bed. I wanted to press "Send" on my typo-filled resignation letter and book the next flight out of here. I wanted to forget that I was ever stupid enough to let my heart fall for Declan Gallagher.

But I promised.

So I looked.

Oisin had pulled up the front page of *The Irish Times*. I nearly fell out of my chair when I saw my own face smiling back at me from the red carpet. But once the shock of that faded, my eyes moved slowly over to Declan.

He wasn't smiling for the camera, but he was smiling. Scooting up closer to the counter, I adjusted the laptop screen and clicked to zoom in on Declan's face. I'd never seen him smile like he was smiling in the photo.

His lips, always frozen in a dark scowl, were pulled up into a wide, unfiltered grin as if he wasn't surrounded by dozens of cameras and instead, he was just alone with close friends. The dark bags I'd grown accustomed to seeing under his eyes were replaced with fine laugh lines as his eyes crinkled in joy. Even the colour of his eyes seemed different to me. Normally, a storm waged in those icy blues, but his beaming smile brought rays of sunshine to crystal-clear aquamarine waters. The past that followed him like a heavy weight around his ankle and creased his forehead was gone. He seemed happy.

Oisin thought this proved that Declan had feelings for me,

because Declan wasn't smiling at the camera; he was smiling at me. As I stared at the picture, alone in the kitchen for who knows how long, I wanted more than anything to believe that. But I wasn't sure I could.

Because the truth that I couldn't avoid was—Declan never let me see him smile like this. The camera caught him with his guard down and it was a beautiful, rare, special moment, no doubt. But every good fighter knows he'll fall without his defences, without his protection, without his guard up, always up.

So would Declan Gallagher be willing to fall?

Willing to fall for *me*?

Declan

"I can't sleep. I can't eat. I can't focus on training. I can barely stay still long enough for my physiotherapy." Sagging in my char, I closed my eyes and rubbed my throbbing temples.

"I just don't know what's wrong with me," I continued, feeling weary even as my heart pounded rapidly in my chest like it was about to burst out. "I must be sick. Doc says I'm fine, but I'm not fine."

I felt my forehead for a fever. It had to be a fever after all. What else burned your body and dried your mouth one minute and then froze your veins and poured oil over your palms the next?

"Something is wrong," I groaned. "Something is terribly wrong."

Opening my eyes, I looked between my two best friends on the split screen video call on the computer in my room. Each was silent as I waited.

Danny rubbed at the back of his neck, his dark hair falling over his blue eyes, his muscled limbs hanging over the guitar in his lap; always the guitar. Or these days, Ailis, his wife. I barely recognised his Dublin apartment in the background now that it *actually* had furniture, throws, candles, and art on the walls in it—thanks to Ailis.

Diarmuid, dark hair pulled back into a man bun, scratched his beard and cleared his throat quietly so as not to wake Saoirse, the girl he chased halfway across the world. It was in the middle of the night where he was in Brisbane, Australia, but he woke his ass up just because I needed him. Any time I needed him, he was there for me. I'd do the same for him. He knew that.

My eyebrows furrowed as I looked again between them. "What?" I asked. "You know what it is?"

"Dex," Diarmuid started, his words measured. "Anything new going on with you? Anything different?"

"What the bollocks does that have to do with anything?"

Danny strummed a chord and shrugged. "You get a reaction and you go to the doctor, yeah?" he said. "He asks you if you've changed your detergent or cologne, right?"

I narrowed my eyes. "Yeah…"

"Well…" Diarmuid gave me a pointed look through the screen. "What's your new detergent, Dex?"

I threw my hands up in frustration. "Are you two fecking kidding me? I call you for help for a serious problem, a fecking serious problem, and you suggest it's because of a new *detergent*?"

"Dex, you eejit." Danny sighed. "How did you make it out of high school? It's a metaphor."

Diarmuid nodded and explained, "We're talking about that girl."

"What girl?" I asked, the tips of my ears suddenly feeling hot.

Both Danny and Diarmuid laughed.

"Oh, come on!" Diarmuid's ring-covered hand thudded the table. "We've all seen the pictures."

"I don't even watch TV and *I've* seen them," Danny added.

"River?" It wasn't a good sign that saying her name aloud sent a jolt of electricity down my spine. "My personal assistant? What does she have to do with my illness?"

Shaking his head, Danny chuckled and then asked, "Tell me this, Dex. Did you experience any of these symptoms of yours before she showed up?"

I considered his question. My life without River seemed to be lifetimes ago. I couldn't remember feeling like this: panicked, restless, anxious, excited, and *alive*. I remembered waking up, training, sleep. Repeat. It was like living in a fog. Everything was grey. Everything was out of focus.

I was numb.

"I guess not," I answered slowly before finally looking up at my two friends, suddenly feeling lost.

Diarmuid smiled. "You've got it bad, my friend," he said.

"There's no hope for you." Danny grinned. "No hope at all."

Diarmuid nodded. "No recovery."

"No one survives what you've got, Dex." Danny winked.

Unblinking, I stared at each of them as I considered what exactly they were implying. I slowly shook my head. "No, no," I insisted. "That can't be it. With Giselle, I never felt like this."

Both Danny and Diarmuid just continued to stare at me, not saying a single word.

"I never felt this way with Giselle," I repeated softly.

Diarmuid finally leaned forward closer to the webcam and smiled before saying simply, "Exactly."

My hands shook as I wiped my damp brow. Why was I sweating so terribly? Maybe Danny and Diarmuid were wrong. Maybe it was the flu. Maybe it was the onset of food poisoning. Maybe it was a rare brain condition never known to exist before now.

Anything felt like a more promising diagnosis than…*that.*

If it were the flu, I would know what to do. I'd sleep it off. I'd drink lots of water, place a hot towel over my eyes and moan and groan till it eventually passed. And it wasn't like I wanted to cling desperately to a toilet for the next twenty-four hours, but I at least understood what food poisoning was and how to deal with it. Hell, even if it were an incurable brain condition, I'd at least get some goddamn morphine.

What the fuck was I supposed to take for…this?

My voice was quiet as I stared at my fingers, clammy and shaking in my lap. "I don't know what I'm supposed to do," I admitted in a hushed whisper.

A laugh from Danny brought my gaze back up to the computer screen. "Fuck, Dex," he said. "Nobody does. That's the mystery of it."

"The beauty of it," Danny joined in.

I sighed. "The agony of it."

Both of my friends chuckled.

"It hurts like hell," Diarmuid nodded. "But—"

"It hurts so fucking good," Danny finished for him.

I buried my face in my hands and groaned. What the fuck had I gotten myself into?

"You have to go to her," Diarmuid said as I squeezed my eyes tighter shut. "You have to tell her."

"He's right," Danny said. "As much as I hate to admit it, Diarmuid's right, Dex."

I groaned even louder. I wasn't sure I could do it. Going to her, looking into her sweet, soft eyes that always seemed to be searching for something in mine… I wasn't sure I could lower my defences, drop my guard, remove the mask I'd grown so accustomed to wearing. *I couldn't even admit my feelings to myself*, I thought. How the hell was I supposed to admit them to her?

My heart pounded painfully in my chest and I rubbed at it with one hand while dragging the other across my eyes. "I think I'm having a heart attack," I told my friends. "Is that normal?"

I checked the screen with one eye peeked open to find them both laughing and nodding.

"Perfectly," Diarmuid said.

"Just wait for the nausea," Danny joked.

Or at least I hoped he was joking…

"How do I tell her?" I asked, staring at the ceiling with my neck resting against the back of the chair. Maybe there were answers somehow written up there. But I didn't have a chance to see, because my phone vibrated on the desk.

"All you can do is be honest," Diarmuid was explaining as I glanced at the screen.

It was a text from Seamus. I was going to ignore it till I was done talk to the boys, but River's name in the message caught my eye. I was pushing my chair out from the desk before I had even finished reading the message. "I've got to go," I said hurriedly.

"What? Now?" Danny asked with a half laugh. "Right this second?"

I didn't answer. I barely registered the concern on their faces as I stood and dialled Seamus's number.

"Declan, what's going on?" Diarmuid called as I ran toward the door, not even bothering to hang up the video chat. "What's wrong?"

I sprinted down the hall and pressed the phone to my ear, begging Seamus to answer quickly because each ring was like a knife in my heart. Hurry. *Hurry!*

River was leaving.

River

Alone in the darkroom I had only one photograph to develop before I left the manor.

It was a photograph of Oisin, Joan, and David at the local pub one rainy night, the only image of my time in Ireland that I wanted to keep. The rest I would do my best to forget: the image of piercing blue eyes, of callused, scared hands, the image of lips, soft and full, drawing closer, closer, clos—

If only those images could be as easily destroyed as the delicate film in my camera.

I'd already gone through most of the steps needed to develop the photo. I'd measured out the chemicals, used the enlarger, positioned the image on the masking frame, checked the sharpness, and made the test strip. But I'd hesitated before putting the exposed paper into the developer. I wasn't entirely sure why. The sooner I did that the sooner I could leave this place.

That was what I wanted, wasn't it?

Before I could answer the question rolling around inside my head, I plunged the paper into the tray of developer and gently rocked it back and forth to submerge the whole sheet. I wouldn't admit it aloud to anyone, but truthfully, I was afraid of what my answer would have been. So to drown out my thoughts, I busied myself the only way I knew how…with my work.

There was a peace, after all, to working steadily, gently, carefully in a darkroom; a peace that I hoped would calm my heart after making the decision to leave.

A peace that was, of course, promptly destroyed.

The door to the darkroom swung open, slamming against the wall.

I winced at the flood of light from the hallway outside as Declan stormed inside, waving a piece of paper wildly in the air.

"Declan, what the—"

"No!" he shouted as he stalked toward me. "I do not accept this."

I stumbled back in surprise when he shoved the piece of paper against my chest.

He pointed a finger at me. His voice shook when he repeated, "No."

I looked down at the space between our feet where the paper had fallen to the ground. It was the resignation letter I sent to Seamus. Slowly, I moved my eyes back up to Declan's face, no more than a darkened silhouette against the light from the hallway. Anger burned in my chest and I clenched my hands into tight fists.

I hadn't seen him in days, *days*. And he had the nerve to burst in here in a wild fury like a Category 5 hurricane, destroying my photographs and demanding that I stay.

No.

Fuck no.

"Are you going to tie me up in the kitchen, Declan?" I hissed, glaring up at him.

He loomed over me, still and silent save the rapid rise and fall of his chest and his raspy breath.

"Huh?" I stepped closer, the sole of my sneaker crushing the resignation letter. "Are you going to lock me in the cell you call my office?"

I could feel the heat from his skin as I moved even closer to him.

"What are you going to do to stop me?" I whispered. "Put handcuffs around my wrists and chains around my ankles?"

Declan's breath caught in his throat. Still, he did not speak as my chest grazed his. I had to tilt my head back to see up into his face, I was so close.

"Because that's what you're going to have to do to get me to stay." I waited for another tense, quiet moment.

Declan remained motionless, frozen.

My shoulder shoved into his as I slid past him toward the door. I would go to my room and pack right then and there. I'd stay in town till my flight home.

Declan caught my wrist. He turned his head, but his piercing blue eyes were still hidden in the shadow. His voice was dark as he repeated, "I do not accept."

I tried to tug my arm away from him, but his grasp was far too strong to escape from. If Declan wanted to hold me in place all afternoon, I would be helpless to stop him. If he wanted to pin me there in the darkroom all through the night, there was nothing I could do. If he wanted us to starve together in that dim light, well then, we would starve.

"Let me go." I tried and failed to keep my voice from shaking in anger.

Declan was quiet for a few seconds that each felt like years before he said again, "I do not accept."

"Stop saying that," I said through gritted teeth as I yanked my arm again to free myself.

"I do not accept," Declan repeated.

I pressed my face close to his and hissed, "I. Do. Not. Care."

Declan glared down at me.

I glared up at him, not intimidated by the face that men three times my size had cowered from in the cage. "You have been the worst employer I've ever had," I said. "The absolute worst." I felt my heart rate begin to beat out of control as I grew more and more frustrated. "You're moody and unpredictable," I started. "You're impossible to please and refuse to adhere to even basic standards of manners. A 'thank you' or 'please' from you is as rare as a sunny day in this country."

You're passionate and untamable and there's a fire in your soul that lures me in like a moth to a flame. I can't explain why but you're irresistible to me. You're impossible to get out of my mind, no matter how hard I try. A day without a thought of you, a night without you in my dreams is as rare as a sunny day in this godforsaken country.

I jutted my chin up defiantly at Declan as I went on, "You're stubborn as an ass and can't admit when you're wrong, which is, by the way, far more often than you realise. You never laugh. You never joke. You never smile."

You laugh, but never when I am close enough to hear it. You joke, but never with me. You smile, but the only reason I know you smile is because a camera was lucky enough to catch it. I want to see you smiling down at me. I want to see it with my own eyes. I want it more than maybe anything. But you're as stubborn as an ass!

"You're demanding."

You're intoxicating.

"You're rude."

You're seductive.

"You're selfish."

You're driving me wild.

I growled in frustration when I again tried to tug my hand free, only to have Declan's grip on my wrist tighten. What made me even more furious was that I *liked* it.

"You've reduced your whole world, your entire existence to a thirty-foot diameter," I growled. "You've literally caged yourself in, Declan, and you've convinced yourself that you like it, that you *need* it. You train and you train and you train and you think it will make you happy. You think a fucking belt will complete you. And you think if you let anyone in, it will all fall apart, and you have no fucking clue that maybe that's exactly what you need."

By the end of this, I was left gasping, my lungs burning for air. As I gulped in greedy breaths in the ensuing silence, nothing seemed to fill them. They burned and burned and I felt like I was trapped underwater.

Declan stared darkly down at me, red hot embers in his eyes. "And you are infuriating." He took a step toward me.

I stood my ground.

"You're annoying."

Even as the truth spilled from his mouth, I lifted my chin.

"You're always bleedin' late 'cause you get distracted by feckin' raindrops."

Closer he moved. Stronger I stood.

"You come in here not even knowing what my sport is and yet you're arrogant enough to believe you know what's best for me—*for me.*" He stopped right in front of me.

My eyes were wide as I stared up at him, hardly daring to breathe as his anger rolled over me in palpable waves.

"You don't take things seriously. You're always joking instead of doing what you are supposed to be doing. That pesky little smile is rarely off your face..." Declan grabbed my shoulders, his eyes dark, his voice a pained growl. "But what I hate most of all about you is..." His mouth wavered, whatever words yet unspoken clinging to his lips.

My breath fluttered nervously as I waited, each second of silence was pure agony.

He yanked me closer to him.

I stumbled, falling against his solid chest.

"...I don't hate you at all."

His lips crashed onto mine. Rough. Savage. Claiming me.

I could do nothing but let him. More than let him, I kissed him back. With all the frustration and need that had built up over the last few weeks of working for him.

He broke the kiss and whispered, "I want to get under your skin, just like you've gotten under mine." His fingers dug greedily into my skin and his mouth moved hungrily against mine. I moaned against him as my fingers clawed down his back.

He spoke to my lips, "I want to obsess you, like you somehow obsess me." With his hands against my waist and my arms around his neck, Declan walked me back till my shoulders collided with the wall of the darkroom.

I was pinned. Helpless as he ravaged my mouth, his hands roaming down my body, finding its way under my skirt and up the sides of my thighs to grip my hips, his erection hard and hot between us.

"I want to get inside you—your head, your heart, *your body*—the way you're inside me."

Jesus Christ. Was I going to let him fuck me against this wall?

Yes. I just might.

No. My rules.

His knee pressed at my thighs, firmly demanding I part them.

I moaned, my blood singing with need.

Yes…

But no…

Somehow, I managed to keep my shaking thighs shut. If he got between my legs, if I let him press that huge—dear God, was it even going to fit—cock of his against the aching centre of me, I was a goner. Willpower, *poof*. Sanity, out the window. I might as well hand over my soul to him to blend up with his morning protein shakes.

"Spread them," he growled.

I shook my head, my bottom lip sucked up into my teeth, afraid to speak unless I gave in.

"Now." He shoved up my top and bra in one rough move.

"Bossy." I gasped as his mouth closed around one nipple and sucked.

He stared up at me, a deep frown creasing his strong brow. "I am still your boss." He nipped my nipple with his teeth as if to make a point.

Shit.

"Which is why we can't do this," I managed to blurt out.

He froze. "What?"

"You're my boss. It's unprofessional."

"You're fired."

"*What?*" It was my turn to yelp. I let out another moan as he swirled his tongue around my nipple.

"You heard me. Now spread them."

His gravelly voice and that command. The expert way he was

alternating between licking, sucking and biting my nipple.

It was all I could do to protest one last time. "You're not my boss anymore. You can't tell me what to do."

He grabbed either side of my face and moved his close to mine so his scowl was all that I saw. His growl reverberated through me in warning. "Spread. Them."

I whimpered. I tried to resist. I really did. God help me for what came next.

The second I relaxed my thighs his knee slipped in between, pushing them farther apart, his muscular thigh pressing right up against my pussy. I moaned and my hips moved of their own volition, rubbing against him. A few minutes of this—*just this*—and I'd come.

I whimpered as his thigh retracted. Gasping the next second as he replaced it with his hand. His fingers slipped inside of my panties and I arched up against him like a cat.

"Christ, River," he cursed as he discovered just how embarrassingly wet I was.

My knees began to shake the moment he began to circle my clit, then my entrance. Closing my eyes, I leaned against the wall as my breath grew ragged as his fingers brought me speeding toward the edge.

Out of instinct, I wrapped one leg around his waist, balancing on the other, my hips tilting in a desperate plea for more.

"Jesus Christ, River." he muttered. "I can't..." His hand withdrew.

I whimpered. He couldn't do this. He changed his mind. Never mind. Just leave me here to die of embarrassment. Or blue balls. Did women get blue balls?

"I can't wait." His hand moved between us. In two seconds flat he'd freed himself, pushed aside my soaking panties. And slid his cock inside me.

We both groaned, long and low.

His forehead sagged on mine, his hot breath swirling around me. "Fuck," he mumbled, his voice groaning with remorse. "River, is this okay? Is this—"

"Shut up and fuck me."

My words were like cold water to him—his gaze sharpened, the hungry gleam returning to his eyes. His fingers curled around my hips, pulling up my other thigh so they were both wrapped around him, causing me to sink deeper onto him. I wasn't going anywhere though. I was pinned to that wall by his glorious wide frame.

He began to slam into me, a brutal, punishing pace that hit at that sensitive spot inside me and made my toes curl.

"Demanding, infuriating woman. Don't forget who's the boss," he said, punctuating every word with a thrust.

I scowled back at him, even as waves of pleasure roared through my body, even as I tilted my hips to meet him. "Stubborn, rude bastard. You already fired me. Remember?"

"You're rehired."

"I quit then."

"Shut up and grab onto my neck."

"I—"

He slammed his mouth against mine, effectively shutting me up. Our tongues wrestled. I wrestled between wanting to obey him and wanting to slap him for being so obnoxious.

I tore my mouth away from his and glared at him. "Please," I corrected him.

"What?"

"Grab onto my neck, *please*."

He rolled his eyes. "Just feckin' do it, woman."

"*Say please*."

"Or you'll be dropped."

I clutched onto his neck, deliberately digging my nails into his skin, making him hiss. His eyes flashed with fire, sending a thrill down my spine.

"Rude bastard." I cursed at him.

"Stubborn woman." He walked us away from the wall, his huge strong hands palming my ass to hold me against him.

My nails dug in harder and I locked my feet behind his back as he carried me across the darkroom.

"I'll replace it," he said.

Before I could ask what he meant, expensive equipment crashed to the floor as he swept his muscular arm across the workbench.

I whimpered. All my beautiful equipment!

I didn't have time to mourn though. Declan threw me down on the hard surface, not letting me catch my breath before he was dragging me to the edge of the bench by my ankles, throwing my legs over his shoulders, and thrusting deep inside of me again.

I moaned and clawed for something to hold onto as Declan fucked me fast and hard. The table rattled against the wall noisily as he pushed in deeper and deeper, squeezing my waist tighter and tighter. My tits bounced, my bra still pushed up, and my toes curled. I could already feel the muscles along my stomach tensing, my thighs tightening, my lips tingling as my teeth sank into them to bite off my loud moans.

"Come," he demanded.

"Bossy asshole," I said through my teeth. Damn him. Part of me wanted to hold the incoming wave off just to spite him. The other part of me realised that this was going to be im-fucking-possible.

His brow narrowed over his hooded eyes. And I knew I was in trouble.

"Stubborn woman." His hand slipped between us, his thumb finding my clit and drawing fast little circles over it. "You *will* come."

"Fuck!" I gasped, eyes squeezed shut as the orgasm crashed

over me like a giant wave, heaving all the air from my lungs. I gripped his forearms, nails digging in so deeply I feared I drew blood, as my back arched and my body shook. "Fuck, Declan."

He looked glorious, sweat glistening on his chest, muscles twitching, dark eyes staring at me with such intensity, groaning as he, too, came. His chest collapsed against me. He held my head tight against him as his hips twitched and finally stilled.

That was messy, rough, and raw. And we hadn't even bothered to get naked. But it was perfect.

Just perfect.

"Fuck," Declan said, pushing himself up onto his elbows. "That's not how I wanted…"

My heart seized.

He was regretting this while he was still inside me?

"…this isn't how I wanted our first time to go."

The grip around my heart released. "Well…" I said, tracing his shoulder, a sly smile on my lips. "You have the rest of the night to make it up to me."

River

I was surprised to wake up with sheets and blankets and a comforter piled high on top of me, because I most definitely kicked them off Declan's bed the night before.

My shoes had been the first to hit the floor as we came crashing in through the bedroom door, hands on each other's faces, lips pressed tight against one another, breath already gone. Declan walked me back till the back of my knees hit the edge of the mattress and we toppled down together.

His shirt was next. I could still feel the tingle in the tips of my fingers as I fumbled with each and every infuriating button. We parted lips just long enough for me to sit up and Declan to pull my top up over my arms, then toss it onto the floor. As his hot tongue made its way from my neck down to my chest, his belt, his shoes, and my bra and skirt joined them.

My back arched up off the bed as Declan's teeth scraped against my hard, straining nipple, so I was barely aware of his pants hitting the floor. All I knew was that I wanted his naked body against mine close, closer, *closer*.

"Your socks," I gasped as he slid down between my legs and nipped at my hipbone. "You forgot your socks."

I moaned when he dragged his tongue, slowly, so fucking slowly, across my pussy through my panties. He hooked a finger inside the waistband and grinned up at me from between my legs, his eyes dark from his wide pupils.

"And you forgot *these*, love."

So Declan's socks and my wet panties made their hurried way to the floor as well. And it wasn't long after Declan's tongue went to work on my clit that my thrashing legs got rid of the comforter, the sheets, any and all blankets, throws, or decorative rugs.

For the rest of the night it was just him and me on the bed and nothing else.

But as I blinked awake and rolled over, panic flooded through my veins, because as the early morning rays flooded through windows, it was just me. Me and no one else.

I sat up and scanned the room. Declan wasn't there. I leaned over to check the cracked bathroom door. The light was off. Thoughts I couldn't control filled my brain.

He changed his mind.

He doesn't want you after all.

He never wanted you…

As I was about to give in to the hysterics of my mind, the bedroom door opened and Declan, shirtless with the hottest bed head I'd ever seen, walked in carrying a large silver platter.

"Shite," he said when he saw me awake. "I had hoped to wake you up myself." His eyes glinted darkly.

I squirmed at the thought of just how he would have accomplished that.

"It was the smell of bacon coming down the hall, wasn't it?" he asked as he sat on the side of the bed and arranged the silver tray between us.

"There's bacon on there?" I asked, practically licking my lips.

With a wide smile at me that melted my heart, Declan lifted the cover.

I greedily scanned the silver tray, trying not to drool at the sight of piles of glistening bacon, stacks of golden pancakes dripping in melted butter, and a verifiable mountain of freshly picked fruit topped with homemade whipped cream and shavings of the finest Belgian dark chocolate.

"Oisin has really outdone himself this morning," I whispered in awe of the glorious spectacle.

"Chef's probably shaking the walls of his cottage with his monstrous snoring right now," Declan said in response.

I dragged my attention away from the food—as difficult as that was—and lifted an eyebrow up at him. "What do you mean?"

He smiled and I thought I noticed some pink in his cheeks where it hadn't been just moments ago. "I, um…" He cleared his throat and looked down at a loose thread in the comforter he twisted around his finger. "I told him to take the morning off."

In confusion I looked from the array of beautifully cooked food to Declan: pancakes, Declan, butter, Declan, fresh fruit, Declan, chocolate, Declan, butter, Declan, *butter*...Declan?

"Joan?" I asked.

"At home with her son," Declan answered.

My mind was scrambling for another explanation for this breakfast. "Not David?"

Declan grinned, looking up at me through those thick, dark eyelashes. "No."

My mouth hung open, unbelieving. "Gordon Ramsey is here?"

Laughing, Declan shook his head.

I narrowed my eyes. No…it couldn't be. Could it? I shook my head. No. It definitely wasn't possible. "You didn't even know where the blender was in the kitchen," I said, crossing my arms.

MMA Champion, Declan Gallagher, did *not* just make me breakfast in bed. Nope. No way. No siree Bob, whatever in the world that meant.

"True, true." Declan laughed, leaning forward to kiss my shoulder. "But the other day I had Chef give me a tour." His lips made their way along my clavicle up to that delicious hollow between the chest and the throat.

I moaned as his hot tongue circled my skin.

"Last week when I told you I was busy watching an old film," he said while sucking at my neck, "I was actually watching cooking videos online."

I used most of my self-control reserves for the day to push his skilful tongue away from me. I searched his eyes for any hint of a lie and found none. "Why?"

Declan laughed at my question. "What do you mean 'why'?"

"I mean, why would you do that?"

He shrugged and again looked away, shifting on the bed uncomfortably. "I don't know. Food is important to you." Declan glanced up at me before continuing. "I'm not always great with words."

I snorted, unable to stop myself. Understatement of the century or what?

Declan smiled over at me. "I'm working at it, I guess. As best I can, at least. But for now, I thought I could at least learn to be good with a spatula…for you."

While Declan was distracted by staring at the bed sheets, I launched forward and pulled him into a deep kiss.

"What was that for?" he asked when I finally came up for air.

I grinned as I grabbed a piece of bacon from the breakfast platter. "Maybe I'm not so good at words either."

He smiled and together in bed, we ate breakfast, feeding each other fresh, bright-red juicy strawberries. When we were laughing, it was perfect. When we were talking, it was perfect. When we were silent, staring into each other's eyes in the soft morning light, it was perfect.

I didn't want it to end, but inevitably, I caught sight of the time on the bedside table clock. I began to stack the dirty dishes on the platter with a sad sigh. When I tried to crawl to the edge of the bed, Declan stopped me with a hand on my thigh. "Where in the world do you think you're off to?"

I nodded at the clock. "We're late for work."

Declan raised an eyebrow at me. "Last time I checked, River, I was the boss here."

I rolled my eyes. "Well, yeah, but do you see what time—hey!"

The silver tray and all the dishes clattered to floor after Declan reached over and pushed them off the bed.

I stared at him with wide eyes. "What are you doing?"

Declan's eyes flashed mischievously as he pressed me down against the mattress and straddled my hips. "We have a very busy day ahead of us," he said from above me, his hands pinning my wrists above my head.

I squirmed in delight as he lowered his lips to mine and whispered against me.

"We best get to work, dear."

River

I lowered the camera from my eye and laughed. "You've got to stop smiling."

Across the cage, Declan, wearing just his training shorts, jumped lightly from foot to foot and grinned over at me as he gave the air a jab or two. "And why's that?"

"Because you're a goddamn fighter, man," Seamus barked behind me before I could answer.

Sighing, I looked over my shoulder to find Seamus pacing just outside the cage.

The colour of his cheeks rivalled his hair for the brightest red as he pointed a finger at Declan. "And a loopy grin and puppy dog eyes don't exactly convey the intended message," he continued irritably. "We're going for, 'Watch out or I'll bite your ear off'."

I rolled my eyes.

Declan laughed as Seamus walked up to the cage and gripped the mesh.

"This was all your bleedin' idea," he grumbled at me. "Get him to focus, will ye? We're already behind on our *actual* training for the day."

"That reminds me, Seamus," Declan called from the other side of the cage where he was grabbing a drink of water. "I'm going on a hike with River this afternoon."

"*Again?*" Seamus's clawed fingers shook so terribly that the cage rattled. "You've got strength training this afternoon," he shouted.

Declan winked over at me. "I'll get some strength training in today, don't you worry." Declan's eyes trailed up and down my body.

He might as well have been using the delicate tip of a black feather, the way the hairs along my arms raised in response. I hoped Seamus didn't notice the way I shivered.

"How?" Seamus resumed his pacing, arms crossed and

eyebrows furrowed.

"River will help," Declan said between rapid uppercuts. "Won't you, River?" He glanced over at me, hunger in his eyes.

My throat went dry as I imagined Declan pinning me to the wall of the cage, stripping me of my clothes. My nipples strained against my bra at the thought of his strong hands on my hips lifting me up and pulling me roughly back down onto him as I rode him right here in the centre of the cage. "Yeah," I said, slowly, my voice low and rough. "I think I could help with that."

Behind me, Seamus threw his hands up in frustration. "She's got arms like twigs!" he bellowed. "How is she going to spot you when the weights are twice her size?"

His shouts echoed through the gym, but I barely heard him because I was too busy grinning at Declan, who was grinning at me.

"She'll do just fine," Declan spoke to Seamus, but his lust-filled gaze didn't leave me. "She'll do *just* fine."

"Those weights will crush your chest if she's the one spot—"

Out of the corner of my eye, I caught the moment realisation hit Seamus like a right hook as he glanced between Declan and me. "You nasty fuckers," he grumbled.

I tried to stifle a giggle as Seamus grabbed his jacket, ready to march out in a fit.

"I hope you're at least getting in some good cardio, Declan," he called over his shoulder as he stormed across the gym toward the door. "Let me know when you're ready to train for real."

I winced at the resounding slam of the door.

Declan waved his hand dismissively. "Don't give him any mind," he said. "He's always been a cranky fucker."

I glanced nervously toward the door and bit my lip. "Declan, are you—"

Lips pressed against mine, interrupting me. I sighed happily, as I sagged against Declan's chest.

He pulled away and lifted my chin, making sure I was focused on him and him alone. "I'm right where I should be," he said, his blue eyes clear with honesty. "Doing exactly what I should be doing, with exactly who I should be doing it with." He squeezed my chin gently and smiled. "Alright?" he asked, earnestly searching my eyes.

I nodded. "Alright."

"Good," he said. "Let's get back to it then."

I picked up my camera and adjusted the settings as he got back into place opposite me in the cage. Lowering myself to one knee, I closed an eye and looked through the lens to again find Declan.

Ever since we made love days ago, I kept waiting for the bubble to burst. Every smile I expected to be the last. When he laughed, I held onto the sound, because I wanted to remember it for when cold, distant silence came flooding back in. My fingers lingered every time I traced his soft, full lips because I feared they wouldn't be mine to touch for very long.

But each night as I fell asleep, he was there, breath gentle against the back of my neck. Each morning, I awoke and he was there, arms wrapped tightly around me. He skipped scheduled training to go on hikes with me. He stayed up late to talk to me, both of us cuddled under a blanket on the terrace under the stars. He woke up early to disappear beneath the sheets and wake me up with his hot tongue between my legs.

It was all so surprising, wonderful and surprising, delightful and did I mention surprising?

Then Declan really stunned me when one evening during dinner, he casually asked me to take photographs of him for his social media accounts.

"Are you sure?" I had asked, nearly choking on my green beans. I knew it meant vulnerability to him, and vulnerability wasn't exactly something Declan was comfortable with.

He had reached over and squeezed my hand. "If you're the one taking them, I am."

His words still made my heart leap as I remembered them in the gym as I focused the camera, only to immediately lower it back down. "You're still smiling," I said. My attempts to remain professional were made difficult by the infectious, joy-filled grin across Declan's face.

"I can't stop." He laughed. "I'm sorry, but I really can't."

I couldn't keep myself from smiling at this. "What if you don't look at me?" I tried.

Declan shook his head. "I see you everywhere I look."

I drummed my fingers along the side of my camera. "What if I say no 'strength training' till we get the shot?" I asked with a wink.

Declan ran his fingers through his hair and exhaled. "You wouldn't be able to stop me," he said, his eyes darkening.

I raised an eyebrow. "No?"

Declan shook his head as he walked slowly, ever so slowly toward me. "Why don't we take this camera to my bedroom and you can show me how to use it?"

I groaned as he pushed me against the wall of the cage and I felt his growing erection against my hip. "What exactly would you want to take pictures of in your bedroom?" I asked as my lips found his, hot and desperate.

"The closet, obviously," Declan joked. "I want *so badly*," he punctuated these words with a roll of his hips against me, "to take pictures of my closet."

"We're not going to get any work done, are we?" I whispered.

"Not a fecking chance." Declan kissed down my neck to my chest, divesting me of my shirt and bra as he went.

I squealed and grabbed at my naked chest, a half-hearted attempt at modesty.

Even as he nuzzled at my breasts and peeled my fingers away, he chided, "Don't hide them, baby."

"What if Seamus comes back?"

"Fuck him." Declan slid my skirt down to my ankles. My panties followed.

"I'd rather you fuck me," I hissed as he slid his fingers along my soaking slit.

Declan grinned up at me from between my legs. "As you command, *boss*." Before pushing his tongue into my aching pussy.

As Declan fucked me against the cage with his tongue, then his fingers, and finally his cock, I couldn't seem to care that we wouldn't be getting the shot that morning, yet again.

It didn't even matter that this was, after all, not our first, but our *second* attempt at a photoshoot. Yesterday, I'd developed some samples from the first session, but as I laid them out across the kitchen island to study them with a glass of wine while Oisin cooked dinner, I'd realised not a single one of them would do. I'd been standing there, arms crossed and frowning, when Oisin, drying his hands on his apron, had come up behind me.

"I can't figure it out," he said.

I turned to look over my shoulder at him. "What?"

"This," he said, circling a finger around my face. "All of this."

I patted a hand on my cheeks as if there was leftover chocolate ice cream from lunch or something. "What?" I asked. "What about it?"

"Well, there's this." He pointed to my lips. "And then there's this…" He tapped my eyebrows.

I shook my head and sighed in frustration. "Oisin, what in the world are you talking about?"

He nodded at the pictures on the counter behind me. "Let me put it this way, my little voodoo queen." He laid a hand on my shoulder. "If a man was smiling at me with that much love the way Declan is smiling at you there, I certainly wouldn't be giving myself unnecessary wrinkles from frowning so hard."

He returned to the stove and I glanced down at the pictures. "They're for his social media," I explained. "He can't be smiling."

Oisin gave me a look over his shoulder. "You're avoiding the truth, girl."

I crossed my arms. "I am not."

"You're afraid to accept it," Oisin said as he tossed a pan of bright peppers, red, yellow, and orange. "I get it."

"I am not," I insisted. "I'm not afraid of…*it*."

Oisin laughed.

"I am not," I repeated defensively. "He hasn't said anything."

And it was true. As perfectly as the last few days with Declan had been, neither of us had said…*that* word.

"He doesn't have to." Oisin glanced toward the photos laid out on the island. "Those right there say everything."

Whenever Declan kissed me and slid inside me, I dared not say it aloud, but I hoped against hope that Oisin was right.

River

Outside on the terrace under the first twinkle of stars, I stepped back from little table and tapped a finger against my lips as my eyes scanned over the white linen, the fine china, the candles, the wine glasses, and the furs resting on each chair.

It was missing something.

Frowning, my head tilted from side to side as I tried to figure out exactly what it was. I wanted tonight to be perfect. To thank Declan for everything he'd done for me, I'd insisted that I make dinner for us.

I'd finished up work early that afternoon to leave myself time to cook, shower, and get ready before he was ready after his physiotherapy session with Niall. Everything was done.

There was just some—

Snapping my fingers, I ran inside, grabbed a vase, and filled it not with flowers like usual, but instead snipped branches from the sweet cherry tree in the backyard. Frost coated them like raw sugar and tiny buds of bright red shone in the candlelight like rubies. I was smiling at the completed picture when I heard the French doors swing open.

I turned around, ready to rush forward into Declan's arms, when I suddenly stopped mid-step. "Seamus."

Stretching onto my tiptoes, I glanced over his shoulder to see if Declan was behind him. But the dark hallway of the manor was empty.

"I hate the cold," Seamus grumbled, tugging the lapel of his jacket tighter around his neck as he shivered. "Everything's ugly in the cold."

I watched in confusion as he disapprovingly flicked a finger against the delicate cherry tree branches in the vase.

"Lots of things are beautiful in the cold," I said slowly, again turning toward the motionless hallway before warily studying Seamus.

Something was wrong and it wasn't something as simple as

missing flowers.

"The snow is beautiful," I argued as Seamus poured himself a glass of red wine intended for Declan and my dinner.

He took a swig before shrugging. "For a moment, maybe," he said before turning his eyes to me. "But then it melts and mixes with dirt, turning to slush and slush just makes a mess of everything now, doesn't it? Makes that unique little snowflake, so pretty and so delicate in the moment, not even really worth it after all, doesn't it?" Seamus did not blink as he stared intently at me.

I swallowed, suddenly nervous. "Where is Declan?" I asked, my voice sounding small even to my own ears. My eyes darted to the hallway, hoping to see Declan there. He would swing open the doors with that smile I'd become so accustomed to seeing this last week and yell at Seamus to get lost.

"I'm going to make love to my woman under the stars," he'd say. "Our asses might freeze, but we'll freeze together," he'd say with a wink.

"That wine's not for you, Seamus," he'd say. "It's for her tongue and mine. So beat it."

But no one burst through the doors. No one entered the hallway. There was no smile.

"He should be done with his session with Niall by now," I said, returning my eyes to Seamus.

He lazily took another sip of wine and stared up at the stars. "I underestimated you, River," he said. "I would have hired you for PR if I knew you were so good at it."

I frowned. "What do you mean?"

Seamus waved his hand in front of him.

"This whole relationship with Declan," he said. "It was quite the brilliant move. He needed some humanizing."

I shifted uncomfortably from foot to foot as I watched Seamus stroke his fiery red beard. Moments ago, I hadn't felt the cold, but now it seeped into my sneakers, bit at the tips of my fingers, clawed at my cheeks.

"Um..." I wondered if rabbits heard the same alarms in their head when they sensed a trap nearby. "Thanks, but—"

"Yes, yes." Seamus nodded. "It was very calculated. Very impressive."

I shook my head. "No, that wasn't—"

"Planned out brilliantly," Seamus interrupted, raising his glass of wine to me. "And wonderful acting, if I do say so myself."

I took a step forward, cheeks turning red and fingers curling into tight fists. "It wasn't planned and it wasn't acting."

He held up his hands as if to plead his innocence. "No, no, of course not," he said.

I sighed and fell back on my heel.

But then he added a wink. "I'll see about getting you a raise for your efforts. You certainly deserve it."

Frustration flooded my chest as I marched over to the table. "You don't understand, Declan and I—"

"Stop!" In the light of the candles, Seamus's eyes flashed darkly. "Sit down."

"I don't want to sit down," I said. "I'm going to find Dec—"

"*Sit* down, girl."

The look in Seamus's eyes made me pause, and for reasons I couldn't explain in the moment, I slowly sank into the chair across from him.

"Now, you listen to me," he hissed. "If you know what's good for ye, you'll listen good."

I studied Seamus's face as he poured me a glass of wine. He sighed and rubbed at his temples before looking over at me. "I understand, okay?" he said, raising his eyebrows and leaning forward. "I get it. I know exactly what's going on. I understand, I do."

My heart pounded in my chest as I waited for him to go on.

"But I also understand Declan," he continued. "More than anyone, maybe. Certainly more than you."

I wanted to protest, but I couldn't seem to make my lips move. Perhaps the cold had frozen them shut.

"I understand that he likes you," Seamus said. "I'm not saying he doesn't. Why wouldn't he? You're something new. Something different. Something pretty and colourful and sweet. Something unique. Something rare…"

The flames of the candles fluttered in the wind between the two of us.

Seamus seemed to be searching for what to say before snapping his fingers as if it just hit him. "Like a snowflake," he said.

My eyes moved to the branches of the cherry tree, the frost already beginning to melt in the heat of the candles.

Seamus reached across the table and pushed my wine glass closer to my numb fingers. "Right now Declan is with Niall, who is explaining to him that since his last session he's lost muscle mass, he's lost flexibility, he's lost strength and power and speed," he informed me. "And Declan will understand that the reason for that is you." His voice as he spoke was unemotional. He was simply stating facts. And that made it all the more terrible.

Seamus didn't have to push the glass of wine any farther toward me; I reached forward and grabbed it myself. I needed the burn of the red down my throat before I froze entirely.

Seamus continued, "I also understand Giselle wasn't like you. Declan's connection to her wasn't like his connection with you. But he married her, and I'll add as well, is *still* married to her. I understand why that is. Do you want to understand why that is, River?"

I stared across the table at Seamus, unable to speak.

"Because Declan wants to win," he said, leaning back in his chair and peaking his fingers over his chest. "It's all he wants. Giselle did not interfere with his training. She brought the media attention, the fame, the tits and hips and legs for fucking days, but she did not get in the way of the one thing, the one fucking thing in all of existence, he needs to goddamn *survive*...winning."

When he stopped speaking the wind from the distant hills felt a little colder, the moonlight through the branches a little weaker, the red of the cherry buds a little duller.

After several moments of silence, Seamus sighed. "I like you, River." He reached across and patted my hand. "I do. But you're going to get hurt if you don't understand your place in all of this, right?"

I nodded numbly. I wasn't even sure what the fuck I was nodding in regard to.

"Good," Seamus said before tipping back his wine glass and emptying the rest of it. "Good, good."

I winced at the sound of his chair screeching against the stones as he pushed it back. It was ten times worse than nails on a chalkboard.

"So we're agreed?" he asked, standing over me. "You're a brilliant personal assistant. A smart, hardworking, dedicated personal assistant. A clever personal assistant who pretended to fall for her boss for the cameras. Quite the clever *personal assistant*, wouldn't you say?"

I again nodded, again with no idea why.

"Good." Seamus smiled and turned to leave. "I'll see about that raise then."

I heard the doors open and then close and then I was alone on the terrace in the cold. The wind blew out the candles and then I was alone on the terrace in the cold, in the dark.

River

Despite how often I insisted otherwise, Declan knew something was wrong.

My lips didn't move quite as passionately against his and my body didn't respond quite as sensitively to his touch and my eyes didn't seek his as we each neared our climaxes amongst steam-covered windows. As we lay together afterward, he would hold me close, stroking his hand up and down my arm sweetly before asking me if everything was alright.

I would say "yes".

"Yes, of course."

"Yes. Why wouldn't it be?"

"Yes, yes, yes."

But he knew. He knew something had changed.

Our journey together was surely ending, but it seemed that only one of us realised this. To Declan, the path we walked along side by side stretched far into a hazy, golden horizon. But I knew the fork in the road lay just around the next bend.

Still, I hadn't thought it would be that night. I hadn't thought it would be quite so soon.

It was just past midnight when my cell phone vibrated on the nightstand next to Declan's bed. It didn't wake me because I was still awake. For the last hour, I'd been fighting the sleep that weighed down my eyelids and clouded my mind because I couldn't fall asleep. Not yet, at least.

I had to stay awake until I could trace the feeling of Declan's arms around me in my head. I had to stay awake until I could recall from memory exactly the way his fingers looked intertwined with mine on the pillow in the soft moonlight. Until I could memorize the rhythm of his gentle, peaceful breathing against the nape of my neck, until I could count precisely how many hairs along my arms each exhale raised, etched into my mind so I wouldn't forget how his body next to mine made me feel each night—safe.

Until then I was determined not to sleep, because I wasn't sure how many more nights I would have. I knew it wasn't much. But I hadn't known that tonight would be the last.

Declan mumbled something in his sleep and stirred slightly against me as I stretched a hand to silence my cell phone. I could have had a few more hours of blissful pretending if I hadn't happened to glance at the screen.

Miley: *The media found out.*

My blood ran cold as I frantically read and reread her words, hoping, praying, *begging* that I somehow got something wrong in my tiredness. But there they were: undeniable in black and white.

I wanted to throw my cell phone across the room. I wanted it to shatter against the wall. I wanted it to fall onto the floor in a million pieces I could never manage to fit back together.

But I had to look. I had to see. I had to know.

My fingers trembled in the harsh blue glare of the screen. I typed my name into the search bar, my thumb hesitating over the "Enter" button. I squeezed my eyes shut and focused on Declan's strong arms around me one last time. Everything was about to change.

But for that one moment, he was still mine. I could still believe we had a future of morning hikes through sun-filled mist and evenings beneath the cherry trees with nothing but a bottle of wine between us. I could still imagine, for just that moment, that this impossibility could still be possible.

I opened my eyes and pressed "Enter" and the world was again righted: up was again up, down was again down, and the impossible was again as it always was, as it always would be...impossible.

The media found out.

The past I tried so hard to run from stared me straight in the face. I could look away from the screen. I could look out the window at the tops of the softly swaying trees. I could even turn around and look at Declan's sleeping face. But all I would see, no matter where I turned, was those headlines flashing brighter, brighter, brighter.

The Dark Truth About Gallagher's Bright Light

The Delta of Gallagher's River Isn't So Pure After All

We Know All the Dirty Secrets of Gallagher's New Fuck Buddy and They're Juicy!

I scrolled through the articles, one after the next, even though it was nothing I didn't already know. It was *my* story, after all: Orphaned at a young age, River always found a way to get herself in trouble. At the age of sixteen, she ran away from her orphanage and did whatever it took to earn a buck, bouncing from city to city. No attachments, no strings, no commitment. No family, no education, no money. A nobody. An absolute nobody.

"River?"

Behind me I felt Declan shift. I quickly wiped the gathering tears from my eyes as I heard him push himself up onto his elbow, his hand rubbing up and down my arm.

"River, baby, what is it?" he whispered. "Why are you awake?"

I turned over my cell phone onto the pillow, plunging us back into darkness to hide my face. Even the moon, knowing like I did that it was finally the end, had moved on from us, replaced by dark, heavy clouds in the night sky.

"Nothing," I answered, keeping my voice soft to hide the tightness swelling in my throat. "I was just checking the time. You can go back to sleep."

Sensing Declan's eyes searching my face in the dim light, I kept perfectly still so the tears at the tips of my eyelashes like dewdrops on blades of grass would not fall onto my cheek. I would leave in the morning, when it was easier, when I didn't have to face him. I just had to get through these next few moments.

"You're sure you're okay?" he asked, his thumb tracing comforting circles on the back of my hand.

"Of course."

Declan hesitated a few moments longer, but then he whispered "okay" and rested his head back on the pillow.

I made it. That was it. I made it. He was going back to sleep now. I resisted the urge to sigh in relief as the tears came hot and fast and most importantly, silently. I let them fall.

I was intending to let them fall till morning when I would leave only a wet pillow behind me, but suddenly Declan pushed himself up behind me.

"Nope," he said, his voice loud in the silence. "Nope, I'm not going to make it easy. If you want to push me away, I'm going to make it hell on you. That's a promise, River."

I squeezed my eyes shut. "Declan, please, everything's fi—"

"Don't say fine," he interrupted. "Something is wrong. Something's been wrong since our dinner on the terrace."

"Everything's fine," I insisted. It was all I could say, all I knew how to say.

Declan tried to pull me over to look at him, but I resisted his touch. "River, please," he begged. "Why are you pushing me away?"

"I'm not!" I cried. "Let's just go back to sleep." I couldn't look into his eyes and say goodbye. I just couldn't. Not even in the dark.

"River, you're worth holding onto," Declan said. "I won't let you push me away. You're worth holding onto with everything I have and mo—"

"I'm not!" I shouted, sitting up, yanking my phone screen up, illumining the tension between us with blue light.

Declan stared in surprise at my tear-stained cheeks as I grabbed his hand and slammed my phone into his palm. "I'm not," I said.

Weariness crashed down on my shoulders like a boulder as

Declan lowered his eyes to my screen. I wanted to sleep. I just wanted to close my eyes and dream of a world where Declan wasn't realising what he should have realised from the very start.

"I don't deserve you," I whispered. "Everyone knows it. The media knows it. Seamus knows it. I know it. It's about time you know it as well."

Declan was silent as his thumb moved over the screen, over my secrets laid bare for the world to pore over.

"You deserve someone like Giselle," I said, remembering what Seamus told me on the terrace. "I was just a distraction."

Still Declan said nothing.

"Someone from your world," I continued. "Someone from the world of the rich, the world of the famous, the world of the successful. Not someone from the gutters." I sighed and bit back the tears, feeling embarrassed, ashamed, pitiful, absolutely pitiful.

"You're Declan Gallagher," I sniffed. "You deserve better than…" I swallowed. "Everyone knows it now."

Declan's fingers typed something on my phone and without a word he handed it over to me. I frowned in confusion, but he pushed my cell phone into my hand. I blinked away the tears until the text on the screen was clear enough to read.

"My life hasn't always been fast cars and expensive suits," he said as I read. "I'm more than well accustomed to the gutters."

I looked up from the phone, the tips of my fingers so numb I could barely hold it. "This is true?" I whispered.

Declan nodded. "All of it."

The phone fell between us, quickly forgotten, as I pulled him into a tight, if shaky, hug. We clung to each other as if we'd been apart for years and were just reunited again.

"I tried to hide it, too, River." Declan's voice against my hair was thick with emotion, and I could feel his heart fluttering against mine. "I tried to hide the fact that my mother always struggled with drugs. I tried to hide the truth that my father abused her, and then me, when I tried to defend her. I tried to hide the memory of constant bruises because of my father's fist and a constant grumbling stomach because there was no food on the table."

I squeezed Declan closer to me.

"I wanted to hide from them, River," he continued. "But I don't want to hide from you." Declan's fingers dug deeper into the flesh of my back. "There's something the media doesn't know," he said so quietly I could barely hear him.

With my cheek against his chest, I waited.

"My mother," he whispered, "she died in my arms of an overdose."

"Declan—"

"I want you to know," he interrupted, clearing his throat. "I want you to know that if anyone is undeserving, River, it's me."

I shook my head against his chest. "No, no, don't say that."

"We're more alike than you think," he whispered with a sad smile.

"How can you stand it?" I asked, leaning back and holding him away from me so I could see his face. "How can you stand them knowing everything? Your past being thrown back in your face again and again? Their constant judgement, as if they know, as if they have even the slightest clue what it's like?" Anger filled my voice as my fingers shook. It wasn't fair. It wasn't fair at all. I found tears filling my eyes again.

Declan smiled gently and reached over to tuck a strand of my hair behind my ear. "I use it as a reminder," he said softly.

I wiped at my tears in frustration, because they were betraying my weakness. "A reminder?"

As the next tear began to trail down my cheek, I reached up to push it away, but Declan caught my wrist.

"Let it fall," he whispered. "Let it fall."

This brought even more tears and I sagged forward against Declan's strong, steady chest as I cried and cried and couldn't stop.

"It's a reminder that there are types of people in the world," he continued. "There's the type that criticize and judge and stare from the shadows. They're scared, frightened, weak people." Declan's fingers carded through my hair and he spoke softly against the crown of my head. "But then there's another type. The type that dare to step into the light and fight, love, laugh, breathe, cry, sing, *live*. These are the brave, the bold, the strong, no matter how weak the world makes them seem."

Declan gently lifted my chin so my shining eyes met his, so I couldn't turn away from him.

"I'm not with you because you're from the world of diamonds," he said. "I'm with you because you're from the world of mud and darkness, deep, deep darkness, and yet you're strong enough to shine brighter than any of their silly stones."

I stared up into his eyes, barely able to believe what he was saying. "But Declan, everyone knows."

"So let them know, River." Declan laughed. "Let them know you're strong, stronger than they'll ever be. Let them know you live, truly *live*. Do not shy away from *that* truth. Let them know. Shout it in their goddamn faces." He paused with his hands on either side of my face, his thumbs moving over my cheekbones as he smiled. "Show those fuckers what it means to shine."

Declan's lips sealed off any further protest from me as he pulled me into a deep, passionate kiss. His fingers tangled into my hair and tugged slightly as his tongue twisted against mine.

I surprised myself when a growl escaped my lips.

I was strong.

I clawed at Declan's back and he groaned in response.

I wasn't going to watch life go by from the sidelines.

I pressed my chest tight against his.

I was going to take what I wanted, no matter what anyone had to say about it.

I pulled Declan down with me to the sheets.

And he followed.

River

The first thud shook the aged wooden floorboards beneath my sneakers in the hallway just outside the gym.

The second thundering boom shook dust from the gold chandeliers above my head and created ripples in the peppermint tea I held cupped between my palms.

The third crash seized my heart, but not because of the volume of the sound itself, it was because of what came after it—a roar.

A roar of pure agony.

My fallen teacup shattered on the shaking wooden floorboards behind me as I sprinted beneath the quivering chandeliers toward the gym. I flung the doors open and stopped dead in my tracks just behind Seamus, who clutched at his hair at the sight before us.

It was as if a tornado tore through the gym. Tornado Gallagher.

Half the cage was ripped down and lay in a mangled mess on the floor. A treadmill was overturned, a window was shattered, and one of several punching bags lay on the ground covered in drywall from where the thick metal chain had been wrenched from the ceiling. In the midst of the wreckage, Declan stalked back and forth like a caged animal.

His face was red. His eyes were wide and unseeing as his chest heaved in ragged, uneven breaths. His shoulders were slumped forward, making him appear more beast than man as he lifted a fifty-pound kettlebell over his head and slammed it repeatedly against the concrete floor, which shattered as if it were glass. The kettlebell seemed to weigh nothing when Declan tossed it to the side, but when it slammed into the towel stand, the wooden shelves exploded from the force. Declan was a dangerous man when in complete control of himself, but he was deadly when he lost even an ounce of that control.

From the guttural raw, unrestrained, blood-chilling roar that ripped through his throat, I knew he'd lost control so completely, so utterly, so wholly that he might never be able to gain it back. That noise alone shook me more than the weight rack toppling over beneath his rippling muscles and rattling the very floor beneath my feet.

"What happened?" I asked as I hovered in the doorway, half in, half out.

Seamus turned to me and his eyes widened in a sort of panic at the realisation that I was standing there.

A normal person would run. A normal person wouldn't even stay long enough to ask what happened, what went wrong. A normal person would immediately know that this was not a safe place and run, run, run.

A stubborn ass like me would want to stay.

A stubborn ass like me, and me alone, would want to get *closer.*

Closer to him.

The moment I took a step forward, Seamus rushed toward me and stood in my path. "No, no, no," he said quickly as he shook his head. "You can't be here. You need to leave. *Now.*"

I tried to step around him to get to Declan, but Seamus easily blocked my path and held up his hands. "Leave, River," he said. "I'm serious."

"What's going on?" I demanded over the sound of more equipment crashing.

"River, please just go," Seamus insisted. "It's not safe for you."

I levelled a glare at him and jutted my chin up toward him. "Tell me."

Seamus sighed and dragged his fingers through his wiry red hair. "I knew it would be bad when I told him," he started, glancing at Declan's continued rampage over his shoulder. "But I didn't know it would be this bad. Fuck, he's out of his mind. He's out of his goddamn mind."

"Tell him what?"

The floor shook again and the windows rattled as a loud thud echoed throughout the gym. Declan roared again and I thought my heart would break at his obvious pain.

"Seamus, tell me what is wrong," I demanded. "Tell me *now*."

"His title," Seamus finally admitted. "It's his title, okay? They stripped it from him."

My stomach dropped. Declan's MMA title meant everything to him, *everything*.

"How?" I asked. "He hasn't lost."

Seamus scratched impatiently at his fiery red beard, then after checking nervously again over his shoulder, he answered, "Yeah, well he's hasn't won lately either." When he saw my confusion, he sighed loudly and explained, "You can't keep the title if you don't win. You can't win if you don't fight. And, as you know, Declan can't fight, so…"

I nodded numbly. A question hit me like a bolt of lightning and my eyes darted up to Seamus's. "That means someone else now has the title," I said, barely daring to utter the words aloud.

Seamus lifted his eyebrows and crossed his arms over his chest.

"Indeed it does."

I didn't want to ask. I didn't want to hear the answer I already knew, I already feared. It was like a train barrelling toward me on the tracks—looking away wouldn't change the inevitability of it crashing into me. "Who?" I whispered.

Seamus sighed. "Who do you think?"

"Dominic."

Declan's greatest rival. Stealing his wife wasn't enough. Stealing his health, his strength, his body wasn't enough. The thief wanted Declan's title. And now he had it.

He had it all.

I craned my neck around Seamus just enough to watch as Declan hurled a dumbbell across the room. It crashed into the stationary bike, toppling it over as easily as a feather in a fierce gust of wind. I stared at the warped frame and it didn't take much imagination to predict the effect the impact of the dumbbell would have had on bone versus metal, and yet I spoke without hesitation. "I need to get to him."

I stepped forward.

Seamus grabbed my shoulders and shook me so I was forced to peel my eyes off of Declan and focus on him instead. "River, you're not thinking straight," he said, earnestly trying to get through to me. "He will hurt you. He will hurt you."

"No, he won't."

Seamus spit out a dark laugh. "Don't be foolish, girl. He'll rip you in two should you get within arm's reach."

But I wasn't trying to get within arm's reach. I was trying to get much, much closer. I needed to touch him, I needed to hold him, I needed to wrap my arms around him and guide him back to me, the beating of my heart his path in the dark.

"He won't hurt me," I repeated. I pushed his hands from my shoulders.

"I'm not allowing you to go near him," Seamus growled, grabbing my wrist. "It's not safe." He tried to drag me back toward the door, but I wrenched my hand free again.

"I'm not asking!" I snapped back. "He needs me. And I'm going to him."

Seamus was close at my heels as I marched toward the back of the gym where Declan was punching hole after hole in the wall along the row of thick black stretching mats.

"You're being reckless, girl," Seamus warned just behind me. "You're going to get yourself hurt. Or worse."

Declan growled before crashing his fist into the drywall.

Seamus grabbed my shoulder, spinning me around to face him.

I shoved him back and continued toward Declan.

"River, stop!" he called after me.

But I wasn't going to stop. Declan helped me in my time of need and I was hellbent on never letting him down. Enough people in his life had already done that and I wasn't intending on being another.

"He's not thinking straight!" Seamus shouted. "River, stop!"

I stepped onto the mats without hesitation. Declan would not hurt me. I knew he would never hurt me. Declan's fist pounded the wall as I approached him cautiously. The muscles along the length of his arm and down his back rippled like a wild animal's. His skin was covered in sweat, his hair matted down against his forehead, his knuckles were bloody. I stared with nervous eyes at the red stains marring the holes in the wall before glancing back to see Seamus stopped at the edge of the mats.

He shook his head and mouthed, *"It's not worth it."*

But it was, I told myself as I turned back around and took another step toward Declan. *He* was worth it.

"Declan," I said as softly as my careful steps. "Declan, it's me. Let me help you."

Blood splattered the mat just in front of the toes of my sneakers when Declan lifted his fist again before slamming it against the wall with a guttural cry. Drywall sprinkled the floor as his hand disappeared between a pair of two-by-fours.

A shiver travelled down my spine, but I clenched my hands into fists and stepped forward.

He wouldn't hurt me. I knew he wouldn't.

"Declan," I dared to speak a little louder. "Declan, I'm here."

I was no more than a few feet away from him. If I stretched out my arm completely, I probably would have been just an inch or two shy of touching him. The hurt in Declan's cries wrenched my heart even more this close. I bit my lip to keep tears from pooling in the corners of my eyes. Declan's forehead rested against the wall as both his fists wailed against the wall on either side of him. I knew any one of those punches could break bones. I knew any single one of those punches could break *my* bones.

I knew I needed to get closer.

Three steps to him. Three and no more.

One. One step closer. Two left.

Two. Two steps closer. One left.

Three…

I reached out a hand.

"Declan…"

I didn't scream when Declan whirled around and grabbed me by the back of my neck, despite the flare of pain as his fingers tore at my hair. I wouldn't scream, I wouldn't cry out. Black pupils dominated his eyes so I couldn't see a trace of blue, just my frightened reflection staring back at me. His grip tightened and I winced.

"Declan, don't!" Seamus shouted behind me.

But Seamus wasn't even there. It was Declan and me. Just him and me.

Declan's unseeing eyes narrowed in anger and his ragged breath quickened.

"Declan!"

Just him and me.

Him and me.

"You won't hurt me," I whispered as I reached up with both hands and ran my hands over his cheeks. "You won't hurt me, Declan. You won't. I know you won't. Declan, please…"

Declan raised his fist.

Declan

"Declan, please…"

I blinked as if I was awakening from a horrible dream: sudden, frantic, and panicked. But it wasn't a nightmare I was escaping. It was a nightmare I was entering. My eyes widened in horror as I saw the one person I never wanted to hurt right there in front of me, her face tight with obvious pain as my fingers dug into the back of her neck.

"River," I gasped.

"I'm here," she whispered, her hands cupping my cheeks.

"River," I exhaled like a desperate plea.

My body shook with fear at the realisation of what I could have done as I released my grip on her and sagged against her, hands running again and again over her hair.

"It's okay," she cooed against my chest. "It's okay, it's okay."

We sagged to the floor together when my knees buckled and gave way.

River eased my head into her lap as my desperate fingers clung to the hem of her shirt. She leaned over me, cocooning me in her sweet perfume like a field of wildflowers as far as the eye could see, and kissed my temple.

"River, I—"

"Shh…" she cooed. "I'm here."

"You shouldn't be," I said with an uncontrollable shiver. "You shouldn't be—you shouldn't…"

"Seamus, can you give us a minute?"

River's voice above me sounded far away.

"It's alright now."

Through vision that blurred at the edges, I looked up to see Seamus shaking his head as he made his way to the exit of the gym. Why did Seamus let her near me? If Seamus was here, he should have done anything and everything to keep River away from me. He should have known when I lose control like that, I can't see anything but red, I can't hear anything but hot blood rushing in my ears. I can't do anything but destroy. Seamus should have known I wouldn't even have recognised the girl. I shouldn't have recognised her…

Why did I stop?

Why was her neck not snapped in two?

How did she reach me?

"River, I could have hurt you." I shuddered even as I said the words aloud. "I could have…"

"You didn't," River said, quickly catching my hands before I could rake my nails over my eyes. As she kissed each of my bloodied knuckles, she said, "I knew you wouldn't hurt me, Declan. I knew."

How did I not hurt her? How did I see her when I was blinded by rage?

I could have hurt her. I could have—

I tried to suck in desperate breaths, but none of it went to my lungs, as if I didn't deserve air. Perhaps I didn't. Perhaps I didn't even deserve goddamn air.

I felt a gentle hand at my heaving chest and blinked up through wide eyes as I gasped for air to see River looking down at me.

"Breathe, Declan," she whispered. "Just breathe." She traced small circles at my temples.

I felt my heartbeat slowly even out. "I let them down," I finally said with a shaky breath.

River looked down at me at the sound of my voice. "Who?"

I dragged a weary hand over my face and sighed. "My fans," I explained. "Myself."

Her.

"Declan, you were in a car crash," River tried to reason with me, but I shook my head. "They understand your body has limitations. They understand you'll be back in the cage when you're ready, when your body is ready. They love you. They'll be patient. But you need to be patient, too."

"No, no, I've deceived them," I continued. "I've pretended to be someone I'm not, someone stronger, someone braver, someone better. I've deceived them. I've deceived myself."

You deceived her. Most of all, you deceived her. You deceived River.

I couldn't escape the voice in the back of my mind. It was a voice I worked for years to push down. It was a voice that sent chills down my spine.

But it was a voice I knew was right.

"Declan, I know you." River wrapped her arms around my head and rested her cheek against my cheek. "I know who you are. I know."

I again shook my head.

"You'll be back to number one in no time," she tried to reassure me. "I know you'll be strong enough, you'll be back on top. I know you."

She doesn't. She can't. Or she wouldn't love you.

I wanted to tell the voice to shut the fuck up. I wanted to tell the voice to get lost. I never wanted to hear the sound of the voice in my head ever again. But the voice was right. The voice was right…

"I don't deserve it," I whispered, more to myself than to River.

More to the voice than myself.

"I don't deserve yo—*their* love."

River squeezed me more tightly and I exhaled shakily. I almost revealed the truth, the horrifying, terrifying truth that this wasn't about my fans. This wasn't about my fans at all. I feared it never was.

I cared about my fans, I did. They made my career and I wanted to keep fighting for them. I did. But it wasn't them I feared letting down. It wasn't them I wanted love from.

It was River.

You've got to earn it.

The voice.

Have you earned it?

His voice.

What have you done to deserve my love?

I closed my eyes and my father's fist was raised high above his head. It was about to crash into my stomach; he was smart enough to know not to leave a mark where the teachers would see it. Love was a night without a beating. Love was an hour without that constant terror. Love was that moment of peace when he passed out in front of the television with a beer still in his hand.

Love was earned.

Love needed to be deserved.

Love wasn't just freely given.

How could I have been so foolish? River wouldn't just love me, no strings, no demands, no requirements. That was a childish fantasy. She wouldn't stay with me if I didn't give her a reason to stay. She wouldn't hold me if I wasn't worth holding. She wouldn't love me if I didn't earn it.

And there was only one way I knew how to earn River's love—win.

As River gently eased me down and laid behind me on the mat, a sudden peace that had nothing to do with her arms tight around my chest fell over me. I breathed deeply and evenly once more, not because of the steady pace of her heart beating against my back, but because I knew what I needed to do. It wasn't her whispered affirmations just beneath the nape of my neck that caused my heavy eyelids to sink down…it was the scene I wanted to imagine.

A dark arena. A cage surrounded by cheering fans. A belt held over my head as Dominic lay unconscious at my feet.

River would love me then, I thought as she rocked me gently in the gym. She would love me when I won back my title. I'll deserve it then.

I'll deserve it.

River

I was sleeping with a ghost.

I hadn't known that there on the mat in the gym would be the last time I would hold flesh and blood against my chest. From then on, it was just the memory of an arm, strong and protective, holding me tight as the moon journeyed along those emerald hills shining with midnight dew. Any whisper that raised hairs along the back of my neck was just the wind sweeping softly against the curtains. Like the faintest perfume of rain from a passing storm, his ghost was there in bed, pressed against me.

I wanted more. I wanted rain against my face. I wanted drops tracing every curve of my naked body. I wanted to drown in him.

I was tired of sleeping with a ghost.

With an irritated exhale, I opened my eyes and rolled over in bed to find the sheets on Declan's side still perfectly made, every decorative pillow still perfectly in place. Ghosts didn't leave an impression, after all. The moonlight drifted over the untouched comforter and I tried to remember the last time Declan had come to bed with me.

I easily recalled the night before when he tiptoed silently across the room and slipped under the sheets just past three in the morning. I expected him to wiggle close to the heat of my body and sigh against my neck. But after a few empty moments passed, I'd checked over my shoulder to find him huddled into a ball as far from me as possible.

It didn't take much to bring to mind the night before that when he missed dinner for another round in the cage, missed our nightly talks on the balcony for an extra physio session with Niall, missed whispering "goodnight, baby" after breathing in deeply the scent of my damp hair for "a few more reps, baby."

And I had no problem at all remembering all the nights before that when I'd fallen asleep waiting for him to come to bed from studying film in the theatre, only to wake up with him already up and in the gym room, training, training, always training.

With the date of his fight with Dominic set and everything now on the line, Declan had thrown himself into his preparations. But to make time for heavier weightlifting and longer sprints and faster combos, he had to reallocate time. He was already getting the minimum hours of sleep and eating his pulverized meals while stretching before practice, so the answer was obvious…he had to steal hours from me, from *us*.

His kisses were still sweet, but rushed. He still brushed his thumb along my cheekbone, but only while saying he was sorry. He had to go. *Again.* His eyes still found me, locked onto me as if there was no one else in the world but the two of us, but there was always something between us—a rack of dumbbells, the mesh of the cage, the screen of his laptop with the audio of a fight, fists against bone, loud and harsh against my ears.

I wanted a kiss so agonisingly slow that I was begging him on my knees for more. I wanted his hands on my cheek, but I also wanted them on my waist, my hip, my neck. I wanted his fingers digging into my thighs, I wanted his thumb against my clit, I wanted the pad of his pinkie teasing my hard nipple as I bucked and squirmed beneath him. I wanted his eyes, but I wanted them in the silence of the night interrupted only by our harsh breathing as we careened wildly toward the edge together.

I wanted *him*.

Throwing the comforter back with a sudden determination, I grabbed the silk robe Declan had ordered for me and marched straight out of the bedroom. In the dim light of the hallway, I winced at the cold floor beneath my bare toes as I made my way down the stairs to the first floor. The sound of a crowd cheering echoed toward me and light from a single room spilled across the dark hallway. I entered the theatre room to find Declan on the couch, furiously scribbling on a notepad resting on his knee. A dust-filled beam of light above him projected a video onto the opposite wall of Dominic standing over his knocked-out opponent in the cage, his teeth bared like a savage animal as the roar of the crowd rose to deafening.

A pang of fear stabbed at my heart as I silently watched the doctors rush to the unconscious man, only to check his eyes and hurriedly wave for more help. Declan wanted to fight him?

With the click of a remote, Declan changed the video just as a stretcher was brought into the cage. His eyes fixed on the screen as a bell rang and Dominic charged another opponent.

Pushing away the image of the blood running down his last victim's nose, I strode forward confidently and stood directly between the projector and the wall.

Declan looked up from his notepad in surprise. "Baby, wha—"

"I'm here to renegotiate the terms of my deal, Mr Gallagher," I said firmly.

Declan frowned. "River, honey, go back to bed. It's late."

My fingers moved to the knot of the silk robe around my waist and I pulled slowly. "I will be representing myself in these proceedings," I said, holding back a grin as Declan's eyes followed the silk robe as it slipped from my shoulders to pool at my feet.

"Fuck," he muttered, perhaps without being able to stop himself, as I stepped forward, hips swaying seductively, and leaned over to force his knees apart. The notepad and pen tumbled to the floor.

"River, baby," Declan tried, throat tight as I knelt between his legs. "I have to finish wa—" He hissed and his hips bucked into the air when I dragged my nails down his inner thighs.

"This is serious," I said, running my fingers lightly back up his sweatpants to his crotch, which was already tented. "I haven't come to mess around."

I caught Declan's wrist when his hand reached out to cup my breast. Behind me, a fist landed on flesh and the crowd cheered, the noise filling the space around us. I stretched out a hand and fumbled for the remote. We were plunged into silence when I hit the power button.

"Baby…" Declan sighed.

"I only have one demand," I said, softly. "One single demand." I climbed up so my mouth was just above Declan's growing erection. I licked one slow line up his length and was rewarded with his fingers tightening in my curls. I kissed a trail up his bare chest as I straddled his legs and bit back a groan when he gripped my hips.

I pressed my tits against him as I whispered, "I'm not leaving until you agree to it."

I rolled my hips over Declan's cock and his fingers clawed down my spine.

"I want something greater than diamonds, greater than rubies and emeralds and sapphires." I sighed against his neck. "Do you want to know what I want?"

"Yes," Declan exhaled.

I kissed just below his ear. "A hike."

Declan's hands paused on my ass. "A hike?"

I leaned back and nodded. "A hike."

Declan sighed as he rubbed his hand over his eyes. "I know I've been busy, baby. And I know for goddamn sure I haven't spent as much time with you as I've wanted to. But it will all be worth it when I win back my title. You'll see." He interlaced his fingers with mine, raising my hand up to kiss it. "I promise you'll see."

"I'm worried about you," I said. "Don't think I haven't noticed the bags under your eyes or the way your fingers shake around your fork on the rare occasion you have dinner with me. A hike would be good for you."

A hike *with me.*

Declan pulled my head down so that my forehead rested against his. He breathed in deeply. "A hike, huh?" he asked.

I nodded.

He guided my lips to his and kissed me sweetly, softly, *slowly.*

I cupped the sides of his face as I melted into the warmth of his mouth.

Declan pulled back and squeezed my chin between his thumb and forefinger. "Tomorrow then."

My eyebrows lifted in surprise. "Tomorrow?" I asked. "A hike tomorrow? Really?"

Declan laughed. "What can I say, you're a tough negotiator." He grinned. "Tomorrow morning, alright?"

I smiled. "Perfect." I climbed off of his lap, reaching for his hand to continue what we had started back in bed. I jumped at the sudden burst of sound as Declan turned the projector back on. "You're…not coming to bed?" I asked, my hand still outstretched, empty of his.

"I'll be there in just a few minutes," he answered, already with his notepad and pen back in hand, eyes fixed on Dominic's fight. "I just need to finish studying this fight first. I'll see you tomorrow morning for our hike, alright?"

I nodded slowly. "Okay then," I said, leaning down to grab my robe, suddenly self-conscious of my nakedness.

I was halfway out the door of the theatre when Declan called out to me, "Goodnight, baby."

It wasn't whispered with his full lips hot against my earlobe. It sounded far away, very far away.

So I went back to bed with his ghost. The memory of his arms alone held me as I fell asleep on a pillow quickly turning wet. And when I awoke at the first light of dawn it was not to his steady breath against my back, but the wind shuffling the curtains.

I got dressed and packed for our hike, assuming Declan had gotten up early to get in a run before we left. But in the quiet of the morning I found the gym empty. He wasn't in the spa, the office or even the kitchen.

I found Declan asleep on the couch in the theatre, a video still playing and his notepad still balancing on his knee. With a sigh, I placed a blanket carefully over his shoulders, and after a ghost of a kiss on his forehead, I closed the door as quietly as I could behind me.

He needed his sleep.

He needed his sleep more than I needed him.

I was rounding the corner toward the staircase when I ran into Niall with his medical bag slung over his shoulder.

"You're up early," he said with a happy smile.

"So are you," I answered with a frown of confusion as I stared up at him.

Niall shrugged with a good-natured grin. "Declan called me yesterday afternoon to come in for an extra session this morning. He's been experiencing a lot of pain with the added training."

I nodded. He was going to hurt himself. And it terrified me. "Well, you might have come in early for nothing," I said, leaning tiredly against the wall. "Declan's asleep. He stayed up all night studying film."

"Eejit." Niall shook his head disapprovingly.

“I can wake him, I suppose,” I said, glancing over my shoulder down the hallway.

“No, no,” Niall quickly said. “He needs to sleep.”

Rubbing at the back of my neck, I smiled.

“Looks like you could use some more sleep, too,” Niall said, staring down at me with concern in his eyes. “You going back to bed?”

I laughed. “I was on my way to go for a hike, actually.”

“Well, if I’m not working on Declan for a while…” Niall then glanced at his watch, set down his bag, and offered me a friendly smile. “How do you feel about a hiking buddy?”

Declan

After Giselle cheated on me, I never thought I'd wake up again in the arms of a woman. I was doomed to cold mornings alone, snapping upright to attention, pain throbbing through my veins, grey shadows looming in my empty room.

But River gave me hope again. I would blink slowly awake, her skin warming my back better than any ray of sunlight ever could. Her legs, intertwined with mine under the sheets, seemed to fit better than any two puzzle pieces ever would. She was my still waters when I'd known only churning seas. She was a melody when all I could hear before was the screech of tires, the moan of warped metal, the wail of sirens on a lonely road. She was my sliver of peace in a cage of violence.

But that morning there was no calm. There was no music. There was no peace, not even the tiniest glimmer of it in the dark.

That morning, I jolted awake in a cold sweat at the sound of bone cracking. I cried out in terror, falling to the floor to find myself alone and confused. In the flashing light, my wide, frantic eyes darted around me as I raised my arms over my head, a protective instinct I learned from my father, perfected with my trainer, and used only in the cage and my darkest nightmares.

I sagged against the couch, chest heaving. I was still in the theatre room. A video of Dominic's last fight played on the wall from the projector. I must have fallen asleep by accident. Rubbing my eyes, which were puffy and stinging, I pointed the remote blindly and switched off the video.

It was when I was plunged into silence that I remembered River, remembered the hike, remembered my promise.

Hurrying to scramble to my feet, I stumbled over a blanket and rushed to the door. Wrenching it open, I cursed when bright light from the tall windows overlooking the garden in the back of the manor blinded me. Through squinted eyes, I saw that it must be close to noon.

"Fuck," I growled as I stalked toward the gym to find River to apologise. "Fuck, fuck, fuck!"

I felt jittery, panicked, anxious as I hurried down the sun-filled hallway, which hurt my eyes. An invisible knife stabbed my shoulder, retribution for sleeping on a hard couch, and I oscillated from freezing cold to burning hot, and that wasn't even the worst of it. A hammer pounded in my head that grew louder and more painful with each echoing step.

Despite the warning signals from my body, all I could think about was all the time I wasted oversleeping. I told River that I just needed to finish this video of Dominic fighting. But that video turned into "one last one," and that "one last one" turned into ""just another" and that "just another" turned into a loop of teeth-shattering uppercuts, nose-breaking hooks, and crosses so brutal and violent that the poor fucker who faced him was out even before his head hit the mat. At some point, I fell asleep, only to be trapped in a maze of blood and bruises, and above me, Dominic's taunting laugh followed me everywhere I went.

So I got a little less fucking shuteye than I intended. That wasn't an excuse. There were no excuses. Not now. Not anymore.

I wouldn't take back my title from Dominic by easing up. I wouldn't win by being gentle on myself. I wouldn't prove myself worthy of River's love by sleeping in late, by sleeping into feckin' noon, despite how late I was up working.

I needed to work harder, push myself harder. I needed to be faster, stronger, meaner, so I could win. I needed to—

Halfway across the wide, airy foyer, I froze mid-step. I shook my head, suddenly fearful like a child. I was hallucinating. Overtired. Because what I saw was simply impossible.

She wouldn't do that to me. She couldn't.

But when I looked back across the foyer through the windows on either side of the double door, I stared at the impossible: River returning down the gravel drive from her hike, smiling and laughing and staring up at Niall.

My body trembled in growing rage. The only logical thought that managed to cross my mind as I rushed to the front doors in a blind fury was, *don't kill him, Declan. Whatever you do, just don't fucking kill him.*

The door rattled on its hinges as I slammed it open. I barely heard the boom that echoed in the marble foyer and shook the crystal chandelier because of the hot, boiling hot blood that rushed past my ears. Stones cut at my bare feet but I felt no pain.

I saw no dazzling sunlight. Heard no singing birds. Felt no cool, gentle breeze on my face.

I was back in a hot, dimly lit room that smelled of sweat and cum. *She* was moaning Dominic's name when I walked in. The perfect roses I'd held in my hand hit the floor. I felt numb, completely numb when she looked over, her tits still bouncing as he thrust into her.

"Declan."

She pushed at Dominic's chest to distance herself from him an inch or two, as if that would change anything.

As if an inch or two would undo the deed that could not be undone.

As if an inch or two would sew together my already broken heart.

"What the fuck is this?" I shouted across the front lawn.

River and Niall looked up from their intimate eye contact to see me for the first time. River's laugh died and she moved away from Niall. It was just an inch or two that she moved. But I knew what an inch or two meant. I knew the pain an inch or two could inflict.

"Declan," she said.

"Declan."

It was happening again. Fuck. It was happening all over again. They say lightning doesn't strike twice, but this wasn't like lightning. It wasn't a jolt—painful, but over in an instant.

This was quicksand and it was slow.

I pointed a shaking finger at Niall because I couldn't bear to look at River. I wasn't ready for that kind of agony. Not yet. Not again. "You're fired," I shouted at my physio, who had stopped at the sight of me.

He held up his hands in a pathetic last-ditch defence of his betrayal. "What?" he said as I walked straight up to him.

I walked straight up to him as black played at the edges of my vision. "You're fired," I repeated, voice shaking. "Get the fuck out of my sight."

A hand at my arm startled me. River. I jerked away as if her touch burned me.

"Declan," she said softly, calmly. "Declan, calm down, okay?"

I scoffed at her words. "I think I've been calm long enough," I said. "I think I'm done with being calm. I'm done with letting people walk all over me."

Niall tried to step forward, but River stopped him with a hand on his chest.

Look how easily she touched him!

"Declan, we just went on a hike," she tried to explain. "That's all that happened, a hike."

I clenched my fists so tightly that my fingernails pierced the skin of my palms. "You said *we* were going to go hiking."

"Baby, you were asleep. I didn't wake you because I thought you needed it." She tried to reach for me.

I stepped back out of her grasp.

"She's right, Declan," Niall added, moving closer to her. "Your body can't handle this."

"No!" I shook my head before pointing to each of them. "My body can't handle *this*."

"Baby, nothing happened." River's voice rose higher. "It was just a hike."

I laughed darkly. "And tomorrow?"

River glanced at Niall in confusion. "What?"

"Today, it was nothing," I crossed my arms over my chest and leaned forward. "But what about tomorrow?"

River frowned. "What do you mean?"

I ignored her and continued, "What about the day after tomorrow?" I said. "And the day after the day after tomorrow? Will it be 'nothing' then? How long before it isn't 'nothing' anymore?"

There was silence among the three of us as my implications sank in.

River's face darkened and I saw anger building inside of her. "This isn't you," she said in a low tone. "This isn't you right now, Declan. I know you."

"But do I know you?"

This seemed to hurt her worse than anything I'd said up until that point. "Don't say that," she whispered. "Declan, don't you dare say that."

"I thought I knew *her*," I said nonetheless. "*She* smiled at me the way you smile at me."

"That's not true and you know it." Tears came to her eyes, but she angrily swiped at them before they could fall.

"*She* held me the way you hold me, too," I continued, far past the point of stopping myself no matter how much I knew I was hurting her. I held the final dagger in my fist and I knew I was going to plunge it into her heart. "*She* told me she loved me," I said with no emotion. "Just the way you tell me that you love me."

River glared at me for a long, drawn-out moment.

I wanted to fight. Fuck, I needed to fight. She must have known that; she must have seen that. Because she spoke to Niall while staring straight at me, straight fucking at me. "Niall, would you mind giving me a ride to Oisin's place?" she asked. "I can't be here right now."

Out of the corner of my eye, I saw Niall nod as he mumbled, "Yeah, sure," before stuffing his hands into his pockets, ducking his head, and walking toward his car.

I continued to stare at River. I kept my face blank, expressionless, nonchalant and uncaring, but inside my mind, I was begging her to fight back. I screamed for her to slap my face, to curse me out, to swear me out of her life forever. I wanted her to tell me I deserved to be alone, I deserved to be betrayed, I deserved to be unloved.

Above all else, I wanted her to say something…anything.

Without a word, River turned and followed Niall.

I stood there, motionless, as he held the passenger side door open for her and she got inside. I stood there, silent, not even opening my mouth to stop her, as the car disappeared between the trees. I stood there, numb, completely numb as she left.

She left because of me.

The vase of flowers she picked during our last hike—arranged delicately as I watched her in the kitchen and placed on the marble table beneath the crystal chandelier in the manor's foyer before I swept her over my shoulder and carried her giggling to my bedroom—was the first thing I destroyed.

With a roar, I hurled it against the wall, relishing the sound of the glass shattering and the water dripping down to pool amongst the petals that would shrivel and die. I upturned the marble table. It cracked the floor when it fell.

I destroyed the art hanging along the curved staircase on my way to the second floor next. I punched a hole in the drywall of the hall outside my bedroom before destroying the antique clock she loved, the nightstand where she'd left her stack of books with the dog-eared pages, the four-post bed she gripped with those petite hands the last time I fucked her.

I hadn't known at the time that it would be the last. I would have let my eyes linger on her for a moment longer. I would have kissed her a little more sweetly. I would have held her just a bit tighter as she called out my name.

My name…she called out my name.

I destroyed it all because I couldn't destroy the one thing I truly wanted to destroy fast enough.

Me.

A verifiable *barrel* of carbonara sat in front of me on the round wooden table in Oisin's airy kitchen nook, and all I could muster was a despondent sigh as I twirled my spoon around and around in the pasta.

Next to me, Oisin looked from me to the food and back, frowning with his chin resting in his hands. "Not enough parmesan?" he asked.

I shook my head.

"Wait…" He leaned back against the cushioned banquette as the rain made pitter-patter sounds against the shuttered windows overlooking an impressive herb garden. "Wait, *too much* parmesan?"

I managed a sad smile as I glanced over at him. "I'm afraid this is a pain that can't be cured with carbonara."

"Bullshite." Oisin contradicted me with such gusto that it took me by surprise.

"Every world problem can be solved with more carbonara, my little voodoo queen," he said, and then tapped the tip of my nose. "I'll just go get more bacon."

I laughed as Oisin slid out of the banquette with a snap of his fingers and crossed the short distance to the kitchen. His cottage on the edge of the closest town to Declan's property was 80 percent kitchen, 15 percent wine cellar, and 5 percent bed.

As he grabbed a frying pan from the hanging rack above the massive marble island, I sighed again and pushed my pasta away to rest my forehead against the table. "I don't know what to do," I mumbled. "I thought I knew him. I really thought I saw the real Declan past all of that irritability, anger, and dark, moody stares. I thought there was…more."

More kindness. More gentleness. Softness, tender caresses in the morning, more rough, callused fingers tracing circles along my palm on a starlit balcony, more whispered "I love you's" when he thought I was asleep.

"But the man I saw on the lawn when I returned from my hike with Niall," I continued, squeezing my eyes shut to push away the image. "I just don't know, Oisin. I just don't know anymore."

Bacon sizzled in the pan and not even that glorious smell could revive my normally cheery outlook.

Oisin glanced over at me from the stovetop. "I do know one thing," he said. "Declan takes the weight of the world on his shoulders. Sometimes it weighs just a little bit heavier than he can handle, than anyone could ever handle."

I chewed at the inside of my cheek and sagged against the back of the banquette as I considered this. In my head, I pieced together a timeline and pinpointed the change in Declan's behaviour to one moment…setting the date of the fight with Dominic for his title.

"Why won't he let me take some of that weight from his shoulders?" I asked Oisin as he flipped the thick bacon. "I can handle some of it. Why won't he let me help him?"

Oisin shook his head. "You'll have to work some of that voodoo magic of yours to get Declan Gallagher to let even you help, little lady."

I leaned forward and scooted to the edge of my seat. "But why?" I pushed. "Why?"

Before Oisin could answer, my cell phone in my back jeans pocket vibrated. Irritably, I pulled it out, ready to press "Ignore" so I could finish my conversation with Oisin and perhaps stomach a few bites, or a few bowls, of healing carbonara. My thumb above the cell phone screen froze when I saw the name on the caller ID.

"Who is it?" Oisin casually asked over his shoulder.

I looked up at him with wide eyes. "University Hospital Kerry."

Oisin dropped his spatula and rushed over to me as I forced myself to answer, "Hello?"

"Is this Ms River Moore?" a female voice asked curtly.

I glanced fearfully at Oisin, who was huddled in close to me to hear. "Yes," I said, throat tight.

"Ms Moore, I'm calling from the ER at University Hospital because you were listed as next of kin for, um, yes, for a Mr Declan Gallagher. Are you his wife, ma'am?"

"*What?*" It was all I could manage to say as cold fear swept over me.

"What happened?" Oisin whispered. "Is he okay?

"If you could please come as soon as possible, Ms Moore," the woman insisted.

His wife?

He listed me as his *wife*?

My mind clung to this question because the alternative was a question I couldn't bear to ask—was he *alive*?

My fingers were numb as the woman's voice drifted farther

and farther away.

"Hello?" I heard as if a faint echo down a long tunnel. "Ms Moore? Are you still there?"

I stared blindly at the black smoke coming from the burning bacon.

Oisin slipped the cell phone from my loose grip and placed it against his own ear. "Hi, yes, can you tell me what happened?" he said, his fear obvious. "Is he all right? Is he alive?"

I winced. No. I couldn't think about that. I focused again on the fact that he listed me as his kin. It was easier. It was safer. My mind was doing what I always did—I ran.

"River, River, we have to go," Oisin said, holding the phone away from his ear.

"What happened?" I asked as panic started to give my body an unwelcome jolt. I wanted the numbness back. I didn't want to feel. I didn't want to hurt.

"They can't tell us anything over the phone. We have to get to the ER."

"What happened, Oisin?" I asked, turning to him with tears already pooling in my eyes, nails cutting half-moons in my palms. "What happened?"

Oisin had already hung up. He grabbed his coat and mine along with his keys before hurrying back to me and offering his hand to me.

"I don't know, darling," he said as tugged me to my feet.

"They won't tell me. We have to go."

Oisin's fingers in mine was the only thing that got me out of the cottage, down the lane, and into his car. If it weren't for him, I would be a shaking mess on the floor of his kitchen.

"Oh, my God!" I gasped in the passenger seat as he floored it down the muddy country road. "Oh my God, Oisin, I just left. I just left him without saying anything."

Oisin tried to comfort me by running his hand up and down my arm as the engine whined in protest at the speed. But I was far past being able to be comforted.

"I was just mad," I said, struggling to breathe as I rocked forward and back. "But—but—but—fuck, I can't breathe."

I squeezed my eyes shut and my mind went immediately back to Declan's face just before I turned and walked away. His eyes were calling out to me and I knew it. I fucking knew it.

And I walked away.

"What if that was the last time?" I cried, nearing hysterics. "What if that was my last chance to hold him and I fucking walked away?"

The drive to the hospital was agony.

I feared it was nothing compared to the pain I'd feel forever if Declan was—if he was…

I couldn't say it.

I wouldn't say it.

Why did I walk away?

Declan

I winced at the flash of the light and irritably shoved the doctor's hand away to stop him from tugging at my eyelid. A low growl and a dark glare were all it took to keep him from trying to touch me again. We both already knew the obvious truth: I had a concussion. On my very first goddamn practice spar since the accident…

He'd been one of the up-and-coming fighters who'd trained at one of my gyms. At least he'd have a story to tell about how he knocked out the World number 1…ex-number 1, I reminded myself bitterly. *Soon to be again number 1*, I echoed in my head like a chant.

"I told you," I grumbled, sagging forward on the edge of the exam table with a sigh and resting my elbows on my knees so I could rub at my pounding temples. "I'm fine."

"You're not," the doctor said.

I stared up at the ceiling to avoid that frown of concern that was the exact same frown of concern as the semi-circle of doctors who trapped me in that bed that night after the accident. The glare of those unnatural phosphorescent bulbs and the rows of water-stained squares above me were exactly the same as the ones I stared at for days in my prison of agony, so I dropped my head to stare at the floor instead.

I couldn't escape. No matter where I looked—I couldn't escape it.

That grey speckled linoleum between my legs was the same. The wires and cords, like a pit of snakes, inches from my toes were the same. The stark white sheets, whiter than any corpse could ever be, that hung from the bed were the same, the exact fucking same.

Memories of being trapped in that car flooded my mind…smoke searing my eyes, tightening my throat, burning my lungs. The heart rate on the monitor next to me leaped as I felt that panic again. I was trapped.

I was fucking trapped.

In the hospital room, I clenched my eyes closed so tightly that it hurt. The darkness did nothing for the sounds that brought me right back to the night of the accident. The harsh beep of machines, the low whispers of nurses passing in the halls, the clang of metal tools on metal stands.

I tried covering my ears with my hands, but a memory just grew louder and louder. It wasn't from my accident. It was earlier. Much earlier.

"I fell."

The doctor's thumb pressed at the bruises along my ribcage as I tried not to breathe to avoid the stabbing knives.

"I fell."

I shook my head as the fear consumed me. The whispers, the beeps, the frowns. Louder and louder.

"I fell. That's all. I just fell. It was my fault. I swear I just fell."

He was going to be mad. He was going to be so mad.

"I fell."

A cold hand grabbed my arm and I jerked back, chest heaving.

The doctor, a needle in one gloved hand, stepped back at the sight of my raised fist. "I'm just going to give you something to calm you down," he said in a voice I knew was meant to soothe.

They all used that same fucking voice; it gave me the same terrified tremors.

"We want to help."

They only made it worse. Far worse. I shuddered when I remembered my father closing the door slowly, so slowly, after we got home from the hospital, his dark eyes narrowed on me.

"I told them I fell."

It did no good.

"Get that feckin' thing away from me," I said to the doctor. I only lowered my fist when he finally sighed and dropped the needle into the neon-orange disposal bin.

"Look," the doctor said as he sagged into the same chair as before and crossed his arms. "You're obviously on edge. I suspect we can add sleep deprivation and anxiety attacks to the diagnosis here today. But I need you to hear what I'm about to say, alright, Mr Gallagher?"

I didn't have time for this. How much training time had I already lost with this trip to the hospital? I told Seamus when I came to that I was grand. I'm grand.

I'm grand.

"Is there some form you need to sign or can I just leave now?" I asked as I tried to stand.

A wave of dizziness and nausea washed over me. The doctor rushed to grab my arm to steady me as I stumbled back to the exam table. The hammers in my head went into overtime on my skull and black dots appeared in my blurry vision. I was trapped.

"Mr Gallagher," the doctor bent over so he was face to face with me as I tried not to gag, "I believe your condition is far more serious than you take it to be."

I barely heard his words. I needed to get out of there. "Bollocks. It's a bump on the head, Doc." I attempted a casual tone, but it was undercut when I ducked my head from the harsh light. "I'm a fighter. It's kind of in the job description."

The doctor rubbed tiredly at his eyes underneath his glasses. "Does the job description include brain trauma, Mr Gallagher?" he asked. "What about death?"

"What are you talking about?" I asked, glancing at the door next to the window overlooking the hall and the nurses' station.

"I've looked at your MRIs," he said slowly. "If you sustain another hit like you did today, I'm afraid there is a very substantial chance of both of those things, Mr Gallagher."

Blinking against the harsh light, I stared at the doctor. "What are you saying?"

"I'm saying that you can't fight."

I laughed and immediately regretted it as pain erupted in my head. "Good thing that's not up to you," I said with a wink.

I again pushed myself to my feet and leaned against the table, waiting for the nausea to pass so I could leave.

"I'm afraid it is up to me, Mr Gallagher," he said.

The doctor's voice was soft, but I heard him crystal clear even over those goddamn hammers. I took a wobbling step toward him that was meant to be threatening but failed when I was forced to reach out to the counter to steady myself. "What the fuck did you say?"

The doctor avoided my eyes as he fidgeted with his pen. "You need doctor's approval to compete," he explained. "And I can't, in good conscience, Mr Gallagher, give that, knowing what I know about your health."

I shook my head as I tried to comprehend what he was saying. "But I'm a fighter," I said, eyes darting across the grey linoleum that was always the same, always the same. "I'm a fighter."

The doctor gave me a soft smile. "You *were* a fighter, Mr Gallagher."

I was trapped. The beeping. The wires. The goddamn phosphorescent lightbulbs darkened only by the trapped moths. I was one of those moths. I was one of those fucking moths.

My heart began to race painfully when the door to the hospital room suddenly opened and I heard my name like a lighthouse in the dark.

"Declan!"

River rushed into my arms and we crashed together back to the exam table. She squeezed me tight, and all it took was one inhale of her lavender shampoo to escape—escape the sterile room, the haunting memories, escape the fear that was dragging me down deeper, deeper, deeper into a cage of darkness.

Tears stained her cheeks and her eyes were red and puffy when she pulled herself back and looked me over. "Are you hurt?" she asked worriedly. "Baby, they called and I was terrified because we fought and I walked away without saying anything and what if that was the last time and—" She broke down crying.

I grabbed her quivering chin. "River, I'm grand," I said with a gentle smile. "I'm grand." Over her shoulder, I saw the doctor's obvious disapproval.

"Are you sure?" River sniffled. "They said it was bad. On the phone they said it was really bad." She looked up into my eyes, searching for the truth.

I laughed casually and pulled her tight to my chest, running my hands up and down her back. "They were just being cautious," I told her while staring down the doctor. "I got knocked about a bit in practice and they just wanted to be cautious. I'm all cleared."

The doctor stood and opened his mouth to speak, but I quickly interrupted him.

"I'm grand."

He looked between me and River in my arms before sighing in defeat. "I'll give you two some time alone then," he said, heading toward the door.

"Thanks for everything, Doc."

He shook his head as he closed the door behind him. I was

fighter. That was what I *was*. No one would take that from me. Not even goddamn Death himself.

"Declan, you have no idea how terrified I was," River whispered against my chest. Her fingers shook as she clung to me as if she wasn't certain that I was truly there in flesh and blood. She peered up at me with those wide, sweet eyes beneath eyelashes dotted with tears…more beautiful than the dew-dotted blades of grass in the quiet, mist-filled glen just north of the manor. "I shouldn't have left like that, I shouldn't have—"

"River."

"I never want to leave like that again," she continued, tears streaming down her face. "I never, never want to—"

"River."

"I could have lost you and—"

"River, you could use braces."

That did the trick. River blinked slowly as she stared up at me, her mouth frozen open with half a word forever unspoken. A small frown tugged her eyebrows together.

I tried not to smile at how adorable it made her look.

"Huh?" she asked.

"There's a small gap between your two front teeth," I said, lifting her up easily by the waist and setting her on my lap as she continued staring at me in bewilderment. "And you're going to get wrinkles, you know?"

"Wrinkles?"

I nodded. "When you smile, you scrunch your nose, so you'll definitely get wrinkles here." I pointed to each place on her face. "And because you smile all the goddamn time, you're definitely going to get lines around these lips here and around these eyes here."

As my thumb trailed along her cheek, I wiped away as many of her tears as I could. I wanted to erase them all. I wanted to take them all away. I wanted to believe they weren't because of me. But they were because of me.

I had to make things right.

"You drink red wine and coffee like they're not making any more of it," I said.

River frowned. "You want me to stop drinking red wine?"

I smiled and shook my head. "No. I want you to have all the red wine in the world. I want you to have red wine from Argentina and Spain and California. And I want to go there with you. I want to see everything with you, taste everything with you, experience everything with you because you're *you*, River. You're completely and utterly you and no one else is like you."

She shook her head. "I don't understand."

I tucked a stray curl behind her ear and cupped the back of her neck. "I'm trying to say I'm sorry, baby," I said. "Trying badly."

"Go on then." River placed her gentle, petite hands on my

chest and looked at me as she waited.

"I was wrong. Your smile is nothing like hers," I whispered. "You are nothing like her. I said it because I was tired and angry and a feckin' eejit."

The corners of her lips tipped up. There it was…that smile.

"I mean, look at you," I said. "That smile is nothing like anyone's. Not even close."

She grinned. "Even with the gap between my teeth?"

"Especially because of the gap between your teeth."

She narrowed her eyes. "And the red wine and coffee stains?"

"Perfection."

River laughed as she wiggled closer to me on my lap. "What about when those wrinkles come in?" she asked as she ran her fingers down the sides of my face. "What about then?"

My fingers tightened on her back. "I'll love each one more than the last," I answered truthfully. "Because each one will mean you're still smiling. And that's all I want, River. I want you to smile."

She leaned in, her hair falling down to curtain us from the world, and her eyes fluttered closed as she tenderly pressed her lips to mine.

We kissed and everything fell away.

The sterile, bare, stark-white hospital room walls collapsed.

The metal frame of that burning, mangled car disappeared.

The mesh link sides of the cage rattling with the cheers of the crowd fell, and I was no longer trapped.

I was free.

Declan

My finger traced constellations across the light freckles that dotted River's back. The stars, so bright, so sparkling, so dazzling in the sky outside my bedroom window held no appeal for me when she was beside me. If I never saw the North Star ever again, I would be fine, knowing I had her body to guide my way.

River sighed in her sleep and nestled closer to me beneath the sheets. Her soft, steady breath was like a metronome for me, keeping time when all the clocks in the room seemed to spin, spin, spin. Staring down at her sweet face, I gently pushed a curl from her cheek and tucked it behind her ear.

After a moment of peace and tranquillity, I glanced over at my nightstand and the bottle of pain medication pills the doctor prescribed when I was discharged from the hospital to help me sleep. But the dull throbbing in my head wasn't the reason I was still awake at that late hour, despite the exhaustion that weighed down my eyelids as if tied to boulders.

It was guilt.

It was guilt that ate at my stomach, made my legs restless, and buzzed like a thousand bees in my head.

I should tell her. I should tell her what the doctor said.

You're lying to her. You're keeping secrets from the woman you love.

She'll find out. You should tell her the doctor's prognosis before she finds out from someone else.

Lies...secrets...lies...secrets...lies...lies...lies...

I knew why, of course. I knew why I was hesitant, fearful even, to tell River about the true seriousness of my injury and the potential danger of stepping back into the cage to fight Dominic. I knew why I didn't open my mouth.

It wasn't because I thought she would try to convince me not to risk my health, my life; I knew she would. I knew with absolute certainty that she would. I didn't tell River, not because I knew she would try to convince me, but because I knew I would *listen.*

I would step away from the cage. I would walk away from the challenge of my greatest rival. I would leave my title, the title I deserved, the title I earned, in the hands of another.

I *was* a fighter. All I'd ever known was fighting. Who would I be without my fists? What would be left when my entire identity was stripped away?

What would be left for her to love?

Who would be left for River to love?

Closing my eyes, I focused on the sound of her breathing and told myself I didn't need the roar of a crowd when I had those tiniest of exhales from the pinkest of lips. I laid my palm against the small of her back and told myself that there was no need for the pain of knuckles against jawbone when I had the pleasure of warm, soft skin that goose bumped so deliciously at the faintest of touches. I told myself I didn't need a title when I had her.

She was right there, right there beside me.

But for how long?

The voice snuck up on me like a king punch from behind, the most brutal act of violence. I tried to shove away the image of River and Niall emerging together from the forest, smiling, laughing, and whispering lovers' secrets. I'd overreacted. I was tired, that was all. River wouldn't do that to me. She wasn't Giselle. She wasn't Giselle. River was not Giselle.

But no matter how many times I repeated that as I lay there

paralysed in bed, I couldn't stop myself from seeing my hand wrapping around the handle of my bedroom door. The door swinging open to a hot room with dense, sticky, perfumed air, River's legs wrapped around Niall's hips as he fucked her, her back arching as he pinched her nipples, her throat straining as she screamed his name, not mine.

I climbed out of bed as if it were on fire and hurried across the room after grabbing my cell phone from the nightstand. My fingers were already fumbling for Seamus's number before I'd even closed the door behind me. My frantic, panicked breathing filled the otherwise silent hallway while I paced back and forth in the dark as I waited anxiously for Seamus to pick up. I was seconds away from tugging out my hair when the dial tone stopped.

"Jaysus fuck, Declan, it's past three in the mornin'," he complained. "I was dead asleep you ass—"

"Yes," I whispered hurriedly.

"Yes what?" Seamus asked. "Yes you're an asshole? That wasn't a question, *asshole.*"

I cupped my hand over the receiver so as not to wake River and quickly glanced back at my bedroom door. It remained closed and still. "Yes to what we talked about in the hospital," I said in a low, hushed voice. "I want to fight."

It wasn't what I wanted to say. I wanted to say, "I need to fight. I need it like air, I need it like goddamn oxygen.'

"Now yer suckin' diesel," Seamus said. "I knew yer man couldn't have hit you that bleedin' hard that you'd give up everything just like that."

Back in the hospital, Seamus had come into my room. In what I thought was a rare moment of unselfish kindness, he gave River some money to go get a drink.

"I know how shite this all has been on ye," he'd said to her.

But the moment the door closed behind her, Seamus sat next to me and whispered fast, his tongue rapid in his mouth like a snake, "Don't worry about that feckin' doctor, Declan," he'd said, checking the window next to the door. "There's more than one way to get a signature to appease the federation." He'd clamped his hand on my shoulder with a grin. "You'll fight," he'd hissed. "You'll fight. I'll see to it."

"Don't."

The word was out of my mouth before I could stop it. The sound of it in the quiet hospital had surprised even me.

Seamus stared at me, his eyes searching mine. "What?"

The question wasn't just a question; it was a challenge. I hesitated, but only for as long as it took to remember River's smile…I wanted her to be happy. That's all I wanted. Facing Seamus, I squared my shoulders, set my jaw, and spoke clearly and confidently. "I'm done, Seamus. I'm done."

He immediately stood, pacing in front of me and shaking his head. "No, no, no," he had said. "Not when we're this close. Not now."

"I'm done."

Seamus had then snapped his fingers and hurried back to my side.

"Just think about it, alright?" he'd insisted. "As a favour to your old friend, eh? Just take a little while to ponder such a big decision, okay?"

"Seamus, Riv—"

"Just a day." He'd stopped me with his fingers clawing into my shoulder. "Don't decide yet. That's all I ask ye."

I'd finally relented with a sigh. "Fine. One day."

Seamus had smiled.

I couldn't help but think I'd just struck a deal with the devil.

"Consider who you are," he'd said with a wink. "Consider *what* you are, Declan."

In the darkness of my hallway, I closed my eyes. "I'm a fighter," I said. "I need to fight." I breathed in deeply. "I need to win."

I could practically see Seamus's smile, his white teeth between his red beard and mustache, flashing in the dark like daggers. "I'll get you that fight with Dominic. I'll get you your revenge, Declan."

I was about to end the call, my finger an inch from the red button on the screen, when I heard Seamus's voice, harsh like clanking of shackles around my ankles, around my wrists, around my throat.

"What about the girl?" he asked.

Sagging against the wall in the hallway, I dragged my hand wearily over my face and sighed. It was for her good. She'd understand in the end. She would understand.

"She doesn't need to know," I said and hung up.

Careful not to make a sound, I slipped back inside my bedroom, crossed the cold floor on tiptoes, and climbed back into bed beside River. I wouldn't be sleeping that night, that much I knew. I'd sleep once it was done—once I'd defeated Dominic, when I had my title back, once I'd earned her love. Then I could stop lying.

Then I could sleep once more.

I was no longer tracing Orion's Belt along River's back as she slept next to me. I wasn't tracing the Big Dipper or the Little Bear either. I wasn't tracing any constellation.

With the pad of my finger along her smooth, cool skin, I was writing letters, tenderly, softly, gently.

As she sighed and nestled in closer to me, so full of trust that it made my chest hurt worse than the ache in my head, I wrote across her bare back:

I - A - M - S - O - R - R – Y

Declan

I was ready.

Weeks of training later and I was finally ready. Weeks of weightlifting, push-ups, and burpees later…I was finally strong enough. Weeks of speed exercises and sprints and footwork practice later and I was finally fast enough. Weeks of sparring and film watching and strategizing later and I was finally mentally tough enough.

I was enough.

I was finally enough.

Enough to beat Dominic. Enough to win back my MMA title. Enough to deserve River's love.

After a last light training the day before the flight to Dublin for the big fight, Seamus set up a small folding table in the centre of the cage to finalize all the details.

"Where's River?" I asked as I used the towel around my neck to wipe sweat from my brow after getting in one last squat set and then sat down.

Seamus, arranging a stack of papers in front of him, didn't look over at me as he answered nonchalantly with a wave of his hand, "Oh, she said she didn't need to be here or something like that. I don't know, busy with something else, I guess. Now your jet is all set to take off tomorrow morning for Dublin so we can get in a walkthrough of the stadium before dinner." Seamus ran his finger down a checklist, clicking his tongue. "Our driver will pick you and me up at—"

"And River," I interjected.

Seamus looked up at me. "Huh?"

"And River," I repeated with extra emphasis. "River is coming, too."

Seamus waved his hand at me dismissively and mumbled a "Yeah, yeah" before continuing on down the checklist.

As he droned on about things I didn't care about, I glanced

around the empty gym and leaned back to see the light of the little office in the back already turned off.

I frowned. "Where did you say she was?"

Seamus smiled over at me as he slapped a piece of paper down in front of me. "Doesn't matter where she is," he said, jamming a finger down on the paper. "All that matters right now is this baby right here."

With my mind still preoccupied with River's mysterious absence, it took Seamus's irritated snaps in front of my nose for me to finally glance down at the single sheet of white paper on the little table between us. My eyes quickly glossed over the doctor's note clearing me for the fight with Dominic, and I nodded.

"Good," I said. "I think I'm going to go find River. She should be here for this." I pushed my chair back.

Seamus stood and immediately blocked my path out of the cage. "Come on, sit down, alright?" He held his two hands out in front of him as if I were a wild animal he was trying to tame. "I think I deserve a bit more than 'good', eh?"

I dragged my hand over my face and begrudgingly slumped back into the chair. When he sat back down across from me, I reached across and grabbed his beefy, freckled hands. "Thank you, Seamus, my darling petal, Seamus," I mocked. "Thank you for getting this signature in a manner that I'm sure was *entirely* legal, I might add. I owe you my life, my everything."

Seamus rolled his eyes and grumbled, "That's more bleedin' like it."

He tried to pull his hands back from my grasp, but I held him tight. "I swear in this cage on this very day that in order to convey my undying gratitude, I shall name my first child after you and my second child and maybe, just maybe, thir—"

"Alright, you fucker. Alright, alright." Seamus wrenched his hands free and rubbed his wrists. "Before that girl came, you used to be so sulky and forlorn and far too 'woe is me' to joke around." He paused to sigh dramatically. "I miss that."

I laughed. "Get used to it, Seamus, *baby*."

"Fuck me," he muttered under his breath, running his hand through his coarse red hair.

I slapped my palms on the table and grinned. "We all done then?" I asked. "I have to go find River."

As I was again moving to leave, Seamus stopped me. "Wait, wait," he said. "I still want to go over some last-minute breakdowns of Dominic's surprise attacks. He's a sneaky motherfucker and if he's going to beat you, that's how it'll happen."

I dismissed Seamus with a wave of my hand. "I've watched all the films," I explained. "I know every dirty trick in his filthy little book. I'm going to go for a quick hike with River to relax before dinner. It's been too long."

Seamus lunged across the table to catch my wrist as I tried to stand. "That right hook after that jab combo of his has knocked out three competitors in the last month, Declan. We should stay focused and go over it again. Plus, we really can't forget about that king hit. That poor kid is still in the hospital."

I peeled Seamus's fingers one by one from my wrist as I clearly articulated, "One, he stole that right hook from me. Two, I'm not those fighters he knocked out. I'm Declan Fucking Gallagher. And three, king hit or not, Dominic does not scare me. Now I'm leaving."

I stepped around the little table set up in the centre of the cage, excited to find River and wrap her up in my arms.

Seamus turned in his seat to call after me. "Declan, this is the very moment where we can't have any distractions. It's crucial we stayed focused solely on the fight and nothing or no one else. Declan!"

"I'll see ya, Seamus."

I was halfway out of the cage when Seamus shouted once more, "River doesn't want to go!"

I didn't think that anything he had to say at that point would stop me from running to those sweet lips and gentle arms, but I immediately froze. Glancing back over my shoulder, I stared in confusion at him. "What?" I asked, my voice barely recognisable to me.

Seamus sighed and rested his elbows on the table to bury his face in his hands. "I hadn't wanted to tell you like this, Declan," he mumbled. "I really hadn't."

My feet felt like lead as I moved back toward the table and sat rigidly in the chair. I narrowed my eyes at Seamus. "What do you mean she doesn't want to go?"

Leaning back in his chair, Seamus shook his head. "I shouldn't even have told you," he said. "This was a mista—"

"River hasn't told me anything," I interrupted.

"And she's not going to," Seamus interlaced his fingers and placed them behind his neck. "She knows how it would upset you."

"Upset me?" I blinked as I searched the little table for answers I couldn't find. "She can tell me anything. She knows that…" She knew that, right?

"This life just isn't for her," Seamus said. "The media. The fame. The *violence*."

I glanced up at Seamus. "She said this to you?" I asked in a soft voice, almost afraid to even ask the question.

Seamus nodded. "She said she had to tell someone." He shrugged. "And, well, she couldn't tell you."

Had I pressured her without knowing it? I'd wanted her to go with me, of course I had. She was the only person who could calm me and I wanted that, needed that, before my fight. In her presence, there was stillness. Waves could crash around me, winds whip around me, lightning strike on every horizon, but one touch from her soft hand, and there was stillness, silence, *peace*.

"Declan, we can't change who we are," Seamus said in a low voice, reaching over to pat my shoulder. "You know this more than most."

No, I thought. No, I didn't. I thought I *had* changed. I thought I had become kinder, gentler, more selfless. I really thought I had changed, changed because of her.

Because of River.

"You're a fighter and you'll always be a fighter," Seamus continued. "You have brutality in your blood, anger in your heart, violence in your soul."

Not with River. Not with her arms around me.

"You need the cage, my friend. You need it like oxygen," he whispered. "You need to fight."

No, no, no... I needed her. I needed *her.*

"At least that's what she said," Seamus concluded.

Did River not know I needed her? Did she not believe I'd changed? Did she not trust I could ever be anything more than a fighter?

"What do I do?" I asked, my voice the voice of a child.

Seamus crossed his arms over his chest. "She'll never admit she said any of this, that's for sure," he started. "But if you love her, I'd think you'd find a way to give her what she truly wants."

To stay. She wants to stay.

I wanted her to go, to be by my side, but more than that, I wanted her to be happy. That's truly what I wanted.

"I mean, that's just my opinion, of course," Seamus said. "But what do I know? Bring her with if you wan—"

"No."

Seamus raised his bushy red eyebrow. "What was that?"

"She'll stay."

"Are you sure?" he asked, staring up at me as I stood, numb. I felt his eyes on me as I moved toward the cage door. "Declan, are you sure?"

"She'll stay."

I would go alone.

Alone in the dark.

Again, alone in the dark.

In the dim light of my bedroom lamp, I wiped my sweaty brow and squeezed at the pinch in my side.

No, I hadn't just returned from a long hike through the forest.

I wasn't practicing the combos Declan taught me while we trained together in the cage.

It wasn't even particularly hot in my room that night as a cool breeze carrying the first scent of spring blossoms swept in through the windows.

It was the suitcase stuffed to the brim on the end of my bed that caused me to huff and heave and reach for my deodorant.

I'd jumped on it, stomped on it, sat on it, squished my knees and then my elbows into it and no matter what I tried, I couldn't quite seem to tug that pesky zipper closed.

Knowing how stressed Declan would be before the big fight in Dublin, I'd wanted to pack everything I could to help him relax. I'd raided Oisin's herb garden to make calming teas, I'd ordered several essential oils to rub along his tense shoulders and neck, I'd gathered up fuzzy socks and a photobook of our hikes through the peaceful trees and noise-cancelling headphones. Grunting the whole while, I'd attempted to stuff my acupuncture set, two yoga mats, and a set of chakra quartz bowls. Anything and everything I wanted to bring to Dublin to keep Declan in the right headspace.

I knew the risk if he wasn't.

I was straddling the suitcase, face red and muscles strained as a long string of curse words tumbled out from between my lips when a knock at my open door made me look up from my failed efforts.

"Thank goodness you're here," I exhaled with a relieved smile as Declan stepped inside. "Can you please close this for me?"

I rolled off the suitcase and collapsed on my sheets next to it. I was pushing my damp curls off my forehead when Declan came to stand next to the bed. I barely noticed his hands stuffed into his pockets, shoulders slumped forward as my mind ran wild with my potential packing list.

"I debated back and forth on bringing the bath salts I made with that orange zest you like so much," I babbled. "Do you think we'll have time to soak before the fight?"

Nerves of my own taking over, I interrupted Declan before he could even answer.

"I obviously can't take a whole massage table, but I thought I could bring some sweet mint oils," I continued.

"River—"

"I mean we can't take the whole massage table, right?" I shook my head. "No, no, we can't. I mean, unless—"

"River—"

"Maybe if there's room, we can consider it then."

When Declan remained unmoving above me, I nodded my head toward the suitcase. "Do you mind?" I asked. "Alright, so how do you feel about my famous blueberry pan…"

I frowned slightly as I noticed Declan's fingers paused on the zipper. I looked up to see him biting his lower lip. "What?" I asked. "Is it too full? Is it not going to fit?"

Concern grew in my chest when Declan continued to awkwardly avoid eye contact with me, and I quickly sat up. "Declan…" I reached for his hand. "Declan, what's wrong?" I scooted back on my bed and pulled him gently toward me.

With a sigh, he sat down at the very edge of the mattress.

"Declan, you're scaring me," I whispered.

"River…" Declan's eyes flashed over to me before he rubbed at his temples and rested his chin on his chest. "River, I think you should stay."

I dropped his hand in surprise. "Stay?"

As I watched Declan's downturned face with wide, panicked eyes, I sensed turmoil and uncertainty as he searched for his next words to me. "You distract me, baby," he finally said softly, glancing over at me.

I shook my head in confusion. "Distract you?"

"Yes."

"And…that's not what you want…with you…in Dublin…"

I couldn't keep the hurt from my voice. My mind flashed over the times Declan had paused his training to kiss me, to yank his shirt off his body so I could kiss the sweat off his chest, the mornings I rolled over him, mewling in his ear to stay in bed longer. Yes, I suppose I was. But I thought being his distraction was a *good thing.*

"It's important that I stay as focused as possible for the fight."

It took me a moment to realise that Declan was speaking again. I looked up to find him watching my reaction with searching eyes…that blue, vivid and deep.

"And when you're around me all I want to do is spend time with you, baby," he went on.

"Oh. Right." My hands instead fell limply into my lap and all I could manage to do was stare at my slightly quivering fingers.

It shouldn't have affected me that way; Declan's words shouldn't have made my breath quicken like each one was the last gasp before I went underwater. My heart would accelerate like it was speeding toward a cliff I wouldn't survive the fall from. It shouldn't have affected me at all. I should have been used to it by now—being left behind, pushed away, set aside, *abandoned.*

My parents. All the orphanages, foster families, institution after institution. All those bright white, fake smiles that promised each and every time "I was home, finally home."

Why did I ever believe that Declan Gallagher would be any different?

My fingernails dug painfully into my palms as I bit back tears. There on the bed with Declan inches away, I told myself that I deserved to feel that knife pressed deeper and deeper into my heart for being so stupid, so ignorant, so goddamn naïve.

I knew better.

I fucking knew better.

"You're the most beautiful, wonderful, rare distraction, River," Declan continued, trying to appease me. "But you're still a—"

"I get it," I interrupted, forcing a casual, carefree smile.

Declan blinked in surprise and studied me, hesitated, and then asked, "You do?"

I tugged the corners of my lips up higher. "Of course," I

answered, laying a hand on Declan's thigh.

Over the years, I'd perfected goodbyes. I knew just how to make them fast, the right words, the right smile, the right tilt of my chin, so I could get a head start on the pain that followed after me like a bloodhound.

"I understand completely," I insisted.

Declan rested his hand over mine and weakly squeezed my fingers. "You're just too stunning is all," he said lamely.

He spoke with a sweet smile, but I could hear the strain in his voice. There was something he wasn't telling me. But that didn't matter.

All that mattered was that I kept smiling.

"I'll stay," I said, getting to the point. "It's fine."

Declan's eyes met mine and his mouth opened as if to speak, but then he closed it and dropped his gaze from mine. "Alright, well, are you ready to come to bed then?" He stood and reached his hand out to me.

I kept my tone casual despite the lump in my throat that was only growing and growing. "Um, actually, I think you should really get some good rest tonight," I said. "You know how my cold toes wake you up at night," I added with a laugh I hoped sounded real.

Declan's smile was barely there as he nodded and laughed, too. "Okay, then," he agreed too quickly…far too quickly. "I'll come say goodbye in the morning then."

He was already heading toward the door when I spoke. "Maybe we should just say goodbye now."

Pain was on my heels. It was time to run, time again to run.

I watched, fingers fidgeting, as Declan turned around and looked over at me.

I shrugged with a smile and said, "I haven't had a morning to sleep in with all the preparations. Need those beauty z's, you know?"

Declan remained silent as I chewed at the inside of my mouth.

"We can say goodbye now, right?" I asked softly.

After another tense moment without words, Declan finally nodded and grinned. "Of course."

My heart rate spiked as he neared me, closer, closer, closer. I could do this, I told myself. I'd done this before. I'd done this before more times than I could count; I wasn't sure why this one seemed to be infinitely harder.

Standing in front of him, we awkwardly grinned, laughed, and wrapped our arms around each other more like we were close co-workers than lovers destined to be together.

"Good luck then," I said, fighting down the emotion.

"Yeah," Declan said against my hair before clearing his throat. "Yeah, thanks."

I should have pulled back then. I should have ended the embrace, smiled, and said one simple word—"Goodbye."

But with his arms around me and mine around his, I couldn't help the sting of tears at my eyes as I buried my head against his strong shoulder I had mistakenly thought would be around to cry on for forever. The smell of his cologne, the security of his hands on my back, the steady beat of his heart against mine, it was all too much.

I wanted to tell him that I wanted to go with him.

I wanted to tell him that I feared him leaving me behind.

I wanted to tell him that I needed him.

But I couldn't get the words out, I *feared* getting the words out, and so I just clung to him. It was all I could do.

I bit my lip to keep a ragged, wretched sob from escaping my lips as my fingers grasped as much of his sweatshirt as I could hold. I held my breath so he wouldn't hear my shaky exhale. I made sure not to rest my cheek entirely on his chest despite how terribly I wanted to for fear that a tear would slip from my damp eyelashes and wet his clothes, because then he'd know. I had to keep space between us so he wouldn't know, so he wouldn't know I needed him.

I needed him.

I needed him.

When we finally pulled away from one another, my tears were replaced with a smile, just like I'd always done.

"Goodbye," I said, kissing his cheek. "Good luck."

Declan lingered. I could practically see the words on the tip of his tongue, but I prayed he would swallow them; I couldn't bear to hear them. My eyes fluttered closed when he leaned over and pressed his lips to the crown of my head.

"Goodbye," he said.

We were two magnets, I supposed as I crawled beneath the sheets, scrunching up my legs to accommodate the suitcase I didn't yet have the strength to unpack. The connection between us was only hard to sever for a moment. But with more distance between us, it'd get easier and easier as the draw lessened and lessened until there was no way at all to find our way back to one another.

No way at all.

Declan

I prayed Seamus put his credit card, and not mine, on file for any damages inside my suite at the Merrion in Dublin, because the night before the fight I was wearing a hole in the luxurious carpet between the crackling fireplace and the burgundy suede couch as I paced back and forth...back and forth...back and forth...

My darting eyes glanced again and again at the manila folder on the glass coffee table. I wrung my sweaty hands before turning yet again on my heel and marching back in the opposite direction. I had already tried just sitting and waiting, but I found myself growing more and more restless as I watched the second hand of the ornate grandfather clock tick around and around. I quickly stood up and started pacing when I had thoroughly convinced myself that time itself was slowing down as I continued to wait.

This was inevitable, I told myself. I couldn't avoid it any longer. This was bound to happen at some point or another.

The knock at my hotel door simultaneously drew a relieved sigh from my tight lungs and sent cold chills down my spine. After exhaling a shaky breath and dragging my fingers through my hair, I reluctantly walked across the suite's expansive living room and forced myself to open the door.

Before I even invited her in, Giselle strode confidently past me into the suite. "About damn time," she said as she slipped her black fur coat from her shoulders.

It fell to the floor, pooling around her five-inch Louis Vuitton stilettos. I watched, stunned, as Giselle immediately stepped out of the fur coat and continued toward the bedroom, her long red nails already at the gold zipper of her skin-tight black minidress. She paused just before the door and glanced over her shoulder at me.

"Shit, Declan, I know you've been hit in the head one too many times," she said with that condescending click of her tongue I used to dread, "but even you should have come to your senses sooner than this."

Giselle then dropped her dress, revealing a red lace thong and bra that left little to my imagination. Before I could even manage to open my mouth, she disappeared into the darkness of the bedroom.

Left alone in the living space of the Merrion suite, I glanced at the door behind me. *I should leave*, I thought. I shouldn't be here, with just her and me. I should leave.

Now.

The clink of ice echoed from the bedroom as I reached for the door handle. I paused when out of the corner of my eye I caught the manila folder still on the couch. With a sigh, I squeezed my eyes shut and pulled my hand from the handle.

Marching across the room, I scooped up the folder and hurried to the bedroom. "Giselle, I—"

"Have you missed me, darling?" Covered in the warm, flickering light of several candles set around the bed, Giselle smiled up at me from the centre of the large, silk-sheeted bed while swirling a martini from the minibar in her long, narrow fingers. After taking a delicate sip, she laughed.

I always hated the way she laughed.

"I knew that simple little thing wouldn't keep you entertained for very long." Her eyes, dark in the dim light, flashed up at me. "What was her name again? Tree? Pebble?"

I swallowed as I watched Giselle fish the olive from the bottom of her glass with her pinkie. "Her name is River," I whispered.

Giselle's head fell back as she laughed again. "Yes, that was it!" She shook her head in obvious amusement.

"Giselle," I said quickly as I feared I would lose the nerve, "I need to talk to you about why I asked you here tonight."

"Declan, honey," Giselle said after finishing her martini. "I already know why you called me here."

I frowned as she placed her glass on the bedside table and crawled toward me on all fours, licking her tongue seductively over her dark red lips. I flinched when her nails dug into my thighs as they travelled up toward my groin.

"You're tired of playing in the shallow waters," she whispered, her voice low and raspy. "You want to dive back into the depths of a real woman, of a real woman's body."

She was what I wanted, what I thought I wanted. When she left me, I lost everything, I thought I lost everything. I imagined winning her back and it brought me happiness, I thought it would bring me happiness.

But then I met River and I *knew* I was wrong, so terribly wrong.

"You're back on top, Declan," Giselle whispered. "And you know how much I like to be on top."

As she reached for the waistband of my sweatpants, I grabbed her wrist. "Stop."

A flicker of doubt flashed across Giselle's dramatic eyebrows, but it quickly disappeared as she laughed. "Playing hard to get, Declan, darling?" She clicked her tongue again. "That's a dangerous game, love."

I barely saw her reach behind her back for the clasp of her bra, because my vision grew red at the mention of that word. Any word could come from those traitorous lips, any single word in the world. But not *that* word. Never that word.

How dare she? How fucking dare she?

My fingers clenched tightly on the manila folder.

That word was reserved for quiet forest groves in misty mornings. It was saved for sleepy mornings doing nothing but watching the fog roll over the emerald hills. That word was only for sweet, pink lips, kinky, uncontrollable curls, and a laugh, pure and joyful.

"I didn't call you over here tonight because I want to get back with you, Giselle," I said. "I want a divorce."

Giselle paused, her hands alone holding up her bra, and stared up at me in surprise as I tossed the manila folder with the divorce papers on the bed next to her. Her eyes narrowed as she assessed the seriousness in my own. Then she stood and pressed herself up close to me. "Let me show you what you want, Declan, darling," she whispered against my lips.

I stared darkly at her as she pulled the strap of her bra off her shoulder and slowly stepped back, revealing her exposed chest. She grinned as I followed after her till the back of her knees hit the edge of the bed and she fell back. Her long blonde hair spread around her pretty face as she bit her lip, watching me straddle her hips.

"I know exactly what I want, *darling*," I leaned over to whisper into her ear.

Giselle squirmed underneath me and gasped, "Show me, darling."

Lips just an inch from hers, eyes locked on hers, I grabbed the manila folder with the divorce papers and covered her naked tits with them.

"I want a divorce."

Without another word, I pushed myself up and away from her. Without another glance back toward her, I walked out of the bedroom. I only had a few moments of peace, relief, and ecstasy before Giselle came running out after me, waving the divorce papers as she stood in my way, her bra and dress pressed to her chest.

"What does that little nobody give you that an international model, millionaire entrepreneur, and one of *People*'s 100 Most Beautiful can't?" She huffed and puffed and jutted her chin up at me.

Standing my ground, I stared at her, pitying her more than hating her. "Love, *love*," I answered softly.

There was nothing more to say than that. It was love, plain and simple. It was love, quiet and gentle. It was love, pure and delicate. It was love.

Her love.

Giselle spit out a dark laugh and shook her head. I held the hotel door open for her. She slipped her coat over her half-naked body and stalked past me, the rest of her clothes over her arm. I was closing the door when she spun toward me one more time.

"Where is she then?"

The question caught me off guard. "What?"

A smug smile of victory wrenched up the corners of her overdrawn lips as she leaned toward me in the hallway. "If she loves you, Declan, then where is she?" she hissed.

When I had no immediate answer, Giselle shook her head and walked away toward the elevator at the end of the hallway. "I'll be at the fight tomorrow," she called back to me as the doors closed on her. "Will she?"

The hotel door closed with a dull click behind me and I suddenly didn't know where to go, what to do. It was the night before the biggest fight of my life and I just felt numb.

My fingers itched to call River.

To tell her what I wanted to, but didn't, *couldn't* tell her when we said goodbye the night before because I was too afraid.

Because I was too afraid to tell her I needed her.

Declan

After an early workout the morning of the fight, I sat on a bench in the stadium locker room, rubbing at my sore shoulder and trying to ignore the dull thud in my head as I imagined entering the cage that night to face Dominic.

The door to the stadium's locker room burst open, and Danny and Diarmuid strode in with giant grins.

"Who the feck let you two in here?" I asked with a smile as I stood from the bench and embraced each of them in back-thudding hugs.

"We gave the security guard a fifty and a swig of Danny's naggin'," Diarmuid said. "I'd had him flown all the way from Australia where he lived with his missus for this fight."

Danny winked at me as he pulled a silver flask from the inner pocket of his worn black leather motorcycle jacket and tipped it back to his lips.

"Jaysus, Danny, it's 7:30 a.m.," I said with a laugh.

"Relax, Dex. You know I'll share with ye." Danny offered me the flask.

"No, thanks." I pushed the flask back.

Danny raised an eyebrow at me. "Since when did you become a dry shite, old man?"

I snorted. "Since my title is on the line, asshole."

Danny shrugged and took another shot for himself.

"So what's the story?" Diarmuid asked me.

"Well," I started, "I think I'm going to win. I prepared for this fight—"

"Ah, shite on," Danny interrupted. "We're not ESPN, ye big eejit. Tell us about this woman of yours." Danny raised his eyes suggestively up and down.

Diarmuid groaned. "Dex, is there any way to switch my seat, so I don't have to sit next to this eejit for the whole fight?"

Danny laughed and flopped his long arm over Diarmuid's shoulder. "You'll be sittin' next to the sexiest thing in that stadium, you lucky bastard."

Diarmuid snorted as he tried and failed to push him away.

"Go on, Dex." Danny grinned. "Out with it."

I took the towel from around my shoulders and wiped at my still sweaty forehead.

"Lay off, Danny," Diarmuid shoved at him before quickly grabbing him as he nearly toppled off the narrow bench. "You know Dex isn't ready for that again after…" Diarmuid's voice trailed off and I watched as he cleared his throat, ducked his eyes, and awkwardly scratched at the back of his neck.

"Hell, I'm not saying he's got to propose tomorrow or something, but—"

"Danny!"

Danny threw his hands up into the air. "I mean, we didn't think Dex would even date anyone ever again and yet, here we are. Don't tell me you're not dying to know, too."

I held back a grin as best I could as they bantered.

"Just not today," Diarmuid hissed while elbowing Danny in the ribs. "You know that wound hasn't healed and with his fight in just a few hours…"

As Danny shoved back at Diarmuid, I slowly dropped my head and pushed myself off my knees to stand up. It took everything in me to keep my lips in the scowl both of them had become so accustomed to seeing ever since the accident.

"Look what you did, ye feckin' eejit," Diarmuid whispered angrily as I crossed my arms over my chest and made my way around the bench toward my gym bag in the locker.

"Dex," Danny started, "I'm sorry. I didn't mean to upset you. I'll stop talking about it, alright?"

Keeping deathly silent, I unzipped my gym bag and packed up my sneakers, my water bottle, my tape, and ice packs.

"Dex, don't leave," Diarmuid tried next. "You know Danny's just fucking around. Tell us about the fight."

"Yeah, tell us about the fight," Danny added. "We want to know about the fight."

Slipping my hand secretly into a small pocket in the inner lining of my gym bag, I rummaged for the box as I shook my head and grumbled, "I don't want to talk about the fight." My back turned to my two friends, I grinned when my fingers grazed the soft black velvet. As Danny and Diarmuid continued trying to smooth things over, I hid the box in my fist and turned around.

"We know you need to focus," Diarmuid was saying. "So walk us through your strategy."

Danny nodded eagerly. "Yeah, how are you going to take down that fucker, Dex?"

Glaring at each of them, I repeated, "I said, I don't want to talk about the goddamn fight right now."

Diarmuid stood to move toward me. "Dex—"

"I want to talk about this." With an unstoppable grin, I held the tiny black velvet box in front of me and pulled open the lid to reveal a ring.

The night before, after Giselle left, I was so restless with excitement, nervousness, and anticipation that I couldn't sit still. Regardless of my fight the next night and the risk of sleep deprivation, I grabbed my coat, slipped out of the hotel, and strode along the empty streets of Dublin in the early hours of the morning, tracking down jewellery shop after jewellery shop.

Amongst shadows and in the glare of streetlamps, I stood outside window displays lit perfectly to make each and every diamond shimmer and shine. All were beautiful, and none were *River.*

Shoulders slumped forward in defeat and feet weary from my fruitless quest, I began to make my way back to the hotel. But no more than a block away, a dress on display at a small vintage shop caught my eye. I couldn't help but imagine River wearing it, another for her collection of "dancing in the rain dresses."

I almost missed the ring on display beneath it.

It wasn't well lit, it didn't sparkle, and it wasn't surrounded by other expensive jewellery. It was all by itself and the second I laid eyes on it, I knew there was none like it in the world.

It had an intricately carved silver band with an uncut, unpolished emerald, and it was perfectly imperfect.

I waited, pacing back and forth, impatiently glancing again and again at my watch, till the shopkeeper arrived early that morning as the streetlamps in Dublin finally flickered off. I bought it right then and there without hesitation.

Now in the locker room at the stadium, Danny's eyes immediately went wide at the sight of the ring in my palm as he fell off the back of the bench in surprise, banging his head nosily against a locker before trying to scramble to his feet.

Diarmuid's mouth fell open and he lifted a finger toward the ring. "Is that—is that a—a…" He shook his head at his loss of words. "A—"

"A bleedin' engagement ring!" Danny shouted as he scrambled to his feet. He rushed over to me, leaning over to shove his finger at the shining gem. "That right there is a bleedin' *engagement* ring!"

With a boisterous, echoing laugh, Danny turned to a still shocked Diarmuid. "I told ye so. Huh?" He grinned. "Didn't I say so?" Wrapping his long arms around both Diarmuid's and my shoulders, Danny pulled us tight, leaned his head back, and howled, "A feckin' engagement ring!"

Diarmuid squeezed my shoulder and levelled his gaze on me. "This is real?" he asked me, his eyes searching mine.

"Of course it's real." Danny jerked me back and forth in excitement. "It's a feckin' engag—"

"Dex?" Diarmuid interrupted, focusing intently on me.

Looking him square in the eye, I smiled and nodded. "I haven't known love till River loved me. I'm not going to find anything more real than her love. I got Giselle to sign the divorce papers last night," I explained. "And I'm planning to propose to River once I win tonight."

A smile of his own lit up Diarmuid's face as he again squeezed my shoulder. He then clapped his hand on Danny's back.

Danny still beamed from ear to ear.

"I suppose that a congratulation is in order," Diarmuid said.

"More importantly," Danny interjected, holding up his finger, "a bachelor party."

Both Diarmuid and I groaned. Danny laughed and unscrewed the cap of his whiskey.

"To happiness at last," he said, raising the flask before knocking back a shot.

He passed it to Diarmuid, who shrugged and tipped it back himself before adding, "To healing at last."

Diarmuid lifted an eyebrow in the form of a question.

I extended my hand for the flask. It was early enough to not affect me tonight, and if anything was worth celebrating, it was this. I held onto the feel of that delicious burn as I lifted the flask myself. I looked from Danny to Diarmuid and smiled. "To love, at last," I said. "At long, long last."

"To love," Danny and Diarmuid chimed in.

"So…" Diarmuid grinned. "Are we going to get to meet River tonight then?"

My smile faltered at the question. "Umm," I cleared my throat.

"She's not actually here."

"At the stadium?" Danny asked with a frown.

"In Dublin," I admitted.

Diarmuid took a step back and crossed his arms over his chest. "She's not coming to the fight?"

I shook my head. "She doesn't want to be a part of this world," I added.

Danny's frown intensified. "*Your* world, you mean?" he asked. "She said that?"

I shrugged. "Yea—well, no," I corrected when I realised River had never actually said that. "No, she didn't say that."

Diarmuid lifted his eyebrow. "Then why d'ye say that the woman who *loves you*—"

"Clearly, she'd have to to be with ye," Danny teased.

"—doesn't want to be part of your world?" Diarmuid finished.

I looked between the two of them. River hadn't told me. Seamus had. He said she told him…but had she?

I only realised I'd been muttering out loud when Danny spoke.

"So your manager told you that your woman didn't want to be here by your side supportin' ye on what is probably the biggest feckin' fight of yer life, and you believed him? Did ye even ask her if that were true?"

Heaviness descended over my shoulders.

Seamus had been with me for almost a decade of my career. Why would he lie to me?

I ignored the loud, urgent beep of my cell phone still tucked away in my gym bag. My head was still reeling, still trying to process whether someone I trusted had been dishonest with me and why.

Then my phone pinged again. And again.

Danny and Diarmuid's phones each went off, too. Several pings. Leaving us to frown in confusion at one another.

Diarmuid reached into his back pocket to pull out his phone.

Both Danny and I watched him as his eyes scanned the screen.

"Jaysus," he muttered, looking up from his phone. "Dex, you need to see this."

River

To say I'd slept poorly the night before Declan's fight would be one hell of an understatement. Hour after hour till dawn blinked weakly on the horizon, I tossed and turned till my sheets were on the floor, my hair was in tangles, and my mind was so anxious I could no longer remain in bed, despite the exhaustion that tugged at my eyelids.

I thought a hike through the misty morning would help. It

didn't.

I thought a yoga session in the gym might bring me some sense of inner calm. It didn't.

Not even a long, hot shower could cleanse the worried thoughts that clung to me like the dark clouds that seemed to skim the roof of the manor.

My last resort to ease my tumultuous mind really should have been my first…food.

In my fluffiest, warmest slippers and Declan's softest, cosiest sweatshirt, I tiptoed in the dim light of early morning toward the kitchen to busy myself with making a feast of anything and everything: pancakes, French toast, bacon, and eggs.

Hell, I was even committed to slaving over an intricate rustic berry pie that took hours if it meant focusing on something other than Declan and his fight, Declan and Dominic, Declan and me.

But as I turned down the last hallway, I was surprised to find light from the kitchen already spilling across the marble floors bathed in shadows. My eyebrows knitted together in confusion as I approached slowly. When I first heard the hushed voices of Oisin and Joan I was relieved that they were already up this morning; they could distract me for sure. Joan with a mimosa or Bloody Mary or a "hell, who cares that it's 7 a.m., have a whiskey, dear" and Oisin with story after story of Declan's greatest victories as he stirred his homemade oatmeal with lemon zest and blueberries over the stovetop.

That sense of relief quickly soured and contorted into an even more intense level of stress, though, when I got close enough to hear exactly what they were whispering about, huddled close together at the large kitchen island.

"—devastating, it'd be devastating to her," Oisin said in a hushed voice as he tried to pull the newspaper away from Joan. "We have to hide this, at least till after the fight."

I leaned closer to hear Joan after she tugged it back from Oisin.

"She deserves to know. And you know it."

"We don't even know what this is!" Oisin hissed.

Joan scoffed. "Looks pretty obvious to me."

"Joan, we can't assume—"

"Assume what?" I asked.

Both Joan and Oisin jumped before turning around with wide, guilty eyes to find me with arms crossed, leaning against the door frame to the kitchen.

Joan was still wearing her coat, which dripped raindrops onto the floor around her muddy work sneakers as if she hadn't even taken the time to wipe them off at the door.

I lifted an eyebrow at both of them.

Pink coloured the tops of Joan's cheeks, and Oisin not so inconspicuously slipped the newspaper behind his back.

"It's nothing," he lied. Badly.

"It's not exactly 'nothing.'" Joan ducked her eyes.

"Let me see." I strode toward them and held out my open hand, indicating for Oisin to give me the paper and whatever news he wanted to hide from me. I tried to keep my hand from shaking, but even I noticed the tips of my fingers quivering slightly as I waited. "Oisin."

"We can't judge anything from this—"

"Oisin."

"We don't have the whole story right now and—"

"Oisin, give me the paper," I commanded, thankful that my voice didn't crack from the growing lump of concern in my throat.

"You have to give it to her, Chef," Joan whispered, glancing up at Oisin, who still wore his silk sleep mask around his neck.

With a defeated sigh, he rubbed tiredly at his eyes and flopped the rolled-up newspaper, slightly damp from the rain, into my open hand. "This isn't a good idea, my little voodoo queen."

I ignored him as I moved between the two of them and spread the newspaper out on the kitchen island.

After just a single glance at the large pictures that encompassed the majority of the front page, I was already reaching blindly behind me for a bar stool as my knees wobbled and my face paled.

"It's okay, dear," Joan cooed as she guided me to sit down. She rubbed at my back as my head collapsed into my hands.

"River," Oisin said softly as he pulled up another bar stool close to me. "River, baby, you of all people know a photo isn't the whole story. Any good photographer knows it's just a sliver of the whole story and—"

"And what?" I said, emotion obvious in my voice as I looked over at him and jabbed my finger at the photograph of Declan opening his hotel room at the Merrion for none other than his ex, Giselle. "What's the rest of the story here, Oisin? Do you really want me to know what happened once she went inside?"

I fought back tears as I shoved the newspaper away from me. I didn't want to see the headline: *Ireland's Perfect Couple Reunites at Long Last?* I didn't want to read any more of the text than I'd inadvertently read as I skimmed the page:

"It looks like Declan Gallagher wants to win back not just his title, but his wife."

"With River Moore nowhere in sight, does this mean Declan has moved on?"

"Sources close to Giselle reveal he called her as soon as he arrived in Dublin for his big comeback fight saying, 'I can't wait any longer. I need you to come over tonight.'"

I didn't want to see the picture of them together: her in a luxurious black fur coat, heels, red lipstick.

No picture of me looked like that, not even close.

"Confront him," Joan said suddenly from the liquor cabinet across the island. "Get right up in his face and demand the truth."

I blinked back tears as I stared at her.

"That's what you need to do." She pointed a finger at me as she walked over with the coffee pot and a bottle of Baileys. "You need to get to Dublin, confront Declan, and make him tell you what happened, straight to your face." Joan nodded at me as she pushed a cup of mostly Baileys and a little bit of coffee toward me. "That way, he has to be honest," she insisted. "I'll drive you. We'll go right now." Joan immediately started searching her pockets for her keys.

Oisin stretched his hand across me to stop her. "Let's all just take a breath for a second. We can simply call him to clarify this photo. Declan has his fight today and we can't go rushing in there, guns blazing."

"Bollocks we can't," Joan countered. "If he did this to my sweet little River, then he can shove his fight up his hoop. I'll end him before Dominic even has a chance to."

"I'm telling you." Oisin slapped his palm on the island. "This just doesn't sound like Declan. I've known him for years and he just wouldn't do this!"

"Then explain the photo now." Joan jutted her chin toward Oisin.

They began to argue, but I heard less and less of it as I sat numbly on the bar stool and stared at my fingers shaking slightly in my lap. I fidgeted with the loose hem of Declan's sweatshirt as I itched to just take it off.

I didn't want to call Declan. I didn't want to go to Dublin to confront him either.

I wanted to run.

I wanted to leave the manor, packed or not packed; I didn't care. I wanted to get out of here as soon as possible, even if it meant walking along the long gravel pathway in the rain to town. I wanted to book a bus, any bus leaving Kerry, get on it and run, run, run.

Run away from the memories.

Run away from the pain.

Run away from the photograph of him with her, the images in my mind of him with her, the realisation that I never stood a chance, because it was always going to be him with *her*.

As Oisin and Joan continued to fight over what I should do about the photograph in the papers, I pushed my bar stool back from the island and without a word, climbed off of it. Silent with eyes focused on the door, I walked forward with stiff, robotic movements as if my soul itself had left my body.

I was nearly at the door when Oisin called after me, "River, what are you doing?"

I didn't stop.

"Where are you going?" Joan asked.

Squeezing my eyes shut, I sighed and turned around to face them; they deserved at least to know for everything they'd done for me. They deserved to know I was leaving.

Their concerned eyes fell on me as I opened my eyes.

"I'm lea—"

I didn't finish my sentence because just then my cell phone in the pocket of Declan's sweatshirt rang.

"Who is it?"

I stared down at the screen of my phone.

Incoming Call: My fighter

Dammit. I had to change Declan's contact name in my phone. Even better, I had to delete his number. Block it. Smash my phone into pieces.

I looked up from my still vibrating cell phone to find Oisin's and Joan's eyes fixed on me.

"Answer it." Oisin stepped forward, and with gentle hands cupped around my open palm, pushed the phone closer to me.

"No, no." Joan hurried to my side, squeezing my shoulders. "Make him sweat."

Oisin leaned down so his eyes were level with mine. "At least hear him out," he insisted, again urging my cell phone closer.

No part of me in that moment had any desire at all to answer. My ears wanted to hear wild winds and the screech of bus tires outside some stop along some country road, not Declan's voice. My lips wanted to stay sealed as if that could somehow keep the hurt from pouring out of me; I didn't want to open my mouth to utter even a single raspy *hello*. My hands wanted to hold the worn leather handle of my duffel bag or a plane ticket, damp from the pouring rain outside, not my cell phone that vibrated, vibrated, vibrated.

"He'll surprise you," Oisin whispered. "River, let him surprise you."

Those words shouldn't have worked. No words at all should have worked. But despite Joan's exacerbated groan of protest, I found myself, with eyes still locked on Oisin's, lifting my cell phone up, pressing the green "Answer" button, and with shaking fingers holding it to my ear. I opened my mouth, but no words came out.

"River?"

The sound of Declan's voice was pure agony to me, because it filled me with hope. Hope that things could be the way they were when he grabbed my waist in the darkroom, hope that he would once again look at me like he did that sunny morning in his bed, hope that he was somehow still mine. But hope was a nasty bitch. It raised you up just so you could fall…

"Hello? River?" Declan asked again, a slight note of panic in his voice. "Are you there?"

In the background, I heard two more men talking over each other. *"Did she answer?" "Tell her." "Is she there? Dex? Did she answer?" "Call her again; you have to call her again." "Don't stop till she answers. Until you tell her."*

I heard Declan's voice low, hushed, and closer than before to the receiver. "River, please, if you're there," he paused, "please, just hear me out. I can explain everything."

He tried to hide it, but I heard it: he was begging, pleading, praying.

Huddled close to me in the kitchen, Oisin whispered loudly, "What is he saying?"

"You make sure he understands that you're not taking any of his shite," Joan added, jabbing an angry finger toward me. "You tell him right now. You tell him if he hurt you, I'm personally coming to chop off his balls—"

"Joan O'Sullivan!" Oisin chastised.

Again, on the other line, I heard voices prodding Declan, *"What did she say?" "Did you tell her? Dex? Dex, where are you going?"*

Oisin bumped Joan out of the way to move in front of me, his concerned eyes consuming my field of vision.

"What did he say?" he pressed. "Did he explain the picture?"

"Did you tell him about his balls?" Joan interjected.

"River?" Declan's voice was soft as the other voices grew fainter. "Can it just be you and me for a minute? Just you and me."

Without answering, I turned from Oisin and Joan to walk out of the kitchen. They called after me, wanting to know what was going on, but I kept going, leaving them behind. On the line, Declan's echoing footsteps matched mine as I made my way down the dimly lit hallway as long streams of rain created a grey curtain against the tall windows. A door closed on his end and I turned a corner on my end. The voices around both of us faded and died. I think we both understood without putting it into words that it was just the two of us now.

I felt the way I felt when his eyes found mine in the crowd of the red carpet. I breathed deeper the way I did when it was just him and me at the overlook at the top of the hill, our shoulders brushing against one another. A stillness I'd only ever experienced in the first light of morning with Declan's arm around me, his soft exhales warm against my back, washed over me.

I was certain Declan felt the same.

Sagging against the wall, I slid down, pulled my knees tight to my chest, and tucked them under the warm fleece of his faded sweatshirt as I waited.

"River, I know how the photograph looks," he started. "I know what they're writing in the papers about it, about me, about her."

About *them*, I thought. About them reuniting, the perfect love story. About them fitting together. About them moving past their respective rebounds, their distractions, their temporary playthings…

"I want to be honest with you, okay?"

I nodded as if he could see me. I still couldn't manage to speak—I still wasn't sure I even wanted to speak.

"River, I invited Giselle over to my hotel room last night," Declan admitted. "It was me."

Almost before his words were even out of his mouth, I was already biting down on my pointer finger to hold back a devastated sob. I clenched my eyes shut as fresh tears, hot and stinging, slipped down my cheeks.

"I invited her over because I needed her signature."

Opening my eyes, I stared out at the garden in the rain. "What?" I choked out.

It was the first word I'd uttered to him since our goodbye two nights before. It wasn't exactly Shakespearean, let alone even poetic in the slightest, but for some unknown reason, Declan acted like that single word rivalled the entirety of Sonnet 18 after a prolonged moment of silence.

"Hi," he whispered, his voice heavy with emotion.

I could almost hear the tears in his eyes, the tightness in his throat, the relieved weight in his heart.

Swallowing and leaning my head back against the wall to stare up at the intricately carved ceiling, I sighed. "Hi."

Declan laughed softly. "It's ridiculous how much I love the sound of your voice," he said. "It's completely bonkers how much I wake up every morning longing for you just to open your mouth, to say anything, to say everything. It's mental how much I missed it the moment I left your bedroom the other night. It makes no sense, no sense at all."

I held my cell phone to my ear with quivering fingers. I wasn't sure if I was shaking because of fear of what Declan would say next or hope for what he might say.

"It makes no sense at all why you would love me the way you do, River," Declan continued. "It makes no sense at all."

"Declan…" I whispered softly in the empty grey hallway.

"But I realised yesterday that I want it, I need it," he said. "I need that improbable, irrational, ridiculous love."

I waited, listening, yearning.

"I realised yesterday that I need you, River."

Tears streamed down my cheeks, but this time a smile tugging at the corners of my lips accompanied them.

"So I called Giselle over to finally have her sign the divorce papers," he explained. "I've had them for a long time, but I'd never had a reason to let go. I thought my victory in the cage would finally be the reason, but it's you. River, you're my reason."

I laughed a laugh of pure joy, happiness, elation.

"I'm ready to have a new life, a new start with you," he said. "You're all I need. I'm ready. I'm finally ready to be free. Free with you. Free *because* of you."

My heart pounded when I pondered what he could mean by that—a new life…a new start…could he mean…?

"So you're coming back?" I asked despite the lingering fear for his answer.

"Of course!" He laughed. "You're the only place I want to be."

I smiled. "This afternoon then?" I asked.

There was pause on the line. "What's that?"

"This afternoon," I repeated. "Would the jet be ready to bring you home this afternoon?"

Another pause renewed the anxiousness that made my fingers fidget.

"River, I still have the fight," he said slowly.

I frowned. "Oh, I thought you said—"

"I have to win," he interjected. "I have to win and then I'm coming home. Once I win we can be together, truly be together."

I silently ran his words over and over in my mind as the rain fell and fell.

"River? Baby?"

Realising I hadn't said anything for a while, I smiled and laughed softly. "Right, right, of course," I said quickly. "I'll be watching, baby."

"I love you," Declan whispered.

I squeezed my eyes shut. "I love you, too."

We hung up, but I couldn't quite find the energy yet to stand. The same thought kept me frozen where I sat, shivering on the cold, hard floor, alone:

If all he needed was me, then why did he need to win?

River

In the manor's theatre room, I was watching the pre-fight press coverage with Oisin and Joan, who thankfully was no longer gunning for Declan's balls after I explained the misunderstanding and told her what he had hinted at. My phone rang again.

Handing the bowl of popcorn smothered with homemade salted caramel sauce to Oisin, I fished my cell phone out of my hoodie, fully expecting it to be another call from Declan.

I frowned. It wasn't Declan, but Niall.

Joan reached for the controller to turn down the volume on the reporter at the stadium in Dublin as I answered.

"Um, Niall, hi," I said.

Oisin lifted his eyebrow in surprise of his own as he stared at me.

"How are you?" I asked.

"River, I have to tell you something."

The serious, urgent, worried tone in Niall's voice immediately made me sit up and return my wine glass to the chair's arm rest cup holder. "What's wrong?" I asked, trying not to let my voice sound the exact same way.

On the line, Niall sighed and the longer he waited to speak, the harder and harder my heart thudded in my chest.

"Niall?" I couldn't wait any longer; I couldn't. "Niall, is it Declan? Is he okay?"

"Yes, yes," Niall immediately answered. "Well, no. I mean, right now he's all right. But—"

"But *what*?"

"Shite," Niall said, "Declan's going to murder me for this, but I thought you needed to know, or at least, that you deserved to know."

I narrowed my eyes, suddenly adding suspicion to my anxiousness. "Know what, Niall?" I asked slowly.

Oisin turned in his chair at the tone of my voice.

I glanced over at him as the silence on the line grew longer and longer. "Niall?"

There was another pause. Then I heard him sigh. "Look, River, I'm still on Declan's doctor's notification list. I guess in all the preparation for the fight, Seamus forgot to take me off of it when Declan fired me or something. Or, I don't know, maybe it takes a few days for those requests to go through and—"

"Niall," I interrupted, unable to take the drawn-out uncertainty any longer. "Why are you telling me this?"

"Because I know about Declan's concussion a few weeks back and, like I said, I think it's fair you do, too," Niall said.

Relief flooded my body as I sagged into the chair, running a hand over my face. "I already know about it," I said. "He got a concussion from sparring with a new partner. I was at the hospital when they released him."

I heard Niall mutter "shite", and it was clear I wasn't intended to hear it.

"The doctor said he was fine," I continued, frowning in confusion.

"Is that what the doctor said or Declan?" Niall asked.

"The doc—" I paused as I recalled the moment I rushed into the hospital room, tears already in my eyes. I fell into Declan's arms and…

"River, despite whatever Declan told you, he's not fine," Niall said.

Any sense of relief disappeared as my body tensed, as if about to receive a physical punch to the gut. "What do you mean?" I whispered.

"When he was admitted, they performed a CT scan and—"

"I don't know what any of that is," I interrupted in frustration. Frustration and fear. "Just tell me what it means." I could sense Niall's hesitation as my palms grew slick with sweat, my cell phone suddenly slippery in my shaky grip.

"It means that because of the trauma from his past fights and the accident, if Declan takes another hit to the head there's a high possibility it could result in serious brain damage…" Niall paused. "Or…death."

The blood in my veins ran cold as I hung up immediately, barely even aware of what I was doing as my fingers fumbled to dial Declan's number. I could hardly hear Joan and Oisin's concerned prodding from the rush of blood in my ears. My foot tapped impatiently as the time between each ring stretched into an infinity after infinity.

"Fuck," I groaned when I reached Declan's voicemail. "Fuck, fuck, fuck." I didn't bother with leaving a message. "How long till the fight starts?" I asked Oisin as my numb brain tried to find the contacts on my phone to call Seamus.

"Baby girl, what's wrong?" Oisin asked, gently touching my arm.

"Just tell me how long!" I snapped, panic flooding my voice.

"About three hours now," Joan answered for him as I lifted the phone to my ear.

My prayers grew more and more desperate as each ring passed. "Please, please, please," I whispered, clenching my eyes shut to avoid seeing Dominic's deranged eyes at his pre-fight press conference on the screen in front of me. "Please pick up."

"River, what's going on?" Joan asked, leaning forward in her reclining chair. "Riv—"

"Seamus!" I shouted the second I heard him pick up. "Seamus, I have to talk to Declan."

"River?" Seamus asked over the pounding of heavy rock in the background.

"Yeah, yeah, it's me," I said. "Seamus, is Declan there? I really need to talk to Declan before—"

"Bummer you're not here, River," Seamus interrupted. "The fight is going to be spectacular."

"Okay, but that's why I'm call—"

"Hey, did you post to his social this morning?" Seamus interrupted me yet again. "We really want to make sure we're engaging fans all throughout today. It's crucial you link everything to his merch site, yeah?"

I grinded my teeth in frustration and pinched the bridge of my nose. "Seamus, I don't give a fuck about selling some goddamn t-shirts!" I shouted. "Niall just called me and—"

"What? Who?"

"Niall," I repeated. "He said—"

"He said exactly what the doctor said to Declan, sweetheart." Seamus spoke to me as if I was a five-year-old and it caught me off guard.

I glanced at my cell phone in confusion before pulling it back to my ear. "But—"

"You didn't think Declan knew?" Seamus asked, his voice dripping with condescension, each word coated with poison.

I hated him in that moment. I hated even more the fact I couldn't avoid…he wasn't lying.

Still, I fought against it, because it was all I could do.

"If he knew, he wouldn't fight," I whispered, sounding uncertain even to myself.

Seamus's laugh was cruel, cruel like kicking a helpless, wounded dog. "Because of you?" He chuckled darkly. "Because of his undying love for some vagabond assistant?"

I stared numbly at my fingers in my lap. They were useless. Declan was out of reach. Perhaps he would always be out of reach. Perhaps he had never truly been in reach of my touch.

"Listen, girl," Seamus hissed. "Declan Gallagher is a fighter. He is going to fight no matter the risk, because it's all he knows."

It isn't, I protested weakly in my head. He knows my finger tracing little circles on his palm as we lay together in bed. He knows the sound of my footsteps by his side as we hike through the forest outside the manor. He knows my love.

He must know my love.

"It's just a stupid title," I muttered, already feeling defeat creep in like a heavy fog in the night to hide the path I thought I knew by heart. "It's not worth it."

Seamus paused. "To him, it's worth everything."

These words brought the sting of tears to my eyes and I refused to believe them. They couldn't be true. Because if the title was everything—that meant I was nothing.

I'd been nothing my whole life.

"Just let me talk to him," I pleaded as my one last dying gasp. "Please, Seamus, just—"

"Who's that?" I heard Declan's voice suddenly in the background, a swift wind to sweep away the fog.

I was shouting Declan's name when the line went dead. "Declan?" I cried out. "Declan?" Even after checking the screen and seeing with my own two eyes the "Call Ended" message, I still shouted his name again as I pushed myself hastily out of the chair. "Declan? Declan! Fuck!"

Slamming my phone to the plush carpet in the theatre room with a whimper, I covered my face with my hands as hot tears of frustration and pain streamed down my cheeks.

Joan and Oisin were at my side, arms trying and failing to wrap me into a tight hug as I squirmed away.

Pacing in front of the large screen that now displayed footage from Declan's old fights, I shook my head. "I'm helpless," I said as I tugged at my hair. "I'm helpless, always fucking helpless."

"River?" Joan reached for me, but her hand fell limply to her side when I marched past her.

I couldn't stay still. Not now.

"I thought I was done being helpless. With Declan I felt…" I laughed after my voice trailed off. "Who was I kidding? Who was I fucking kidding?"

As I spun on my heel to impatiently march the other direction across the screen, Oisin suddenly grabbed my shoulders, stopping me in my tracks. "Now listen here…" He pointed a finger at me. "You're helpless only when you don't have fabulous friends—say, one with impeccable style and one who could lay off the gin—"

"Hey!" Joan protested behind me.

"Who will do anything in the world for you," Oisin finished. He levelled his eyes intently on mine. "Let us help you, my little voodoo queen."

Fresh tears sprang to my eyes as I collapsed into Oisin's outstretched arms. "You don't understand!" I sobbed, sniffling against his silk robe that was indeed rather impeccable. "He wasn't cleared from his last concussion. They fudged the doctor's certificate somehow. If Declan fights tonight, he could…"

I couldn't bear to utter the word.

Oisin gasped.

Joan cursed.

"I need to get to him, but he won't answer and Seamus won't let me talk to him and there's no other way I know how to—"

"I'll get the keys," Joan interrupted.

Cheek still against Oisin's chest, I blinked slowly in confusion and craned my neck to stare back at her. "Huh?"

"I'll get my driving loafers," Oisin said next.

"Huh?" I asked again.

Joan was ignoring my raised eyebrow as she looked over me at Oisin. "But how are we going to get her in?" she asked him.

"In where?" I asked, still not comprehending.

"No bother, darling." Oisin winked at Joan.

Why was nobody answering my very reasonable questions? Had I become invisible all of a fucking sudden?

"No bother?" Joan smirked.

A tiny grin tugged at the corner of Oisin's lips as he casually assessed the cuticles on his right hand. "I may have made a certain stadium head event planner a pancake or two back in the day."

I frowned. "Stadium?"

"Then it's settled?" Joan asked Oisin, both still ignoring me.

"What's settled?!" I stomped my foot in protest as I glared first at Oisin, then Joan for answers.

Joan bumped into me as she hurried past.

"Hello?" I shouted. "Anyone?"

Joan paused at the door and snapped her fingers. "Yes, yes, of course!" She leaned back inside the theatre room.

Finally, some answers!

"River, dear, bring that popcorn for snacks, won't you?"

I shook my head, dumbfounded. "Snacks?"

Oisin grinned at me. "We're going on a road trip."

Declan

The concrete floors beneath my feet shook as the roar of the crowd rattled the set of double doors in front of me. Two security guards, each with a beefy hand on one of the handles, nodded toward me after I heard an inaudible crackle from the radios clipped on their belts.

Next to me, Seamus gripped my shoulder with flashing eyes and a blood-hungry grin. "Ready?" he asked.

No.

"Open the doors," I commanded the security guards, my voice a low growl.

I blinked against the blinding spotlight that followed my every step out of the locker room. In front of me, lights swept back and forth along a wild, cheering crowd on either side of the narrow aisle. Outstretched arms and pounding fists and hands cupped over screaming mouths pushed back against metal barriers as two rows of security guards attempted to keep everyone back.

But it was like trying to hold back the sea itself. As I walked toward the cage, illuminated in the centre of the arena like a lighthouse in the dark, I found my chest tightening and my breath escaping my parched lips in desperate pants.

There were too many people; they were too close. I needed room. I needed air.

I needed River.

I stepped toward the cage, toward that glowing beacon in the storm, and I knew the closer I drew to it, the closer I drew to the rocky cliffside that would break my bones, rip me apart and leave me to drown in murky waters. But still I went to it, drawn in as if by some siren's spell. I went toward the pain. I went toward the agony. I went toward the suffering.

Because I deserved it.

The stadium roared with my name as the announcer with a stretched out, booming voice shouted, "Get to your feet, ladies and gentlemen, for the long-awaited return of Declan 'The

Homewrecker' Gallagher!"

I didn't hear my fans. I didn't hear the calls of encouragement. I didn't hear the applause, the cheering, the echoing chant of my name again and again as I approached the cage.

I heard my father.

"You deserve that black eye, you little shit."

I heard the crack of his knuckles against my cheekbone.

"You bleedin' deserve it, d'ye hear me?"

I heard my mother's cries when he didn't stop. I heard them fading away as black specks covered my vision. I heard my head hit the floor and then my father's voice before it all went silent.

"He shouldn't have gotten in my way."

"Declan! Declan! Declan!"

It wasn't the crowd.

It was my doctor. *"Declan, you shouldn't step back into that cage. You could get seriously injured if you do. Even killed."*

"He deserves it," my father sneered in my head.

"Declan!"

It wasn't the young kid to my right, waving a poster he made to support me. It was Niall. *"Declan, you're pushing yourself too hard. You'll hurt yourself."*

"He deserves it," my father scoffed. *"He deserves nothing but pain."* I

could hear his slurred voice, feel the heat of his whiskey-stenched breath on my ear as if he was standing right there.

"Declan!"

It wasn't a fan who shouted my name with a bloodthirsty grin as I stepped up to the cage.

It was River. *"Declan, you don't have to fight."*

As I gripped the cage door with sweat-slick fingers, I couldn't escape my father's spitting laugh, harsh and grating against my ears despite the deafening roar of the crowd.

"Stop fighting?" my father hissed. *"You're worthless without it. Nothing without it. How else are you supposed to deserve her love?"*

The memory of my father leaned against the mesh side of the cage as I opened the door and stepped inside for the first time in almost a year as the stadium rose to its feet around me.

"Prove to her you're not weak," he shouted after me.

I tried to ignore the sound in my head of him shaking the cage behind me as Dominic's name was announced. He wasn't there. He wasn't here.

"Just like I taught you, my boy," my father called out behind me. *"Kill him. Kill that fucker who stole everything from you and you'll finally earn my love, son."*

I shook my head, frozen against the side of the cage, as not one but two opponents stepped inside to face me.

There was Dominic, teeth gnashing and mouth foaming like a rabid junkyard dog chained up to some rusted metal post. He stalked back and forth in front of me, shouting profanities the noise of the stadium drowned out as he flexed and jutted out his beefy, scarred chin.

He didn't scare me.

It was the little boy beside him that sent ice through my veins.

A tangle of dark auburn hair flopped over one of his piercing blue eyes, swollen and ringed in purple and green and black. His lip was busted and he tenderly held his left arm that hung lower than his right. He stared at me and I stared at him, two sides of one mirror, as the referee stepped between Dominic and me. I barely listened to him outlining the rules I knew by heart and reiterating the need for a clean, respectful fight that night. Dominic sneered at me, but I only had eyes for the little boy.

He was my real opponent.

He was the one I needed to kill. He was the one I needed to defeat to finally earn love. From my father. From River. He was weak, pathetic, helpless. He deserved to be beaten, to be abandoned, to be left alone with his mother dying in his arms as his tears ran down her cold cheeks.

I would become the fighter I was meant to be. I would embrace the only identity I knew. I would fight for River's love.

I would win.

Dominic was staring at me in confusion as the referee instructed us to shake hands before the fight began. Up until that point, I'd been petrified. I'd stood there unmoving, shaking like a frightened little boy in front of the schoolyard bully. My eyes hadn't even dared to meet Dominic's as I quivered at the sound of my father's voice, at the haunting blue eyes of my pitiful past self. My shoulders had been slumped forward, my chin tucked low to my chest like all I desired was to curl into a ball of defeat at Dominic's feet right there on the floor of the cage.

But as I realised who I was truly fighting and why, I came alive. A devilish smirk played at my lips as Dominic stretched out his hand for mine and I grinned when his hand flinched back slightly. Standing straight so we were eye to eye, I grabbed his hand and pulled him in tight to slap my hand against his back in what would look to everyone, including the referee, as a friendly embrace.

But as I held him, I whispered in his ear, "You have no idea who you're about to fight, boy. No fucking clue."

I caught the mix of confusion and delicious, delicious fear in his wide, stupid eyes as I stepped back and turned around to raise my arms to the crowd.

If I had thought it couldn't get any louder than before in the already rocking stadium, I was wrong as the volume rose to ear-bleeding levels around me. As I bounced lightly, swiftly from foot to foot and pumped my arms, the crowd erupted—this was the fighter they knew, the fighter they wanted. This was Declan "The Homewrecker" Gallagher they expected, out for revenge, out for justice, out for his title.

They wanted blood and I was going to give it to them.

I shook the side of the cage in front of each section of the stands and even found a camera to send a cocky, bold smirk. I shouldered past Dominic, whose face reddened in anger.

Good. I wanted it to at least be a challenge.

"Alright, gentlemen, alright, alright," the referee shouted as I took my place across from Dominic, who shoved at my chest. I saw pure rage in his eyes when I laughed.

"Gentlemen, let's save it for the fight, shall we?" The referee, wedged between us and holding out his arms to keep us separated, glanced over his shoulder and checked with the film producer to make sure the on-demand viewers were all ready with the near certain flood of viewers trying to order last minute.

I could see the VIP boxes past Dominic where I knew Danny and Diarmuid and their wives were watching. A pang of regret shot through my chest as I wished River was up there with them, but I shoved the thought aside. I could win without her here. I could show her I was strong enough. I could prove I was worthy of her love.

The referee stepped from between Dominic and me, wishing us both good luck. The bell dinged as even more frantic cheering flooded over the cage hitting me in the chest like a crashing wave. Whereas before the enormity of the crowd made me feel small and unworthy and undeserving—it now fuelled the anger in my blood and fire in my soul.

I slipped my mouth guard between my teeth and flexed my fingers as Dominic lowered into his stance. I danced from foot to foot as I waited for his first attack, relishing the doubt that coloured his narrowed eyes.

When he led with a half-hearted jab at my chin, I easily feigned and blocked his normally deadly uppercut. Catching him off guard, I landed a bone-rattling hook to his jaw. Dominic stumbled to the floor as the crowd roared and I turned and raised my hands to the stands, knowing full well Dominic couldn't resist attacking while my back was turned.

He, of course, tried a push kick to my torso, and all I had to do was watch the faces of the front row to time my move perfectly. At the last minute, I twisted to the side, grabbed Dominic's leg mid-kick, and yanked it up, sending him crashing to the floor. He expected me to fall on him and deliver a series of punches to his face till his nose ran red, and I knew this.

With just the tiniest flinch, Dominic shielded his face, but I didn't attack. Instead, I let the crowd break out in laughter and boos at the sight of him cowering on the floor. I circled the cage as I waited for Dominic to rise to his feet.

It wasn't a smart move to let my opponent stick around when I could finish him off. But I wasn't ready for this moment to be over. I was getting everything I wanted—revenge on Dominic, my title, and River.

"Giselle wanted to wish you good luck last night," Dominic smirked as he pushed himself to his feet and stalked toward me, "but her lips were busy with my cock."

Before River, this would have gotten to me. His words would have wormed their way under my skin, making me squirm and tear at my flesh. The way he licked his mouth while grinning across the cage at me would have made me lose all self-control and fly off into an uncontrollable fit of anger. The image he painted unwillingly in my mind would have blinded my vision with flashes of the brightest red, leaving me vulnerable to the brutality of Dominic's fist.

But in that moment, his words rolled off me like rain off the roof of the manor. Instead of imagining Dominic and Giselle, I imagined River and me, legs intertwined beneath the covers, holding each other tight and falling asleep to the rhythm of the steady patter against the window panes. Instead of losing control, his taunting reminded me just what, just *who* I was fighting for.

Dominic reddened in frustration when he saw that his lame attempt to throw me off my game failed entirely. His next few attacks were desperate ones, wild, uncontrolled, swinging punches, and it was child's play to land a jab to his nose, drawing a stream of blood.

Soon enough I lost myself in the rhythm of the fight, and as the final seconds of the first round wound down, Dominic had barely landed a solid blow. My right eye was swelling slightly, but it was nothing compared to the black and blue mess of Dominic's face.

Everything was perfect in that moment; it was going exactly how I had hoped. I was leaving behind my weakness, my unworthiness, my helplessness, and it felt fucking *good.* I was going to put a ring on River's finger and she would say "yes" because I won, right now.

I was in my fighting trance and it seemed like nothing could stop me, nothing at all.

Until I heard, like an arrow slicing impossibly through the head of a needle, her voice.

"Declan!"

River

In the middle of the aisle just ten feet from the cage where Declan and Dominic fought, two massive security guards with arms the size of tree trunks held me back with unperturbed glares as I kicked, punched, and pushed against them with everything I had.

Being miles and miles away from the man I loved hurt, but a few mere feet?

That was agony.

I'd come all this way with Joan and Oisin's help and I couldn't reach him… I just couldn't reach him.

"I have to get to him," I shouted at the security guards above me as I shoved at their bulging chests. "Please, I have to get to him!"

They couldn't hear me…they just couldn't hear me.

With eyes wide with fear, I caught sight of Declan and clenched my eyes shut as Dominic's fist raced toward him. I couldn't lose him—I just couldn't lose him.

Not like this.

I panted from the effort of fighting against the security guards who I hadn't even managed to force back an inch. Panic coursed through my veins at the realisation that I couldn't get past them. If I didn't get to Declan and I didn't tell him what I needed to tell him and he got hurt…

I couldn't live with myself, I just couldn't.

The dark stadium shook around me as the stands rattled and the cheers of the crowd pounded against my eardrum and I couldn't even hear my own voice, but the moment I called out to him in one last desperate gasp, I knew.

"Declan!"

I knew he heard.

As I pushed myself between the shoulders of the two security guards still easily holding me back, I watched in amazement as

Declan's head immediately turned toward me. But my relieved smile immediately turned into a scream of horror as Dominic took advantage of Declan's distraction and landed a punch to his ribs just as the bell announcing the end of the round echoed throughout the stadium. I covered my mouth in horror as Declan sagged against the side of the cage as the referee forced a cursing Dominic away even while his fists still swung and clawed like a rabid animal.

"Declan!" I called again, stretching out an arm for him.

I needed to reach him, finally, *finally* reach him. I needed to hold him. I needed to get him away from here.

His eyes, wide in surprise, met mine, and I was suddenly tumbling forward as the security guards each shifted to the side after a simple nod from Declan. My fingers grazed the concrete floor of the aisle and I quickly pushed myself up to race toward the cage.

Declan kneeled as I came crashing in. The wall of the cage vibrated as if with electricity as I pushed myself as tightly as I could against it. Even the fine plastic-coated metal separating us, no wider than the tip of my pinkie, was too much.

"Declan." I gasped his name as if it were my first breath of precious air after being submerged in dark, churning, rock-riddled rapids for days, weeks, even. Through the side of the cage, Declan brushed his finger along my cheek as I leaned into his touch.

"Baby, what are you doing here?" Declan whispered as his finger lifted my chin.

I bit back tears at the swelling around his right eye and reached out a hand to gently run my thumb along the blossoming purples and blues. I never again wanted him to feel pain. I wanted him to feel sunshine, cool breezes, and sand between his toes—and my love. Above all else, I wanted him to feel my love.

"River?" Declan prodded.

Looking into those piercing blue eyes, I pressed myself as close to him as the mesh of the cage would allow. "Let's go home," I whispered.

The noise of the stadium thundered around us, but I knew he heard me. His eyes searched mine and I knew in them there was a plea greater than I could ever find the words to express.

"Please," I begged. "Declan, let's go—"

"Declan, wrap it up," Seamus suddenly interrupted. His eyes burned with anger at the sight of me as he pointed emphatically toward the referee, who indicated to both Declan and Dominic that the second round would begin in one more minute. "Remember what you're here for," Seamus barked.

Declan glanced toward a display just to the left of the cage in front of the judge's table holding an oversized gold and silver encrusted belt. When he looked back at me, I saw it reflected back at me in his dark pupils.

"River, I don't understand what you mea—"

"Declan, I know about your prognosis," I said hurriedly as Dominic pounded his gloves together on the opposite side of the cage.

I could feel the rush of the clock counting down the seconds I had left to save the man I loved. It was a ticking time bomb I didn't know how to defuse. I was racing the clock—and I was losing.

"What?" Declan asked, shaking his head and pulling away slightly from me as he fell back on his heels.

I tried to close the distance he made between us, but the cage would not let me, no matter how hard I tried. "You can't fight," I said. "Please, baby, please, don't fight. I don't want you to fight. I want you to come be safe in my arms. Please."

His brows were furled in confusion as he continued to shake his head, as if he couldn't quite believe what he was hearing. "River, I'm winning," he said, his tone defensive like his posture. "I'm going to be just fine. In the first round, I dominated Dominic. It wasn't even a challenge. I'm win—"

"Are you?"

"What?" Declan said, clearly taken aback.

I pressed my palms against the mesh and silently begged him to do the same, but he remained still as he assessed me through the cage. "Declan, you've already won," I whispered. "Please, come home."

His eyes darted to mine and I could see the indecision deep within those blue seas. I was reaching him. I couldn't touch him, but I was reaching him. I could see it.

He'd listen to me.

He'd step out of the cage.

He'd leave the title behind.

He'd be safe.

He'd be *loved.*

I just had to push a little further… I just had to try a little harder… I just had to reach a little farther…

"Declan, you'll lose everything if you fight," I said.

I meant those words to be a gentle, guiding light, but I could see immediately that they were a violent strike of lightning.

The moment they fell from my lips, unheard to anyone, Declan jerked back as if I struck him. "Everything?" he asked, his voice so soft I could barely hear him. "Everything?"

"Declan, I—"

"Everything?"

I flinched as his tone grew louder, harsher, *angrier.*

I glanced over my shoulder at the two security guards watching me before turning back to Declan who was breathing heavily to the point of panting. "Declan, please—"

"Everything?" he roared. "I have nothing!"

It was my turn to step back in shock. "Declan, what do you mean?"

"Without my title I have nothing," he said, pupils wide, cheeks flushed. "Without my title I don't have fame. Without my title, I don't have money. Without it I don't have success."

I shook my head, "Baby, I don't—"

"Without my title," he interrupted before pausing and hanging his head between his arms which quivered as he gripped the mesh of the cage with a white-knuckle grip. "Without my title I don't have a single reason for you to stay, for you to be with me, for you to ever lov—"

His voice trailed off as I stared at him in horror.

"I don't deserve you, River," he whispered.

I stared mutely at him. I swallowed heavily to fight back the emotion that caught in my throat. "Declan, why would I want a silly, shiny belt when I already have your strong arms around me at night?"

He kept his head bowed as I sucked in a shaky breath.

"Why would I want fancy shoes when all I want is to be barefoot in the wild grasses with you?" I reached out, interlaced my fingers with his through the cage, and leaned close so my lips grazed the mesh. "I don't want the world, Declan," I whispered, "I just want you."

"River…" He squeezed my fingers through the mesh of the cage wall. "I'm fighting *for* you."

"Don't," I said, softly but firmly. "Declan, if you have to fight, fight *with* me, not *for* me."

I smiled when he lifted his head just enough for me to see his raised eyebrow.

"We'll fight about what flowers to plant in the backyard if you want to fight," I continued.

I grinned when I noticed the intensity of his gaze soften.

"I'll fight with you over the acceptable volume to play Whitney in the morning."

This earned a small chuckle. I moved in closer.

"We'll fight about everything, alright?" I promised. "Oisin's best dish, the colour of the walls in the foyer, how many chickens we can keep, the hiking path we take each morning, the names of our children one day…"

Declan's eyes met mine.

I pressed my palm against the mess of the cage, fingers reaching for him. "Come fight with me, Declan," I whispered.

I watched the struggle play out in his eyes. I knew his past; I knew how difficult this was for him to let go of. But I also believed he knew I loved him and that I would catch him when he fell. It took everything in my power to hold back a sigh of relief as Declan lifted his hand to me.

"Time out's over, Gallagher," the referee called behind him. "We fighting or what?"

Declan's eyes again met mine as he dropped his hand. "I…can't," he said simply.

Who knew it took only two tiny, little words to break a human heart? I stared at him from across the barrier between us. Despite the bruising and swelling around his right eye, he did, in fact, look fine, perfectly healthy. And yet, in that moment, it seemed to me as if I'd already lost him.

With a shaking voice, I said, "Neither can I."

I couldn't watch him risk his life for a silly title.

I couldn't stand by as he hurt himself in my name.

I couldn't be with a man who didn't trust my love was enough.

I wanted to say goodbye. I wanted to tell him what he'd meant to me. I wanted to utter the three words I knew he didn't believe. But my throat was tight and I couldn't.

So without another word, I dropped my hands from the cage, from Declan's cage, and turned around.

Declan

Just moments before, she seemed to hear the softest whisper from my lips, the faintest pulse from my heart, the tiniest flutter of my eyelashes as I stared deep into those sweet almond eyes.

But as I called out to her as she turned, it was as if no sound came out at all. Her head did not flinch toward me, her shoulders did not make even the slightest turn, her footsteps did not pause, did not hesitate, did not slow.

"River!"

I screamed at the top of my lungs, but I might as well have been shouting her name deep underwater the way the noise of the crowd swallowed it whole mere inches from my lips. I clutched at my throat as if she'd stolen my vocal cords and dragged them behind her across the concrete floor as she disappeared into the sea of fans hurrying back to their seats for the start of the second round.

"River!" I tried again.

If I could have heard myself, I would have heard panic. If I could have heard myself, I would have heard pain. If I could have heard myself, I would have heard anger.

But I couldn't hear a goddamn thing.

I sure as hell could feel it, though.

Still kneeling at the edge of the cage, I rattled the mesh and pounded my fists violently against it, startling some fans in the first few rows like some wild beast at the zoo. To me the cage had always been a place of freedom. When I was fighting, I barely saw it surrounding me.

But in that moment as I shouted for River till my throat grew sore and my lungs burned, the cage was my prison. And yet that wasn't what made my blood boil with rage and my old scars burn with fury.

It was the fact that I was in a fucking prison I could get up and walk straight out of if I wanted to.

I pushed myself to my feet. I could step out of the cage, my cage. I could run after River.

But I didn't want to.

I wanted to stay. I wanted to fight. I wanted to *win*.

I wanted to show her she was wrong. I wanted to show her I needed this title. To show her this was who I was, who I am, who I always would be: a fighter.

"Gallagher, time's up," the referee said behind me.

I whirled around, face hot, fists clenched. "Just give me a goddamn minute!" I shouted.

As the referee fell back on his heel and lifted his hands in front of him at the sight of me, I noticed the judges' table just past him. My eyes fell again on the belt displayed there for all to see.

The referee braved a step toward me and said as I continued to stare at the belt, "Look, Gallagher, we have millions of people watching who paid a shit ton of money. We have to sta—"

"What's that thing made of?" I interrupted, eyes transfixed over his shoulder.

The referee frowned and followed the path of my intense gaze. "What? The belt?" he asked. "Gallagher, stop fucking around."

"What's it made of?" I repeated.

"Um, I—I don't know?" The referee moved to grab my arm, but I tugged it away. "Gallagher, I'm going to have to start deducting points if you—"

"Just tell me what the fuck it's made out of!" I shouted.

"Let's go, Gallagher!" Dominic bellowed from the other side of the cage.

My mind whirled and I couldn't look away from the belt.

Plastic? Was it made of goddamn plastic? Aluminium? Gold? Fucking platinum?

I tugged at my hair as I tried to remember what it felt like holding that belt after one of my victories, after any of my victories. I dug through the deepest corners of my mind and for the life of me couldn't remember what it felt like to lift that stupid thing over my head as a stadium of faceless spectators chanted my name.

But I could remember what River felt like. Closing my eyes, I could feel her in my arms as if she was physically there. I could imagine the softness of her breath against my neck, the whisper of her kisses along my collarbone, the heat of her body on mine as we made love.

I tried to remember how I felt winning the title, but there was only an emptiness. A loneliness. A darkness.

With River, there was fullness. Her laugh filled a room, her music filled the manor, her smile filled my vision till it was all I could see, even when I closed my eyes. With her, there was closeness: her chair close to mine on the balcony, her footsteps close to mine on the hiking trail, her fingers close to mine when I thought no one could reach me, when I thought no one would ever try. With her, there was light, beautiful, pure, unending light. The rain may fall and the bad memories may cascade like sleet and the old scars may sting like the howling wind on the darkest of nights, but with River—there was always light.

I'd done nothing at all to deserve it.

I'd earned none of it.

And now I wanted to throw all of that away for a hollow piece of plastic and a deafening roar from the darkness surrounding me that would soon fade and die, leaving me again alone, empty, and still inside my cage.

I looked around the stadium and realised I wanted none of it, I needed none of it. Without a word to either the referee or Dominic, who were both staring at me in bewilderment, I turned toward the door of the cage.

I was ready to be free.

"Where the fuck are you going?" Dominic shouted after me.

I ignored him.

"Gallagher, we're starting in thirty seconds," the referee added. "Whether you're ready or not."

I ignored him, too.

"Fight me!" Dominic screeched. "Goddamn it, come back and fight me!"

Anger dominated his voice, but I heard something else there, too…fear. I knew that feeling all too well and for a moment, I actually felt bad for Dominic. Fighting was his life, his everything, and I was taking it away from him. A title meant nothing if the other fighter forfeited, and what was he without a title?

"What is that pretty little thing of yours going to think if you walk out?" Dominic called, growing desperate as I pushed open the cage door. "Aren't you going to fight for her?"

No, I thought with a grin. No, I wasn't.

I didn't have to.

Just as I was about to step down the stairs to run toward River, Seamus blocked my path. The colour of his face burned a brighter red than even his fiery beard as he jabbed a vicious finger into my chest, forcing me backwards. "Don't you fucking dare!" he hissed. "Don't you dare fuck this up for me over some bitch."

Narrowing my eyes, I stared down at him. "For *you*, Seamus?" I asked darkly.

"Goddamn right, for me," he said, practically shaking with anger as he gripped the sides of the door. "I've given everything for this title, made sacrifice after sacrifice, and I'm not going to lose it. I will not let you take it away from me."

His words sounded familiar to me as I assessed him silently. The anger, frustration, and drive stirred what felt like a long, distant memory. His pupils blown wide, his ragged breath, his quivering fingers all reminded me of someone I used to know…me.

Me, without a curly-haired girl who danced into my life. Me without loud music at 7 a.m., without wet footprints across my expensive rugs, without sunshine-yellow paint on my white walls. Me, without fullness, closeness, *light*.

"Ten seconds, Gallagher!" the referee shouted as the announcer indicated on the speakers the start of the second round.

Me without River.

I grinned down at Seamus and patted him on the shoulder as he looked up expectantly at me. "You're fired, Seamus."

His eyes narrowed immediately in anger. "What?"

"If you'll excuse me," I said, nodding for him to move aside. "I have a title to forfeit."

His face was a full-blown red. "Get back inside that cage right now or—"

"I'm never fighting again." I leaned close to him and said as calmly as possible, "But if you don't move, I suppose I have one last brawl left in me."

Seamus's face darkened as he finally shifted to the side. "You'll regret this."

I barely registered the bell for the start of the second round—it was as if the noise was already fading far, far into a past I never wanted to return to. I was going toward my present, my future.

I was going toward my River.

As I took the first step out of the cage, I noticed Seamus's eyes widen in surprise and his mouth open to shout my name. But it was too late to realise my mistake; it was too late to realise the cage would never let me go.

There was a blinding pain in the back of my head.

Then there was nothing.

River

I expected him to stop me.

As I turned my back on him, on *us*, I expected to hear the rattle of the mesh behind me as he pulled himself to his feet. To feel the floor shake beneath me, and not from the pounding of the crowd in the stands, but from the pounding of Declan's feet as he ran across the cage to rip open the door, leap down the stairs, and sprint to me.

I expected his hands, rough in his gloves, to grab my arm and whip me around to face him…to stumble into his chest as Declan lifted my chin so my eyes, already wet with tears, met his. I expected him to say, *"I don't need the title. I need you. Nothing in this world is worth losing you. Your love is enough, River. Your love will always be enough."*

I was ready to say, *"I knew you'd come after me."*

I expected him to kiss me as Dominic screamed at him to fight, as the referee screamed at him to fight, as the stadium and the whole goddamn world screamed at him to fight. That he would kiss me as his insecurities, doubts, and feelings of unworthiness screamed and screamed and screamed at him to fight. I expected him to kiss me and hear only the rhythm of my heart beating against his amongst the noise.

I expected too much.

Because as I turned my back on him, on *us*, I heard nothing.

As I faced the double set of doors down the long concrete aisle, I sensed no movement behind me.

As I took a step toward the exit, glowing a slickly neon-green above me, I felt not even the faintest brush against my skin.

I passed the two security guards and glanced up at each of them, sending a quick, desperate prayer that maybe they'd stop me as I walked past. They held me back before when I was trying to get to Declan. So why couldn't they stop me, just for a second or two, when Declan was trying to get to me?

They could check my purse. They could step in front of me to inform me that I needed a stamp to get back inside once I left the arena floor. They could just ask for my name even, as a security precaution, of course.

I'd pretend like I hadn't heard them in the noise of the stadium, filling up again for the start of the second round.

"What's that?" I'd shout.

I'd give Declan a few more seconds, a few more seconds to stop me from leaving.

But I moved past the two security guards and their dark, focused eyes, which scanned the crowd, didn't even bother glancing down at me.

Tears started to pool in my eyes as I moved closer and closer to the double doors. Soon, I would be pushing them open. I would be walking through them—they would be closing behind me with one final, definite thud.

Soon, it would be over.

He might still be coming to me, I reassured myself even as a heavy sadness settled in my heart. He's just explaining to the referee that he's forfeiting.

But I refused to look back over my shoulder to check. I couldn't. It was the Number One Rule of Running:

Never look back.

Never.

As I slipped through a large group of VIP fans with lanyards hanging from their necks lingering in front of the set of double doors, I listened for my name.

I heard only Declan's.

The first tear of what I knew would be more than I could count, trailed down my cheek as my hand grasped the door handle. "He's still coming," I whispered to myself as I squeezed my eyes shut. *He's still coming…*

I lingered there for longer than I should have. No matter how much my fingers quivered and my chest ached, I should have shoved open those doors and marched out. But I waited…

He won't let me leave.

One…

His feet are carrying him toward me, his hand is stretching out for me, his lips are calling my name.

Two…

He loves me. Declan Gallagher loves me.

Three.

If it weren't so damned loud in there, perhaps I would have heard my heart breaking. As it was, I just felt it.

I shoved open the doors.

I stumbled out.

I didn't even hear them close behind me.

My footsteps echoed in the long, empty corridor as I walked, then ran, then sprinted toward the back exit where earlier, the head event planner had slipped me in.

I never wanted the hallway to end. I wanted to run and never stop. I wanted to stop and curl up into a tiny ball on the floor…scream at the top of my lungs. To never utter a single word ever again. I wanted to punch a wall, to kick and fight, to bloody my knuckles and drink in the pain. Too feel nothing. I wanted to be numb forever.

The air inside the concrete corridor felt unmoving, heavy, and oppressive, and so when I finally escaped the stadium, I breathed in deeply, only to find the air in the open parking lot the exact same. I folded over and rested my hands on my knees, trying to catch my breath.

"River?"

I heard again the roar of the crowd and the voice of the announcer. For a moment, I thought that the last few minutes were but a terrible, terrible nightmare. I thought I'd imagined it and really, I was back inside, and this time—Declan really was going to follow after me.

So it was agony all over again to glance up and see through tear-stained eyes, Oisin calling me from his car just across the street.

Joan sat in the passenger's seat as the radio blared commentary from the fight inside.

"River, where's Declan?" Oisin asked before checking the street to walk toward me.

"Can you turn that off?" I asked in a weak voice.

Oisin jogged across the street. "What?" He ran up to me and placed a hand on my back while checking the exit behind me.

"Where's Declan?"

"Please," I begged. "Can you turn that off?"

I could hear the commentator from the radio say, "Alright, folks, it looks like Declan is up again and ready to continue this fight after all."

Oisin looked from me to the door, from me to the door that wasn't moving, from me to the door that wouldn't move. "Oh, baby girl..."

I sobbed as he wrapped his arms around me. "Turn that shit off!" I screamed.

It only took a second for the radio to cut out, but a second is plenty long enough to stab a knife straight through a heart—the bell for the second round.

Oisin squeezed me tight as my tears stained his suede jacket. His hands smoothed over my hair…over and over again. "I'm sorry," he whispered, his cheek against the top of my head. "I'm sorry. I'm so sorry."

"He didn't come after me," I whimpered, barely able to get the words out. "I thought he'd come after me. I thought…" Fresh tears poured out of my closed eyes as I clung to Oisin's back. "Fuck, I was so stupid! So stupid."

"Hey, hey, hey." Oisin tugged himself away from my grasp, even as I scrambled to pull him in close again. With his hands firmly on my shoulders, he held me far enough away from him that he could look down at me. "Believing in the power of love is never stupid, my little voodoo queen," he said. "I won't have you talking nonsense like that ever again, no matter what. Do you hear me?"

I tried to nod but couldn't as I again broke down into pathetic sobs. "It hurts," I groaned.

Oisin smiled softly and cupped my cheek. "Come with me," he said, guiding me with his hand on my back toward Joan and the car.

I moved forward with numb, stumbling feet.

"I can't help you with tomorrow or the day after or the day after that or even the day after that," he said gently. "But I can help with tonight."

River

For the longest time, I couldn't tell if the ringing was from my phone or from the hangover of the century. Either way, I groaned at the shrill, piercing, head-stabbing noise. Rolling over on the plush couch I didn't remember passing out on, I tugged over my head the blanket I didn't remember covering myself with and I didn't remember ever causing me this much pain.

I "enjoyed" a few moments of nausea-filled silence before the ringing started again. Cursing, I covered my ears as best I could and prayed for it to stop.

Finally, it did.

"Looks like you're having a fun morning," an unfamiliar voice said *way* too cheerfully.

With a groan, I peeled back the blanket and peeked open one eye to squint up at a man who approached me with a glass of water and a bottle of aspirin.

He sat across from me on the coffee table.

I frowned at the sideways image of him. He was clothed. Good-looking. Cute dimples. Reminded me of that actor who played Thor. A little bit too pretty for me. I, apparently, only had eyes for brutal-looking fighters who obliterated hearts as easily as they blended protein smoothies.

"Who are you?" I asked. Glancing around the room, I realised I wasn't back at the manor. What the hell happened last night?

"I'm Noah," he laughed. "Noah O'Sullivan? We met last night."

I tried to dig through my memories and came up blank. I shook my head.

Noah raised an eyebrow. "I own The Jar," he offered up as explanation, which ended up being no explanation at all.

"The Jar?"

He whistled, probably in amazement at my level of blackout.

I was quite amazed myself, to be honest.

"The Dublin college bar?" Noah tried to jog my memory.

"Nope."

"The Dublin college bar where you finished my Teeling 29-Year-Old Vintage Reserve Single Malt?"

I shrugged.

Noah leaned in closer. "The Dublin college bar where you finished my Teeling 29-Year-Old Vintage Reserve Single Malt and set off the fire alarms with a bachelorette party's sparkling champagne bottle so you could 'dance in the rain' atop my bar?"

This caused me to blush as I fingered my still damp curls. I was about to utter a long string of apologies and promises to pay for any damage, but Noah spoke before I could start. "Oisin swore you were American, but after last night I'm still not sure you're not 100 percent Irish." He laughed. "You put on quite the holy show."

"Fuck…" I muttered under my breath before looking back up at Noah and asking, "Where is Oisin, by the way? And Joan? What happened to her?"

"Joan had to drive back to get her son to school, and Oisin is asleep in the guest room," Noah answered. "We offered it to you first when we got back this morning, but you said, and I quote, 'I only have half a heart left so the couch is plenty big for me.'"

As embarrassment hit me like a truck, I groaned and I flopped back down onto the couch.

"Here." Noah handed over the glass of water with a sympathetic chuckle and then poured out a couple of aspirin from the bottle. "These should help with the pain."

I swallowed them down after a quick "thanks". Right after, that goddamn ringing started up again, and it somehow seemed louder than before. "Do you hear that too, or is that my brain exploding?" I asked.

Noah laughed as he ducked beneath the coffee table and returned, waving my cell phone in his hand. He glanced at the screen and said, "Umm, 'Asshole Boss' is trying to reach you."

Apparently, I'd had enough sense to change his name in my contacts. Not enough to smash my phone though.

Sighing, I held out my hand for the shrill devil-box.

Noah jumped in surprise when I promptly ripped the phone apart and slung the battery across the room. Leaning my head carefully against the armrest, I covered my eyes with my hands and whimpered.

"Headache?" Noah asked.

"Yes," I said. "But it's not that bad compared to the pain of knowing that the person you love didn't choose you." I parted my fingers just enough to see Noah through one eye that still narrowed in the harsh morning rays. "I'd take a whiskey knife to the head any day over this," I said softly.

Noah crossed his arms. "Could you just make it a bit of a cheaper whiskey knife next time?" he asked with a playful twinkle in his eyes.

This caused me to laugh a little and I pointed a finger at him. "Stop that," I chastised. "I'm trying to be miserable and pitiful over here and you're ruining it."

He laughed. "Trust me, River, I know what's it like to be in your shoes." He paused. "Oh, by the way, you kicked off your shoes to Whiskey in the Jar and one got caught in the rafters, so I'll have to find a ladder to get it down."

"Ugh, please make it stop," I grumbled with another groan.

How *embarrassing*!

Noah laughed but then patted my shoulder. "But really," he continued, his tone suddenly serious, "I know this part is rough, but believe me, love always wins out in the end."

I shook my head and immediately regretted it as pain stabbed through my brain. "Not for me," I said, remaining as still as possible. "Never for me."

When Noah didn't reply, I glanced over at him. I watched as he played with his fingers in his lap. I sensed he wasn't there with me any longer; he was somewhere else, in some distant memory.

"Sometimes people are just scared," he finally said, looking over at me with a smile. "Fear makes us all do silly things, like take the wrong path when the right one was standing, *waiting* in front of them the whole time."

I frowned at his words. I wanted to ask him what he meant by them, but just then the front door slammed open and a frantic voice called from outside the living room.

"Noah?"

"Who's that?" I asked.

"Aubrey, my wife," Noah answered with obvious concern in his voice. "She just ducked out to get everyone coffees from the café around the corner. Rey?"

"Noah!"

Footsteps pounded in the hallway and suddenly a pretty woman, red-faced and with hair dishevelled, appeared with a to-go container of half-spilled coffees dripping onto the hardwood floors at her feet. "We have to go," she said hurriedly. "We have to go now."

Noah stood immediately, reaching for his wife. "Woah, woah, honey," he cooed. "What's wrong? What happened? Where are we going?"

Sucking in a breath as her chest heaved, Aubrey shook her head and nodded toward the couch. "Not you, babe," she gasped. "Her."

Noah turned around to stare at me in confusion.

I, equally confused, pointed a finger at my own chest. "Me?"

"Yes, you, River," she said, stumbling over her words she was speaking so quickly. "We'll take his car. Come on."

Noah calmly stepped to his wife's side and took the dripping coffees from her. "Aubrey, slow down," he said softly. "What's going on?"

"I heard at the coffee shop," she answered. "We have to go."

"Heard what?" Noah prodded.

"It's all over the news," she said, looking between her husband and me. "You don't know?"

I shook my head, cursing at the pain that lashed through me.

"Last night, Dominic king hit Declan from behind and he was rushed to the hospital."

I flung off the blanket. I didn't care that I only had one shoe as I stood. I didn't care that he didn't choose me. I didn't care about the pain, the heartache, and the sadness I wasn't sure I would ever heal from.

I didn't care about anything but Declan.

"Take me to him."

River

It had all been a blur.

The sprint to Noah's car, the mad dash through Dublin traffic, the fumbling of my fingers over the keypad of my cell—battery retrieved and restored—as I tried to reach Declan.

The numbers on the screen blurred like this was all a dream, a horrible, horrible dream.

"Is he okay?" I desperately asked Aubrey from the backseat as Noah whipped the steering wheel to switch lanes, only to slam on the brakes half a second later.

Aubrey braced herself on the glove box before tugging at her locked seatbelt so she could turn back to me. "Honey, I don't know," she said, reaching a hand back to squeeze my knee that bounced rapidly up and down.

"But what did the news say?" I insisted as I finally managed to get Declan's number up.

From the backseat, I watched Aubrey's eyes flick over toward Noah as the phone rang.

"Do they know—anything?" My voice cracked. My heart would be next, then my soul. I'd shatter into a million pieces if Declan standing in that cage was my last image of him.

"River, I know it's hard, but we'll know once we—"

"Fuck!" I shouted and slammed my cell phone on the seat cushion next to me. "He's not answering his phone. Fuck!"

Why didn't I answer it earlier? Why?

I leaned over to see through the windshield an infinite stretch of goddamn red brake lights below the low-hanging grey clouds that erased the tops of buildings, as if it didn't already feel like my world was collapsing. "How much longer till we're to the hospital?" I asked, eyeing Noah's speedometer creep down, down, down.

"Soon," Noah lied, avoiding my eyes in the rearview mirror. "Soon."

Biting back the threat of tears, I grabbed my phone and again dialled Declan's number. "Please pick up," I begged as Noah laid on the horn when the car in front of us hesitated for just a moment as the light turned green. "Please, please, please. Please pick up."

We received the middle finger as the tires screeched and the engine accelerated to get around the slow car.

I squeezed my eyes shut on the fifth ring, dreading the sound of Declan's voicemail. But the sixth ring stopped halfway through.

"Declan!" I shouted, collapsing against the headrest in relief.

Both Noah and Aubrey twisted their necks around to silently ask with wide, imploring eyes, "He's okay?"

Covering my eyes, I smiled as I exhaled, "Oh my God, Declan, I—"

"Hello?"

I froze.

That wasn't the voice that whispered my name into my ear as I pressed up against the wall in my darkroom. Not the voice that grumbled at me to turn down my music even as a grin played at his lips…the voice that told me I was his, and he was mine.

This wasn't Declan.

"Hello?" the stranger's voice repeated.

"River?" Aubrey hissed from the passenger seat. "River, is he all right?"

Everything was suddenly loud again. The pitter-patter of rain against the roof of the car, the back and forth, back and forth of the wipers against the windshield, the blare of horns and screech of tires and growl of engines from the traffic surrounding us, all of it beat down on me as my heart rate surged.

"River, what's going on?" Noah asked, his head moving between me and the road, black with the slick of rain.

"Hello?" the stranger's voice was louder. "Hello, is this River?"

I swallowed. "Yes." I wasn't sure if I managed to say it aloud or if it remained a quivering gasp in my head.

"Thank Jaysus," the stranger replied. "I've been trying to reach you all night."

He was a doctor at the hospital. He was calling to tell me the bad news. He was a lawyer from the MMA. He was calling to ask me not to sue. He was a reporter. He was calling to get a quote about the tragic death of Declan "The Homewrecker" Gallagher.

"You still there?" he asked. "River, you still there?"

I ignored the questioning looks from Noah and Aubrey. "I'm here," I whispered.

I wished I wasn't. I wished I was anywhere else. That I could open the car door, sprint out into traffic, and escape into the dark, churning clouds.

"My name is Danny," the stranger said. "I'm a good friend of Declan's. He's, um..."

When Danny's voice grew thin from emotion it was like a sucker punch to the gut. I sank my teeth into my lower lip as my eyes watered.

"Can you get to the hospital?" Danny asked. "I can send a car to you. I'll be here in the ER waiting room."

I wanted to ask the question so terribly—I needed to ask it. It was on the tip of my tongue… I was about to ask it. But I didn't… I couldn't.

"I'm already on my way," I said, numb to everything.

I hung up and stared without seeing at the back of Aubrey's headrest, ignoring the wave of anxious questions tossed back at me till there was nothing but silence and doubt in the car. For the rest of the ride to the hospital, I repeated the question I was too afraid to ask again and again and again: *Is Declan alive?*

Twenty minutes later, the screech of tires like a dagger through my brain was a welcome relief because it interrupted the question that repeated again and again… *Is Declan alive? Is Declan alive? Is Dec—*

I opened the door of Noah's still moving car in front of the ER.

"River! Wait! You can't just—"

I stumbled onto the pavement, scraping my palms and knees, but quickly pushed myself to my feet and without even bothering to close the car door as I ran toward the glass sliding entrance amongst the shouts of hospital personnel and the wail of ambulance sirens.

Inside the waiting room was chaos. Phones rang behind the busy front desk, gurneys rattled across the stained linoleum floor as attendants called for people to move, babies cried in the arms of parents with fast-tapping feet. Nurses bellowed orders as a wheelchair emerged from the ER where machines beeped, alarms blared, and moans of pain cut through all the noise like a knife.

It was all so loud. Standing there just inside the double doors, I was brought back to the stadium the night before—the thousands of feet pounding the bleachers, the crushing wave of cheers pouring over me, the vile shouting from Dominic as I begged for Declan to come with me, just come with me. I ran then.

I wanted to run now.

I wanted to escape to a place of quiet with green leaves above me and green blades of grass between my toes. I wanted peace, but there was none to be found here, in this ER waiting room.

Whirling around on my heels, I stepped toward the glass sliding doors, only to hear my name called out over the din.

I hesitated.

I could still leave. I could still slip through the doors, get lost in the traffic of gurneys, ambulances, doctors, nurses, and hospital staff. I could still run.

But a hand on my shoulder erased any dreams of softly swaying trees and replaced them with white, sterile walls.

"River?"

I turned around to find a tall, darkly handsome man wearing a motorcycle jacket with messy midnight hair and the bluest eyes I'd ever seen, staring down at me with wide, bloodshot eyes.

"I'm Danny," he said as I considered just lying and telling him my name wasn't River. "We talked on the phone."

He laid his hand on my shoulder, but all I managed to do was blink mutely up at his dark eyes.

"I know this is a lot," he said softly. "Come with me."

Danny moved to my side and slid his arm around my still quivering shoulders. Him next to me was the only thing keeping my heavy, clumsy feet moving one after the other as we passed through the chaotic traffic of the waiting room.

Ask him, I told myself. Say the words, *Is he alive? Is Declan alive?*

But I didn't.

Danny spoke quietly with the nurse at the front desk as I stared at my slightly too big sneakers borrowed from Aubrey. I should redo these laces. I'd made a mess of them, barely doing them up.

The doors to the ER opened and Danny guided me through.

Ask him now, my mind screamed. You need to know. *Is he alive?* It's a simple question. Ask it! *Is Declan alive?*

I couldn't open my lips.

My shoes squeaked on the linoleum floors as Danny gently eased me past hospital beds, curtains drawn shut, and hallways lined with imposing-looking medical equipment. We stopped at an elevator.

How bad is he hurt?

Danny helped me into the elevator when my knees wobbled beneath me. I didn't look at which number he pushed. If Danny spoke to me on the elevator ride, I didn't hear him over the rush of blood in my ears.

The elevator doors parted and we were immediately greeted with two security guards. They went to block our path but immediately moved when they saw it was Danny and me.

It wasn't loud on this floor of the hospital, but I suddenly wished it were…I could hear myself too loudly here.

How bad is it?

My throat was dry and my head was pounding when halfway down the dimly lit hallway, Danny gently guided my shoulders to a closed door. I stared at his hand as he reached for the door handle, silently praying for it to stop.

He pushed the door open.

We stepped inside.

Despite how hard I bit my quivering lower lip, I couldn't prevent the tears, hot and fast, from falling this time at the sight of Declan on that bed in that room as a nurse adjusted a stark white sheet over him next to a doctor who pushed some button on some machine. Desperately, I scanned his pale body for signs of life. I searched his purple-ringed eyes for the slightest quiver of his eyelids. But my vision wavered and I couldn't be sure of anything.

Is he okay? Is there brain activity? Danny's arm around me held me in place as I tried to peddle backwards as the chest rattling sobs started.

The doctor hurried toward me and with Danny's help, eased me into a chair against the window with its blinds drawn. "This is Ms Moore?" the doctor asked, kneeling in front of me.

Danny nodded. "River."

I buried my hands in my face so I couldn't see Declan. "Is he alive?" I gasped against my wet fingers, unable to avoid the question any longer. "Is Declan okay?"

"Mr Gallagher is presently in a coma," the doctor started. "He entered the ER with a very serious head injury and given his medical history, we transferred him immediately into the ICU."

This my fault. I should have stayed and fought harder for him. I shouldn't have run; run like I always do.

I felt a hand rubbing comforting circles on my back and knew it must be Danny.

"When will he wake up?" I whispered in the warm darkness behind my hands.

There was a pause that grew and grew and grew.

"To be honest, River, Mr Gallagher could wake up this afternoon," he explained. "But there is also the real possibility that he might never wake up. Head injuries like these are…difficult to predict."

I sagged in the chair in grief, in despair, in helplessness.

"Doctor," Danny finally spoke, "would it be possible for River to have a moment alone with Declan?"

The doctor pushed himself to his feet in front of me. "We'll be back in a bit to monitor any changes in his condition."

"Thank you," Danny said.

Shoes rapped on the linoleum floor, and then I heard the door open before clicking shut.

"River?"

Danny's quiet voice was close to my ear.

"River, I know he would have wanted you to be here," Danny whispered. "I think he…he needs you." His hand squeezed my shoulder. "I'll go get us some coffees from the cafeteria downstairs to give you two some time together, alright?"

I didn't reply, not even a nod, but Danny still patted my shoulder and again, I heard the door open before clicking shut as I remained hidden behind my hands. My breath was loud, fast, and raspy in my dark cocoon.

I couldn't do this.

I couldn't.

Pulling my hands from my face and without glancing back toward Declan, I hurried to the door. My fingers wrapped around the door handle and I was about to tug it open when I paused. I rested my forehead against the window and exhaled shakily.

"I'm sorry, Declan," I whispered. "I don't know how to stop

running."

I looked over my shoulder at Declan lying unconscious in the hospital bed.

"I ran last night."

Without realising it, my hand had dropped from the door handle. I found my feet moving toward the chair at Declan's bedside. I frowned as my messy thoughts whirled around my head.

"I ran last night and yet, here I am," I said aloud as it all dawned on me suddenly. "I ran right back to you."

Sinking into the chair next to him, I laid my hand across the tubes and wires following his forearm. I shook my head in confusion as I stared at his closed eyelids.

"My whole life I thought I was running from something, from someone," I whispered. "But maybe I'd just never known the truth…I was running to you, Declan."

I slid my fingers down to his and gently interlaced ours together.

"I don't think I'll ever stop running," I admitted, "but I think I'll always be running to you, no matter how hard I try to stop."

My throat tightened with emotion and I swiped fresh tears from my cheek.

"I tried to run from the manor, but instead I ran into your arms. To run from my fear of judgement, but instead I ran into your acceptance. I tried to run from my insecurities, but then I ran into a love so deep, I'm afraid I'll never stop falling."

My tears trailed down Declan's chest as I rested my cheek against his shoulder, my body shaking.

"I can't stop," I sobbed. "Declan, I can't stop running to you. So please…" I gasped and clenched my eyes shut. "Baby, please don't go where I can't follow."

I was trying to catch my breath as panic, love, fear, devotion, hope, and despair all flooded my heart when I felt Declan's thumb move to trace slow, uncoordinated circles on the back of my hand. Chest seizing, I looked up to find his eyes, tired and pain-filled but awake and waiting for mine.

"Run to me," he whispered, his voice hoarse and rough. "River, run to me."

Declan

The rolling green horizon hadn't even seen the first touch of golden morning rays when I flung back the sheets and slipped out of bed. My whole body buzzed from the top of my head to the tips of my fingers all the way down to the last inch of my pinkie toe. I needed to move—I needed to move *now*.

I'd already slept too long.

As I tugged on my sweats, I watched River sleepily push a stray curl from her face and blink in the still dim light.

"What are you doing?" she asked when I sat back down on the bed next to her to slip on my sneakers. "Is it your head?"

I shook my head, leaned over to lace my sneakers, and answered, "I have to get to work."

River pushed herself up onto her elbows as she frowned in concern. "Work?" My oversized t-shirt she slept in slipped off her shoulder.

My fingers froze halfway through tightening the knot on my left shoe. The sight of her messy bed head haloing in the soft light, her hooded eyes, and the promise of her naked body just under that flimsy material almost made me kick back off my sneakers and crawl right back underneath the covers with her.

Focus. I couldn't let her distract me, no matter how tempting her nipples were peaked like that against the thin material of my t-shirt in the cold of the morning.

"Declan?"

"It's time to work on my title, baby," I said in a rush as I leaned across the bed and pressed a quick peck to her forehead, which was furled in confusion. "I've got to go."

I stood to leave, but she caught my arm and tugged me back toward her. "Declan, you already have the title," she said softly as if I was fragile and a word any louder than a whisper might break me. "Dominic was stripped of the title because of the king hit and it transferred to you. They're shipping the belt to the manor, remember?"

River ran her thumb in circles on the underside of my forearm. Her touch alone almost wiped out all my drive to leave her by herself in our room.

"Baby, do you feel okay?" River asked, concern obvious now. "Is it your head? Should we call the doctor?"

I unwrapped her fingers from my arm and kissed the back of her hand. "It was just a bad concussion, River," I said as her eyes searched mine in the dim light.

I got lucky. Dominic's hit could have killed me. I could have easily died without ever winning the title that was more important to me than anything else in the world.

That was why I wasn't going to waste my second chance at it. I had to get to work.

River again reached for me.

This time, I stepped back and her hand fell to the bed. "I've got to go," I repeated.

"Declan, please," she whispered. "Just come back to bed. You have the title."

I shook my head. "It's not enough. I want more."

River sank back into the bed, defeated, as I made my way in the dark toward the door.

Halfway through, I ducked my head back into the room. "Oh, and I'll have some things for you to do today, so I'll need you in the office."

The door clicked shut before I could hear her response, if

there even was one. Leaning against the door, in the silent hallway, I squeezed my eyes shut and reassured myself it was worth it, it would all be worth it.

As I requested, Chef was already up and cooking in the kitchen when I made my way downstairs for my morning smoothie.

"You sure you're ready for all of this?" he asked, looking back over his shoulder at me from the stovetop.

My only answer was to start guzzling the thick green drink and try to keep my foot from tapping nervously on the kitchen tiles.

"Did you sleep at all?" Chef pressed. "You look like you didn't sleep."

Does tossing and turning all night and replaying terrible scenario after terrible scenario about what could happen in the cage count as sleeping?

"Just make sure dinner's ready when it's supposed to be, okay?" I grumbled as I tossed the dirty smoothie cup into the sink and stalked out of the kitchen, making sure not to let Chef see my shaking hands.

What if it all went wrong again? What if I couldn't do it? What if my past snuck its long, rotting fingers through the mesh of the cage and ripped my feet from underneath me?

"Declan, your delivery came," Joan called out from the dining room as I passed by. "I tried to move it from the front door to the gym, but it was too heavy."

"Great, great," I said distractedly. "I'll get it."

I lugged the big box to the gym and placed it by the cage. Just that effort alone made my brow sweat and my heart rate leap. *I'm not ready for this*, I thought as I stared through the mesh walls in the silence of the gym.

I stood there and remembered the deafening roar of the crowd that night. I remembered the way the floor shook beneath my feet. I remembered what I lost, what I almost lost forever.

I vowed right then and there never to make the same mistake twice.

As I suspected she would, River avoided me most of the morning and well into the afternoon. When I texted her to tell her I needed some help, she delayed in arriving to the gym and marched straight to the office without making eye contact, just as I guessed would happen. I busied myself at the punching bag till the door to her little office in the back slammed shut.

Me: *I need you to post some updates on my social media.*

River: *Fine.*

Sure that she was determined to stay in the office instead of coming out to talk to me, I figured it was safe to lug the brown box into the cage. *I'll text you what to say.*

I can't read your mind, her text replied.

I was typing when my cell phone buzzed again with another text from River.

Clearly.

It's going to be worth it, I repeated. It's going to be worth it.

Anyone who thought I would stop after this MMA title doesn't know me. I texted again, *Hey, while you're working on that, can you check the delivery status of my belt?*

Shoving my cell phone into my pocket, I pulled the tape from the box as quietly as I could. I had to work quickly. I was halfway done when River texted back.

I'm checking now. Anything else you wanna say?

The words came easily. *'My next title will be my greatest yet.' Post that.*

Her text read, *Yes, master...*

I had to hold back a grin.

I went back to work, checking every once in a while to make sure the door to the little office stayed closed. I wasn't done yet, so I quickly texted again… *Add, 'I'm terrified about going after it, but I won't be able to live with myself if I don't, no matter the cost.'*

This time, I didn't receive a response back from River.

Slipping out of the cage, I hurried on tiptoes toward the front of the gym and switched off the large overhead lights. Reds and purples from the deepening sunset poured across the cage, a stark contrast from the glare of the phosphorescent.

Me: *'It's the only thing that matters to me now.'*

I pulled a lighter from my pocket. I was halfway around the cage when my phone buzzed.

River: *Umm, there's been some sort of mistake. They said the shipment for your belt to the manor was cancelled.*

I hurriedly finished what I was doing before I responded, *Figure out who cancelled it then.*

I'm on the line with them now, she texted back.

I want to post a picture of the next title I'm going after on social media.

River's response, *Kinda busy.*

I typed in the words, *I'll send you a picture of it.*

It almost slipped from my fingers as I pulled it from my back pocket. I laid it gently in my open palm and positioned my cell phone's camera above it. The photo came out a little blurry because of my shaking hands, but I simply couldn't wait long enough to try again. My phone buzzed one after the other before I could send it.

River: *What's this?*

River: *You cancelled the shipment for your MMA belt?*

River: *Declan, why would you do that?*

Smiling, I pressed "Send" for the picture and stood in the centre of the cage as I waited for a reply. I waited. And waited. And waited…

I was staring at the screen of my cell, worry and doubt creeping into the back of my mind, when I heard not the buzz of my phone, but the creak of the little back office door as it slowly opened.

Looking up, I found River in the doorway, staring across the gym at me.

When she saw me smile back over at her and drop to one knee in the centre of the cage that was ringed with flickering candles, her cell phone fell from her hand.

My heart thudded faster and faster as she made her way slowly through the weight equipment toward me. My palms grew slick with sweat as she stepped into the cage with me. My throat tightened as she came to a stop in front of me.

Her eyes, soft in the candlelight, found mine.

In a simple cherry blossom-pink dress and her scuffed sneakers with her hair loose and wild around her face, I'd never found her more beautiful. I reached out my hand for her. Her fingers quivered as she placed them gently in mine. I held her like she was the most delicate petal of the rarest mountain flower.

I breathed in deeply. "River."

I rotated the ring nervously in my other hand when River sucked in a gasping breath.

"River," I started again, "before you crashed into my life, the thought of being on my knees in this cage meant weakness, submission, defeat."

River stared down sweetly at me as I gained the courage to continue.

"I thought I always had to be standing tall in here, strong and proud and victorious," I said, my voice soft. "I thought I would never willingly drop down onto my knees."

"Declan…" River whispered.

"But you've shown me that there is a different kind of strength than muscles and brutality, and that's the strength of kindness. You've shown me that there is a different kind of victory than an arm raised high in a cage, and that's the victory of devotion. You've shown me that there is a different kind of success than money and fame and silly plastic belts, and that's the kind of success I want, that I hope you'll give me here tonight."

River's eyes were shining in the candlelight. Her fingers squeezed mine.

I squeezed hers. My voice wavered a bit as I continued, but I no longer cared. "The only I title I care about now is the title of having the gentlest touch on a Sunday morning, the title of bringing you the best pancakes in bed. Of making you the richest chicken soup when you're sick and cracking the lamest jokes when you're sad. I want the title of best shoulder to cry on, best lover, best dance partner in the rain."

A tear ran down River's cheek as she laughed. She quickly caught it and smiled down at me.

"The only title I want now…" I paused as I held out the vintage ring I'd bought for River in Dublin, "…is the title of husband."

I breathed in deeply for the first time in a long time, because I was finally free.

"Marry me?"

Epilogue: River

Several years later…

"Declan! Declan, over here!"

The bright flash of lights from the line of cameras blinded me, but Declan's arm around me comforted me like nothing ever could. I smiled up at him and laid my hand on his baby-blue sweatshirt; we were long past dressing up in constricting suits and skin-tight dresses for public events. I was wearing a tulle skirt painted with wildflowers local to Ireland that I found in the same vintage store where Declan bought the ring I wore on my left hand. We promised each other to always be ourselves and ourselves alone…the world be damned.

"They love you," I whispered up at him as the cameras went crazy as Declan leaned over to kiss my cheek. "Just the way you are."

"Over here!" a cameraman shouted. "River! River! Over here!"

Declan grinned down at me and winked. "They love you," he said. "They're all here for you tonight. *I'm* here for you always."

Declan's lips found mine and we kissed on the red carpet before we turned the corner arm in arm and stepped inside a brightly lit, art-filled gallery…*my* gallery.

Cheers erupted from the gathered crowd the moment Declan and I entered. I couldn't help but blush, turning my red cheek against Declan's chest.

Oisin stepped up to us with two glasses of champagne.

Declan and I each took one.

Oisin squeezed my shoulders and kissed me on the cheek. "I barely managed to snatch these from Joan," he whispered before giving me a quick wink.

I glanced over his shoulder to find Joan stopping a waiter in a fine black-and-white suit to fill her hands with as many champagne glasses as she could. I laughed as Joan then shouted for me to give a speech.

I was shaking my head, about to explain that I couldn't when Miley, already next to a fine-ass Irishman, shouted, "Speech, bitch!"

I resisted the urge to retreat into Declan's arms, but this was my work and I was proud of it. I could speak to a room packed with more people than I could count who would be judging my every wor— "Hi, everyone," I said before I could completely chicken out. "Thank you for coming."

Applause burst out as I smiled at all the faces I recognised and loved: Joan and Oisin, Miley, Danny and Diarmuid and their lovely wives, Noah and Aubrey. I was briefly overwhelmed by all their support.

"This project was inspired by my husband, Declan. Maybe you know him?"

Laughter filled my airy gallery and I chuckled at my own lame joke. *Why didn't I practice this?* I silently chastised myself. I cleared my throat before continuing, "But seriously, do you know him?" I paused and glanced around the room. "Because the world thought they knew who Declan 'The Homewrecker' Gallagher was."

I looked up at my husband.

"But I saw someone entirely different…" My voice was softer now. "Someone kinder, gentler, more tender. And I wanted the world to see that."

Declan and I stared into each other's eyes. The room was so silent.

"I love you," I mouthed up to him.

He smiled. *"I love you, too,"* he mouthed back.

I turned back to the crowd and raised my glass. "So thank you for coming, and I hope you like this study of the private and public lives of some famous Irish we all *think* we know!"

Cheers again filled my ears along with clinking glasses.

Declan hugged me tight to him. "You're brilliant, River," he said against the top of my head. "Come with me. I want to show you my favourite photograph." He interlaced his fingers with mine.

I followed after him, curious which photograph could be his favourite. We passed photographs that I considered my most artistic, my most technically advanced, my most unique, my most well edited. We passed all of those and finally stopped in front of a photograph I never would have guessed.

After staring at the photograph for a moment in the silence between Declan and me in the loud, busy gallery, I looked up at him.

He was already looking down at me.

"This one?" I asked, my voice but a whisper.

Declan nodded.

I glanced between the photograph and him, then back again. "Why?"

Declan wrapped his arm around my shoulders and looked back toward the photograph himself.

It was a simple black-and-white photograph of a large, muscular forearm, and resting on that forearm was a tiny, naked newborn baby boy.

"Because, my love," he said. "It's the moment when I gained my greatest title yet…dad."

The End

Dear Readers

Thank you for your patience in waiting for this story. It took me four rewrites and so many frustrated tears to get this one right. Declan is such a wonderfully complicated character that he just needed—*needed*—the right story and the right woman. I hope I did him justice. I hope you love River and Declan's story as much as I do!

Please post a review!

Did you enjoy Fighter's Kiss?

Please consider leaving a review! Just one sentence. One word. An emoji!

It really helps other readers to decide whether my books are for them. And the number of reviews I get is super important.

Thank you!

Stay sexy,
xoxo Sienna

www.siennablake.com
www.facebook.com/SiennaBlakeAuthor
www.instagram.com/SiennaBlakeAuthor

Join my Newsletter

Never miss a new release again!

No spam. No junky emails. Ever.

www.siennablake.com

Join my Reader Group

You'll get access to Advanced Review Copies of my books, exclusive giveaways, sneak peeks into what's coming up next, and get to vote on covers, titles and blurbs.

http://bit.ly/SiennasDarkAngels

Join my Bloggers List

If you're a Blogger, please sign up to my Bloggers List for ARC opportunity alerts in your inbox.

http://bit.ly/SiennaVIPBloggers

Blogs will be verified.

Books by Sienna Blake

Irish Kiss (Standalone Series)
Irish Kiss
Professor's Kiss
Fighter's Kiss
The Irish Lottery
My Brother's Girl ~ *coming soon*

Quick & Dirty (Standalone Series)
Three Irish Brothers
My Irish Kings
Royally Screwed

A Good Wife (Standalone Series)
Beautiful Revenge
Mr. Blackwell's Bride

Bound Duet
Bound by Lies (#1)
Bound Forever (#2)

Dark Romeo Trilogy
Love Sprung From Hate (#1)
The Scent of Roses (#2)
Hanging in the Stars (#3)

Paper Dolls

About Sienna

Sienna Blake is a dirty girl, a wordspinner of smexy love stories and an Amazon Top 20 & USA Today Bestselling Author.

She's an Australian living in Dublin, Ireland, where she enjoys reading, exploring this gorgeous country and adding to her personal harem of Irish hotties ;)

Printed in Great Britain
by Amazon